MW00658466

# AN Obvious TELL

# AN Obvious TELL

BRITT
BARTILSON

First published in February 2024 by Britt Bartilson
Cover design by Kari March
Editing and formatting by Allusion Publishing, www.allusionpublishing.com

ISBN (paperback): 979-8-9891968-0-7

www.brittbartilson.com
Instagram: @brittbartilson
TikTok: @brittwrites

To Dirty Little Secrets, 'popcorn' romance novels, Taylor Swift, and Cosmopolitans, without which there would be no inspiration. To my friends, family, and especially my husband, who read and reread countless chapters every time I asked. Your sacrifice was worth it. These characters and stories wouldn't exist without your continued support and love.

# Chapter One

## DIMPLES

### Lucas

"Well, my friends," Chase says with a wide grin, showing off his stupid smile and white teeth. "You might as well give in and pay up." His laugh quickly permeates the air in my garage. Leaning forward, with that dumb grin plastered all over his face, he pushes all his chips toward the center of my old, felt-covered folding table. "All in."

The look on his face says enough. It's a little bit sly and *way* too confident. Also, who shoves all-in this early in the game? My brother, Chase. That's who.

My heart picks up, and my blood pumps in silent excitement when Kit follows it with his usual "Good luck, all in." He somehow makes the words sound both supportive and a threat all at the same time. I find myself admiring that unique skill. There aren't many people I know who can be threatening in a thoroughly approachable way. Though given his job as a local sheriff, it is probably more of a learned skill than an innate one.

This moment is the rush I crave when we play together. I'm clearly not in it for the money—not with a twenty-five-dollar buy-in. It's the feeling of winning when the odds are stacked against you, or when you're relying solely on the luck of the deal that keeps me coming back. Well, that and the company.

All the guys at this table have been entrenched in my life in ways that cemented them permanently. Most of us have known each other since grade school, and while college, careers, and women pulled us in different directions, we've all somehow ended up back here. And without the women, I might add.

Poker night for now is strictly "Dads only," with the exception of Chase, my baby brother, and my best friend Harley, who is the closest thing to a father-figure that his niece has. He runs the local watering hole, and also keeps Chase gainfully employed. We have been best friends since before either of us could walk.

Kit, Tyler, and Damian round out the "Dad" table. Kit is the only one of us who is still married, and surprisingly, happily so.

The other guys at the table groan, almost in unison at the "all-in" shove, and a few lower their hands, obviously not needing to remember whatever cards they had been planning on chasing with. The poor bastards limped in to see a cheap flop, and it shows. Their eye rolls and semi-pathetic sounds instantly let me know what they have... or don't have, in this case.

No one likes it when Chase wins.

First off, while I love my kid brother, he is all jokes. All the time. Chase is endless tales of 'good times' and 'YOLO' or whatever. Well, maybe not YOLO, but definitely a shade too heavy on his carefree-life attitude. Add that to the fact that he is younger than the rest of us, and less tied down. It can be rough. To be honest, I am not above judging him... slightly, given that he is a little bit of a mess and the guys and I just can't find it in us to cut him any slack. Especially not at cards.

If I remember correctly, I'm sure his last one-night stand needed a restraining order. Sadly, that was just one of the *many* broken hearts left in his bachelor's wake.

Really, more like a Bachelor's Tsunami.

I have no interest in kidding myself or turning an intentional blind eye to my own inferiorities. My life is *far* from perfect, and I'm not on some high horse or anything. Not by a long shot.

I am a divorced, single dad. Chasing a second-choice career—even if it was and is the better choice. I barely know what to do as a parent on the best days. Sure... I've got pieces of my life together, but it's not where I thought I'd be in my thirties, not to mention the fact that I'm raising my kid with my bitter ex, Sherry, who's more of an emotional train wreck than I am.

In my mental spiral, it is not lost on me that I conveniently leave out the fact that it's been two years, and neither of us has *really* moved on, leaving our family in this weird perpetual state of incomplete brokenness.

Jasper, my son, is the highlight of my life and better than anything I've achieved to date. Having him in my life is what has made everything... and I do mean all of it, worth doing. But Sherry makes everything more complicated than it has to be. Tonight included.

I could tell she was itching for drama from the moment she dropped Jasper off. No one has perfected her unique way of pointing out my flaws as a man and a father in one go while still somehow making me think she's right.

Coming back from that depressing start of the evening, I look down at my hand as the betting finishes moving around the table. I know I can win this. No one else seems to have anything to take Chase down. Even Harley, the 'lucky' one of us, doesn't seem to have anything, and he silently folds before it comes back to me. I'm holding a premium hand, Ace-Queen of Hearts, and there are two more hearts staring up at me from the felt. My odds of hitting the flush are good, and even without it, I'm sitting on the top pair.

There's a world where I let all of this go. That world is a fictional place, where Skittles are food-safe, and ex-wives with Pilates-toned bodies don't try to ruin your night with an inebriated attitude and a few choice words.

But then again, what are big brothers for?

My lips *almost* twitch as I effortlessly suppress my smile, inwardly chuckling at the thought that a 'tell' like that would slip out. My poker face has *always* been better than that.

Chase's blue eyes level on me and I lazily shove all my chips toward the center.

"Call." I intentionally lace my voice with boredom. It's not my usual play at diversion, but these guys can gauge my shit mood any day of the week, and more so on poker days, so I'm laying it on a little thick tonight.

Chase's face is a crystal clear, 4K picture of a lousy bluff. Twitching and flushing with excitement, thinking he's won. His eyes gleefully scan his cards again, checking to make sure he has what he believes he has. I swear I can see his pulse visibly pounding in his neck.

God, this is too easy.

Ignoring his overly apparent tells, I study the board again. With what's flopped, it's clear what he's got, at least to me. The only possible thing he would play is the straight, especially this early. It's painful that he is missing the flush draw on the board. Poor guy.

This is where he loses his money every time—forgetting to see the board's potential. Or life's potential, for that matter. Living and jumping in with whatever he sees at first glance. A tight ass, nice chest, blonde hair—making bad choices without looking at the *obvious* probable and highly likely potential outcomes.

*Jesus, Lucas,* I scold myself. It's just a poker game, and not even a high-stakes one.

He lays his hand down, and my suspicions are spot on. He's got the straight. Two more cards to go.

His stare holds mine, and when he blinks, I swear I see a hint of desperation before it clears, and his excited flush takes over his face again.

"Nice try," I croon. "Pathetic, really." My voice lets out a touch of what I like to call 'condescending humor', and I lay my hand down a card at a time—aiming for more of a dramatic finish than this game requires. Chase immediately sees what he missed and goes a little pale. One more heart and he's finished.

Kit turns over the last two cards, in rapid succession. I soak up the looks from each pair of eyes at the table as they follow the cards with rapt attention. Ten of Clubs, and the Jack of Hearts, completing my beautiful hand. The table loses it when that last card hits. Chase—the poor guy, (literally poorer now that I've won)—cries out with a string of curses, reluctantly admitting his loss.

After he takes a large gulp of his amber drink, he confesses, "Looks like I'm sleeping on your couch again, Lucas, since I can't afford the Uber home anymore." His tone is carefree, and I know I didn't offend him... at least not too much. It's not lost on me that he could easily walk home. I don't bother pointing it out, though. He's always welcome here, and it's better than him trying to drive home tipsy or getting lost on the walk and winding up in a bush. Which may or may not have happened before.

Even with all that flitting through my head, my smile is the only response he gets as I slide my winnings toward me, the sound of cards shuffling and mindless chatter filling my ears. Tyler is telling us about his latest Tinder experience, and even though I can't say I envy him even in the slightest, at least he was getting out there. That was absolutely something worth bragging about. I'll probably point out later that he might want to raise his standards... at least slightly.

Zoning out when he reaches the part of the story where they get to second base sitting on a pair of boxer briefs from her last date that she left in the backseat of her car, I let my eyes slide across the table. I'm always curious to see who invests what at these poker nights. Both Harley and I were substantially up, with Damian trailing pretty close behind.

Damian was an enigma, always had been. He kept to himself mostly and was incredibly private, but he is, without a doubt, the most intelligent guy I know, and loyal to a fault. None of us were surprised when he moved to a big city to go to school at the end of graduation. However, he did garner a few looks when he returned five years later with a three-year-old daughter in tow and refused to answer any questions.

Seeing me staring, he raises a silent, dark eyebrow in question, but I just shake my head and look back at my piles, pretending unnecessarily to count them. They are neat enough that I could tell you, almost without looking at them, how much I was up or down. The little round discs are stacked by amount, and all lined up against the edge of the table. They don't hold a candle to Damian's—which are so organized I am half-tempted to knock them over just to get a rise out of him, but I know it isn't worth the drama. Knowing him, he'd probably just get up and leave. Definitely not worth it.

The fact that I'm up for the night has me deciding to take a break so I don't find the need to play crap, the hidden danger of any lucky streak.

As I get up to refresh my drink, the smell of beer and chips hits my nose. It's a familiar scent, almost homey despite its cliché combination. Our weekly poker nights have become comforting to me, and like most things in my life, the fact that it is predictable and consistent goes a small way toward improving my mood, whatever it may be.

Sometimes it's better if I just acknowledge that Sherry has put me in a funk. Though tonight, even cleaning out my little brother's winnings hasn't been able to clear the cloud of chaos and drama that she left in her wake when she dropped Jasper off.

Cracking the lid of my fresh beer on the workbench in the corner, I turn and watch the table continue to deal without me. The buzz hits smooth, and I settle in, silently observing from the sidelines. These guys know me well enough that they don't even need to ask if I want to be dealt in, or if they should go on without me.

The air is crisp and comfortable in the cramped garage. Fall had finally settled in a few weeks ago, making the enclosed space far more bearable than it was in the summer heat waves. The weather in Camden is as unpredictable as the rest of Maine, but at least you can count on having every season.

When it is my turn to host in the hotter months, we usually have to squeeze around my small kitchen table to play so that we aren't suffocated by the humid air that tries desperately to drown anyone dumb enough to stay in it for too long.

Part of the unspoken agreement with these games is that hosting switches up so that the need for a babysitter alternates.

It's funny that I've known all of these people basically my whole life. Even when we all went our separate ways for school, that small-town life called us all back. Each one of us said we'd 'get out' or swore we would never come back, at least until we saw what we were missing. No surprise that we all came running home. Though each of us for different reasons.

The only downside of the low populace that sticks with me is that there isn't much to do outside of Harley's bar. There are restaurants and other nightlife places, but they usually cater to tourists looking for precisely what we treasure about this place—and ruining it with their curiosity in the process. And sure, we could drive a ways and go to some Minor League baseball games, or even make it to an NFL game. But when the reality of life sets in, who has time for that? Alas, we make our own entertainment, and one or two random poker nights for someone's birthday eventually turned into a weekly social activity that we all use as an outlet to escape our daily life.

"How do you always do that?" Harley comments, pulling me out of my own head, as he leans over to grab the bottle opener.

"Do what, win?" My reply is casual, and I hold back a smile. His eyes roll at my response, but he doesn't let me get away with it. "Annihilate your little brother," he volleys back lightly. "Even for the two of you, that was cold."

He's not wrong. Most of the time, I humor Chase. But then, maybe that's why his life is such a mess. No one is preparing him for when *his* Sherry is going to come over, drunk off her ass, throwing herself at him again.

I feel like an asshole for taking it out on Chase, but the thoughts in my head are engulfing all rational thoughts and sensible feelings.

"It's not him," I breathe as I stare down at my bottle, absentmindedly wiping the condensation off the sides in slow, even lines.

"Sherry?" His voice is low as he pivots topics easily, tracking my mood.

"Fuck, isn't it always fucking Sherry? I swear she's out to ruin my life one insult at a time."

His eyes catch mine when I look up, and I know he gets it. We've been best friends long enough that if anyone knows the ins and outs of what she and I have gone through, it's him.

"It's time you move on." He's making the same point he makes every *single* time this comes up, and like every time before, I know he's right.

"It's not like I'm still with her," I argue weakly. My reply is pathetic, even to me. I can't imagine how it sounds to Harley.

"Look..." He turns to face the dust-covered workbench behind me so that his voice doesn't carry to the table. "It's been what... two years since you split? And somehow, she still feels justified coming over here and trying to rekindle things every time she has a glass of Pino? That's not normal."

What is he getting at? Of course, she comes over. We have a fucking kid together.

I ignore the rest of his incredibly valid point. "It's not like we didn't end things," I breathe defensively. "We got a divorce. If that's not ending things, what is?"

"Maybe going out with someone, anyone else since then? Like literally anyone."

Ouch.

I know he's right, but still. "It's not like women are lining up to date a single dad with baggage." I can't meet his eyes as I say it. Revealing that small insecurity feels a little too real for poker night.

"Man, you're not undateable, and if you don't do *something* to move forward, everything in life will keep pulling you back into the same shit." His eyes are unwavering, and I chuckle quietly when he tacks on, "Also, don't call my godson baggage."

"When did you get so prolific?"

"All I do is listen to people at the bar. You'd be surprised at the shit people share when they're two or three drinks in." Harley's tone is light, but there is something in the way he says it that makes me think I should probably pull on that string later. We've had enough deep conversations in this one night to last the month.

My mind turns as I think over his perpetual point, the silence stretching effortlessly as we both nurse our drinks, happy to let the quiet build.

"So, what do you propose I do? Blind dating? Tinder?" I finally blurt minutes later. The thought of both makes me cringe, and he rolls his eyes for what feels like the hundredth time in this conversation alone.

"Just start by being open to it. I'm sure your 'natural charm' and 'magnetic energy' will have flocks of girls flying your way in no time." He doesn't get or expect a response to his sarcastic comment as we both head back to the table.

The rest of the night goes by in a blur, and if I am being honest with myself, I didn't really have my head in the game after that.

Is my life with Sherry so difficult because I'm not moving on? What about Jasper? How would he feel if I suddenly start seeing other women? Am I even ready to move on?

Surprisingly, Chase is the first to call it a night, bidding the guys farewell as he makes his way to my couch, already texting on his phone. I beat myself up a bit for being so hard on him, even if it was mostly in my head.

Once the guys have cleared out, I start folding the chairs and cleaning up the empty bottles scattered around the garage, *completely* obsessing over how in the world someone gets back into the dating scene after this much of a dry spell. Is it even possible to go from a washed-up divorcee to an eligible bachelor?

*Damn it, Harley.*

I do not need to be in my head about this. He's mentioned it countless times over the years, and I never sway from my utter disinterest, but now, here I am considering the possibility.

Could I finally be done with being alone?

"See you at practice tomorrow?" Tyler calls, pulling me out of my mental shit show.

"For sure, we'll be at our usual field." The brief mention of the youth football season starting improves my mood instantly.

"I'm excited about this year. It will be great to get those boys through some of the plays you introduced last season." I can hear the genuine excitement in his voice. "Asher and I have been practicing his running play. Hopefully, the team picks up where we left off."

"We've only got one new player, a new kid in town. I'm pretty sure with the rest of the team, we can get him up to speed pretty quick."

"If anyone can, it's you. I'll tell Asher to keep an eye out and help him. No one likes being the new kid."

"You're a great dad, Ty. One of these days, I'm gonna get you to coach the team with me."

His laugh comes easy, and I know he's still not sold, but he really is great with the kids and has a natural talent for coaching. I'm not going to give up without a fight. He is such an interesting mix of a person. As a father, he is more hands-on than anyone I have ever seen, but somehow when it comes to the rest of his relationships, he has a no-strings-attached policy that baffles me. I can't even maintain my life as it is with a single personality trait and a penchant for extreme consistency. Yet here he is, separating his worlds like it takes no effort at all. Even the family-run ski lodge he oversees is a constant battle of ups and downs, with long off seasons and a low population in Camden. But you never see the stress he is under keeping his family business afloat when he is with Asher or here playing cards with us.

Tyler's constant good mood doesn't falter when he adds on, "Honestly, I'm just not sure I have the time, even though it would be a dream."

I almost thank him for snapping me out of my mental funk by bringing up one of the few things outside of Jasper that always improves my mood, even though he has no idea what he's done. He smiles in that happy, puppy-dog way again, putting his dimples on display before he turns and leaves.

I find myself wondering if the dimples in his cheeks are what makes him so good at the dating game. He never has any trouble 'getting out there,' as Harley said. Plus, he is always going on about whatever chick he is seeing.

Do I even have fucking dimples? Probably not knowing my luck.

I hit the garage light before closing the door, reminding myself to check the dimple thing later, and then maybe I will *consider* downloading the Tinder app... a few swipes left or right probably wouldn't kill me.

# Chapter Two

## SCORE KEEPING

### Maddie

"Mom?" a hesitant voice calls from the small bedroom at the back of the house. The weighted emotion in it has me putting down the taped-up box of books I am carrying to the living room without a second thought.

Thankfully, it doesn't take long to make it to his room from the front of the old 'cozy' house, where our boxes and belongings are strewn all over.

I think when the realtor showed it to us weeks ago, she used that word more times than it's ever been said in history—and honestly, by the twentieth, 'Isn't it just so cozy' I started to wonder what the heck she thought it meant. She didn't use that word when she showed me the rundown bakery that I am now working on refinishing and reopening. 'The Sweet Shop' as it will be rechristened, is *charming* but not 'cozy'. Well, it will be charming once I'm done with it.

To her credit, the house is indeed homey, quaint, and... well, cozy. It is in an upscale neighborhood and has the exact right amount of space Mikey and I need for our fresh start. While yes, I did pick it because of its charm, I also chose it because of how close it is to Mikey's new school—and to the new shop. Not that anything in this town is *particularly* far away from anything else. A town-trait I have firmly categorized in the 'pros' column.

When I reach Mikey, he's perched against the far wall, sitting 'criss-cross applesauce' on the floor of his new room, surrounded by open boxes, pillows, and an unzipped suitcase bursting with unfolded clothes and shoes.

"What's up, kiddo?" I ask softly.

His eyes meet mine dead on, and I scan him head to toe. Every mom instinct in me says that something isn't right. I recognize the picture in his hand instantly. The shattered frame is familiar enough that I don't need any further explanation to know why he called for me. The fact that it broke during the move is oddly fitting and only adds to the emotion we are both hiding below the surface.

Mikey is silent as he passes it to me, and shattered pieces of glass fall to the floor when he does. The faint 'tink, tink, tink' of the shards falling fills the silence that has stretched between us.

His eyes are misty, but I can tell he's unsure if he should be sad or angry, and boy, do I get it. This whole thing is a crap pile of epic proportions. I mean, how in the world is he supposed to prepare for this at the age of ten, especially if I never even thought we'd be here?

"I'm okay," he rushes before I can ask, nodding and pulling his lips between his teeth. My tight smile doesn't really make anything better, but it is all I have to give back to his comment. None of this is something a ten-year-old should be dealing with, yet here he is, looking much braver than I feel.

"You are such a great kid." My voice is quiet in the silent room, and I grasp his hand, pulling him up for the biggest hug I can muster. "What would I do without you?" The words come out muffled in his hair, and he squeezes me tighter in response.

Pulling him back, I stare at eyes that are little mirrors of my own. He always resembled me more than his father because of them, something I have been grateful for lately. Really though, it is his eyes and his hair. It's hard to ignore the blond curls that flop over his forehead in a shade that is almost a perfect match to mine.

"Let's do this later," I whisper, waving around the room. "Pizza?" The suggestion is my attempt at trying to lighten the mood with the promise of food. A frequent habit of mine. His nod is emphatic, and I know he needs the comfort just as much as I do. "Get some shoes on and meet me at the front."

Taking the shattered photo with me, I decide to dump it in the first trash can I find. That's where it belongs. Something that is only pretty when you don't look at it too closely. Like the future I had painted in my mind when the family picture in the destroyed frame was taken.

Just garbage.

Keeping my promise to myself, the frame... and the photo in it, go into the first empty box I pass as my phone buzzes in the back pocket of heavily worn jeans shorts

Pulling it out, I glance at the screen, knowing who it is before I look. Nope. Not a freaking chance. Without a second of hesitation, I silence the call and slide the dumb electronic back into my pocket. Not picking it up won't actually change how much Zach calls, and I know I will have to answer him soon. But it's looking like there is only one brave person in this house today, and that is Mikey.

"Ready!" Mikey's now chipper voice calls from behind me. Pizza is clearly the right choice as a mood improver.

"Perfect! I think I saw a pizza shop down the street. You up for a walk?" His blond curls bounce as he nods eagerly, and we make our way out the front door and down the worn brick steps.

I glance back at the *cozy* house. The house that I am determined to make feel like home sooner rather than later. For Mikey, I vow that I will not sleep a wink until it is everything he needs and more.

It takes less than five minutes for us to reach the main road that runs through the middle of our new small town. The whole center of it is overflowing with tiny streets packed with cute restaurants and coffee shops. All of these are tucked into historic houses that had, at some point, been converted into shops and restaurants over time. It is funny to me to see the little cottage-like structures sandwiched between each other, fighting for space like siblings.

You have to look twice at every home you pass, or you might miss the restaurant you're searching for—mistaking it for the house next to it where, I can only imagine, a happy family has lived for five generations.

I spent more than a few mornings since we arrived walking the streets to get familiar with our new home, loving how the avenues and sidewalks are always bustling with families and tourists. Both intermingled but fully identifiable, walking between meals and cute, Instagram-worthy ice cream shops like they have all the time in the world to get from one place to the other. Not at all like where we moved from.

Our walk is silent, both of us taking in our new surroundings and our new life. When we reach the pizza shop, I turn toward the entrance and open the door. Mikey grabs a table while I make my way to the counter, where I plan on ordering enough food for us... plus six.

This habit is one of my more self-proclaimed generous and loveable personality traits. Feed the world. 'Feed the world treats' is a bit more where I ride that line. But maybe I shouldn't be too specific while I'm pointing out and naming my flaws in a pizza shop that I plan on wallowing my worries in.

The redheaded teenager behind the counter raises an eyebrow right to the brim of his bright red baseball cap when I finish listing off my order. I'm not remotely embarrassed that it consists of three different 'mega slices', a salad, and the brownie pie. Though the look on his face seems to think I should be.

"Umm, ma'am...the slices here are *huge*." His voice doesn't hide his disbelief, and I can tell he's desperately trying not to be offensive. I nod at the display counter where the pizzas are baked, sliced, and waiting. "Well, how are we supposed to decide our favorites if we don't try them all?" He eyes Mikey in the corner at a table for two and stares at me for a minute. "You're gonna need a bigger table."

I bite my lip to keep from laughing and repeat the line back to him in Martin Brody's voice from *Jaws*, "You're gonna need a bigger boat..." Picturing myself in his signature glasses with a cigarette perched on the edge of his mouth as he says the line.

Nothing.

The poor kid's eyes are blank, empty as an undecorated cake. "You know from the movie," I press, trying to salvage the moment and not gain the 'weird new lady' title before I've truly met anyone here. But the teen still gives me nothing.

"*Jaws*? You know... 'You're gonna need a bigger boat...'" I hedge, desperate at this point.

He smiles politely. "Isn't that movie from like the 80s?"

I am *officially* uncool to the redhead pizza boy. Shame. But maybe this is one of those things that we'll do every time Mikey and I come in here, and in a month or two, he'll be reciting the lines back to me when we walk in.

Hoping for that envisioned future, I respond back, "Well, actually, it's from the 70s, but that doesn't mean it isn't good!" I hand him cash for the food with a hopeful smile that, unfortunately, is followed by an awkward silence.

"Umm, sure, ma'am," he finally says, breaking the brewing social chasm, though he couldn't sound less interested or even slightly convinced.

Well, there goes my hope of being future besties with the pizza kid. I take the plastic number he hands me, smiling brightly in an effort to undo the earlier, very obvious age gap I highlighted by my ancient movie reference.

"Enjoy your pizza." His voice is flat, and before I can make an even bigger fool of myself, he turns and walks into the kitchen—no doubt planning to tell every person back there about the odd bird up at the front.

Luckily for me, Mikey is smiling up at me by the time I make it back to the table.

"You weirded him out, didn't you?"

"I did no such thing!" The words come out quickly and are laced with guilt.

"Uh-huh," he mumbles in response with a giant eye roll.

My phone buzzes in my back pocket again. It will stress Mikey out if he sees who it is, but I know I can't put the call off indefinitely. Whether it is the awkward social exchange I just had, or me needing to take a leap toward self-preservation, I suddenly want to get it over with sooner rather than later. Despite what I told myself an hour ago.

Mikey doesn't bat an eyelash when I tell him I'm going to step outside for a call. He has his phone in hand and is playing something with a consistent tune before I'm even all the way out the door. I send a silent thank you to my virtual babysitter and wait for the door to close behind me before I answer the phone without looking.

I know who it is, and I know I'm only trying to delay the inevitable by pretending I don't, hoping to give myself a small ounce of deniability at who could possibly be on the other line.

"Hello?"

*You are a strong, independent woman, Maddie.* I tell myself this on repeat. *You can't be weak if you don't show weakness.* Right?

"What the fuck, Madelyn!" Zach's voice yells through the phone and I close my eyes in response. I can't help it when my body tenses in anticipation. Anticipation of what? Who knows. But there's tension in every inch of me. Maybe it's the worry that he'll keep yelling, or perhaps it's guilt that I haven't talked to him since we left. Really though, it's probably all of those things and then some.

*I am a strong, independent woman,* I remind myself again.

Despite the reminder, my heart rate picks up, and my palms start sweating. Great, sweaty, and tense. There's nothing I can do to stop the physical response. Too many memories are dug up at Zach's tone, so I do what any woman would do and take a deep breath, not so much a cleansing one, but a reaffirming breath.

I can do this. He's not here. He doesn't even know where *here* is. That is the point.

"Zach." I don't have any idea what to say back. Honestly, that is one of the reasons I keep ignoring his calls. I'm not sure that only saying his name is enough, but it's probably better than nothing.

"Where the fuck are you?" He is angry. Like, *really* angry. I can tell by his tone, even if he hadn't screamed it. Which he did, by the way. Loudly. I absently lower the phone volume and glance around the sidewalk at the families passing by hoping no one noticed. Not that it would mean anything to any of them if they did. I'm sure the teenage redhead already spread word through the small-town network to ignore the odd blonde in ragged shorts.

I clear my throat before trying again, knowing I'll likely just aggravate him more if I continue to say nothing. Why did I answer the phone again?

"Zach, I told you we would leave. I'm done. I'm not doing this with you anymore." Keeping my voice steady, I get the words out without so much as a hitch or stumble. Yay me.

*Maddie: One*

*World... (or Zach): Zero*

"You're a bitch, Maddie. You can't just leave me and take my son. We fought. You're making it something bigger than it is." There's not even an attempt from him to hide the venom in his voice. The name-calling hurts, but I remind myself they are just words. Words through a tiny piece of metal that I can easily turn off.

"Zach," I repeat his name like it's apparently the only word I know. I don't want to fight. I hate confrontation, and he knows it. But I keep going while my steady voice is still in my corner, "Beyond the fact that our relationship hasn't been healthy for years, you went too far. The first time I gave you a free pass, you had a shitty week. The second time you convinced me it was my fault. But the third time? I made it clear we would leave if it happened again."

His quiet breaths on the other end bring back even more vicious memories than any nearly silent sound should, and I block them out as his voice comes through, pleading and as sweet as honey. "Baby… I miss you. Look, I'm sorry I yelled. You know how it is at work, and when you get me worked up, I can't help how I respond." The personality shift stopped giving me whiplash years ago, but his pause after he finishes gives me enough time to register his words. Is he really taking *that* as his arguing stance? That this was somehow no fault of his?

Since I left, I'd been able to see through his gaslighting, and lucky for me, the phone put a filter on his honey-coated voice—leaving me an unhindered view of the words he'd often say behind it. Plus, not seeing him took out the physical attraction we would often fall back on. Hearing the words and what they really mean while he was actually saying them, and not just *remembering* old conversations, gives me the confidence to straighten my shoulders and breathe a little easier.

*Maddie: Two*

*World…basically just Zach right now: Minus One*

"We can go to that couples' thing. We can work on us." Those words, and so many just like them over the years, were the trap I kept falling into before we left. *This* was how I pretended it wasn't what it so clearly was for so long. Zach would turn it on me and agree to put in 'effort', making me out to the bad guy when I got upset.

No, thank you, good sir. I am done.

Taking a genuinely cleansing breath this time, I stop my mindless pacing and turn, finding Mikey smiling at me through the window. His big eyes are alight with sheer joy as he motions to all the pizza I ordered. Crap, those slices *were* huge...

Seeing the scene on display in the restaurant window, my kid, happy and not scared, gives me all the unwavering resolve I didn't know I needed.

"Zach, we're gone. We're not coming back. There is no *us*. There never will be. You need to fix yourself and fix yourself for *you*. Until you do, you will have nothing to do with Mikey. And as for me, I'm going to *finally* move on and maybe someday find a healthy relationship to move on to." I almost cheer for myself when I don't show a hint of doubt through all of it.

I am not going to cave this time. There is no doubt in my mind. Somewhere between that last fight and now, that messed-up piece of me that thought I deserved the violence—the dark place inside me that felt that I deserved the blame, clicked back into place. I will not put Mikey or myself through that ever again.

*Maddie: ONE THOUSAND*

*Zach: GONE*

Seconds, minutes, what feels like forever passes before he finally responds. The silence so loud it makes my ears ring.

He doesn't scream or yell, but when he does speak, his tone is even and subtly savage. I realize in that moment that I haven't seen the dark bottom of this well yet. I've been scared of his reactions before, but I've never been scared of him. Not until now.

"It doesn't matter how far you've gone, Madelyn. I will find you both. You are a spoiled brat who doesn't deserve any better than I gave you. I gave you our kid. I gave you our home and paid for our lives while you worked on your 'passion.' You will never be good enough to survive on your own. This attempt is pathetic. Your family's money will run out, you'll be alone, and when all that happens, I'll be waiting to put you back in your place."

Maybe he's right. Maybe I am only worth *his* brand of love. Maybe all I have is what others have given me. Maybe I'll never become anything on my own.

But as I watch Mikey take another bite of his pizza through the window, a long string of cheese pulling from the slice, he looks back at me with a giant grin on his face. My heart fills with unhindered happiness, something I honestly haven't felt in so long.

I start walking back to the front door of the pizza place, pausing before I reach for the handle. "Maybe you're right, Zach, but I'm more than enough for Mikey. I'm more than enough for me. And that's all I need." I hang up without waiting for his response and open the door to a life that will never again have him in it.

# Chapter Three

## NICKNAMES

### Lucas

"Okay, guys, listen up…" The faces of two-dozen little boys look back at me, faces eager and eyes attentive. "Today, we are focusing on our footwork and learning our basic plays. I don't want any of you, even for a second, thinking about *anything* other than those two things." My tone is level and firm. Not harsh. But I want to start this year off right, and they need to have the right mindset if this is going to be a worthwhile year.

They all nod, determined looks filling their stares.

It's easy to see who's nervous about the new season and who isn't fazed in the slightest. The chewing on a mouth guard, tiny fidgeting of feet and fingers, breaking eye contact. Jesus. These boys should definitely *never* play poker.

"All right, we're going to start with sprints. Go from the first cone over there to the far one. Anyone caught turning early has to do twenty push-ups. Each time." Their eyes widen at me as they look at each other, trying to tell if I'm being serious. Jasper nods emphatically, giving them some inside skinny before they all think I'm joking and end up caught on the ground with shaking arms. I think they got lax with all the play dates we had during the off season. The curse of most of these kids being friends with my son. My coaching style is consistent, so it should not be a surprise, but I'll get them back in shape in no time.

"What are you waiting for?" I ask briskly before they take off like little rockets.

"Hey, Mikey," I call, stopping the new kid, who turns around and hurries back.

"I know we met when you first got here, but I wanted to welcome you to the team. Where are your parents?" His light greenish-brown eyes look back at me. He's got quite a mop of unruly blond curly hair, a big smile, and freckles for days.

"My mom is parking the car," he answers shyly before continuing. "I made her drop me off before she parked since I didn't want to be late on my first day." His face falls, and he chews on his lip, immediately breaking eye contact with me, looking at his shoes. I get the idea he's expecting to get in trouble for that.

"No problem at all." My easy response seems to appease him, and he visibly perks up—mental note to keep an eye on that. Football is a demanding sport, even this young. Between coaches, your teammates, parents, the other team, and even the refs—there are tons of people who will be hollering at you. Frequently. And that is the *best-case* scenario.

"Well, as I said when you first arrived, my name is Lucas. You can call me Coach, Coach Lucas, just Lucas, or any variation of that. My son Jasper is on the team. I think you were talking to him earlier. He can help if you have any questions and I'm with another player."

His eyes meet mine again, and that big smile fills his face, showing one crooked incisor and dimples. "Okay, Just Lucas," he quips, and I chuckle lowly. He's got one hell of a shit-eating grin on his face, and I know for sure that I'm going to like this kid. Hell, I already do.

"Get out of here and go work on those sprints," I laugh, sending him off.

Turning to the parents seated at the sidelines, I scan the group of familiar faces looking unsuccessfully for his mom. I make a point not to linger too long at Cash's dad since the last thing I want to start the season with is another one of his lectures on how we need to have a more aggressive offensive line and how all my plays are 'soft'. Thankfully he's too busy chatting Tyler's ear off. I remind myself to buy my friend a beer next time we're out.

I don't worry about seeing Sherry here. She isn't into any part of Jasper's extra-curricular activities, especially football. She says it's too 'violent' for her baby... but really, I don't think she wants the time commitment that comes with it. Three nights of practice a week plus home and away games is a lot to commit to, and her social calendar can't take that kind of hit. Though I'm sure if it were important to Jasper, she would come to the games, but he has never seemed to care one way or another. Which I am perfectly fine with.

After the boys do sprints for a few more minutes, we get into some footwork exercises and then move on to practicing last season's plays.

I put in some one-on-one time with Mikey, walking him through each of our main plays so he can catch up quickly. He's a little shy on defensive but is fast as hell, and I'm more than hopeful that skill will only improve as his confidence does. With some drilling and practice, he's definitely going to be an excellent asset to our team.

In youth football, it is always a hit or miss on the quality and commitment of the players you get, and so many times, all parents really care about is a posed Instagram photo and a jersey to fill their kids 'childhood memories' with. Thankfully though, the kids all still seemed to be in it and the season is looking promising.

Practice is over before I know it, and we huddle up. Our usual end-of-practice huddle is filled with some pep talks, reviewing what they exceled at and pinpointing what we want to work on next week. Then the kids run off to get snacks and return to their parents.

Following their speedy steps, I walk directly into the 'hornet's nest', knowing it can't be avoided any longer.

Pete, Cash's dad, corners me first—big surprise. I spend more than a few minutes assuring him the kids will run through the plays more before our first game and that we'll work on our offensive line. I don't owe him either, but in my experience, it is easier to give him something. Otherwise, he corners me repeatedly. His constant belt adjusting while we talk is something I can only assume he thinks makes him look tough and confident. But, the sweaty brow, nervous throat clearing, and constant sideways glances at his wife give away his insecurities. I could clean him out in under an hour, easy.

After I'm sure I've given him far more minutes than he deserves, I move on. Getting through the cursory 'hi's' and 'how are you's'. I pause for a second and nod to Tyler, letting him know I am wrapping up. We have a standing dinner with the boys after practice. He nods back and walks onto the field to help me gather up the cones and flags.

After a few more scans through the remaining parents, folding chairs, and kids again, I finally spot who I assume is Mikey's mom at the far corner of the field. Being the only unknown face among a sea of familiar features, she stands out sharply. The back of her blonde ponytail and white tee sticks out like a glowing beacon on the muted fall tones of the slowly yellowing grass. Even with the red color of the boys practice jerseys, her dark jeans and white sneakers stick out sharply against the freshly mowed field.

The conversation from last night with Harley lingers in the back of my mind, followed by the hour or so that I spent mindlessly swiping through endless 'copy and paste' Tinder profiles has me checking her out in a rather indecent way. Especially considering her husband or partner could be coming from any direction for all I know. That thought doesn't stop me though. I admire her curvy hips, which are very visibly on display, being that she's crouched down in those tight skinny jeans. I can't see her front, but given Mikey's features, I am positive she is not unattractive.

Her blonde hair whips over her shoulder as she looks behind her, eyes scanning the thinning crowd sprinkled on the sidelines of the field before she faces the kids again. When she does, her arms begin waving as she animatedly resumes whatever she was telling Mikey and Jasper. Catching a glance at her swooping profile and wide, lash-framed eyes, I find myself *riveted* in her mannerisms and not 'copy and paste' features. The boys sit crisscrossed in front of her, eating apple slices from sandwich baggies and drinking juice pouches. They may be shoveling food into their mouths, but their full attention is on whatever it she is saying.

Curious at what could have them both so enamored, I watch silently from afar until they both throw their heads back in laughter, right before they both keel over at the mysterious punch line. Before I make a conscious decision to do so, my feet are heading toward them, my curiosity clearly getting the better of me.

How she got onto the field without me seeing her perplexes me. I can only guess she walked out while we were running the defensive plays on the far side because otherwise, I wouldn't have—scratch that, I *couldn't* have missed her.

Even though I'm still several feet away, her laugh breaks through the space between us, and it takes me aback. It's completely carefree and happy.

God, hearing it reminds me that I can't remember the last time I laughed like that.

"Dad!" Jasper says when he sees me approaching, pulling Mikey with him as they both stand up.

"Hey, boys," I call back, giving Mikey a friendly smile as I do. Throughout practice, we moved past the initial awkward greetings and first conversations and steadily headed toward a comfortable familiar rapport.

Mikey's mom turns and... screw every Tinder profile I swiped through last night. I was right. Attractive. Her round, hazel eyes are framed by lashes that look like they're from a makeup commercial. Freckles dot her tan skin across her nose and cheeks, not nearly as many as Mikey has, but enough that I can tell he gets them from her. Her pink lips and smile light up her whole face. I'm not surprised to find myself smiling back. How can you not when everything about her exudes happiness?

"Hey! I'm Madelyn," she says, diving in and not waiting for me to introduce myself first. It's like a one-two punch when she speaks because her voice is incredible. A paradox, both sweet and mischievous at the same time. "Madelyn Thompson. Well, Maddie... no one calls me Madelyn. Just my parents. I'm Mikey's mom." She is rambling. Maybe she's nervous? Her voice is confident though, so perhaps not nervous—but intimidated?

Somehow, it's adorable and not at all annoying. Oddly.

Before I can stop myself, my eyes move down to her ringless left hand. That pre-Facebook relationship-status check. Unfortunately for me, it's as obvious a move as liking a social media picture from three years ago, and her smile widens when she notices. Too much time in my head fills the space with what is quickly becoming an awkward silence while I fumble to respond, "You must be *Just* Lucas." She presses, saving me while her eyes laugh at the now inside joke, and both boys start cackling behind her... again. Push-ups next practice. For sure. Lots and lots of push-ups.

"Hey...ya. I'm Lucas, Lucas James." *Nice, you fool. Who do you think you are? James Bond? Get it together, James.*

"I see you already met Jasper." I give both boys a look, and they immediately silence, being completely obvious about it when they do. Smooth recovery, kids. "Why don't you guys go help Tyler finish cleaning up." Jasper pulls his lips between his teeth, looking sideways at Mikey, who seems to be having just as hard of a time containing himself. He grabs Mikey's arm before I can even raise my eyebrows at them, and they run back onto the field.

"Well, Lucas James, it is nice to meet you." That voice of hers pulls me back, and I openly stare as she subtly runs her gaze over me in return. Tit for tat, I guess. My name on her lips does something to my stomach, and I run my hand through my hair trying to not make it obvious that she is having an effect on me.

Fuck, since when do I have such an obvious tell?

I feel like a teenager all over again. I'm stumbling over my words and stressing about whether I smell after practice. The thought slams in the realization that I am, in fact, sweaty from practice, *and* I wore my old shorts today. On top of which, I can't remember the last time I went to the gym. Actually, now that I think about it, all the poker nights and mac and cheese with Jasper have softened my efforts at breaking that 'dad bod' stereotype.

*Way to let yourself go,* I scold myself.

All that self-wallowing, and now you finally meet someone new and *gorgeous,* and you've gone soft on kid food, of all things. I've never been like a Greek god or anything. I know I am not rocking your standard dad bod, but as her gaze comes back to my face, I realize I wish I had been putting in more effort all these years. Though if she notices, she doesn't show any sign of it.

"It's nice to meet you too, Maddie." I finally get out. My response was *definitely* delayed, unfortunately obviously so, but I hope not so long that it made things awkward.

She laughs, and my hopes don't make it far. Yep, definitely awkward. Again.

"Mikey did great today." Maybe if I just keep talking, she'll forget about my return to teenage angst? "He's a great addition to the team, and we're happy to have him."

"That's so great to hear. Since we're new in town, I just want him to have every opportunity he can to make friends, and this was the first thing I thought of."

"Well," I say, looking back at the field, finding the boys chasing each other with cones on their hands, wielding them like swords at each other. Asher, Tyler's son, joined them, and they look like they are having the time of their lives. "They seem to have hit it off."

She looks visibly relieved, and I see something pass over her face that I don't quite catch before she smiles again. Catching it feels like a win to me, even if I don't know what the look means. Noticing the small things that show on a person's face is a skill half the guys I play poker with haven't mastered. I pride myself on my ability to read people.

We watch the boys run circles around Tyler for a minute before Maddie breaks the silence again. "It's such a wonderful thing to be young like that. Don't you miss running around, playing in the grass, and never once worrying if there were bugs where you are sitting, or if you are going to get grass stains on your shoes?" She's thoughtful, and I can tell she means it.

Her question hangs in the air for a second, and I try to think of the last time I did just that. When was the last time I just ran around in the grass? Fuck, who knew. But I get it. We get so caught up in life, the worries of it and the day-to-day grind, that grass becomes something other than an open space of opportunities. I notice that her shoes are free of grass stains.

"I know what you mean."

Her eyes meet mine, and that feeling in my stomach hits me again. My hand twitches to run through my hair, but I force it to stay down, not wanting to blatantly appear nervous despite the apparent fact that she's making me feel that way.

"That's why I started coaching," I offer, hoping to distract both her and me from my twitching fingers. "I wanted to spend time with Jasper doing something other than just the usual parenting."

She nods like my response makes sense to her, and I get the idea she knows exactly what I mean.

Tyler walks up to us, arms laden with flags, balls, and cones—that he finally seemed to have wrangled from the boys.

"Ready for dinner?"

"For sure," I say to him as I take some of the balls he carried over and start shoving them into the supply bag, lifting them onto my shoulder. Glancing over at Maddie, I get hit with a pang of jealousy when I see her smiling at Tyler. Damn it.

She is definitely going to notice his dumb dimples, and I still have no idea if she's in a relationship, or if she's *not* and she's looking for...dimples.

Tyler widens his eyes subtly at me and clears his throat before I finally realize how quiet it's gotten and introduce him.

"Tyler, this is Maddie. Maddie, Tyler. His son Asher is on the team." Pointing to the new addition to the three boys, who stopped chasing each other and were now sitting on the grass in the middle of the field, throwing a ball between the three of them.

"It's nice to meet you," Maddie says, nodding at him. Tyler smiles his wide, practiced Tinder smile back at her, and the memory and details of his last date fill my thoughts, replacing the faceless woman in the back of a random car with Maddie's face. I shake my head, trying to get rid of the picture.

Maddie turns back to me, "Before I forget, I brought these for you." She bends down and retrieves a white box from the ground by her feet, passing it to me. I raise an eyebrow questioningly as I take it from her, noticing the weight of it.

"You see, where I'm from, we buy our friends, and what better way to do that than with cookies?" There's humor there, and I'm startled to find myself laughing at her cheeky response.

Tyler gives me a weird look as he laughs, too, eyeing me oddly as I pull the box closer and don't say anything.

*You're acting like a pubescent teen. Pull yourself together.*

"Why don't you and Mikey come to dinner with us?" Tyler offers after the silence has grown, clearly confused at my abnormal conversational handicap. He's not alone. I remind myself to buy him two drinks the next time we go out. Unless he's planning on hitting on her, in which case I'll make him buy me one. Right before I kick his ass. I can't decide if he is being helpful or if I hate him right now.

"That would actually be incredible. We haven't finished unpacking yet, and *somehow,* I didn't end up labeling any of my kitchen boxes." There's something about the way she says it and the face she makes when she does that I get the idea she did it—or didn't do it, in this case, entirely on purpose.

"You guys should absolutely come." I chime in uselessly and way too late for the speed of the conversation. "We're going to Old Sal's."

Mercifully, she doesn't comment, but holds her hand out instead. "I don't think I know that place. Here, give me your phone. I'll add my number and you can text me the address."

Distractedly I hand her my phone, and our fingers brush, eyes meeting in response to the contact before she pulls her hand back and starts tapping away. While she's typing, the boys make their way over to us, and I watch how easily they've settled into chatting.

"All set," she says, handing it back. "We'll meet you there. Come on, Mikey. Let's get you loaded up." Mikey says bye to me, Jasper, and Asher before turning to do the same to Tyler, whom he's already on a first-name basis with, before I watch the two of them walk away. They head to a white crossover on the far side of the parking lot, and I can't help but think that that seems like the exact car I would picture her driving, even though we've just met.

Unlocking my phone to send her the address to Old Sal's—our go-to after practice, I'm not remotely surprised that she's already added herself as a contact and didn't just put in her number. She doesn't seem like the type to mince words or beat around a bush. The contact name she put in has me chuckling again, which is odd since I don't usually find new people funny… or enjoyable at all, actually.

She's put herself in as 'Just Maddie' Thompson.

# Chapter Four

## FOOTSIE

### Maddie

Holy cookie dough. I am in trouble.

"Mom, are we there yet?" Mikey's voice calls from the car's back seat, reminding me *again* how distracted I am.

"Yep! Nearly there. How was practice?" I know I've asked him this already, but if I am being completely real with myself—which I make a point to be at all times—I am distracted. With a capital D... A capital D for Dad, and damnnnn, and umm, other things—obviously.

Here I was, successfully minding my own business for weeks, working on getting the bakery up and running, keeping my head down, trying to be a good and attentive mom... when, hellooo, Coach.

I've had some mile-high security walls up since things got intense with Zach. Honestly, I had them up even before that. But through the barbed wire and armed electric fence, even I could see how hot Lucas is. Cue butterflies and late-night bedroom thoughts.

I mean, come on.

Those arms filled out his shirt in a way that made me wonder if he could lift me as easily as he swung the sack of footballs over his shoulder when we were leaving. That sandy blond hair looked like it was perpetually tousled, the longer ends at the top resting on the edge of his tanned forehead. Drool. A perky butt that was on full display whenever he bent over with his hands on his knees, chatting up the two dozen or so little kids... Not that *that* belonged in my dirty thoughts, but a guy who was good with kids—bake me some brownies, I really am in deep trouble.

It's not that I was daydreaming during the practice per se, but there was at least one moment on the field where I could have sworn he started moving in slow motion. I shake my head trying to clear the drool-worthy image and leaving myself feeling my self-appointed relationship status of 'single'. It truly has never been a lonelier word.

"Mom, you're not going to be weird, are you?" Mikey asks, startling me away from my inappropriately timed 'me time', and straight back firmly into 'mom time'.

I could tell he hit it off with those kids and didn't want me to ruin it unintentionally.

"Buddy, I'm never weird." Our eyes meet in the rearview mirror, and he tries to hide his grimace with a quick smile. I'm sure imagining all the embarrassing things I might say or might have already said at one time or another.

"How about we make a deal," I attempt, trying to appease his unfortunately valid, uneasy thoughts, "I won't say anything about you that's embarrassing, and you don't say anything about me?" He looks seriously doubtful, but nods just the same, and I give him what I hope is a convincing grin in response.

I don't mean to make him uncomfortable or humiliate him. Really. I just have never understood why anyone should say or do anything other than what they mean. And in being true to that self-proclaimed philosophy, I know for a fact that *that* is precisely why we were here. Not 'here' as in the parking lot of a small-town diner. But 'here' in the 'where are you at' in life sense. Hiding from the consequences of *my* lack of honesty with myself. A situation I am adamant that I will not be repeating.

But since I already spend the majority of my time worrying about Zach, or the shop, or all my grown-up problems of one kind or another, I shove the thoughts out of my head. Putting them back inside my 'to deal with later' box. I will not let this brief reprieve and possible adult conversation be drowned out by my own Negative Nancy or my Wendy Worries.

Sliding into an open parking spot, I turn off the engine and glance around at the collection of cars that fill up the worn and compact lot. Gosh, this town is smaller than I thought. This place is a block or two from the bakery, and maybe five minutes from our home. And it is *packed.*

Mikey is out of the car in ten seconds flat, tapping his fingers on the side of his door anxiously when I finally wrangle my purse out from under the passenger seat.

"You like these boys, huh?"

"Ya." He looks at his feet, and I know he's trying not to make me feel bad. "I miss my friends back home, but these guys are cool, and they're in my grade, so it would be nice to have friends already when I start school. There's even a chance we might be in the same class" He tries to hide the vulnerability in the undertone of his voice, and it breaks my heart. "I'm starting late already. I don't want to be the *new* kid who has *no* friends."

"Aw, kiddo." I grab him without a second of hesitation and make every effort possible to squeeze all the sadness out of him. I am very aware that this qualifies as weird and embarrassing, but I chose not to care one bit. It is just us out here, so it definitely doesn't count.

*Maddie: Two... one for each of us*

*World: Nothin'*

"Ugh, Mom," he murmurs from somewhere inside the hug. "This is not going to help them think I'm cool." I can hear him smiling, and I release him with an unapologetic grin. "You're probably right. Let's add 'no hugging' to tonight's deal. But starting now."

With one more sideways glance at each other in silent agreement, we head inside and find the guys at a large booth at the back of the old diner.

Old Sal's is *definitely* a place for locals. There is an air of friendly chatter, but none of the rowdy conversation or noise that comes with trendy restaurants that are meant to appeal to tourists.

The booths and tables are made of dark wood, surrounded by chairs, and hugged by benches covered in well-loved red leather. The countertop bar is front and center when you walk in, with matching red leather stools neatly pushed up against the spotless white Formica counters that are lined in silver trim. Admirably, the floors and surfaces are pristine. From one food establishment to another, this place is run well.

"You guys find the place okay?" Tyler's friendly voice calls, bringing me back into the diner and away from my appreciative glances. Mikey wastes no time sliding into the booth next to Asher, across from an already-established threesome of Tyler, Lucas, and Jasper, leaving one spot open for me.

"I've never been in here but I'm actually pretty familiar with this part of town," I reply, sliding into the booth after Mikey's enthusiastic entrance. The smooth leather is clean and cool, grabbing my appreciation again as I look around and openly admire the old photographs that adorn the walls around us.

"When did you guys move here?" Lucas asks across the table from me. The deep tenor of his voice bringing back with a vengeance some of those 'me time' thoughts from earlier, startling me as I glance up at him. His eyes survey me. All of his attention firmly on me while he waits for my response. I get the idea that he misses very little.

"We got here about four weeks ago. I was born and raised in Boston, and so was Mikey."

"This place is a helluva lot different than a big city," Tyler remarks curiously, and I chuckle in response. He has no idea.

Camden is just like those small-town cities in prime-time TV shows, but also nothing like them simultaneously. I am starting to think that capturing the charm that places like this have is impossible. You have to *live* it to really understand it.

In Boston, I worked at a small bakery that was one of dozens. It was rather unremarkable, but it was my safe haven away from all my home life dramas. Toward the end, Mikey and I spent most evenings there after school, leaving as much time as possible before we went home each night. Once Zach and I finally separated, more like when I eventually left, we stayed for a few weeks with my mom, and the bakery started to feel more like home than home did. That was when I realized that all I needed to be happy in life was Mikey and filling the rest of my time with baking.

I had been sitting on family money from my late grandpa for almost a decade. It pissed Zach off that I had it and that I might not *need* him anymore, so I didn't touch it. Another useless effort to not rock an already tipping boat. But now is the time and I am happy I waited. I searched high and low for small towns with good schools, charming character, and bakeries for sale until I found the old closed-down one here. Mikey and I moved right after.

I don't tell the guys in front of me any of that. Instead, we settle into an easy conversation. Them telling me about the town. The places that should become my staples, and the places that are reserved for tourists and families who came and went. I quickly learn that Tyler works up at the local ski lodge, which his family has owned for generations. It has yearly ski competitions that were once renowned, and he tells me all about his plans to build it up again. He doesn't outright say it's struggling, but I kinda get that idea. He also volunteers as a local park ranger in his spare time, and Asher is his only son. He gives the impression that he and his ex are still on good terms since he talks so effortlessly about her. Wish I could say the same thing.

Lucas is a lot more to unpack. It is obvious that he holds his personal life close to his chest. What I can gather from the little he shares and the stories he does tell is that he played college football but picked a steadier career path and major when Sherry, his ex, got pregnant. Now he runs a small architectural firm that he owns with a partner, some old guy he apprenticed with after college. Not his words *exactly*, but my interpretation of them. He did not call his partner old. I think he called him Gary, actually. But I got lost a little at that point because I found his lips distracting, which is another thing I did not plan on telling either of these two men.

Both Tyler and Lucas grew up here and were tried and true examples of the charm that people retained when they are from small towns. The sort of heartwarming, welcoming attitude and care that big cities beat out of you from the get-go. But with how they talk about the town and its people, I am certain that they both possess the small-town gossip trait.

The boys all hit it off as easy as we do, especially after they realize Mikey will be starting in their class. As soon as he mentions his teacher's name, which we got in a welcome email earlier this week, the conversation and chatter became even more comfortable. Every now and then, I catch snippets of their conversation: Roblox, school, boy things. Perfect.

Mercifully I don't think I embarrass Mikey once. But to be fair, I'm not really trying to chime in on his conversation. Which I am absolutely sure helped.

It's funny how there are times in life when small talk is exactly what people hate, and the minutes become hours, but then there are times when it is as easy as breathing. And by the end of a conversation, you wonder how you were ever strangers in the first place.

This is how it is with Lucas and Tyler.

Tyler is a sweet, intelligent, and charming guy. His chocolate brown hair frames his face, longish and wispy at the ends, and his brown eyes reminded me of brownies—which he is clearly made of since he is just as sweet. Not only has he already convinced me, ME, to go on one of his favorite hikes, but he also offered to give Mikey skiing lessons once the snow season starts. I tried to tell him we'd gladly pay for classes, but he insisted that it is one of the perks of running the lodge.

Lucas James is something else entirely. While Tyler takes time to tell me about the town, his favorite spots, the weather, and what book he is currently reading, Lucas seems to just vibrate with awareness. He has his eyes and attention on everything at all times, and whenever he asks me something, both are zeroed in on me. His answers are definitive and give no more than I ask, but he listens intently to everything I say. Like I am the only thing that exists in that moment. I'm positive that I blush under his stare on more than one occasion. Who knew that undivided attention was a thing for me?

"Why did you pick Knox County?" His eyes once again meet mine while he waits patiently for my reply. Tyler is giving the boys a demonstration on how to 'correctly' get ketchup out of a glass bottle, slapping the bottom so hard that I start to worry about the integrity of the glass, and remembering a particularly spicy book that referenced the same level of ummm... *focus* he was currently using. The muted conversations and laughter starkly contrast against Lucas's quiet and undivided attention.

This question, though...why did *he* have to ask this question? I knew it, and a million others, were bound to come up. "Where is his dad?" "Is he still in the picture?" "Does he have a dad?" These questions have kept me up at night while I try to come up with the perfect answer. And I have, come up with the perfect answers. I just haven't had a chance to use any of them yet.

I know I am fidgeting and probably look as skittish as I feel, while I decide which *perfect* answer I *should* give him. My palms are sweaty, for Pete's sake. Tucking them under my legs, I attempt to plaster on a carefree face.

I don't like to share the fact that we all but fled Boston because of Zach. The only people who know the details are my sister and my mom. I deleted my Facebook, deactivated my Instagram, and changed my number, which did not deter Zach, who somehow found it anyway. I haven't been able to bring myself to block him after he pointed out how childish and petty doing all of that was. Which is pathetic. I know.

My usual efforts to be upfront still have caveats regarding airing all your dirty laundry to new friends right off the bat. Might as well let the red flags come out slowly so they look a little more pink than red. Also, I get the idea that things are either black or white with Lucas. All the gray—or 'pink' areas of my life will never fit.

"Actually, my sister and I bought the old bakery. It's about two blocks from here. My ex-husband—Mikey's dad and I—split up and I was looking for a fresh start, I guess. Hailey and I always talked about having a business together, childhood dreams and all that. She's not as in love with baking as I am. Actually, she hates it. The only thing she can make is coffee cake. It's delicious by the way." I pause to catch my breath and catch the smile that's formed on his face while I was busy rambling on. Before I spend too much time in my head and wonder what he is thinking I keep going. "She's great at the rest of the management stuff. When I was looking at bakeries for sale, I saw photos of this place and I fell in love with its character. We're putting the charm back into it after all these years, at least we will be once it's finished. The grand opening isn't for another several weeks though." I haven't stopped rambling and I definitely keep fidgeting in my attempts to avoid what I don't want to say, but I'm pretty sure I nail it. Right?

I may or may not answer the question, but the words are at least true.

Lucas's eyes narrow slightly at either what I say or my movements—really could be either. Not missing what I thought was a *subtle* tucking of my hands, or my answering without an answer. I smile at him in response as I try to shift and get comfortable...but less obvious this time. Why was I suddenly so unsettled?

In my efforts to *not* draw attention to my fidgeting, my foot bumps his under the table, and I freeze. Swinging my eyes from what's left of my food to his all-too-observant gaze, I'm frozen like a deer in headlights. Those caramel-colored eyes latch onto mine, and my pulse thunders at the innocent contact, both the physical and the visual kind.

Neither of us moves. My foot awkwardly rests on his, and a smile pulls at the corner of his mouth as I feel my cheeks go pink. Keeping his foot in place, he runs his hand through his hair. Back to front. But he doesn't move it, and his eyes don't leave mine. My uncomfortable anxiety slowly starts to turn into a burning fire under his gaze, and that subtle mischievous grin on his face makes me want to know all his secrets.

I know for sure that this moment is going to be far dirtier when I recount it later during my 'me time'. But was this electricity between us just my many months of celibacy, or was it just him?

The boy's conversation with Tyler continues, turning into muffled chatter as Lucas slowly moves his foot without breaking that steadfast gaze. Gliding it up my jean-clad calf as he does.

Holy cake pops... was it getting hotter in here?

When in the world did eye contact and footsie become sexy? Because it sure as hell was. Set me to broil because I was seconds away from burning like a creme brulé.

Tyler's laugh breaks my trance, and I jump like that time I had been caught by my mom doing the dirty in high school. Lucas's face pulls into a wicked grin at my response, which I would have missed if he didn't have every ounce of my attention.

Tyler spares us from awkward silence as he leaves the conversation with the boys—who are building fry towers beside their cheeseburgers—and joins ours. "That place has been empty for years! It makes sense. Those cookies you gave Lucas were gone before we got here. You should have seen the boys splitting up the box before we even left the field."

Right! The bakery. I couldn't have told you what we had been discussing even if I watched the conversation back or had a narrator give me a play-by-play.

"Well, I have high hopes for it. This town is so special. I'll be happy if I can bring something to it, or hopefully back to it. I saw pictures of the place in its heyday, and I'd love to even come close to that." I don't let my insecurities show as I say it. I know I can bake. Hell, I'm really good at it. Running a business, or getting the construction done, or the website, or the menu… that's a different story.

"If you need anything, setting up or anything prior to opening, we would be happy to help," Tyler continues as his large hand gestures to him and the boys. I'm filled with visions of these not unhandsome dads painting the walls while the boys run around the shop in a sugar-high glee. "You could even pay us in cookies," he continues.

The mention of cookies brings the boys out of fry-sword fights and back to our conversation.

"Maybe you could be on snack duty next game?" Jasper chimes in, his charming voice reminding me of sun-filled summers and s'mores. "The parents never say 'no' when someone brings treats. You could bring cookies!" His suggestion is followed by agreeing remarks from both Asher and Mikey. Mikey was so sick of eating my cookies that I knew he was just happy they thought something I did was impressive and not embarrassing.

"I'd be happy to!" There's not a tablespoon of awkwardness in my response, and I decide to chalk the footsie tension up to how lonely I've been lately.

After we finish eating, we make our way to the front. Tyler clues me in that when it comes to small-town spots for locals, no one bothers you until you get up. If you want to leave, you have to practically beg for your check.

Standing at the register, we wait until the owner of Old Sal's comes and takes our cards, ringing them up without asking who ate what or if we were all on the same check. She's a charming older lady with short gray hair and a deep voice that I heard across the restaurant on and off all night. Her round hips show through the sides of her apron, and her pink cheeks make her seem like a sweet old lady. Until she spoke. Then there was no mistaking her for a sweet, soft, grandmotherly woman after that. I got the idea she was more rough-and-tumble.

"Did you boys eat?" she says in her no-nonsense tone. At first, I think she is talking to the kids, but her eyes stay trained on Lucas and Tyler.

A smile of innocence fills Lucas's face as he replies, "Of course, we did, Sunny! I'd never leave a full plate of food in your diner." Her eyebrows raise with a shared joke, and she struggles to hold in her grin. Looking from Lucas to Tyler has me breaking my silence and laughing out loud. The look on Tyler's face is a mirror image of Asher, nodding like getting in trouble would have him sitting in the time-out chair and getting no dessert.

"Good," is her only reply as she finishes running all the cards we handed over, sliding them all back to Lucas, the receipts folded around each individual card, a tidy and seemingly habitual motion that I assume comes from years of going through the motions given she did it all without looking down.

Her eyes sweep from Tyler and Lucas to me, waiting silently and rather impatiently until Tyler speaks, introducing me like we have been friends for years. I shake my head at his antics when he pulls on the end of my ponytail as he mentions the bakery and my cookies.

I don't miss Lucas's eyes darting to his hand on my hair

when he holds onto the end for a second before he goes on to introduce Mikey. The glare he gives Tyler has my cheeks blushing indecently.

"Welcome to Knox County, you two," Sunny says in that not-so-grandmotherly voice of hers, pulling me back into the conversation. I had the feeling that she prevented as much trouble as she caused. "If you ever need anything, you tell me. I've got my eyes and ears all over this town." I believe that more than anything else I've heard today.

"Thank you so much, Sunny, I'll take you up on that." Her look turns quizzical and I press on, ignoring my inner Judgmental Judy who tells me I'm being pushy. "I'm in the middle of renovating the old bakery and would love to talk about supplying you if you have the time." I keep my response cheerful, letting my smile fill up more of my face, hoping she's interested. I have a feeling that we'll be spending a lot of nights eating dinner here and I don't want to get off on the wrong foot.

"Come by any time. I'm always looking for ways to ease my load. These hips and bones aren't what they once were." She reaches across the register and pats my arm twice before she promptly turns, calling out to her kitchen staff without so much as a look back. Tyler leaves as soon as she does, heading outside with the boys before I finish watching her walk away.

Lucas's large hand reaches out, handing me my receipt and card. When I grab it, my fingers brush his, and the heat in my belly from earlier turns into a raging storm of fireflies.

"Thanks for the invite to dinner." Good God, it was taking everything in me not to sound breathy. "Mikey had a great time."

"And you? Did you have a good time?" His curious eyes hold mine, and I find myself studying his face instead of responding. He is stupidly perfect. His strong chin accentuates the slight grin that holds all sorts of meaning. Plus, my dirty, lonely mind keeps going back to his slow-motion moves on the practice field, and all of that together has me unable to shake the lingering heat building in my body. It's making me far bolder than I have any right to be, but when the world gives you a hot single dad, you sure as hell make freaking lemonade.

Smiling innocently, I glance at his feet and then back up to his face before saying, "Better than footsie in the fourth grade."

I feel my eyes widen in my skull as soon as the words leave my lips. *Oh my gosh Maddie! Why would you say that?* I can only picture the embarrassing shade of maroon my face is undoubtedly turning.

His face fills with the first full smile I've seen since meeting him, and it's a wonder that I don't immediately offer to bake him a cake, since I'm obviously weird.

# Chapter Five

## INGREDIENT LISTS

### Lucas

Jesus.

I can't seem to control my face when my cheeks tilt up and a smile breaks through my usually controlled demeanor.

This woman is something else. She is witty and says whatever the hell flits through her mind. Since meeting her, she has met every single joke, remark, and intelligent statement head on. I like that her sass comes out whether she thinks it through or not—especially since she blushes when she rallies back at me. It doesn't make her even a little less attractive. In fact, I think it's giving me a perpetual semi.

Not even remotely sure how to respond to her last quip, I turn, with that grin still plastered on my face, and open the door to the parking lot, gesturing her out with a nod of my head.

The kids are sitting with Tyler on one of the parking blocks, the hood to his truck up.

"She's finally given out, guys." Tyler says to us as we walk toward him, his voice coming out sad like he's announcing the loss of a pet.

Once we make it to the car I peer into the open hood of his old pickup, my cursory gaze at the guts of his truck purely done in a show of solidarity. I wouldn't be able to do more than tell you if the oil needs to be changed—and only that because the sticker in the car or the electronic dash says so.

Making eye contact with Tyler from his seated perch on the ground, I hold his stare as I deadpan, "I think it's terminal."

His eyes roll as he stands, humor filling his voice. "Well, doctor? What are our options?"

"Definitely need to consider a full reconstruction," I respond, my tone grave.

The boys' eyes are volleying between us as they huddle on the cement block.

"Man!" Tyler yells. "She doesn't need a boob job, she's just sick!" The mock grief in his tone is laced heavily with fake disbelief at my *audacity* to judge his car's appearance during such a 'heavy' moment.

Laughing, I shake my head. Tyler, committed as always.

"I can drive you home," Maddie offers with a smile from beside me, having watched our theatrical exchange with rapt attention.

"Oh, that's too far to make anyone drive it," Tyler argues quickly. "Mikey told me you guys are only minutes from here. I'm all the way on the other side of town." He gives her a dimple-full smile and I narrow my eyes at him slightly.

What is he playing at?

"I'll just take Lucas's car and you can take him and Jasper home since they're just down the street," he continues, ignoring my pointed stare. This whole thing was just getting more and more suspicious.

Considering how much he's already thought it through, I'm one-hundred percent certain he is up to something, but I don't plan on looking a gift horse in the mouth. I certainly won't think twice about the opportunity to spend more time with Maddie.

"What about your car?" she replies, sounding genuinely concerned, and all it does is check more boxes for her in the heavily weighted pro column.

"It's fine. I'll just let Sunny know that I'm getting the poor girl towed, and I'll get Lucas his car in the morning. Right, Lucas?"

"Absolutely," I respond lightly. Trying my best to make this sound like this is something that happens all the time, and not a weird personality transplant he's having... all of the white lies he's spewing are so clearly an attempt at trying to set us up.

She seems appeased by his answer and leans over the edge of his beat-up truck to take a look into the open hood—clearly doing so for the same reasons I looked, given the face of confusion that takes over when she pulls back.

"All right, then," she says finally with a beaming smile at him that I'm suddenly envious of. "It has been really great getting to know you and Asher. I think there are many more dinners in our future."

He grins right back with a playful wink that leaves me clenching my jaw. "Hopefully more cookies too." Has he always been this flirty? Maddie's face lights up under his praise and I mentally remind myself to ask her more about it.

The boys start to say their goodbyes and I tuck that train of thought away to think about later. No need to miss out on time with her while we drive home.

Following her lead, she heads across the small parking lot to the white crossover I saw her get into after practice. Making eye contact over the hood of the car, I wait, rocking on my heels while she digs in her purse to get her keys out. The silence isn't uncomfortable to me, and I find myself hoping she feels the same, though I'm a little surprised that I care. Not usual for me at all.

I am completely fine to take people or leave them, and I am usually fine if they do the same with me but the idea that she might not want to see me again, bothers me. Bothers me a lot, actually.

Jasper and Mikey fly into the back seat as soon as the 'click' of the doors unlocking sounds, the two of them chatting away about the game next week, and Jasper telling him all he knows about the teachers at school. It's funny to hear a ten-year-old gossiping about adults. I would pay to hear what they say about me when I'm not around.

When I pull open the door and go to climb in, I hear Maddie curse under her breath as she dives across the center console to move the stacks of papers and cookbooks that cover the passenger seat. The smell of leather, sugar, and vanilla fills her car. It's a combination that I've definitely smelled before... I just can't pinpoint where.

It gives me this wave of happy nostalgia that I want to swaddle myself in and never leave. I almost laugh out loud when it hits me what it reminds me of. Especially since it's the epitome of childhood and happy memories... one of which I seemed to be lacking lately. Maddie's car—and her, for that matter—smell like every single birthday I've ever had. She smells like cupcakes and frosting. The good kind that has you licking your fingers after. Not the ones that coat your tongue in oil once you swallow.

"I'm so sorry! I wasn't really planning on having anyone else in here," she says, after shoving most of the papers and books to the floor of the front seat and giving me an apologetic smile at the crowded foot space. An uncomfortable embarrassment fills her voice, and she sounds slightly defensive. It doesn't bother me even a little since it's literally her job to make these things.

"Hey," I soothe, trying to ease her completely unnecessary stress over some papers. "I've seen worse. Honestly, I've had worse in my own car."

She smiles at me and syncs her phone with the car's stereo before she pulls out of the parking lot. My response seems to appease her, and she only glances back at the pile by my feet once more before she visibly moves on, and her shoulders relax.

"Where to?" she chirps, her earlier tension nowhere to be found.

I rattle off the directions and we settle into a comfortable silence while the boys keep up their chatter behind us.

It's crazy to think I just met this woman today, and now I'm in her car letting her drive me and my son home.

Who am I, and where did the Lucas from last night's poker game go? Remember that guy who cringed at the thought of talking to a new woman, let alone having one come to his house?

"So, when does the bakery open?" I edge. Small talk is safe, right? Does this count as small talk? Shit. When did I get so bad at this? Because I am *notably* bad at it.

Her blonde ponytail sways when she begins talking animatedly about all the things they've got left to do, and the issues she's having with her website designer.

I'm enthralled while she talks. There are clearly things about this that she knows in and out, and then things she's uncertain about, which become clear as day when her voice dips and her tone becomes hesitant. I've never met someone so equally easy and hard to read at the same time.

We arrive on my street quickly and I point out my house, halfway wishing that I lived farther away.

When we pull up the street, Jasper comments enthusiastically, "Mikey, you have to come in and meet Hulk!"

"Mom, can I?" Mikey pleads, his voice as sweet as all the baked goods I'm sure his mom makes. Both boys go silent as they wait eagerly for her response.

"Of course, but we can't stay too long." She turns and smiles at them as she puts the car in park.

I see her glance at my house appraisingly, and I instantly wonder what she sees. Is it impressive to her? Is it too small-town? Is it unkempt or just well-loved? I know the hedges need trimming and crispy fall leaves are scattered around. But it's still clean and in pretty good condition, if I do say so myself. Which I do. Because I work fucking hard to keep it that way.

*Jesus, Lucas.* Why do I care?

The second the car stops moving, the boys are out. I watch the backs of their heads disappear into the house while we are both still in the front seat with our seatbelts on.

Maddie looks over at me with a clever smile. "Okay, I've told you all about the shop. What about you? What is the Lucas recipe?" She sounds insatiably curious, which causes a chuckle to escape me at how she must view the world.

"You want to know my ingredients too?" I ask back, my tone teasing and a tad flirty, and I hold my breath while I wait for her reaction.

A blush fills her cheeks, and she grins. "Are there nuts involved?" She gets the words out completely composed before a barking laugh breaks free, and that flush I'm getting used to graces her cheeks even more.

I can't hold it in, no matter what all my earlier life training or tendencies have led me to, and I keel over laughing until my sides hurt.

Her eyes are brimmed with tears as she clutches her stomach, her face pink from laughing. When we both catch our breath, I give her one more smile before I open the door. Shaking my head in disbelief, I slide out of the seat, already missing the smell of cupcakes when the fresh autumn air hits my face.

When she doesn't follow me out, I lean back in the open door, "Want to come in? Who knows how long they'll be."

Her responding smile is enough before I straighten and softly close the door.

Maddie follows me down the sidewalk before we walk up the walkway to my house, both still giggling off and on like school kids.

"Okay, where to start?" I stop at the top of the porch and motion for her to sit on the wide swing, mentally berating myself *again* for not blowing off the leaves that cover the wood deck and walkways before the practice.

"The beginning is a safe bet," she says, sitting down, pulling her legs up, and hugging them to her chest. "But just like cream-filled pastries, the middle is usually my favorite part." She smiles at me when I sit next to her, leaving enough space between us that I hope doesn't come off as forward. As if I know what direction that is.

Her ponytail has started to come loose, and strands of wispy blonde hair fall around her face. The light hue of them shines in the warm tones of the porch light.

Rubbing my hands on my knees, I wonder which is a worse place to start, the middle or the beginning? I find her round eyes holding mine with a curiosity that makes me feel like going against what my mind is saying to keep to myself, and sharing the things I worry about when the social niceties are gone.

Also, it's crazy that we're starting here. This is the part I haven't made it to with anyone since Sherry. The few dates I have gone on have been either one-night stands, or just first dates where the conversations are solely surface level... in an effort to get to a one-night stand.

No one tells you when you finish school with your high school sweetheart tucked under your arm like a safety blanket, that learning people on an intimate level as an adult sucks. Where do you start? What do you say? What shouldn't you say?

Fuck, why can't I just be easygoing like Tyler or Harley and talk to a woman without wanting or needing them to know who I am inside and out before we even know each other's last names?

My internal thoughts are making this too hard. Note to self. Think less, please.

"Well, I already told you a bit about Sherry at dinner, so that cat is out of the bag—don't get me wrong, there are plenty more gritty details, but it's not more complicated than high school sweethearts who grew up and realized they weren't right for each other. Besides, I should probably save the rest of the details for when we've had a few drinks to cloud your judgment first. Can't have you not liking me now, can I?" She laughs at this before I go on. "We covered work, so that's also off the table. How deep are we getting, Ms. Maddie?"

"I usually like to jump all the way in. Why prolong it?" She smiles reassuringly before she looks around the porch and off into the distance. Her eyes scanning the trees that line the edge of my property. I appreciate the way she so comfortably slides into an easy silence, leaving me time to jump in with her or chicken out. It's not common to find a girl who is willing to just sit with you.

*No time like the present, Lucas. Dive in.*

"I guess I'm that cliché high school jock. Played football in middle school and all through high school. I tried to keep my feet grounded and not let the little skill I did have get to my head, but that life is made to create assholes, and I fell prey to it more times than I should probably admit. Sherry was who you'd expect a jock to date, we went from friends to dating because we felt like it was *expected*. And honestly, I got comfortable with the ease of it."

I don't know if it's her or the breeze and the sound of the trees, but something lulls me into a verbal trance, and I keep going.

"In my second year of college, Sherry got pregnant. With how I was raised, I knew my job from that moment on was to provide a future for that kid. For Jasper. High school me would roll over in his naïve grave for saying this, but I always knew I was just okay at the game and wasn't going to go pro. Truthfully, part of me was sort of relieved at the excuse to switch paths." The words come out easily, and it's cathartic how effortless sharing this with her is.

"It's pretty great you knew that and made the switch so quickly. I think a lot of people in your shoes would have fought the detour. Honestly, I have friends who would have even resented their kid for the 'sacrifice'... May they rot in a shallow grave for that, of course."

It's easy to tell she's kidding. But only kind of.

"What about you?" I ask, needing a break from the avalanche of life stories that suddenly decided to break free from my chest and out of my mouth.

"Well, I'm a born and raised Bostonian. I had just started my first semester of college when I met Mikey's dad, Zach. We were not from the same circles at all. I barely remember how we met, if I'm being honest... I think it was at a friend's party." Maddie looks away from me and back at the trees as she pauses. Her arms squeeze her legs a little tighter when she keeps going. "He's a real estate agent and already had his career going when we met. He was successful and *very* proud. I was so young and the whole thing was a bit of a whirlwind romance. I was drawn to how mature and together his life was. Or seemed. We got pregnant with Mikey pretty quickly, and unintentionally, and after that I just stopped wondering if he was right for me and focused on making us a family."

She takes a big breath that seems to give her a push to go on.

"It wasn't even until Mikey started first grade that I finally got a job with a family friend at her bakery, and I fell in love with it hard and fast. I got through culinary school at night, and when it came time to move, I decided it was as good a time as any to open my own place."

Maddie holds my eyes for longer than a second this time, and I can tell that there is so much *more* there. The thought startles me, but I realize as I look at her that I want to know everything. Every detail. Every nuance. Every thought. Every feeling.

Just know her.

"So naturally you ended up in Maine." This is my way of asking without asking. Why is she here of all places when her whole life was in Boston?

"Naturally," is her only reply. Even though she says it with a smile, I can tell she's punting the rest of this conversation. Her 'non-answer answers' are quickly becoming her biggest tell. Well, that and the blushing. Which was really rekindling something deep inside me that had been dead for a very long time.

Rotating my body, I turn and face her, my hand moving closer to hers on the porch swing as I do. "So, there's nothing waiting back in Boston for you then?" Her gaze meets mine, and I try my best to convey what I'm asking without actually asking it. Like the male version of her non-answer answer.

The smile she gives me back is a new one, and I catalog it. It's flirty, and knowing, and confident. Honestly, it's fucking perfect.

Clearly, I didn't put enough subtlety into my question.

God, my heart was going to beat out of my chest at the rate it was picking up while I impatiently wait for her to answer.

What if she tells me she's *temporarily* separated? Or that she is going back eventually? Dozens of potential answers rush through my mind, each one as unacceptable as the one before it, and I know deep down I only want one answer.

Am I really going to put myself out there?

To Harley's point—it's been two fucking years. I'm ready. And I feel like maybe the reason it's taken this long is that I've been waiting for someone like Maddie.

"Dad!" Sheer excitement calls out from inside the house.

I give Maddie one last look, deciding that this is definitely not the last time I'll be sitting with her on this porch, and turn to the boys coming over to us.

The boys are breathless and quickly recount how Hulk escaped in the kitchen and they had to catch him with the trash can… but not to worry, they 'cleaned up' all the trash. *Yikes.*

"All right, Mikey, time to go home," Maddie says from beside me, rising from the swing. Turning to me before she heads down the steps and back to her car, she adds, "I guess I'll see you at practice."

"Definitely." I say back with a sure smile.

Abso-fucking-lutely, Cupcake.

My heart sinks when I watch her walk away. The feeling growing as she gets into her car and backs out of my driveway. There's no explaining it, and I don't even bother hiding my falling face when she drives away.

As the car disappears from view, Jasper whispers up at me, "I like them, Dad."

"Me too, kid. Me too."

# Chapter Six

## BOSOM BRIGADE

### Lucas

Sherry doesn't bother ringing the doorbell when she walks in, her arms laden with a bowl of salad and two bottles of wine.

I inwardly and outwardly cringe at the direction the night is destined to go, given that I don't drink wine, and it is just us and Jasper.

Smiling coldly, I watch her half distractedly while I finish dinner. She embraces Jasper with more love than I've ever seen her give anyone else, then crouches down in front of him and they whisper back and forth, noses almost touching. Seeing them together serves as a reminder of all the best parts of her, and it settles a little bit of my bitterness at her more-than-comfortable entry.

Truthfully, Sherry always loved Jasper with everything she had and really did try to be a good mom to him. We just never had *that thing*, the special sauce that soul mates or movie love is made of and really, I don't think she had any more love to give anyone other than him, and maybe herself.

I mean, I'm pretty certain that all teenage relationships are selfish on a basic level, and from the second she and I moved past that point, we just hit speed bump after speed bump.

I've come to terms with the fact that it was me who let us crash and burn in the end. Especially given that I put the final nail in the coffin of our dead relationship. I guess I stopped being okay with the kind of relationship that left me empty. Emotionally, that is.

I couldn't… wouldn't let Jasper grow up in a household that was never anything more than screaming matches over who forgot to swap the laundry. Fuck, it took one time of him asking me if we always fought because of him, and I was done. This kiddo was and *is* my life. Sherry and I settling for each other because we were scared of the big 'D' word was not reason enough to stay together and make him think that.

Pulling the lasagna out of the oven, I carry it over to the table, nodding to the single wine glass set on the counter, when Sherry raises the bottles at me. Her action is a silent question, and mine, a response out of expectation. I knew she'd offer me some, she does every time. It was her way of not quite asking for permission. I mean, after a decade of knowing my alcohol preferences, I truly hoped it was more that than it was really thinking I would change my mind about my drink of choice. I don't know.

Sitting down on one side of the square table in my small dining room, I watch her, and Jasper dig into their plates. I'm trying not to let it bother me that this is starting to feel more like a group of people playing pretend family than it is an actual family having dinner together.

These dinners are Sherry's way of keeping us a family, and they have continued since we fully split two years ago. Really, it was fine in theory. It's just that I finally feel like I'm looking outside of my failed attempt at the only real relationship I've ever been in, and these efforts to 'keep it together' seem pointless. How is either of us supposed to move on when we aren't moving on at all? Especially if we keep playing this make-believe game of perfect family—when we are nothing close to that?

Jesus, Lucas, I scold myself. Trying to keep in mind that this much internal monologue is just going to put me in a foul mood, especially when she's already got the two bottles of Pino in her corner making the inescapable fight a knockout.

"So, Jasper! Tell me about your game." Sherry's high-pitched tone pierces through my internal berating, and I settle in knowing that the only way out of tonight is through it. Like the bear hunt in that children's book.

"Mom, we've only had *a* practice. Games don't start until next week."

"Well, you'll win, for sure," she says back with certainty as she beams at him while loading more salad on her plate.

Her glass is already halfway to a refill, and my mind immediately goes to the fact that she drove here.

Dinner continues in small bursts of conversation wholly centered around Jasper. I never mind this part. This is the part we do well. Even together, with all our faults, we excel at being *his* parents. At least since the split. Just this part of us, at these dinners, reminds me again and again of why separating was the healthy choice for both him and us.

Sherry always puts him to bed after we finish. Jasper tells me it's so she feels like this version of his home has her in it too, and I try not to grate over that. But I know... or hope, that her intentions have him at the center of it. In a selfishly kind sort of way.

While she's reading a second chapter of one of the Harry Potter books—far more animatedly than it calls for from what I can hear, I busy myself cleaning up the remnants of our meal. I toss one empty bottle of wine and put the remainder of the other in the fridge. Her plate, per usual, has no signs of anything being eaten other than lettuce, and I dread what state she'll be in when she leaves Jasper's room.

She finally comes out as I'm wiping the table down and props herself on the kitchen counter, legs swaying off the edge and nursing a glass of water as she watches me. Her straight brunette hair frames her doll-like face and round eyes. She is beautiful. That was never a question.

"So, Lucas, what's new with you?"

"Not much, just the usual."

Her flushed pink cheeks and teetering motions as she gets down and walks toward me are the warning signs I was hoping not to see tonight. But the outcome is inevitable.

"Maybe we should spice things up then?" Her breath hits my face as I turn, the sweet smell of wine on her tongue invading my senses.

"Sher, I'm not doing this again." I steady her with a firm grip as she sways toward my chest, her petite hands finding purchase on my biceps.

The slight squeeze is an obvious foretelling before her lips land on mine and I haul her off me, lifting her body slightly off the floor and setting her down farther away.

"Come on, Lucas," she whines. "I need to feel you. Don't you want to just let go for a night?" The alcohol is making her words run together, and I don't know how much of her request is her wanting *me* and how much is just her wanting. Given how easily she got to this state, I have a feeling it is more the latter.

The old version of me—the one who was still in love with her, at least in some way, would have caved to this. I'd *need* to know why she was stressed, or why she was so *desperate* to let go.

But that guy is nowhere in sight right now.

When her drunken gaze moves down my body with a familiarity that she learned over the years, she slides her fingers smoothly through the front buttons of her already-tight black top, undoing them easily to reveal her Pilates-toned body covered in lace. "Just one more time, baby," she purrs as her hips rock and she saunters back toward me, her dark hair contrasting against her pale skin and black lace.

I silently thank the heavens for making me a strong man as I back up, one step at a time. Leaning against the table, I cross my arms in a defiant show of disinterest.

"Sherry, I said no." There's no disdain in my tone, just unyielding decisiveness.

Maybe it's the alcohol, or maybe it's just our history, but she doesn't slow, and before I can grab her again, her hands are on my chest, sliding down to the top button of my jeans.

"I'm not above begging, Lucas. You know that was never a hard line for me." Her voice is a sultry hum that was the source of my wet dreams for so long. I can't help but respond to her physically as I feel myself grow hard.

With one hand groping me under my jeans, Sherry tucks her dark hair behind her ear and looks up at me through her lashes. I instantly see Maddie.

Maddie sitting on my porch swing. Maddie with her legs tucked under a blanket as she gives me that mouth-watering sultry gaze and tucks *her* hair behind her ear. The image is a fucking ice bath.

Shoving her off me, I glare, "Sherry, that's enough. I'm moving on. There is no more us. I can't be the person you use to scratch this itch. And let's be honest, that's all you want me for!" I'm practically shouting when I finish, and it hits her hard. A reminder of a younger, angrier version of me, I'm sure.

She cracks, and tears fueled by rejection, and probably the wine, start streaming down her face while she clutches her shirt together.

"What, am I not *enough* for you anymore?" The words have a bite when she gets them out between sobs.

"We have not been *enough* for each other in years. Don't turn this on me like I'm rejecting you out of nowhere." I'm getting pissed now even as I tone back my temper.

"We haven't actually *slept* together in months, and we've been separated longer than that." My voice softens as I look into her tear-soaked eyes. The same eyes Jasper has. Seeing them like this has *never* not broken my heart.

"Look, I love you, Sher. I always have." Her eyes shine with hope, and I rush to continue. "I love you for our *past* and for Jasper. But, Sher, I don't love you for me or for my future." Her face falls even though my words are kind, and I'm doing my best to convey my gratitude for everything she has given me.

"I'm moving on, and I think it's time you do as well. I'm not going to sit here and ask for those years back, those nights of us screaming at each other when we were obviously unhappy. But I sure as hell want the ones I've got left. We both deserve that."

Her gaze moves to the floor, and the only sound she makes is occasional sniffles as she buttons her shirt and wipes her eyes.

"I'm a catch, Lucas. I don't know why I was never what you wanted. All I've ever done is love *you*. But your point is crystal clear. I'll give you your space." Turning, she shoves her phone into the back pocket of her tight black jeans and grabs her purse from the counter.

Her cooling gaze settles on mine from beside the front door, and I know any attempts to stop her will only result in her getting physical with me.

I breathe a sigh of relief when she pulls her phone back out and orders an Uber. The hassle of her coming back to get her car isn't something I'm going to worry about now. I'd rather she get home safe.

"You might be the world to Jasper, but you have never been able to commit to anything but him, and that's going to catch up with you. Not everything is easy, Lucas. Especially love."

With her voice still hanging in the air, she turns and leaves, slamming the door on her way out.

Something about her words cuts me deep, and I'm calling the sitter before I can think twice.

Not even thirty minutes later, I'm walking through the

doors of River Rats, Harley's bar, in desperate need of a drink, and more honestly, a friend.

Harley has put so much work into this place over the years, and it's been eye-opening watching a kid who came from nothing, who used to sit with me in the grass and talk about his dreams of making a life for himself, build a successful business. A shining example of overcoming a shitty family upbringing.

My drama was self-made. His was inherited.

The place is busy for a Tuesday night, and I briefly scan the crowd, seeing plenty of familiar faces seated at the small tables, booths, and along the bar.

Unsurprisingly, I see Chase at the pool table in the back, his 'uniform' leather apron slung over his shoulder while he chats with two pretty girls—who are clearly not as interested in the game as they are in him.

The décor has rustic brown leather stools lining the worn wood countertop that starts at the front of the room and flows all along the right wall to the back. Metal tables are scattered around the rest of the room, each with a single Edison bulb hanging above them, giving enough light to see by but not too much that would kill the ambience. The place is more of a classy, upscale bar, but still informal enough that it doesn't have a dress code and the locals still come in straight from work. All the bartenders wear button-ups with the Ace of Spades embroidered next to "River Rats" on the right side, and leather aprons wrapped around their waists. Harley is a stickler for that part. He says a distracting bartender only takes away from the art of the drink itself. Heaven, forbid you pay more attention to a pretty waitress than the ratio of gin to tonic. But Harley sure as hell prides himself on his drinks, so all my teasing in the world won't change his stance on it.

A wall of intricately lit shelving filled with bottles reaches to the ceiling and lines the wall behind the bar that Harley and his lead bartender, Carly, man almost every night of the week.

With the exception of poker nights, you'll find him here or at home with his niece and that's about it.

Shaking my head to clear my thoughts, I make my way to the far corner of the bar, propping myself firmly on a stool. Harley's glance meets mine as he nods, letting me know he'll be over in a minute.

I watch silently as he pours drink after drink. The customer he is currently serving is a pretty blonde who is smiling at him eagerly. He seems unfazed and barely makes eye contact with her before moving onto the next person. Surprising, given how she was showing every single sign of possible interest. But less surprising because he couldn't look less enticed by her, or whatever she was rambling about, if he tried. God, I envy him sometimes.

Minutes go by. I spend them people watching and listening, all while pondering my single life. I've never considered it eavesdropping because I can't turn it off, even if I try. I can just *hear* every conversation happening around me at the same time. Tracking each with little effort.

The couple to the left of me is definitely on a first date that seems to be going in his favor. Lucky bastard. The one behind me seems bleaker, and her cheating wasn't made any better by lying about it until he showed her the text messages. All very dramatic.

I heave with a giant sigh of obvious relief when Harley finally makes his way over to me. I'm grateful he has Carly because it allows him time to chat with me. Two birds, one stone. She's a firecracker if ever I've met one. Short blonde hair, tattoos up her neck and arms, gauges in her ears, and the ability to make any drink you could dream of with her eyes closed. Plus, she is funny as hell and puts up with nothing and no one. My eyes move to her as she flips the cocktail shaker around her back and catches it smoothly.

"She really enjoys the show of it all," Harley says, his voice pleased as his eyes follow mine, and he praises her skills in a way only her boss could. Her cropped hair doesn't have a piece out of place, and her thick eyeliner causes her pale blue eyes to stand out enough that I've seen a fair few people do a double-take when they see her for the first time.

He clears his throat, bringing me back, and I just stare at him as reaches to grab a glass from below the counter, filling it with gin before I ask. His sleeves are rolled up per usual, and I notice a few more details he added to his tattoo sleeves. It's funny to think there was a time when he didn't have any ink at all. Over the years, as he expanded his collection, the tattoos became part of him, and I barely remember what he looked like without them.

"So? Am I going to have to ask, or are you going to tell me?"

I roll my eyes as I drink the perfectly made gin and tonic, not that a two-ingredient drink is that much work to perfect. Still though, I've had some bad ones over the years.

"Fine. I'll guess," he continues, leaning back on the back counter and crossing his tattoo-covered forearms across his chest. "It's Tuesday, so it's Sherry night. She brought wine. Got drunk. And now you're sitting here lonely after turning her down *again* and wondering when the spiral will end." He raises his eyebrows as he finishes, daring me to prove him wrong. Almost hoping for it, if I know him at all.

I finally realize that I can't deal with this any longer and I explode, letting it all out.

"First of all, she brought *two* bottles of wine and took care of all of one and half of the other. All on her own. She ate lettuce with a side of my happiness, and by the time Jasper was down she was practically stripping—no, actually stripping, drunk out of her mind. AND when I turned her down and told her I was finally going to move on, she had the fucking nerve to tell me the problem with us was that I couldn't put in the work when things got hard, and that the only thing I have ever committed to is Jasper."

I'm out of breath when I finish and I down the rest of my drink in one gulp, setting it down harder than I mean to.

"You grew a backbone. Fucking finally." He claps his hands together and laughs at me, causing a few people to turn and stare. The response is so out of place, I can't do anything but look at him in disbelief.

His deep chuckle at my expense has heads turning, mostly female ones, and it pisses me off given the direction of my night. Fucking prick.

"For years I've watched her push you for whatever it is she wants. I love Jasper like he was my own kid and will until I die, but I've said it before, and I'll say it again, you can't tell me he wasn't calculated on her part." He rubs his hand through his full beard before he continues. "I hate watching it happen over and over. Someday she'll finally grow up and won't be the same spoiled girl from high school, but it's going to take some rejection to get her there, and the divorce was clearly not enough. Especially if you're still in her life, meeting her whenever she asks. Fucking her whenever she asks."

I silently think over tonight's newest jab at my character, realizing that my rejecting her is what sets her off every time.

Jesus. Maybe I *was* missing a backbone when it came to her.

This realization has me dumbfounded, and I ponder it as Harley makes a fresh drink in front of me. He immediately has a rag that he uses to wipe down the counter out of habit before the glass hits the already-spotless surface.

While he leaves me to my thoughts, I start counting the number of advances he turns down. The drunken women with cleavage exploding from their shirts hardly get a glance. It makes me wonder if he's okay. I mean, I know he is, and he isn't, but I still wonder.

There is no happiness for me in the endless Sherry-cycle of 'who can make the other feel worse'. He's not wrong that I need to do something to break it. Even if I don't find someone else along the way. *THIS* can't continue.

"So, what's the plan now?" His voice brings me back from my spaced-out abyss, and I meet his eyes when I finally spill the beans about Maddie.

The woman seated next to me calls for Harley, interrupting us and asking him to explain the drink menu to her. I look at her with a judgmental eye. Carly is two feet to her left and she still interrupted us. All the women after him tonight must have shopped at the same exploding cleavage store. He patiently describes an Old Fashioned before he ends up making her the pinkest drink I've ever seen come out of the bar and comes back over to me.

"Of course, you would meet someone at a Pee Wee game." He chuckles as I visibly cringe when Cleavage Lady Number 3 waves him down again. I totally want a break from the Bosom Brigade, I can only imagine how Harley feels. He nods as she compliments the drink and asks him if he's free later.

Poor guy.

Once he turns her down, he comes back over, and we pick right back up. "I can't tell where Maddie stands with her ex, though, and that scares me. What if she's got as much baggage as me?" My vulnerability is showing, and it hurts.

"Of course, she does."

*Wait, what?*

"Everyone has baggage, Lucas."

Girly laughter breaks through our conversation, and I turn toward the squeals, watching as Chase carries one of the girls from earlier, whom he's tossed over his shoulder, toward the back room. Her ass wiggles in the air as she makes a pathetic show of attempting to get down. The other blonde follows close behind them, smacking *his* ass when he copies the wiggling motion.

"What the actual fuck?" I can't even be disappointed in his behavior since I've seen worse. But I'm genuinely surprised by the look on Harley's face when he rolls his eyes and wipes the counter down again, flipping the rag over his shoulder when he's done.

"He's taken to *using* that back room more than I do lately. As soon as he clocks out, he finds someone to keep *busy* with. I don't know what his aversion is to his place, but I've started doing my books at one of the booths." He nods at the back booth which currently has a group of businessmen seated around it.

"Is it just me, or is his carefree attitude getting on your nerves too?"

"Nah, let him live his single life. We all should have the chance to try out different relationships." He's stopped wiping and is openly staring at Chase and his blondes. The upside-down one is trying to jimmy a key into the lock to the back room while Chase bounces her.

"We're single," I argue, gesturing at the two of us.

"True, but we don't want to be."

He sets a glass of water in front of me and walks away. Leaving me with my thoughts again.

His last line rings through my skull like a bell.

He's right. I don't want to be single anymore.

I want Maddie.

# Chapter Seven

## KEITH, KYLE, KURT

### Maddie

"There's not much else I can do." The monotone, almost bored voice in front of me says casually. I don't think he means to come across in a condescending way, but there's literally no other word for it. If it looks like a macaroon, tastes like a macaroon, and smells like a macaroon... It's a freaking macaroon.

"I just don't understand why you can't link the social media pages to my website without a personal Facebook?" Why is this hard? I'm not technology ignorant, but I hired him because he stated *confidently* in his interview that he was a wiz with social, and that was what I needed. Well, that and the website and logo and promo pieces. Internally, I ignore the fact that I'm basically begging at this point. There has to be a solution somewhere that doesn't involve what he is asking because I will not waver on this. Nope. No, sir.

Wednesday has somehow become the day of unsolvable problems.

First, my ovens got delayed for six months. SIX. MONTHS. That's one-hundred-and-eighty days. Like the big corporate company, the one who makes said ovens... didn't know—when I ordered—that said ovens would take an extra six months to produce and deliver? The whole process of canceling and reordering with a new vendor is a nightmare that I'm irresponsibly ignoring until next week.

Then the racks and pans that *did* arrive on time came rusted, and now I have to pay to ship them back.

Now this. How do I explain to this twenty-something-year-old, who doesn't look like he's moved out of his mom's house... which I mean in the nicest possible way, that I can't just "make a Facebook account."

You don't stay minimally undercover with a Facebook account. That's like the opposite of undercover. That's over-cover, it's obviously UNcovered. It's how creepy old uncles and weird aunts stalk your photos, telling you how you've gained a few pounds, or post constant updates about their political beliefs in all capital letters. Nope. (More like NOPE.)

It's also how angry ex-husbands find out where you and your son moved to when you fled while he was out of town, leaving divorce papers on the counter, and a copy of a filled-out, but not-yet-filed, domestic abuse report. Which, if that doesn't spell it out, is code for, "don't want to deal with the fallout. Bye, Felicia."

So essentially, Facebook would not be undercover!

Alright, Maddie. It's fine. We've got this.

*Maddie: Minus three*

*World: TEN*

But there's still time. It's only Wednesday, after all.

"Oh, for cake's sake! Just use mine." Hailey's voice rings out from a mountain of boxes, using my signature line as an obvious attempt to appease me.

I look back at the buttoned-up, glasses-wearing almost child sitting in front of me with hopeful eyes. Inwardly pleading to his mother—whom I'm sure he still lives with—that she raised him to be understanding of women with plights.

His unemotional gaze meets mine with a sigh.

"It should be okay as long as you don't mind her having access to the privacy settings and managing the account," he volleys his eyes from my face to the spot the voice came from behind boxes.

"Not at all," my chipper tone rings back to him. "To be honest, she's going to handle all the social media anyway." Relief rushes through me, and my mood instantly brightens.

*Maddie: Five?*

*World: Umm... probably still ten*

"Okay, I can set that up with her, and then we can make the final edits to the logo."

Kurt, at least I think his name is Kurt, (Kyle maybe?), goes back to his computer without another word, and I don't know if I'm supposed to follow or send Hailey...shoot.

My mom always told me that if you forget someone's name, all you have to do is introduce someone to them, and they will introduce themselves back. It literally works every time.

Plus, Keith is probably less likely to help me if he thinks I forgot who he is.

"Hey, Hails, come here for a sec."

"Coming!" she singsongs as her head pops up again, and I finally get a full look at her, realizing she is covered in teal paint. Some of it is coating the ends of her hair, which is barely held at bay by a matching teal scarf she has tied around her head like a headband.

Growing up, Hailey and I always talked about doing some sort of business together. I fell in love with baking and Hailey fell in love with marketing, the 'new-age' kind, as she likes to call it. And when everything blew up with Zach, Hailey stayed right next to me every step of the way. She didn't even bat an eyelash at the thought of us moving and opening up a bakery somewhere new, though she did have quite a few thoughts on the small town. It has crossed my mind on more than one occasion that Zach could find me through her, but I try my best not to think about it. They never liked each other much anyway, so it's not like they would be texting regularly or anything.

My little sister is nearly identical to me. I mean, if you gave me chocolate-colored hair, big hazelnut eyes, and put me in heels. But I swear we look exactly the same, otherwise.

Maybe minus the teal paint, actually.

As she turns the corner of her cardboard tower, I see that her hair isn't the only casualty. Her white tank top and jean shorts are speckled in the same bright hue.

Turning back to Keith, I go in for the introduction, "This is Hailey. She's my sister… and business partner. Give her whatever access she needs to get it all set up." I smile at Kyle/Kurt/Keith as I present my sister to him.

His eyes widen visibly, even with his glasses, and he looks her up and down, being a tad too obvious about it.

"Hey, Hailey," he says, clearing his throat. "I'm Kevin, nice to meet you." He wipes his palm against his pants before presenting it to her.

KEVIN. I knew it!

While they start chatting about the social accounts, I mentally flip through my never-ending to-do list all while grabbing my *actual* written to-do list and settling down at one of the round marble tables by the front windows.

It's not like I didn't expect that getting this run-down shop up and really running wouldn't be work. I knew it would. I was just hoping that *something* would go smoothly today. Like literally anything.

My phone's ringtone brings me out of my internal spiral of doom, and I blindly swipe one-handed while still flipping through my written-out to-do list, already making mental notes to add to my actual ones.

"Maddie Pie!" My mother's bell-like voice calls through the speaker. "How's The Sweet Shop coming along?" I roll my eyes at the same question she's asked me every single call we've had, but that's what I get for letting my mom name my business.

"Hi, Mom. It's good. Just battling with self-imposed deadlines and delivery dates. How's the auction going?" The joy in my voice at her calling is genuine, and I joke, "Is this self-inflicted stress a hereditary thing?"

Her laugh tinkles through the phone as I bathe in the comfort it brings. My whole life she always found the bright side of everything, teaching me to do the same. No matter how busy she got, she'd always find a minute to sit with us and *really* find out how we were. She became my own personal comfort blanket. An emotional one, that is. One I have tried desperately to impart in my own parenting.

My mom was a stay-at-home mom for most of my life, but the one project she would always make time for was a charity she runs for battered women. She holds an annual auction of items made exclusively by women to raise money for a shelter run by the charity.

I always say my sister and I are her pride and joy, but with my new mindset that being honest with yourself is the first step toward leading a happy life, I've started to admit that the Women's Works for Women, or WWW's Yearly Auction is her true accomplishment. And every part of me is nothing but proud of her for it.

Funny how it takes low points in life for you to realize you haven't been honest with yourself. But I've come a long way and am focused on changing that. One self-admitted truth at a time.

She's turned the auction into an annual gala that raises hundreds of thousands of dollars every year to support women who have escaped abusive relationships and gets them back on their feet.

Really, when Zach started getting physical with me, she was the safest person I could turn to, and she knew exactly how to help me start over. Even if I didn't follow all the steps exactly... it was still a huge help. I've never claimed to be brave. Just honest.

"Oh, just working on our advance donations list." She chimes in, pulling me out of my reverie. "It would really be *even* better if you could send me some goodie baskets to woo the big bucks!" Her tone is teasing and light, and I know she's already ordered sweet treats and is just trying to compliment me.

"It will be great, Mom. I'm sure you'll set a new record with your donations this year, especially given all the press you've gotten lately."

Her newest magazine feature is currently taped to my fridge, and I have no plans to take it down anytime soon.

"Oh, sure, sure." The light brush-off of the accomplishment is a poor attempt at modesty, and I'm one-hundred percent positive she's beaming at my mention of it.

"And what about other things..." Her bell voice presses softly at me through the phone, and I know not answering the question will only make her worry more.

"We're okay," I concede, lowering my voice slightly. "Mikey starts school on Monday and he already made some friends at his first football practice. It's nice here. Drama free."

"That's so nice, sweetie. I'm happy for him and you. You both deserve it."

She pauses, filling the line with a ticking bomb as I wait for her next question. One that I know is coming. *Have you heard from Zach?*

"Have you heard from Zach?"

Boom. Mental explosion.

"Only a few times." I don't bother mentioning that he calls and texts me about a dozen times a day. I really am not in the mood for another pep talk or teasing about the things I didn't do, and I definitely don't want to worry her. Plus, then I'd have to talk about it, and I was guaranteed to admit to her that avoiding his calls was only making things worse in the long run... so best to avoid the subject at all costs. I am pretty sure that if I file that last report and a restraining order, he would take his anger to another level and I would feel far too guilty for pushing him toward that. Even if it was warranted.

Hoping my voice sounds sure and confident, I add in, "I've got it all under control."

"Okay, sweetie. Just let me know if I can help."

I pray to all heavenly bodies above that she doesn't press it any further, and dive head-first into telling her about supply issues and how cute the town is.

My mother is a city girl born and raised, and when I told her about my small-town plans, she was in complete support of my decision. But she was legitimately concerned about where I was going to get my hair done. I assured her I would be just fine.

It's not long before she gets another call and bids me farewell, not a minute too soon because a quick glance at Hailey has me overly stressed that KEVIN is going to be too distracted by her and not focused enough on my cute, but modern, logo design.

Walking over to the *extremely* impossible duo, I quietly clear my throat, and Hailey's eyes meet mine in gratitude. She smiles and gets up, promising to update him if she has any troubles, and then scurries away.

Kevin and I go over my notes for the logo and the homepage a few more times before I'm positively certain he's got it, and that I'm not going to wind up with something I hate for all eternity.

Thankfully, the rest of the day goes by in a blur of painting, shelf hanging, and way less arguing with suppliers.

As we're finishing up and wrapping teal paint-covered rollers in layers of Saran Wrap, Hailey's hip bumps mine.

"You've been so quiet today. Don't tell me that that sweet tech guy ruined your whole day over a Facebook page?"

"No, it's not that. I mean, it's not *not* that. It's just that I think I need a me moment. You know?"

"Completely. There are a few high school kids who have come through here, and one named Chloe was looking for a babysitting gig. Why don't you give her a call and we can go out? Get a drink and relax for a night." She hands me a hand-scribbled number from her back pocket when she finishes.

"That does sound nice."

It's not like being on this mom journey by myself is easy. And yes, I know I did it to myself. Go me... but still. I need a cooling minute. My edges are getting a little too crispy under this self-imposed broiler.

"Okay. Let's do it."

I'm a little shocked at how quickly all the pieces fall together. Chloe is great, and she and Mikey hit it off quicker than a microwave brownie. Especially when she responds to his quiz about Minecraft with flying colors.

Honestly, the specifics leave my mind dancing and wandering while they nerd out and set up her computer to join his world. It all sounds like made-up words to me, but I won't be looking a perfectly raised souffle in the mouth.

Looking my reflection up and down in my bedroom mirror, I'm left feeling a little squishy. Being a master of flour and constantly surrounded by doughs and icings has definitely left its mark on my mom figure. Not that it's where it was when I was pregnant, but there is still that permanent evidence that I grew a full human. My skin is a little softer, and my hips are rounder. I've grown to love the curves, but am still working on liking the squishy bits.

My jeans hug the hips I have *learned* to love and are high-waisted enough that they tuck in the squishy middle.

OHMMGOD. I just described a muffin. A mom muffin. I am a mom muffin.

Rolling my eyes at myself, I tuck in the front edge of my white tee. Standard Maddie uniform, as Hails calls it.

"Bitch! You can't wear that!" Hailey's voice rings out and shakes me from my mental safe space. She's standing in the doorway to my room with both hands on her hips.

"What is wrong with this? I wear this all the time!"

"EXACTLY!" She huffs out as she walks her dolled-up ass over to my closet and starts rummaging through various versions of what I am already wearing.

"Ah-ha!" she cries, pulling a black spaghetti-strap dress from the back of the back of my closet.

My face squishes in response, and I groan, knowing there's literally no way I'm leaving the house wearing that. Hails has no compromise button. It is all or nothing. It's a yes, or it's willing to hear about it for the next five days.

"I can't wear that." My protest is half-hearted in my premature defeat.

"Of course you can. It's in *your* closet, and YOU bought it, so don't even try that with me."

"You're insufferable."

She just smiles and nods knowingly in response. Unfazed at my half-hearted attempt at an insult.

Grabbing the dress, I turn away from her evil cackle and change. Begrudgingly.

Hailey busies herself raiding my makeup drawer, and I can't help but admire the way she holds herself. Squeezing my mom muffin hips into the knee-length dress, I admire hers, which are perfectly displayed in a short, frilly pink dress. It looks like a prom dress, one that she somehow wears with a jealousy-inducing level of confidence.

"Okay, here's the plan," she singsongs from my bathroom, where she's adding mascara to her lashes.

"This town is small. And when I say small, I mean TINY. So, we have like three decent options, and I've ruled out two of them. But since you're older, I'm going to pretend to give you a say." Her emphasis on 'older' doesn't go unnoticed, and I roll my eyes as I pull up the straps on the forced outfit.

She laughs to herself as she continues, "The first is a tapas bar on Durbin Street. Which I have renamed 'Tourist Square,' in case you're wondering, since it's drowning in people who can't seem to walk in a straight line, and who look in every single window they pass. Which is exhausting, by the way. The second is a bar called 'River Rats.' It's a few blocks from the bakery and has some pub food. Definitely a local joint. The third is the ONLY club around. It is called The Wave, which I don't need to elaborate on." She finds my eyes in the mirror over her shoulder and gives me a pointed look that is equal parts exasperation and disbelief.

Laughing at her is really the only appropriate response.

"What in the world is so funny? Did you know when you decided to move here that there is literally one person at the grocery store check-out, and it's like *always* the same person?"

"First off, his name is Greg (I think), and he is *super* nice. Second, it's a charming kind of small, and I love it."

She gives me her 'Of course, you do' smile and goes on.

"Be that as it may, it really does limit our *out* options. So, which one do *you* think we're going to?"

"River Rats, it is."

"Perfect!" She sets the mascara down as she says it, effectively dismissing me as she finishes up her lip gloss and saunters out of my room, calling for Mikey as she does.

I pause, mid-strapping my block heels on my foot, considering the name. What would I name a bar? Definitely not River Rats. The Drunken Donut... Maybe.

"MADDIE PIE! Come on!"

I feel like Hails looped Mikey in on her us-going-out plan because he gives Chloe the rest of the house rules before I have a chance to. He goes over his bedtime routine, only pushing it by thirty minutes. I nod in agreement, much to his elation.

Our Uber is here before I know it, and the two of us are sitting in the back of a rather clean Camry. Hailey is uselessly giving our driver directions, even though he's already very aware of where we're going. I mean, even if she hadn't told him, it's not like there are a ton of options.

I tune them out as soon as I hear the driver say, "So, where are you girls from?"

I'm a silent ride option all the way. Hails, not so much.

There's a calming silence in my head as I watch the small buildings go by. I can't help but think that there's something about this town that feeds my soul in a way that Boston never did. Boston is beautiful and lively and full of history. But it was just so crowded and full. Like when you eat too much at Thanksgiving and can't catch your breath. I lose myself in thought as pastel houses pass by in a whirl of color and untold stories.

The car pulls up at a quaint, dark gray brick building. The gold lettering spells out River Rats in a simple logo across the front that I find myself admiring, especially after spending the day with KEVIN. Maybe he did this one too?

The driver continues talking to Hailey as I leave her to fend for herself. I slide out of the car and onto the sidewalk, tugging the dress back into place as I do and cursing the devil-swapped sister who insisted on making me wear it. I hear the door shut behind me as she tells Joe it was nice chatting and I turn to laugh at her... not so silently.

"What is it about me?" she questions. Her voice rising as our e-driver pulls away.

"Do I just scream 'ask me inappropriate questions'?"

It's obvious she's being rhetorical, but I have to reply, "You do have a *friendly* air about you."

"Well, maybe that 'friendly air' will get us free drinks." Her eyes move up to the gold lettering. "What the heck is a River Rat?"

"Beats me. But I don't want any of them in my kitchen. That's for sure."

Hails laughs deep, and I chuckle at my own joke. She stops before I move to open the door, and her smile takes on a sentimental edge that has me looking at her in question. She raises her hands up like she's holding an invisible camera and snaps a pretend photo at whatever expression is on my face. This is her thing. She's been into photography for as long as I can remember, and while she carries her camera pretty much everywhere with her, when she doesn't have it, she still takes what she calls "mental snaps" to remember all the things she never wants to forget. A smile fills my face at her wanting to remember this, and I shake my head at her a little disbelievingly.

"It's just... you finally look happy, and you deserve to look happy, and I'm just happy that you *are* happy," she says it all in a jumble, but I know what she means, and pull her into a side hug as a silent thank you, before we both go through the door.

We make our way into the bar that seems unusually packed for a weeknight. It only takes a minute and some good luck before two seats open up at the bar and we snag them without a second of hesitation.

The *feel* of this place is awesome. The music is just loud enough that you don't have to yell over it, but I also wouldn't be able to hear the conversation at the next table.

"Well, this place is *exactly* what we need!" Hailey chimes as she flags down a pixie-looking bartender who's really bringing badass vibes to womanhood with her entire look.

As she makes it over to us, she's flagged down multiple times and smoothly passes drinks over the bar with an ease that just screams professional. Completely cool and collected. Can I be her when I grow up?

She slides two leather-covered drink menus across the wood tabletop. "What can I get you two?" she asks, giving us a small smile and putting two napkins in front of us. I open the thick menu and start to look it over, impressed at how it's laid out and the font choices. I've clearly spent way too much time with Kevin lately. We're cut off before I can even think of a drink.

"Carly, I've got this one." The voice that cuts through the bar chatter has me stopping my perusal of the cleverly worded drink menu and shifts my focus full force to checking out the tattoo-covered slice of delicious chocolate cake behind the bar without even meaning to.

He smiles at me knowingly before his rich voice assails my senses again. "What can I get you two?" Mr. Tattoo eyes us both with keen eyes that are flirty, but in a closed-door kind of way, and I swear I can hear Hails stop breathing—if that sort of thing had sound.

I turn and stare at her.

Well, isn't this curious? Little Miss *Never Interested* was suddenly *very* interested.

"What would you suggest?" The voice that leaves my little sister is actually mortifying, and I die a little inside knowing that the sultry tone will haunt me in my nightmares for years to come. I narrow my eyes, glaring at her openly, mostly to make sure her clothes are still on. Cause ewww. Not that I blame her, though, this guy should read romance novels. Be on the cover of romance novels? Be the star IN romance novels.

"Hmm." His head tilts as he evaluates us.

His eyes turn to me appraisingly, and I stare back, curious at what his assessment will be.

"Well, given the way you've been looking at that drink menu, I can guess you don't drink very often," he finally replies in his low timbre while nodding at the leather-bound book still clutched in my hand.

"Plus, I can smell your cinnamon gum from here." A shocked laugh slips out of me, and I turn and look at Hails, who's practically drooling in her own kind of embarrassing *to me* way.

All while Mr. Tattoo casually unrolls one of his sleeves.

"But you look a little stressed, and like you've seen a few things." He starts rolling the edges of his crisp white sleeves back up. I catch a little more of his tattoos as he pushes both sides up over his elbows and grabs a glass, going through the motions of making a drink like it's second nature. To be honest, with how easily he does it, it probably is. His read on me was spot on, and even though I'm not interested, unlike Hails, I can definitely admire his game.

His eyes meet mine as he moves things around behind the counter.

"You're definitely new here, and we don't get a lot of newbies. Where you from?" His hands are whirling and mixing and shaking that mixer thing you see people make drinks with on TV. I catch a whiff of apple, and the sweet notes implore me to respond.

"We're from Boston, just moved a few weeks ago." I lean my head toward Hailey, who's moved on from ogling to reading the drink menu. "My sister and I are reopening the bakery off of Magnolia Street."

He smiles and a look of recognition fills his face, followed by what I'm sure is only a hint of what a real grin would look like. "That place has been empty for years. Good for you guys."

A frosty glass hits the countertop in front of me, a cinnamon stick sticking out of the side, and an apple slice perched on the edge.

"Voila. Apple Pie." His light brown eyes twinkle with mischief, and he rubs a hand over his trimmed beard, casually swiping his thumb across his lip as he watches me admire the beverage in front of me.

Lifting the glass to my lips, I take a tentative sip. The warming scent of apple and cinnamon hit my senses and take me back to my kitchen with a strong urge to bake the drink's namesake. I immediately recognize the burn of whisky that goes down warm and smooth.

"Holy custard! That's delicious." I take another sip. Larger and more confident this time. Savoring the warm flavor of pie and happiness on my tongue, I squeal, "Oh my gosh! Do Hails!"

I smile at her as she stares into Mr. Tattoo's deep eyes and furrows her brows in a challenge. "All right," she says coolly, putting the menu down. "Let's see what you've got."

I look back and forth between the two of them, and a weird tennis match of stares and tension volleys back and forth. His gaze finally shifts as he looks her over a little differently, and he seems to find whatever it was he was searching for in their match of visual wits. Something deep passing between those dark eyes. Weird.

Breaking his stare, he shakes his head. "Actually, I've got other customers to tend to." He finishes wiping the glass he was cleaning and turns to the pixie-looking girl who was off helping a group of rowdy men. "Carly, you're up."

She glances our way and nods as he looks back at us.

"It was nice meeting the two of you." As he turns to leave, Hailey calls out to him, "I didn't catch your name."

He spins slowly, walking backward for a second and a real smile breaks across his face, his eyes boring into her. "Probably because I didn't give it." He winks, turns, and walks away.

She scoffs and puts the menu she was white-knuckling back on the countertop.

"What an asshole."

I grin at her, not missing her flushed cheeks and her heated stare directed at Mr. Tattoo as she picks the menu back up. He helps another group of customers, looking back at us occasionally with a disinterested glance. I'm loving that she's this worked up over the first guy who didn't fall willingly at her feet.

"I kinda like him." I laugh back.

She whacks me with her menu and mumbles under her breath about dumb men and alcohol.

Sipping on my Apple Pie, I know for sure we'll be coming back here.

# Chapter Eight

## NOSE-PIERCING REGRETS

### Maddie

"Mom, it's not that big of a deal." His voice is far more confident than I *ever* was on any of my first days of school. "It's not like I've never been to school before," he finishes, while stuffing a sweater into his backpack.

"I know, bud. But it's a *new* school. New friends. New teachers."

"The more you talk about it, the more nervous you're making me!" Exasperation is evident in his words, and I suddenly feel bad for imparting my insecurities onto him when they are clearly not things he's worried about.

"Oh gosh, I'm sorry. I'll stop. Maybe I can be nervous enough for both of us? Right?" My laughter lightens the mood, and he smiles, knowing it's true and there's nothing he or I can do about that.

"All right," Mikey pulls down on his backpack straps, securing the neon-hued pack tighter as he rocks on his heels with a grin. "Ready."

"Okay. Great. We've got this. No! You've got this." The pep in my voice pumps me up, and I skip toward the door.

His beaming smile at my enthusiasm brings out my own a little easier, and we make our way to the car. Backing out with confidence, I only brace a little before we hit the pothole at the end of our driveway. I've somehow not mastered avoiding it in all the weeks since we moved in. But at least I know it's coming now. That's growth, if you ask me.

*Maddie: Two (I only hit snooze twice!)*

*World...aka the driveway: Zero. Like the shape of that dumb pothole.*

I put on the playlist I had Hailey make for today in a totally unobvious way. I define smooth.

He smiles and nods his head to the music as "I Ain't Worried" by OneRepublic plays through the speakers.

The ride to school is quiet as we jam out. I park way too soon for my liking, and Mikey gets out without waiting for me. I have to shuffle quickly to grab my purse before I race out after him. It hits me that this is what I'm going to have to get used to. While he might be my baby, he isn't a little kid anymore. I know I have to go with his flow in this new experience, not make it into what I want for him.

His eyes survey mine over the car. "No weirdness, right?"

I grin at him, tucking my hair behind my ear and narrowing my eyes in seriousness as I agree. "Right! None at all."

His responding smirk back is a 'mom making' moment, and we both turn to head toward the entrance to the school.

As we enter through the large double doors, I glance around the clean yellow hallways lined with beat-up, dented silver lockers. The smell of lemon, bleach, and school supplies wafts over me in a giant wave of nostalgia, bringing back memories of composition notebooks and sharpened pencils. We make our way inside and follow the signs to the front office.

Late-year starts are required to meet with the principal before they enroll. It took me a while to get his transcripts pulled from his other school, and even longer to get the local doctor's office to squeeze us in for a start of term physical and health waiver. I don't expect this to be very, eventful, especially since we've only missed a few weeks. Mikey is a good kid and always has been. He loves school and really works hard at it, which his grades reflect.

The older lady at the reception desk, Mrs. McDaniels, tells us to have a seat while she lets Principal Noll know we're ready for him.

I watch Mikey as he takes in everything around him. This is his last year of elementary school, and I wonder what he is thinking. Knowing it will only annoy him if I asked, I bump his shoulder, smiling when he looks up at me.

Mrs. McDaniels' prim and proper voice reaches us as she says, "He's ready for you. Just go straight in. Her tight smile and smoothed-down hair seem to me like they would only make kids more uncomfortable, but I nod at her just the same and pause when my hand lands on the doorknob.

"No going back now," I whisper at him.

"I'm ready," he says resolutely, nodding and staring forward, his hands holding each side of his backpack straps as he straightens. I admire his freckles and curly blond mop, for some reason feeling a little like I'm saying goodbye to the kid version of my kid.

I turn the knob and open the door, officially moving me and Mikey into this next phase of our life.

Principal Noll is a round, balding man. And I mean that in a nice way. He reminds me a bit of Kevin James but with twenty years on him, in a brown tweed suit with a tie that might be a tad too tight around his neck.

The man seated in front of him to the right is also unfamiliar to me, but he smiles a friendly smile that I return easily.

"Mrs. Thompson, Michael, please have a seat." Principal Noll smiles warmly and looks at the folder in his hand, and my attempt at not cringing does not go unnoticed by Mikey or the smiling stranger beside me. I correct him before it gets weird. "Ms. Thompson and Mikey, actually. But please call me Maddie." I put strength and a lack of emotion in my voice, hoping to remove the need for further questions.

His eyes move back up from the folder and then back down as he flips through pages. "Oh, I am terribly sorry. Please excuse my presumptiveness." His smile is back, and I can tell he didn't take offense. Nailed it.

*Maddie: Three!*

*World: Nada*

Mikey squeezes my elbow in comfort, a move far too mature for the age of ten, and we both seat ourselves in the chairs that are clearly intended for us.

"Let me be the first to welcome you to Knox Elementary. We are a tight community here and our school is something that we are all very proud of." He is genuinely excited, and the enthusiastic hand waving makes it obvious that every word out of his mouth is sincere.

"Well, we're very happy to be here," I say, smiling back and finding that this is not anywhere near as uncomfortable an experience as it could be.

"Mikey, I've gone ahead and taken a look at your transcripts from your prior school. You're a good student, and I don't think that you will have any trouble getting into the groove of the curriculum here." He looks warmly at my kid as he goes on, gesturing to the man seated beside me. "This is Brad Clements. He will be your teacher for the rest of the year."

Turning to look at Mr. Clements, I take in his appearance as he reaches his hand out to me, another smile filling his face. I shake it in return, introducing myself to him. He leans forward and does the same with Mikey.

"I've got a meeting to attend this morning with our, umm, very committed PTA." Principal Noll's eyes dart around, his smile equal parts grimace and guilt, and I can only imagine what a small-town PTA is like. I think I'll pass on that for now.

"Mr. Clements will be showing you around the school and can answer any questions you have for him. He also had the opportunity to look everything over and has tailored some homework to ensure that Mikey is caught up quickly and smoothly." Principal Noll stands, smoothing his hands down his blazer and motioning us all out the door.

I decide I like him. Friendly, to the point, and maybe a little excitable. My kind of person.

Mikey looks totally at ease and moves to stand. I follow his lead.

"It was wonderful to meet you both. Please don't hesitate to reach out to me if there are any issues. My door is always open." He sings the last bit as he comes around the desk to follow us out the door.

Once we're in the hallway, Mr. Clements seems a tad relieved and takes an obvious breath as he loosens his tie a little.

"Those meetings make me feel a little uptight." His laugh borders on awkward, and I nod for lack of a better response.

Mr. Clements's hair sits perfectly motionless on the top of his head, gel keeping his curls from moving as he looks down the hallway.

"My classroom is this way. I'll give you the lay of the land."

He takes us through the lunchroom, shows us other classrooms, and the gym. Honestly, schools all seem laid out pretty much the same to me. Obviously, they vary slightly, but it's more like a check the box sort of thing.

Classrooms. Check.

Lunchroom. Check.

Gymnasium. Check.

Mr. Clements then shows Mikey his locker and explains how to set the combination. The tour continues with the bathrooms, the playground, and finally, we pause outside his classroom.

A trilling bell sounds through the hallway just before countless doors open along the wide corridor we were walking down, and hordes of children begin flying out. I can't help but see the chaos in it all, and it brings a smile to my face. Sheer insanity.

"My class is heading to the gym right now from science," Mr. Clements starts, his deep voice pulling me from the shouts and laughter that I was happily observing. "Mikey, if I send you with another student, would you be okay to head that way on your own?" His voice is deep and friendly when he addresses my son, and I warm a little toward him.

Mikey nods eagerly and seems relieved that he can rejoin some humans closer to his age.

"Perfect." Eyeing various kids around us, he calls out to one. "Jacob! Come here."

A boy, similar to Mikey's size and age, comes walking up. He smiles at Mikey in greeting, "Yeah, Mr. Clements?"

"This is Mikey, he's starting today. Could you walk with him to the gym and let Coach Collins know it's his first day?"

"Sure. Come on." Jacob leads Mikey away and my heart sings when halfway down the hall he turns and waves bye to me.

Buttery biscuits. That's like a major gold star in mom land.

I spot Jasper in the crowd ahead of him and smile big enough to be embarrassing when they start talking. This is already going much better than I expected a first day to go.

*Maddie: Four!*

*World: Who cares*

"Follow me, Ms. Thompson. I'll walk you through my plan to catch Mikey up." Mr. Clements turns, not waiting for me to follow him as he heads into his classroom.

When I walk in, the neatly lined desks bring back memories of lessons, friends, and the smell of books. Mr. Clements busies himself digging though papers on his messy, but uncluttered desk, still not acknowledging me. Finding the folder he was searching for, he grabs it and takes a seat, indicating for me to sit at one of the small desks in front of him.

I eye the desk dubiously. I haven't sat in one of those in a loooong time. I don't mind, but there's something about his demeanor that I find...lacking. Especially when he leans back with this coffee cup and openly stares at me. There's a shift in his demeanor that I almost can't put my finger on, but it's giving me the creeps.

Not wanting to ruin any part of Mikey's first day, I smooth my ruffled feathers and slide into the seat.

"So, Ms. Thompson, what do you hope Mikey will achieve this year? Have the two of you sat down and set academic goals for him? What about with his father?"

Okay, then. I guess we're just diving in.

"Honestly, Mr. Clements," I start.

"Please, call me Brad," he interrupts and smiles, waiting for me to continue despite the interruption.

"Sure...well, Brad, we really just want to have this transition go smoothly. Mikey tries really hard in school and loves learning. I don't want to diminish that because we moved. It's been a big change for the two of us, and I'm hoping his return to school will give him the routine and stability he needs to help to smooth out all the other changes going on in his life."

Brad's smile is reassuring when I finish, and it gives me hope that I won't mess up Mikey's chances of having a good relationship with his teacher by being obvious about the creeps this guy is giving me. I can't tell if he's impressed with my answer, or just happy I responded politely despite the rocky start I had going in my head.

"I think that is a really decent goal to set for the year, and I'm confident that between the two of us, we can make that a reality. I do need to see commitment from you and Mikey if we want to make this work. Are you willing to put in the effort?"

His eyes hold mine from the six feet between us, and he stares at me silently, waiting for my agreement. I get the feeling I'm back in high school and my teacher is about to assign me detention. Definitely wondering where and when this dynamic came from.

"Not a problem at all. I'll do whatever is needed to make sure my kid is doing the best he can." There. Back in the driver's seat. No detention for me.

He pulls out papers from the folder and moves across the gaping teacher-student chasm that exists between his desk and the students' desks. He sits in the single desk next to me, somehow looking completely comfortable in the tiny seat as he places the paper on the desk in front of me. He leans over to walk me through what Mikey has missed so far. It's pretty thorough. Despite his unusual demeanor, he shows me where he thinks he can catch Mikey up and details a homework plan that we'll need to stay on top of. It all makes sense and I easily agree to his plan.

"Perfect," he replies, and his eyes move across my face.

Looking down at the paper, I almost miss it, but I catch his gaze dip and appraise me a little less *teacherly* and a little more *manly*. My mile-high electric fence goes up another foot, and suddenly I have a dire need to check on my suppliers.

"If it's all right with you, I think we'll need at least one or two more parent-teacher conferences, and I might text you occasionally to check in on the homework."

"Well, if that's all you need from me, I better get going." I glance at the clock on the wall hoping to convey that I need to get back to work.

He doesn't move or respond, just smiles at me.

As I gather my purse and the copy of Mikey's plan, I move to stand up. He stands up with me.

"It was really great to meet you, Maddie." He reaches his hand out to shake mine, and I grasp it lightly with a polite smile.

"You too, Mr. Clements."

Trying not to *actually* run out of there from the unwanted male attention, I spin around slowly and casually walk toward the door.

It's probably just a weird intuition, but before I open the door, I turn, hoping that this feeling will just be in my head. But sadly, someone is out to flip the Maddie vs. World score, and Brad's eyes are *glued* to me. He smiles innocently—in only the loosest sense of the word—and I regret looking back more than I regret my decision to have Hailey pierce my nose in sixth grade. Which was a lot.

I open the door and slide out, not daring to look back again.

The beeline from the classroom to my car is as quick as I can make it without running through the halls, and I can't shake the feeling that Mr. Clements is going to make this far more uncomfortable than I would like.

With feelings of annoyance and regret weighing me down, I decide that food is the only answer to improve my mood and direct my car to Old Sal's. Knowing some badass, not-so-grandmotherly vibes will wash it all away.

Hopefully, with carbs.

# Chapter Nine

## TAG

### Lucas

"Okay, team! Eyes on me."

Little eyes, looking through big helmets, meet mine in rapt attention. Their chatter is suddenly silenced, and I catch a few of them eyeing the huddle happening on the other side of the field. Unfortunately, their trepidation is completely founded.

Those kids are *huge* compared to my team, and it was clear before we even started that this was going to be a tough game.

"This team is good. They are big, and they are fast. I need every single one of you to focus out there. No half efforts on any drive or on any play! Do you understand?" Doing my best to hide my first-game nerves and genuine concern about the imbalance of this match from their knowing stares, I make a point to meet each player's eyes as I speak, conveying as much confidence and certainty as I can with a look alone.

"Yes, Coach!" rings out from all of them and I go on.

"I don't want any of you to rush anything you don't have to. Heads locked and shoulders down. Safety is important in a game like this, and I won't have you injured when you could have done something to prevent it." They nod again, knowing this. Safety is something we always go over at practice. I put my hand in the center of the circle and smaller ones fly onto it.

It's easy to feel their excitement and their nerves. Part of this was expected, for sure. The first game of the season is always like this, and I know they are eager to do more than the scrimmage plays we've been running during our practices. But those kids across the field are definitely not the same size as the teams we played last year.

"Titans on three!" I call out, feeling their excitement build. I'm right there with them. Though I'd obviously never show it.

"One! Two! Three!" I yell, my heart thumping with anticipation as I look at them, watching the dread leave slightly and determination fill their eyes.

"TITANS!" They all scream out at the top of their lungs and the parents seated on the bleachers cheer with pride.

The beginning of a game has been and always will be my favorite. Even when I played, it never failed to make me feel like I was getting a fresh start. There was no second half to come back from, no mistakes hanging over your head. Just the team and the game in front of you. A blank slate every time.

The kids run onto the field and smoothly get into formation, and only one of them seems lost for a second before the others chime in, helping him remember where he should be.

My heart is bursting with pride a little at the show of teamwork. In the past, I'd seen kids annihilate each other over something that small, but the kids on our team are good, and they are kind. They are boys, no doubt about it, which of course means some level of hazing and teasing, but none of it so far has been malicious.

The ref goes through the coin toss with Asher and a boy from the other team who towers over him. This is brutal. The top of Asher's helmet barely met this kid's chin, and it is making me wish I could call the game completely. When the coin lands and the ref indicates that the other team is starting with the ball, I'm slightly relieved. Let them get their feet wet with a little defense. It's easier to read a team's coaching style when they started the game on offensive, so from a strategic standpoint I am all in favor of it. There is also the upside that we won't be at as much of a disadvantage in a size sense. I know my kids are fast, I'm hoping that will be enough to keep us in the game.

The game starts and I move through the motions with a form of muscle memory and routine that you only get from years in the game. It soothes me, and like every single time I've coached before, I find part of myself wishing I still played.

The first two plays made by the other team are good, and my guys seem a tad thrown by the size and intensity of their players. We leveled up a division this year, and the change in our opposing team's size alone is enough to make my boys sweat a little. Honestly, the consistent full head of height difference between our team and theirs is something even I find intimidating.

Their quarterback throws long, and it sails right over the heads of our unfortunately short defensive line. We don't stand a chance if they keep playing like that.

Their receiver jumps, catching the ball and sprints toward the end zone.

"Touchdown" the ref's voice calls out over the parents' screams.

I hear Pete behind me, "This is bullshit! These guys are twice our size!"

*Thank you for that, Pete. Very helpful.*

He's lucky his son is a good kid. I'll put up with plenty from parents, but dealing with his constant criticisms of the kids and his loud, obnoxious need to vocalize every opinion he has definitely toes the line of going too far.

As Pete's voice fades, I become momentarily distracted by a familiar female voice yelling on our sidelines. Unable to believe I'm dreaming *her* up, of all people, I break my cardinal rule of ignoring anything but the players on the field, and I sneak a glance. It takes everything in me not to tip over from shock at seeing Sherry camped out on the benches next to Pete, of all people, both of them screaming in full force.

Catching my stare, she gives me a tentative wave and goes back to cheering on the boys. That was not expected at *all*.

In our agreements when it comes to Jasper, football was always mine. I can see she's worried about encroaching on my time, but honestly, I know Jasper will be so happy to see her. Not that I don't have to mentally shake myself back into the game at seeing her here.

Another familiar voice calls out from our sideline, and I find myself turning. Again. Who the hell am I? I'm more than a little thrilled to see Maddie sitting with her feet up and a giant grin on her face as she watches Mikey run down the field after the ball.

Jesus, Lucas. This is not what you need to keep your head in the first game. These boys are counting on me, but between Sherry being here, and Maddie in the crowd of supportive parents, I can't help but be a little more than distracted.

By the end of the first period, we are down by eighteen, and I know that the boys' morale is waning. Honestly, I expected this. Even if you take their size out of the equation, which is impossible, they are skilled and clearly have more experience under those helmets. You never know what you'll get year after year, but this is coming as a slight shock. You can bet that I will be complaining to the division head as soon as the game ends. The jump from eight- to ten-year-olds to ten to twelve means a lot in terms of size, and I know for a fact that this has been brought up in earlier years. But the kids we are playing look like they are twelve going on sixteen.

At the end of the first half, we have the ball, and the boys are getting into the groove a bit. We had at least made it down the field and scored once. The kids on the other team might seem big and scary, but I got the distinct impression that they felt bad about the unfair advantage and started getting easily avoidable penalties. Multiple delay of game calls and false starts when before they barely paused once they got lined up. Even the biggest asshole of a coach would hate to see kids getting pummeled like this.

It grated at me, and I appreciated it.

Calling out the next play, I catch a few of the boys when they look at each other, exhaustion and defeat filling the space between them. It seems like they know where this game is going but I'm determined to help them see it through.

Mikey seems focused on keeping up with the plays, and I know that part of that is bolstered by him having gotten close with Jasper and Asher. But each time they set up to get into formation, he walks a little slower and his shoulders got a little more slumped.

Honestly the whole game was becoming a huge shitshow. Fucking giant opponents, constant distractions, and an inevitable catastrophe.

It was turning into a dichotomy, one where my past conflicts with my new and uncertain hope for a future, and it is more than messing with me. Why, of all games, did Sherry pick this one to come to? One where I saw Maddie and those same feelings sparked back to life.

Once the final quarter starts, my chest fills with a nervous energy that I can't shake. It's fucking distracting, and my coaching is suffering. I've called three absolutely terrible plays, and I'm starting to get concerned that the boys are losing faith in me. How is anyone supposed to navigate this?

The ball flies out, and I watch as it goes sailing into the hands of a defensive player on the other team. My heart sinks when he breaks away and scores another touchdown. There's no returning from this now—even if it was already a long shot—and that's on me. First game in, and I'm already letting the kids down.

"You guys got this!" Sherry calls out, anxiety laced through her words. Her voice permeates my internal berating, and I know this is another thing we'll fight over now. My safe space is gone. I can't just be a parent, or just be a coach, while I'm doing this. With her here, I have to be a better parent than she thinks I am, a better coach than someone else would be, and it's crushing me. I already feel like a failure, and we haven't even lost. Yet.

I don't want to watch the last fifteen minutes play out, and that thought makes me feel like I'm betraying the team.

*Jesus, Lucas.*

That realization wakes me up. This game isn't about the parents or the coaches, and I'm not doing it for them.

Sucking it up, I don't let my eyes leave those kids even once after that and they start going through the final plays. Mentally forcing myself out of the spiral. I can't let her—or a single loss, fair or unfair—get to me. I'm not in college anymore, and these kids are playing their fucking hearts out.

It's not new that Sherry has this effect on me, and I will just have to manage this like I manage the rest of it. Time to man up, Lucas.

The minutes tick by and the game doesn't get any better or any easier. But they keep playing.

The final whistle blows, and the game is called.

We lost: 34 - 12.

It was a solid attempt against a mountain of adversity, and as the boys come in for a huddle, I tell them nothing less than that.

"You guys played well and played hard. We had some tough calls out there, but you put points on the board, and we will learn from this. Right?"

"Yes, Coach," they mumble back.

"Hands in! Titans on three."

Meeting Mikey's tear-filled eyes, I know he needs this more than I do. I nod to him, telling him with my eyes to lead the count.

A small upturn of his lips breaks through his crushed demeanor, and he clears his throat before yelling. "One! Two! Three!" The huddle explodes with the loudest team call I've ever heard from these kids, "TITANS!" That one word bringing back some life into my soul.

They break apart and we shake hands with the other team. Even their coach seems a bit flustered at the size difference and apologizes to me when we finally meet up at the end of the line.

"Those are some good boys you've got on your team. I'm sorry it wasn't as fair of a fight as I would have liked." His mouth folds into a genuine and apologetic smile.

Inwardly, I groan as I turn and make my way to the sea of parents and kids scattered around the bleachers and sideline. Pete catches my eye and makes a beeline for me before Tyler knowingly steps in his way and appears to show him a playbook from last season that we keep on hand for reference. Tyler's support and willingness to dive into that line of fire is one of his best qualities.

Sherry is destined to want to meet Maddie since she's the only the new stranger on the field and, well, everyone wants to meet the new person in a small town. I am pretty sure that she will do anything and everything in her power to make it uncomfortably awkward for every single person within a ten-foot radius, and even those farther away, especially if she knew what was really going on in my head.

Plus, knowing Sherry, she already had everything dialed up to a nine since her coming to a game was such a rarity. I don't want to have to deal with that so early on in whatever potential relationship this could be with Maddie.

Leaving Tyler to it, I skip the parent huddle and head toward Sherry, aiming to cut her off before she has a chance to seek anyone...aka Maddie, out. She's wearing tight bike shorts and a painted-on tank top, neither of which leave much to the imagination. Her hair is pulled back tight in a high ponytail and her makeup is painted on. I would assume she was teaching a Pilates class today, but I know she doesn't work on the weekends. Which leaves the tight outfit and the makeup completely for show. And not a show I bought tickets to.

"What a surprise." My voice is flat even though I say the words with a smile. Her gaze drops and I briefly...so very briefly, wonder if I should try to be nicer, but after the shitshow of a game that left me mentally drained, I just don't have it in me.

She starts before I can say anything else. "I know we agreed that this was your thing. I just figured after last week I could do something to put in some extra effort." Her round eyes meet mine and she continues, "I came to cheer you on too." The small smile that appears when she finishes is like twisting a knife in the wound, she left at dinner earlier this week.

What the actual hell is happening today?

"Sherry." I shake my head and look around.

Maddie is off with Tyler giving him treats from today's box of surprises, and I am hit with a wave of jealousy when they both start laughing at something she says.

Sherry's eyes follow mine, and regret instantly fills me at my inability to stay focused today.

"Who is that?" Her words seem innocent but barbed. I know that tone, and it only means trouble. "Sherry, I'm going to walk away and let you tell Jasper what a good game he played, and then you are going to go home. I don't want to do this here—or at all, for that matter. Please, let's just talk on Tuesday." Without waiting for her reply, I move to get my things from the coaching bench and give her space to talk one on one with Jasper as I start walking toward Tyler and Maddie.

Without turning around, I hear her start to gush over Jasper. Telling him how fast he was and praising how good he looks in his uniform. Not that *that* mattered even a little.

God, was I being an asshole? She showed up for him. That was her job. I need to get my head out of my ass and not take every little thing she does personally. Even when she so clearly wants to make it *personal.*

Finally catching up with Maddie and Tyler, I smile at them as they finish talking with the mom of one of the other kids. Mikey is standing with them, but his normally chipper and mischievous demeanor is missing, and I latch onto that. He busies himself with what looks like the most delicious brownie I have ever seen. Not eating it, though, but breaking it into smaller chunks and pushing the pieces back together.

Reaching out I gently clasp his shoulder to get his attention without interrupting the conversation going on around us, nodding subtly to a spot away from the postgame chatter. He follows, stopping in front of me when I move a few feet away out of ear's reach from the conversation.

His light green eyes meet mine and it doesn't take much looking to notice that they are rimmed red.

"You played really well out there and I am not just saying that," he nods silently, and it tears something in me when he looks at his feet without responding. I'm not able to let it go. I kneel down, getting eye level with him. Actually, from this position he has to look down at me. Much better.

"There are days that are meant to test you. I'm not sure by who or why, but they happen to everyone, even coaches, and I'm not going to try to guess why that is. But *you* have the power to decide how you feel and who you are when those days are over. No one else."

He is looking into me with such intensity that I get the feeling he is not used adults talking to him like his feelings and thoughts matter.

"You handled today like you were willing to grow from it. You didn't run away. You didn't quit. And I can guarantee that at our next game, there will be something, at least one thing, that you will do differently because of today."

His eyes hold mine the entire time, and I can see the moment he realizes what *that* thing is. He pulls his shoulders back slightly and lifts his chin. At my core I want to fuel that emotion. Feed that fire, because that fire is what will forge him into a man who is brave enough to try new things and to follow the important things through.

Moments like these are why I coach, and suddenly it hits me that I had forgotten that until right this second. I'd gotten so lost in the drama of my personal life that my *reason* had gotten lost too.

Putting my hand back on his shoulder, I squeeze it slightly. "Thank you for reminding *me* what I had forgotten today. I needed it."

Mikey's eyes turn to saucers at my praise, and I smile at him as I stand up.

"Come on. Let's get your mom and Tyler and see if they want to go grab some food."

"Sure thing, Coach," he says back. His voice is back to normal and full of confidence.

"Call me Lucas when we aren't practicing or in a game, okay?" There's hesitancy in his look, and it's either one of disbelief or caution. I pocket that little tidbit to reflect on later.

"Lucas. Okay." He tries it out with trepidation, but smiles when I nod in encouragement.

"Where did you get those brownies?"

"Oh! My mom brought them. She said something about needing to finish the *buying friends process* for me? I told her she didn't need to bring something *every* time, but I'm kinda worried she will." He laughs a little at that, and there's no doubt in my mind that she absolutely will.

The comment gives me such a clear insight into their relationship that I can easily picture the entire conversation. "Well, let's not let her think it didn't work. Otherwise, who knows what she'll bring next week!" I'm kidding, but his eyes widen, and he starts to walk faster, "Oh, good point."

When we get back to Tyler and Maddie, Mikey quickly takes the bakery box from her surprised hands and starts passing out brownies like they're going out of style, and I chuckle at his eagerness. She eyes him in confusion while very obviously trying not to smile.

"That's odd, he's normally so adamant that I don't bring people things that I bake."

Almost everyone has a brownie at this point, and Mikey lands on the grass with Jasper and Asher, handing them the rest of the box with relief. Pulling my lips between my teeth, I do my best to hold in a smile.

"Do you think that means I should bring something else next week?"

I crack and a chuckle escapes.

Turning to me in surprise, Maddie starts laughing with me, while Tyler just watches with a grin on his face. There's something easy here. Like this friendship has blossomed in a way that didn't take any effort.

Looking over at her, her hair is pulled back in her usual casual ponytail, and the head-to-toe assessment I give her body is completely involuntary. But I don't even try to hide it.

Today's outfit is incredibly distracting now that I've really gotten to see it. Her jean shorts show off her tan legs, and her Boston Red Sox t-shirt is a statement in itself. The red makes her raspberry-colored lips stand out, and I distractedly wonder if they taste just as sweet.

Pretty sure I just became a Red Sox fan.

"You're dressed for the wrong sport," I comment once I make it all the way up to her face. She's watching me back, and I know she saw my entire perusal. Her cheeks are flushed, but she holds my gaze just the same.

"I guess I wanted to be sure I liked football before I committed," she fires back with a shrug. There's a coy smile there that makes me feel like we're playing a verbal game of tag.

"And? Was it better than hitting balls with sticks?" I respond teasingly. *Tag, Maddie, you're it.*

"Jury is out," she volleys back.

"Okay, room for improvement noted."

"I'm still willing to show up before the second inning, though." She's playing with me, throwing a baseball reference back in.

I laugh but quickly respond again to keep our game going, "Wrong sport…again."

A soft chuckle escapes her berry lips. "Well, maybe next time it'll be more memorable, and I'll stop mixing things up?"

"Noted on the second chance; admittedly, the performance today was slightly subpar."

Her eyes twinkle mischievously. "True, but the view was excellent."

Her flirty quip leaves me momentarily stunned with its honesty, and that is fine with me. Regaining my composure quickly, I decide to give her some back.

"Somehow, I think it's even better now." Her eyes widen excitedly at my reply, and she breaks my stare with flushed cheeks.

*No tag backs, Maddie. I always win.*

# Chapter Ten

## SHATTERED GLASS HEARTS

### Maddie

Our second after-football dinner is making me feel a pleasant sense of normalcy. I'm comforted knowing that I have found something in this little town that could become routine. It really makes me feel like we've made a small step toward this place feeling like a permanent home. The thought gives me a gooey feeling somewhere I haven't braved looking at in a while.

Mikey and the boys are chattering away like they've been friends for life. I know that takes less effort at ten than it would for an adult, but it matters to me nonetheless.

"So, Maddie," Tyler inquires. "How's the build-out going?" His question is filled with curiosity, and I answer back easily, fueled by his interest.

"We've had a few issues with suppliers and my web guy, Kevin. The suppliers I figured out a solution to, but I'm still working on Kevin. Other than that, we are down to some paint and promotion." I can't wait for the actual baking to start. That was what I'm good at. "You know, I never really thought about the behind the scenes and what it takes to run a bakery before, and I just got good at the baking part."

"You definitely got really good at that part," he agrees. "Those brownies are going to do a real number on my figure."

I beam with the rise of pride from his compliment. "Those and my cookies are my pride and joy. I've spent years mastering those babies."

"Come on," Tyler begs. "Tell me what's in them. I won't tell anyone, I swear." He draws a cross over his heart, and a laugh involuntarily bubbles up out of me.

I turn to Lucas and find his eyes stuck on me like glaze on a donut. Meeting his stare across the table, the air changes under the weight of it, and I bite my lip, holding back all sorts of feelings. A second before I say something inappropriate or overly honest, he grunts, "Who's we?"

The deep rumble of his voice does nothing to my increasingly suppressed libido, and his words barely register. Instead, the timbre lures me in like ants to a bowl of caramel and I have to blink myself out of the sugar coma they dip me into.

We? Who said we? Did I say we?

"Oh!" I instantly realize he was talking about me saying we're down to paint and promotion and that I'd never introduced them to my sister. "My sister Hailey. I think I mentioned her before, she runs the business with me." I'm instantly thrown back to our porch-swing conversation. I never answered Lucas's questions about whether or not I was single, so I hurry and keep talking. Now uncomfortable and worried, I think I've ruined things before they even had a chance to get started.

"*We* wanted to keep it in the family and all that. Since my mom can't bake literally anything without turning it black—even in an Easy-Bake Oven, which we did try, by the way. Hails was the only option. Not sure what I would do without her." The words are truer than true, and I look at Lucas hoping to see that my answer appeased the things he wasn't asking out loud.

Unable to stop myself now that I've started, I keep going. "She's the social one of us, and every business needs one of those. Let's be honest, I'm not above poisoning someone if they leave a bad review..."

Oh my God. Maddie. STOP TALKING.

Lucas's eyes haven't left my face the entire time, and I'm very aware of the verbal explosions that are coming out of my mouth. Not that he shows any sign he cares. In fact, my heart rate picks up when he seems to hold in *another* chuckle at my awkward admission.

"You guys would love her. We should go out sometime, all of us. Hails and I went to this bar a few blocks from here earlier this week. The drinking experience was really delightful." I stop myself when I realize that I'm rambling again.

Tyler gives me his megawatt grin again. "That's Harley's place! He's been buddies with me and Lucas since we were kids. His bar is the only place around here worth going to. You probably met him. He's covered in tats."

Now this was the information I wanted!

"Mr. Tattoo has a name?" There's no way to keep the excitement out of my voice, and I watch Lucas narrow his eyes briefly at the nickname. Powder me in sugar! That looks an awful lot like jealousy.

Watching him listen to someone or me... was like having a silent conversation with his emotions. Before I can think any more on it, he schools his expression back to his normal handsome self, leaving his full lips on display. The only sign he's displeased is the visible and noteworthy clenching of his jaw. Something about that motion has fantasies of his lips on my neck, invading all sensible thoughts. I can almost feel them moving their way down my skin if I think about it. Which I obviously am. It is *not* lost on me that again, these thoughts do *not* belong at a dinner table, and I fight the urge to fan myself.

I feel my cheeks flush, and his small smile finds its way into our conversation of looks. Almost saying, *Is that how you would want it, Maddie?*

Oh gosh, I'm in trouble with a capital T.

If Tyler watches our exchange, he doesn't let on. "We could totally go out with you and your sister." Not letting the silence build again, he presses, "So what is the secret ingredient in those brownies then?" He was smooth. Bringing us back to the conversation I was obviously not getting back around to.

"It is just one of the Maddie ingredients that I put into all my baking." I shrug innocently.

Lucas finally chimes in. His voice incredulous. "Is that a real thing? Do we need to be worried? Are you secretly making us addicts?" His teasing tone gives my butterflies, butterflies.

"Ha! Only someone with all sorts of secret ingredients would say something like that!" I say back, my tone flirtier than I was going for, but I can't help it.

"Well," Tyler chimes in, "I can tell you that no matter what you put in them, I will definitely be coming back for more."

The continued complimenting from both of them has me floating somewhere near the ceiling, and my happiness only grows when we spend the rest of dinner talking about the bar and life and all the normal things that I haven't let myself think about missing from my earlier life.

When it's time to go, the boys run outside leaving us to wrap up the checks and I ask Tyler and Lucas, "I'm going to chat with Sunny for a second. Would you guys mind watching Mikey?"

They agree instantly and I make my way up to the counter where I perch myself on the cool leather stool, welcoming the chill and secretly hoping it prevents any further teenage blushing.

When I flag down the waitress and ask for Sunny, she smiles at me before going back to get the old firecracker, her long brown hair trailing behind her.

Sunny comes around the corner like a woman on a mission and talks to no less than three employees and half-a-dozen customers before she stops in front of me with her no-nonsense grin. I'm starting to look forward to seeing that smile on the regular.

"If it isn't my Baking Queen!" Her round cheeks plump up when she tips her lips up and the crinkles around her eyes frame her face, along with her wispy bob of gray hair.

One thing I have learned about this woman is once she likes you, you're hers. She adopts you in every sense of the word. I have heard a baker's dozen different versions of my nickname just sitting here over lunches in the last two weeks. MY baking Queen, MY cookie creator, MY sugar dealer, MY slice of pie... the list went on and on.

We spent my last lunch here going over the very real possibility that I could supply her with pastries in the mornings for her breakfast rush. Which fits into my goals just fine since then I can use my newly hired baker to make sure everything is ready and delivered before I come in. Giving me a chance to spend mornings with Mikey before school.

She gets right to it like always. There are no bushes to beat around in this woman's life. "Okay, I went over everything and I think we have a plan. Obviously, we'll have seasonal requests, but if you're okay with it, I'd love to start before your opening. It might help drum up your name a bit and encourage people to check it out." I had already had the same thought and contain my need to jump for joy at how wonderfully this is all coming together.

"Sounds perfect! I'll swing by this week, and we can go over costs and your requests. I'm so excited, I really can't thank you enough."

Her soft hands grab mine across the counter. "Me too. We're lucky you came to Knox County, Maddie. Those cookies are worth whatever you left behind in Boston!"

I give her one last look of thanks before I turn. I'm yanked back by her shockingly firm grip as it pulls me back around.

She's got a mischievous glint on her face, and it overrides my initial surprise at her strength.

She just stares at me knowingly, eyebrows raising, and I realize how obvious my blush—blushes, plural—must have been earlier.

You can bet I will take that to my grave before I admit it to this woman.

Aiming for the utmost innocence, I try for a soft, "What?"

Her look is all-knowing. When her eyebrows raise again, and she darts her eyes to the door and back to me, that stupid blush comes back. "Oh, don't you try that with me. Every person in this diner could feel whatever is going on with the two, and some of them are far too old to be witnessing things like that, little miss!"

I had been caught red-handed. Well currently, I've been caught Sunny-handed, but it's obvious that denying this will get me nowhere.

There's no way I'm getting out of here without giving her something, so I just dive in. Hoping the water is deep and that I remember how to swim.

"Okay, fine!" I roll my eyes, but I don't mean it, and she knows it.

"Look, what I left behind is better left behind, *but* there are strings I can't cut entirely. No matter how much I am ignoring each one of them. And I can't go there with Lucas until I know that I can handle what is eventually coming for me on the other side of those strings."

"Now you're giving me reasons to worry and not just pry." The look on her seasoned face is too aware of the skeletons that take up residence in closets, and I tense a little knowing she can see my bones clear as day.

"I'm okay," I say. At her dubious look, I add, "I swear it. I just need to be a little braver to face those proverbial strings, and I know that I've been avoiding them for long enough that they seem far scarier than they really are."

Her knowing gaze holds mine and she nods, understanding exactly where I'm coming from.

"I've known that man out there for most of his life. He is a kind, smart, and good man. He deserves to know what and why you are holding back, especially if you plan on moving forward with him. I'm not sure his heart could handle something that was less than honest."

This was what I was afraid of. There's damage that can be done when you open up that part of you to another human being. Even if it's unintentional.

"I'll talk to him, Sunny, I swear. I just need time."

"Little miss, I saw the way he was looking at you. I'm not sure much time is something you can ask for."

The truth in those words settles in. I look across the restaurant and find Lucas and the boys sitting out in front of the windows. They are casually talking to each other and laughing at what *must* be a good joke since even Lucas is smiling slightly.

He finds my eyes like I sort of hoped he would, and stares back. Silently asking me what we could possibly be talking about.

"As much as it pains me to admit, I think you're right."

She gives me a small, once again, all-knowing smile and leaves, heading back to the kitchen to do what she does best.

My brain is spinning. It's hard to face the fact that there is something in my life that I am so obviously NOT facing. And the last thing I want is to get someone like Lucas caught in the crossfire. But even knowing that, there is a fire burning away inside me that only gets hotter every time he looks at me. Even in my most obvious moments of delusion, I can't ignore that that is something I should look at more closely. Especially if I'm keeping with my honesty theme and all that.

Stepping outside, I am knocked back to reality by the warm gust of air that hits my face. A freak of a heat wave has come through and I am happy that I made fixing that air conditioning at the shop a priority.

Lucas catches my eyes when I make my way over to the group of them. Tyler has his truck parked in what I have discovered is his usual spot, and I smile at him and the boys when I see them all seated on the beat-up red hood.

Mikey looks out-of-his-mind happy, and I mentally thank myself for deciding to research sports teams instead of music when I started planning the move.

"Everything go okay in there?" Lucas meets me halfway, and his voice easily reaches over the laughter and chatter that is happening at the truck.

I can feel the things he invokes in me, almost like you can smell rain that's about to start, and the butterflies that are flapping around pick up their pace.

He puts a large hand on my arm, pulling the *very little* attention that I had on the boys over to him. "Maddie, I know you're new here, and it's clear that there are things we haven't talked about, and a whole life you have that I know nothing about. But I need to know what this is." He's staring at me. His eyes barely blinking. His gaze full of questions and wonder boring a hole into my soul—pushing me to talk to him. All while rekindling a dead and forgotten desire that I've tried to pretend no longer existed over the past few years.

There are words I should say back. They're sitting there, weighing down my tongue with the heaviness of what admitting them would do. But after Sunny's direct onslaught of questions— correction, her accusations—and now this, I can't make my mind work past the fear that if I interrupt him, he'll never pursue whatever this is between us. And if he asks me anything, I know that I have to say no. But I don't get a chance to think past that instant when he continues, "I know you feel this thing between us, and I would hate myself if I never took that jump and asked you to go to dinner with me."

My heart soars and sinks all at the same time. I should have handled Zach. I should have released myself of those stupid things that scared me and made me too afraid to let go of my past. But I didn't.

And now there is a chance that I fucked this up, too. This fire will die because I wasn't brave enough to think of myself and the future I could have. I wasn't brave enough to think past the hurt and the heartbreak and believe that I could be loved again.

The sigh that leaves me is completely involuntary, and I know that he takes it the wrong way the second it leaves my shattered-glass heart.

"I'm sorry...I, ummm, I shouldn't have asked." He goes to turn away, and now it's my turn to put a hand on his arm. Not leaving it as a subtle *wait* but making it mean more when I pull him back to me.

"No! Please don't think that." My gaze holds onto his caramel-colored eyes, and I try my best to tell him with my stare how much I mean what comes out of my mouth next.

"Lucas, it is not you. I have spent the last few years trying to light a fire like the one you've rekindled in me, and failing more times than I care to admit. But with you it came to life faster than I was ready."

Hope fills his eyes and I find that I close mine when I keep talking.

"I didn't plan for this. I left a mess behind me, and I can't make this more than it is right now *before* I clean that up."

His face falls and he looks away, running his hands through his hair, back to front in a way that has me wishing I could take it all back and just kiss him senseless.

"Look..." I pull him back to me with a squeeze of his arm.

"This is *not* a no. This is a *please* wait while I sort my shit out. Because I desperately want to." I smile at him and will him to smile back.

His lips turn up slightly and he nods. I know he gets why without me going into detail, but I can't help feeling like I messed this up.

"Are we okay?" The insecurity bleeds through and he looks at me with concern.

"Of course, we are, Maddie. I just wish I had waited, or tried something else, or I don't know, fell for you slower, maybe?" He gives me a small smile and runs his hands through his hair again, which is something I will be adding to my library of frequently used visuals, though it will be a totally different setting there where I say yes instead of pushing him away.

When he turns to head back to the boys, I call out to him. "Lucas?" I keep going before I chicken out, "Give me time, okay?"

"Maddie, take all the time you need. I'm pretty sure you're worth waiting for."

The butterflies that had died as a result of my past mistakes and cowardice come back with a vengeance.

I am determined to give them a permanent home. One where Lucas was there with me.

# Chapter Eleven

## CAKE VS. PIE

### Lucas

"The papers you asked for are on your desk, Lucas," Amy says as she leans her head inside the doorway of the copy room.

"Fantastic. I was worried I wouldn't get everything together in time, but thanks to you, I don't have to stay late." My voice is laced with relief, and Amy smiles at me in response, eyeing my giant stack of papers laid across the table.

"Happy to help," she says back and enters the room. Without hesitation, she starts going through the copies of the blueprints I had been making.

"Is this for that law firm or the Anderson project?" she asks while sorting through the massive sheets of paper.

"The Anderson project. We're running a little behind because of all their requested structural changes, but I think we can still catch up and make the deadline."

Her blonde hair falls around her face when she nods, and for some reason, my eyes latch onto her empty ring finger when she moves to tuck her hair behind her ear. Staring, it hits me that I had no idea she wasn't married. Is she single? Separated? Does she have a boyfriend?

*What the heck, Lucas?*

She's worked as a junior architect at this firm for three years, and I've never once, EVER, even thought about her romantically. Harley's conversation at the bar last week set *something* in motion, and now I'm seeing women everywhere. No, I am *looking* for women everywhere.

I had desperately wanted Maddie to say yes. God, I wanted it so bad. And in all fairness, she didn't say no exactly. Even though I told myself I would gladly wait for whenever she *was* ready, I am clearly not content to forever dance around my relationship—or lack thereof—with Sherry anymore. Thank God.

Amy clears her throat, and I meet her eyes. Without a doubt, she saw *exactly* what I was looking at, and my clusterfuck of a thought process is evident on my face. Not smooth, James. Get it together.

Mercifully, she looks back down and continues sorting as I move the last of the huge copies to the pile. We work in silence for several more minutes, and I start to think that maybe I wasn't as awkward as I thought when she blurts out, "I thought you were married?" She's eyeing my hand like I did hers, but with no attempt to hide it.

"Oh, ummm. No. We separated almost two years ago." I do my best not to make eye contact with her or look at her at all since I've gone and made a complete fool of myself.

This is already incredibly awkward. I can feel her stare boring a hole into the top of my head, and the need to see what her face shows weighs on me. When I man up and finally raise my head, I am more than a little shocked at the smile she's giving me.

"I wish I would have known," she laughs. "I would have asked you out two years ago."

Now I can't *stop* looking at her, and a blush creeps up her cheeks. I'm openly gaping at this point. Hell, we're way past awkward, so I might as well lean into it. I stop all thoughts and concerns of social niceties and *look* at her. Appraise her is more like it.

Amy is beautiful. There's no question. She's on the taller side, with subtle curves, a big smile, and soft blue eyes. Her blond hair is styled in waves around her face, and her makeup is done tastefully. Now that I think about it, I actually like working with her too. She's low drama, very upfront, and intelligent. I have no idea why I never noticed her like this before.

Oh, sure I do. I've been too busy with Sherry the last couple of years to look at anyone else.

Before the stretch of silence makes things any more uncomfortable, I go with the first thought in my head. "Why do you say that?" I'm not sure why that's the response I pick, but it is out of my mouth before I can think about it, and there is no taking it back.

I guess I'm shocked. Which I use as enough of a justification to avoid thinking about how embarrassing my curt reply probably was.

She just smiles again and fidgets a little with her bracelet, and I wonder not for the first time in the last five minutes if I've made her uncomfortable. I can't imagine I did since she came out and said that so freely, but I can see her nerves begin to surface a little until she visibly straightens, shoving them down and continues.

"Well, isn't it obvious?" She stares at me with a now playful smile. All I can do is stare back at her, fully dumbfounded. It's either my pure shock at this entire situation, or my naïveté that makes her laugh, but she does and then presses, "Lucas, come on. You're attractive and smart. You own your own business. Of course, I'd want a shot if it was even a possibility."

Well, holy shit.

Harley was right. Maybe I'm dateable after all. Maddie's rejection earlier put some holes in my sails. Sails that I had literally *just* raised and hoisted like a lost pirate out at sea. And

I'm not one to lie, it was a little deflating to my already-bruised ego when she said, 'not now.' Which, while it still gives me hope that what's between us can be more, it isn't a yes...classifying it firmly in the no category.

But this. This conversation was sewing those little holes right up.

Amy's blue eyes look me over a little more openly. Bravely, even, and in my head, I can hear her having a similar conversation with herself. Her gaze meets mine, and she gives me a flirty smile.

Her tone shifts into something that borders on sultry, "Well, since I was super helpful and am saving you *many* hours of work, would you want to go get dinner with me after this?"

*Could I do this?*

She is beautiful and charming. I may have never thought of her like that, but now that she is presenting the idea to me, I start opening myself up to a vision of what we could be like. We would go out to dinner. We would talk about work. She would tell me more about her life. I would inevitably beat around the bush when it came to my personal life, but I would share enough that the conversation didn't stall or become awkward. The first date would go fine. I'd ask her out on a second, and maybe a third. Maybe we would get intimate by the third, but with the way she is looking at me, probably the second. Then what? I introduce her to Jasper? She has dinner at my place? Neither of those thoughts appeal to me even in the slightest. I just—I can't see it getting past that point. The point where the relationship becomes personal. The point where I have to be honest. Is this worth trying if I can't take it further than that in my head? Not to mention the fact that there's another woman who has already taken up rent-free space in all my available thoughts, or what getting involved with Amy could do to my work life.

Harley's point is ringing around in my brain like an alarm. I truly don't *want* to be single anymore.

She's staring at me expectantly, but she's worked with me for years, and knows that this is my process. I'm not surprised at all when she waits patiently for my answer. This is like every meeting we've ever had. It's just that the answer she's looking for will change our dynamic, and that matters. Matters enough to think it all the way through before I open my mouth.

Amy's eyes sweep me over from head to toe, and it's only slightly uncomfortable. Running my hands through my hair, I try to ignore the fact that it does nothing for me.

But maybe I just need to dive in and get into the groove.

*You didn't with Maddie.* My mind chimes in.

*Shut up, Lucas.*

"So?" The word is simple and has a soft lure. Enticing me to *want* to say yes.

If I say yes, there is no getting off this train now. I'm officially back on the market, and the thought of that absolutely terrifies me. But what amazing things in life worth doing *aren't* scary?

Here goes nothing.

"Yeah, that would be great. Besides, buying you dinner is the least I can do for your help."

Her responsive smile is contagious, and I smile back, becoming a little more excited at the prospect of building a life outside of work.

She takes everything from there with a level of precision and skill that I admire every day in her work.

Before I know it, we're locking up the office together, and I'm walking with her down the street to La Cabanita, the local Mexican restaurant that is just a few blocks from the office.

We maintain an easy conversation along the way, and she asks me about our upcoming projects. The work talk is easy for us. It's just the usual. Honestly, it's starting to feel not much different from our weekly work lunches.

"Table for two?" Cesar, the usual manager at the restaurant, asks when we walk in. His thick accent is telling of the quality and authenticity of the food at this place. Jasper and I come here a few times a month, and I'm never disappointed in the meal or the service.

We sit down, and she orders a mango margarita on the rocks with extra salt. It's weird watching her take control. It's not my usual dynamic and honestly, I'm not sure it's for me. She orders us tableside guacamole to start, and I'm instantly aware that this is not just two people having dinner together. It's not dinner with Harley. It's not dinner with Sherry or my mom. It's a shared dinner with two people, where you aren't having two separate dinners at the same time at the same table. The point is to have one dinner together. The thought makes me uneasy.

I try not to mind the shared appetizer, and we talk about all our current projects. But when Cesar comes to take our order, I violate all manners my mom ever taught me and order first before she gets the idea that I want to share my actual meal with her.

She chuckles a little when I do but takes it in stride. At least, having worked with me for a while, she's not instantly put off or unaware of my quirks.

After we place our orders, she takes over the conversation, keeping us moving forward. She tells me about her dog, a small white Malti-poo she named Beyonce. She tells me about her dream to move to New York and work for a larger firm—something that doesn't grate on me even slightly since she's been honest about that since we hired her. She tells me about her ex, a guy named David, who didn't work out because he wouldn't move out of his mom's house. There's a pause when she finishes. Gently leaving the door open for me. I don't walk through it.

It's after our entrees arrive that I start allowing myself to admit that this won't work. It's no fault of Amy's. It's one hundred percent a *me* problem.

The problem is that no matter what Amy tells me or does, I don't see her. When she bites her lip as she talks about her dreams, I see Maddie's face when she says something she didn't mean to. When she confesses her disappointment in her ex, I think of Maddie's fire she needs to fix before we can be a 'we.' When she tucks a strand of hair behind her ear, I see Maddie doing the same thing on my porch swing.

Maddie, Maddie, Maddie.

Shit. There are very few things I'm not comparing to that girl.

When Cesar brings the check, he smiles at me knowingly. It's not like I know him that well or anything, but there is definitely a wall I am keeping up, and you'd have to be blind not to notice it. I pay the check and walk side by side with Amy out of the restaurant.

Stopping once we're on the sidewalk, she turns, "Lucas, thanks for even humoring me on this date." She smiles at me with closed lips. Not sad, but definitely reserved.

"It was nice." Really, Lucas? Nice? Way to take out a player when they're all in.

She laughs at that, and I know I've offended her, even if it was just a little. But being the good person she is, she shakes her head at me and puts her arm in mine.

"Come on, walk me to my car."

We walk back toward the office. A quiet silence filling the space between us, and it's the most comfortable I've been all night. We stop a block away from our building, and she turns to face a little blue car, smiling at me with a sincerity that has me wanting to rethink if I could make this work.

"This is me." She gestures to the little coupe, and I get distracted thinking about whether or not it fits her. She patiently watches me while I do so, and a look fills her face that I can't place.

"I have a feeling I shouldn't take this personally." Her soft voice cuts through my mental assessment.

It isn't lost on me that I'm not necessarily obligated to explain anything. I also know how much of a plus point that would be if this was...something. But I'm not going to lead her on. It's just not who I am.

"No. You shouldn't," I respond casually and a little embarrassed while I stare at my feet. A huge tell, but I let myself slide on it given how out of the box I've been acting lately.

She takes a step toward me, and I put my hands on her shoulders. There really isn't a reason to do anything but walk away. She gets it. I admitted it.

But who makes good decisions all the time? Not me, that's for fucking sure.

Leaning down, I pause a second before my mouth touches hers. Giving her all the control and enough room to pull away... if that's what she wanted.

It is evidently not.

Her lips close the small gap that was slowly filling with the weight of our indecision. I'm honestly a little shocked at how much I lean into the kiss. I meet her mouth at every turn, and when her tongue hesitantly sweeps against mine, I can taste her worry that I'll end it before even trying.

The sweet apprehension does something. The vulnerability chipping away at the things that separate me from a boy and a man. Her responding enthusiasm when I do has me pouring more into the kiss than I would if I were a better person. But here we are.

Our tongues clash, and her body melts against me. My hands move up her body to the nape of her neck, below her hair. Pulling her closer, as I give it everything.

Her moan leaves me spinning with visions of Maddie and me in this same position, her breathy sounds taunting me and spurring me on. My body isn't my own with sounds like that. I become ruled by the things that make me male, both tangible and not. When I move my hands, sliding back down her body and clutching her waist closer, the size of it doesn't fit my fantasy.

I pull out of the kiss, holding her to me as I rest my face against the top of her head.

Our heady breaths are far too indecent for the sidewalk in this small town, and the floral smell of her shampoo is the final straw for my momentary weakness. It should be the scent of vanilla and sugar. Of cupcakes and birthdays.

The reality of how I was replacing her with who I wanted her to be throws me, and I pull back even more. Holding her at arm's length, the shock of my wandering mind hits me like a bucket of ice water.

Jesus, Lucas!

So, I do the respectable thing. Her sigh is audible, and I chuckle when the disappointment reads through loud and clear.

"Still nothing?" she cries out, playfully exasperated.

I can't help but shake my head with a smile on my face as I put the final distance between our bodies. The space putting us back into a socially acceptable friend zone.

"Amy, I'm so sorry." I don't owe her an excuse, but there's something in me that can't help but press on with one. "I'm just getting my head around all this again, and there's someone who's already taken up residence there." My apologetic tone probably isn't necessary with the look she gives me back.

Her playful smirk brings the levity back to what could have become a sad, depressing mess.

"It was worth a shot," she replies with a shrug.

"It really was."

She gives me a look one more time that screams of all that could have been, before walking around her car with her head held high. She gets in without a look back, and it makes me smile even more at her confidence.

I wait until she pulls away, running my hands through my hair when she still doesn't stop or turn around. It feels like we both were trying to see what this could be rather than actually having an expectation that it would work out. I wonder briefly what she was hoping for? Before I turn and head down the street, my thoughts run through all the things she told me at dinner, coming up empty-handed. Figures. You have to actually pay attention to read people, I remind myself.

Walking to clear my head and think the night through is a cathartic process, and I enjoy the quiet moments while I watch the shops and the people I pass. It's nice not to be going anywhere specific. Just walking. I have time on my hands, Jasper is at a sleepover, and there is no rush for me to get home.

As is required in small towns, I say 'Hi' to just as many people as I don't. This place has been my home for so long, and every street of its small-town center brings back memories. I can watch myself grow up as I sort through the images that flood back when I pass the storefronts that were home to so many childhood moments.

Turning down the block, my feet are walking toward Old Sal's before I realize I'm halfway there. It's closing time for most of these places, and a majority of the stores have patrons scattering from them as the lights turn off. Another thing you can expect when the population doesn't pass the overcrowded mark.

The bright glow and faint music coming from across the street pulls me out of my reverie. Turning, my stomach falls out of my shoes when I see which store its coming from.

It's the old bakery. Maddie's bakery. I'm not sure how, in all my pining for her, I haven't made it here. Which is probably why I am currently rooted to the spot, feeling just shy of a creepy peeping Tom. But I keep staring anyway. I can't help it. I just stand there.

I watch Mikey at a small round table by the front window with his pizza. I watch as Maddie's face lights up in joy when some soundless song comes on the little radio they have propped up on the counter. I watch when Maddie leans forward and starts to sing into the paint roller, while Mikey's face lights up with so much happiness the shop glows with it. I can't take my eyes off the two of them.

I'm done.

Hooked.

If I'm being honest with myself, I was hooked from that first meeting. I don't want to go on more dates like tonight. I want to make things happen with Maddie.

Pulling my phone out of my pocket, I pull up her contact name as I formulate a plan, laughing quietly to myself when I again see the nickname, she put herself in under. Just Maddie. Deciding this is the best idea I've had yet, I start typing, putting my plan into action. I can play the long game for her if that's what she wants. But I won't make it easy.

Fingers hovering over the button, I only hesitate for a second before I hit send.

I watch her look at the counter when the text goes through, opening her phone with one hand while the paint roller sits in her other.

**Me: Can't stop thinking about those brownies. What IS that secret ingredient?**

Her face lights up with a smile and she pops her hip against the edge of the unpainted wood. I hold my breath as the three little dots appear on my phone.

**Maddie: Oh, that is Top Secret, Lucas James.**

My grin is probably lighting up the whole freaking street at the moment.

***Me: Give me a hint...***

Her response is instantaneous.

**Maddie: If I told you, I'd have to kill you.**

I look up and watch her put the roller down as she sits

across from Mikey. Her face is still full of that smile that ruins all possible hopes of not being into her.

**Me: Hmmm they were delicious, but it might not be worth dying if I have you around to make them.**

**Me: I'll give up on the brownie recipe if you tell me what else is on your ingredient list.**

**Maddie: hmmm...pretty sure all my ingredients are top secret.**

**Me: What if we trade? I'll tell you one of mine and you tell me one of yours.**

**Maddie: Depends. How good are each of your ingredients?**

I look up again. Unable to decide if I want to stare at the screen, or at her so I can see her reaction to my reply.

**Me: I guess you'll have to play with me to find out.**

The three dots appear and disappear, and I look back up at the window. She's biting her lip and smiling at the phone, and I feel something start to stir inside me.

This is it. I know it is. Like you recognize a core memory when it happens. This is one of those. A moment in time that I'll look back on and it will move in slow motion to my favorite soundtrack. It doesn't matter if she shares something small, or if she lays it all out. I know that if she plays this game with me, I can make this happen. I can win her over.

And, if she doesn't, I make a weak and silent promise to myself that I'll call it and fold. But I know a good tell when I see one, and I'm ready to start counting my chips.

The three dots start again.

Am I folding or am I calling?

I hold my breath, waiting for her to finish typing.

**Maddie: I'm finding that the company here is way better than in Boston.**

My breath leaves me in a whoosh.

All right James, tit for tat.

**Me: I'm realizing that City girls have a lot to offer.**

**Maddie: Maybe football is better than baseball.**

**Me: First, that is obvious... Second, cupcakes are way better than pie.**

**Maddie: Spoken like someone who's never tried my pie...**

Good God. This might be a terrible idea. But it's too late. I've already shoved in my chips, and it's time to play this one out.

# Chapter Twelve

## HEALTHY CHOICE

### Maddie

A moan leaves my mouth when the feeling of two large hands sliding over my arms and around my waist registers.

I know who it is as easily as I know the lines to my favorite movie.

A kiss lands on the soft spot behind my ear, and my heart rate jumps up a degree, which from my experience in the kitchen, can make or overbake anything.

"All right, your turn." His voice purrs in my ears, and it sets those butterflies I've come to love free.

"What do you want me to say," I reply breathlessly. It's half-hearted, but playing coy with him is part of our game. His responses always make it exciting.

I can perfectly picture the silent conversation we *would* be having if he wasn't behind me...

First, his eyebrows would furrow softly, and his eyes would silently say, "Don't you want to tell me, Maddie?"

He always says my name in our silent conversations. The silent version of his gruff voice would fill the broken cracks that make up my heart.

My mouth would part, and I would slowly look up and meet his eyes, holding his gaze... "It'll be more fun if you guess."

My eyes would reply instead. His lips would purse, then smirk slightly, and his look would say, "I'll get it out of you one way or another."

Me? This smirk would *undo* me. I'd inhale a silent gasp... a response that asks, "Promise?"

But I can't see him, and sadly, words are required. His fingers toy with the stretch of skin below my shirt as he patiently waits for me to respond. His touch keeps him placated while I play out these various scenes.

"You didn't ask a question yet, Mr. James. That counts as cheating." The teasing tone in my voice does little to cover up my body's excitement over the fact that his hands are on me.

"Didn't I?" His sultry tone hits deep—below my stomach, and I turn in his arms. The fact that he lets me tells me that he wants this as much as I do.

I can't make my eyes look anywhere other than his lips. He must know that because he pulls the bottom one between his teeth as he wets it. Telling me with his actions that he'd prefer it if I did it instead.

An inferno is growing within me when his hand comes up to my face, and he runs his thumb over my bottom lip, gently gripping it and tugging my chin closer toward his face.

That movement seals the deal, and I willingly accept my fate. I am forever now a pile of chocolate at the sole whim of his wants and desires.

His head dips, and his lips gently touch mine. Barely any contact at all, but what little there is, does *everything*.

Before I can make a move myself, his other hand is tangled in my hair, guiding my head with an almost undetectable amount of pressure, while that first one moves down to my neck. It's obvious the second he gives up prolonging this, and the sound that leaves him an instant before our lips crash again is purely masculine in every sense of the word. The hand on my neck slides down the front of me, pausing just under my rib cage, all while he kisses me like he's trying to prevent me from slowly melting away—me being the pool of liquid that I am. His thumb brushes higher, and I shudder. The involuntary movement leaves him softly chuckling. "This is better than I could have dreamed," I whisper between kisses. There's a breathless quality to my voice that's borderline embarrassing.

"Is it enough for you?"

I pause. That phrase triggers something I can't put my finger on. It hurts trying to pinpoint it, and I struggle to put myself back in the moment, but the thought won't let go. It has strings. I tug and tug, but they won't show me *why* I should remember them. Why do I remember them?

His hand tightens on me. A desperate attempt to bring me back, and I shake my head, trying to free the mental weight that holds me hostage.

This isn't right.

"Come on, Maddie," Lucas's voice tries again. Urging me to focus on him, not the tug of this string that's pulling me away. His fingers dig in with the effort.

Why is he holding me so hard? I'm not going anywhere. Doesn't he remember I told him that? I swore I said it.

"Lucas, that hurts." I try to pull back, but his grip hardens further, and he repeats himself.

"Come on, Maddie," I hold onto Lucas's voice as my mind tries to place the second phrase that has alarm bells going off in my head.

"Is it enough for you?" Zach's voice says as it slips out of Lucas's mouth. His bruising grip on my ribs making me cry out. I can feel the words surrounding me like smoke. Filling my lungs and my heart with poison.

I try to pull back. But Zach just laughs at me. The harsh, condescending tone coming out without effort. My useless struggles fuel their power and his eagerness to hold me there. I try to find that safe space in my mind where I can hide. How am I back here again?

His hand grips my chin, souring the trail left behind when Lucas did the same thing only moments before. A sound leaves me when his lips roughly scrape my face from my mouth to my ear. The movement taunting and so unlike the affectionate caress it was when Lucas did it. He mocks me as he laughs, while the sounds of pleasure that were just leaving me moments ago turn into sad and helpless whimpers.

"You're mine, Maddie."

I bolt upright. My heart is racing. I can't breathe fast enough to fill my lungs with air. Dream. It was just a dream.

Rubbing my hands over my face, I dig my knuckles into my eyes, trying to scrape away the last of the sleep from them and the memory of his hands on my skin. I barely register the fact my fingers come away wet.

Sadly, this isn't the first time, and it probably won't be the last time I dream of some variation of this. Though the Lucas part is new and something I'd gladly repeat. Just without the last bit.

Putting my head between my knees, I count to ten with each inhale and exhale. The time blinking away before I realize my breathing is back to normal. Swinging my legs over the side of my bed, I mindlessly go through the motions of getting dressed, my thoughts and movements still in a numb state of denial.

It must be around five in the morning since the sky peeking through my curtains is still dark.

Sleep will elude me after this, and there is no use chasing it, so I decide to do what brings me peace.

The kitchen is an absolute catastrophe by the time Mikey makes his way to it. Bowls and baking sheets piled high in the sink. I'm pulling another pie out of the oven when he props himself on the stool at the counter and just watches me.

A minute passes before a soft, "Mom? You okay?" makes it to me. His eyes trailing over the stack of dishes with a look of distrust.

"Oh yeah!" I call back from the safe place in front of the oven, aiming for a breezy tone. I'm only half worried it will end up sounding chaotically frazzled.

"Are you sure?" he says as he reaches over the ledge to grab a muffin.

"Really! I'm just making stuff for the team today."

"Mom, there aren't that many of us."

"You know what I mean!" I wave my hand dismissively at the ever-growing pile of baked goods that is way more than enough for the team. Plus, their parents. Plus, half the town.

Mikey doesn't really point it out again between then and when we leave. He's almost supportive of the sweets when he helps me pile them into the back of the car.

"Don't you think three pies plus the muffins is kinda a lot?"

"It's really not if you think that there are three people who want pies!"

"Wait? Three people asked you for pies?" He's staring at me in borderline disbelief.

"Well... no. Not exactly." I bite my lip. I was thinking of it more optimistically than that. "They won't know they *want* pies if there aren't any pies to want!"

He laughs for the first time that morning and shakes his head as he puts the last batch in and closes the door. He moves into his seat and puts on his seatbelt while I balance my coffee on top of the bakery containers and slide in.

Once we get to the practice field, Mikey runs off, dutifully taking a box of muffins with him while I sit in the car, kept company by silence and my own thoughts. The latter of the two being not even close to silent.

Part of me wants to never see another man again. My brain

is currently categorizing them all under the heading of controlling assholes.

It hurts because I was finally warming up to the idea of moving on, and now I am stuck with the reality that my delusional thoughts of moving on are never going to happen as long as Zach is still tainting my life.

The new version of me knows that this is because I have been undoubtably sweeping it, and him, under the proverbial rug rather than really changing anything. There's no rational thought in my mind when my hands are suddenly tapping on my phone, pulling up old voicemails, and harsh words start blaring through the speakers. I jump when Zach's voice bounces off the walls of my car... even though I'm the one who pushed the dumb button and called up the beast.

These messages are from a month ago.

"Madelynn, this isn't funny." His tone really *doesn't* sound like he thinks it is even slightly amusing at all. "I've put up with your childish tantrum for weeks now. Grow the fuck up and call me back."

What was I even doing when I got this call? Hard to say since he calls all the time. Probably a three or four on the 'Zach is pissed' scale. Especially since he still sounds annoyed and not mad.

It's like someone else is controlling my body, and they're out for pain because next thing I know, my fingers are pressing on the next voicemail, and he is filling the car again.

"You can't keep ignoring me, Madelynn. Call. Me. Back."

Almost three weeks ago.

I'm on a crashing plane now. A train wreck. The freaking Titanic? Where's Leo when I need him?

*World - one million*

*Maddie - minus all the points I've ever made*

"Come on, babe. I get it. I got mad, and I know you can't handle that." There it is, me being inferior. Not his anger. Not his violence. Not anything from him ever. Just me. "Please just call me back. I want to make sure you and Mikey are okay."

Ten days ago. This is what comes after he loses. Words that sound sweet... if they were to come from someone else. I know I'm in for it with the next message, this one from last week.

I press it anyway.

"This is enough!" He's *really* mad in this one. I can hear it in the shaking of his voice at the end of his sentence. Right at the punctuation. He's trying to restrain himself. I almost see him behind my closed eyes. He's at his desk. Hands in fists, resting on the dark wood of the tabletop. "You will fucking answer me, or I will come get the two of you and bring your asses back here." The sound of him slamming his fist against the wood fills the car before the line goes dead.

With shaking hands, I click the button for the last one, from two days ago. Might as well finish them.

"Maddie. Honey. Please just call me back." A sob cuts through his slurred words. "I can't do this anymore. I swear I'll get help. We can work this out. Call me." I can almost smell the whiskey. Closing my eyes, it's clear as day, his tie half undone, his crisp button up slightly askew and uncharacteristically wrinkled. His dark hair a mess from him pulling on it when he can't seem to get himself under control. An empty glass to the side.

My heart squeezes. This is where it has been fucking *hard* to hold my ground. He was the love of my life for so long. I worshiped him. I know now that his love for me wasn't what I deserved, but when he was in front of me, I *needed* it to survive. To breathe.

A year ago, maybe more recently, if I'm not going to be naïve with myself... I would have gone to him. Held his head, his hands, his *world*, while he crumbled around me. Letting him breakdown so that together we could bring him back. The week or so that followed one of these breakdowns were the best we had. Every time. He would go back to the man he was when we met. Back to our honeymoon phase. But I know better now. The version that wanted to control me always came back. The drinking came back, and I lost him within the bottle.

He calls every day, but the voicemails are fewer. Thank God. My self-preservation is not nearly strong enough to have kept up not answering if there were countless messages like these. I'd probably throw my phone off the edge of the harbor... or fly back to Boston in a fit of guilt.

I realize that Zach's calls definitely started out more frequent, but I didn't answer after the first week we were here, so I figured he was giving up or giving me time. It hits me suddenly that that is probably not as good of a thing as I had thought it was. He still texts every day, and while I read those, the sound of his voice saying the words is so much worse. I had assumed he was getting used to the idea, but that last voicemail was not from someone who was handling this situation well.

The healthy thing to do would be to block him. *Actually,* the healthy thing to do would be to report him and get a restraining order. But this new me is *honest*, not a health freak. Obviously.

Healthy choices are not my forte... I worship pastries, for Pete's sake.

The idea of making a decision that would cut Mikey's dad out of his life for good feels like a choice I have no right to make. Every time my finger hovers over the block button, or I think about the unfiled restraining order, my mind floods with all the times he whispered sweet words in my ear or surprised us with family trip. Or worse, times when he broke down and needed me just as much as I thought I needed him. It is a weak stance to take and one that is clearly harmful to my mental state.

Deciding to leave the pity party for one I have been having in my car, I shove my phone into my pocket, unclip my seatbelt, and open the door to the crisp fall air.

I close it harder than I mean to, but who the hell cares? It's not like letting my frustration out for a moment will make it visible to everyone else. Part of me has a strong urge to google rage rooms and really let it out, but it sounds like way more physical effort than I am up for, like ever.

After a few deep breaths, I eye the boys across the field, noting how happy Mikey looks as he runs through whatever it was they are doing. Tyler is bent over with the team. A clipboard in his hands. Weird, I wonder why Tyler is there with the kids.

My eyes scan the field, and it's only when I don't see Lucas that I realize I was looking for him. Pulling my cardigan tighter around my shoulders, I close my eyes and lean my head back, giving myself another minute of grace. A throat clears behind me.

"Probably better to let you know I'm here now, rather than in a few minutes when it will seem *way* weirder than it is." The deep voice causes goosebumps to slide against my skin.

Shit.

I open my eyes and turn to face the sound, seeing Lucas on the other side of my car. He gives me a small apologetic smile and runs one hand through his choppy hair. Back to front in his usual move. My fingers itch to do the same.

His recent texts were subtle, but I know it was his way of telling me that he was not going to take my *not now* as a *no*. Asking questions that set little fires inside dead parts of me, shameless flirting which I happily and excitedly did back.

My eyes fixate on his hand. The earlier images from my dream come back in flashes and bring a blush to my cheeks. I can't help but dip my eyes to his chest and then lower. The voicemails fading out of my mind, *almost* forgotten.

"I want to take the speechlessness as a good sign, but you should probably say something soon." His chuckle fills the space from the other side of the car.

I give him a smile and open the door to the back, grabbing the results of my early morning baking session. Hands full, I come around to his side of the car.

"Sorry we're late," I finally say as my smile makes his break free. Handing him the pie I was holding, I keep going before my current wave of bravery leaves me like the tide it came in on. "I felt the need to prove my point." The words from our texts the night before hang in the air as I pass him the pies.

He takes them seamlessly, not looking down once.

"These better be apple." His eyes lower to my mouth just like in my dream, and I swear he can feel my heartbeat through the foot of space between us.

Oh shit.

"And here I thought you preferred cupcakes?" my voice whispers through the space between us, just like in the dream.

"Oh, Maddie, if it's from you, it doesn't matter. My mouth waters, regardless."

Well, double shit.

*Maddie: Who the hell cares?*

*World... or maybe just Lucas: One? Plus, sexy dreams, so... a million?*

He grabs a few more boxes from the back seat before he turns and starts walking toward the field.

"So...why aren't you out there?" I call out ahead of me as I finish balancing the rest of my morning efforts in my hands.

"I finally convinced Tyler to take on the assistant coach position. The league requires two games of supervised coaching before they'll give him the title." He stops and reaches a hand toward me in an offer to take some more of the white boxes from my arms.

I shake my head and turn back to watch Tyler in the middle of the huddle as we keep walking. The boys respond really well to him, and it's obvious he loves it. Mikey tips his head back and laughs with two of the other kids while Tyler sits on one knee, showing them something on his clipboard. I know nothing about football, so I couldn't tell you if he was skilled at what he was telling them to do, but I *can* tell that Mikey likes him, and that is enough for me.

Looking back over at Lucas, I watch him watch Tyler and wonder what he's thinking. The way he is positioned gives me a perfect view of his profile. His strong jaw and contoured cheeks. Honestly, the color of his skin is almost exactly what I go for when I'm making caramel. His eyes are slightly squinted with the sun, and in my head, I know the warm brown is peeking through his lashes.

"It's nice that you bring Mikey to these practices...and that you stay."

The comment brings me out of my ogling. "Thanks. It is easier when he likes whatever it is I want him to do." The words come out with a small laugh as I think back to the first day of school.

"And yet you prefer baseball..." He turns and gives me a small smirk.

When we reach the sidelines of the field, I opt for sitting straight on the grass over standing. Leaving the treats I brought stacked in a pile off to the side. Lucas looks down at me, his eyebrows raising at my choice of position.

I just shrug in response and turn to watch the kids run back and forth between cones while I lean back on my hands, settling in. It takes a lot to hold in my giddy grin when I feel him sit down next to me. His hand landing inches from mine.

It looks like they are having a practice game between two halves of the team. When one kid breaks away and scores a touchdown, the parents cheer, almost all of them clapping loudly while yelling various versions of the same encouraging things. Me, included.

They start the next drill and I peek a glance over at Lucas and see him smiling at the kids as they run through another one of the plays. His hands are wrapped around his knees as he watches everything.

I'm not even remotely embarrassed when he catches me watching him. Smiling at the situation, minutes go by before I feel a finger brush mine between the blades of itchy grass.

My breath catches at the small touch, and I freeze. Lucas holds his hand as still as I hold mine. His finger silently asking me if it's okay.

A million thoughts run through my head. It feels like a question I have no right to answer right now, especially given my morning, but I find myself wanting to have something just for myself that's good. That's healthy. Messy thoughts weed their way in as I hold my finger as still as possible, not giving him an answer while neither of us moves our eyes off the field.

I'm in no place to start something. The *healthy* thing to do would be to fix things and make the Zach problem go away for good before I even consider what Lucas and I have brewing between us. But the butterflies in my chest and the heartbeat in my ears are telling me that healthy choices are boring. Who picks kale over chocolate—over pie?

Fuck it.

I lift my finger off of Lucas's, causing him to stiffen next to me. I want to reassure him, but there really is no need for words, my innocent touch was about to say plenty. So, I put my hand back down, almost on top of his and he tips his lips up in surprise when I use my pinky slide through the space between his last two fingers.

Our silent conversation of touches continues when he wraps his finger around mine, causing my heart to skip a beat at the intimate pinky promise. I squeeze slightly, not looking away from the field as I say everything I need to through the touch of our skin. An unspoken agreement that we are giving this a shot. That I am going to give us a shot. Regardless of all the other messes in my life.

Heat blooms in my chest, and I can't hold in my grin when he squeezes back. And out of the corner of my eye, I see the look of joy on my face is mirrored on his.

# Chapter Thirteen

## BEYONCE

### Lucas

There's mindless chatter around the table in Kit's dining room. Tyler is shuffling, and Chase and Damian are arguing over something—which, even without hearing what it is, I know I side with Damian.

I needed this night with these guys. Somehow there are parts of my life that are sailing smooth as glass, and others that are laying in wait to erupt like some shitty recreation of the decimation of Pompeii.

It's been ages since our last game. We had to postpone the last two due to travel schedules and a round of stomach flu.

The first deal hits the board, and the chatter falls away without preamble. King of spades and the queen of hearts. What a start. The four of spades looks useless now, but you never know.

I chase a few hands that have me riding break even. Damian hits a flush, and then the game starts to slow down after that. Not the most exciting of our nights, but the company makes even the boring ones worth it.

"So, listen to this," Chase starts, leaving the rest of us rolling our eyes before he even gets going.

"This girl I met on Tinder wanted me to meet her mom! We had fucked maybe two or three times, and it was great, but who in the hell wants *me*, of all people, to meet their mother? Unless they want me to fuck her too, in which case I'd have a whole lot more questions." He finishes with a laugh.

"You get tested, right?" Kit replies back without looking up.

"I'll have you know that I wrap it every time." He takes a swig of his beer before dealing out the next hand.

"Thank God. The rest of us don't need you dirtying the playing field," Tyler says only half-jokingly.

"You getting out there, Ty-man?" Chase says to Tyler.

"How many times do I have to tell you not to call me that?" he says back, not bothering to look up from his cards.

"At least twice more."

"Come on, Chase. When are you going to get it together?" I say, slightly distracted, pulling straight from Tyler's handbook and not looking up as I stare at the hand he dealt me. "You're twenty-six. You've got to grow up sometime."

Chase just rolls his eyes while Tyler says, switching sides on us, "Lucas, you should take some of what Chase should give up." The comment annoys me instantly, especially since I've finally made some progress with Maddie, and the idea of seeing someone else curdles my insides.

Damian and Harley both chuckle quietly and the more I think about it, the more I'm aghast that they think I'd ever take Chase's sloppy seconds. I pause, noticing Damian's lack of participation in this. He never talks much about his dating life, but we all know he hooks up with someone when he's on-site at the New York branch of the law firm he works for. Not that I need a reminder that I'm the only one of us who is stuck in this relationship stalemate shitshow.

Ignoring all of that, I respond as immaturely as possible, "I'm not interested in becoming the next man-whore."

"At least I see people," Tyler replies, annoyed at my labeling.

"I wouldn't fucking brag about that." The words come out a little harsher than I intend them, but it's too late now, and it's not like I don't mean them.

I can feel him seething before he even says anything. I might have gone a little too honest with that particular insult.

"You want to call people on their shit, man? Fine. I'll play. What the heck is with you and Maddie?" Tyler's voice is laced with contempt. It hurts deeper since I know that he's not holding back with that jab.

All the eyes at the table land on me. I realize too late that I haven't mentioned her to most of them, and that betrayal shows on a few faces.

"How do you know that there is anything going on?"

Jesus, Lucas. Deny it. That'll help.

"First off, you idiot. I'm not blind. Anyone with eyes on their face can see that the two of you are dancing around each other. Second, since when are we not honest with each other?" He gestures around the table. All of my closest friends are seated in one place, and I instantly feel like a fucking failure.

No one is looking at their cards anymore.

"Fine. You want the truth?" Not a single sound can be heard above the pounding of my heart in my ears and the disappointed silence of the people closest to me. The game completely forgotten.

"Sherry came over for our last round of make-believe family and tried to fuck me in my kitchen *again,* all while she was almost two bottles in, and it hit me that I am fucking miserable. I am tired of being alone, all while playing defense for a marriage that ended years ago to a person who does nothing but make me feel like a failure. Then I met this woman, and I started wondering what it could be like to be happy again."

I can hear one of them exhale with a sigh as I put my face in my hands, utterly exhausted by all of it.

"So, what exactly is stopping you?" Damian asks in his trademark, no-nonsense tone.

I stare at him incredulously. What does he mean? 'What's stopping me?' You can't just go and start a relationship. It has to build. You have to be ready. Lay the foundation and all that shit.

Like he can read my mind, Harley chimes in, "Man, you're on this roller-coaster ride of indecision. You're a grown-ass man and can start a relationship at any point solely because you want to. It doesn't have to be planned and sowed like a vegetable garden."

There are nods of agreement.

"It wouldn't hurt anyone, especially not Jasper, if you went on a date or two. You're not trying to give him a new mom. Just download Tinder or whatever and get out there." Kit's voice of reason has them all muttering in agreement.

Guilt eats at me when I realize I never told them about Amy, either.

I grimace, "About that... I may or may not have gone out with Amy from my office."

"Are you kidding me!" Chase calls out. "I've asked her out at least a dozen times. Should have known that I was the wrong James brother." He sounds disappointed, and all his stops by my office now make sense. The little shit. Of course, he didn't want to see me.

"Well, what the hell happened?" Kit laughs as he casually takes a sip from his beer after he asks, and I can feel the argument fading.

"She stayed late at the office the other night to help me meet a deadline, and I caught myself staring at her ring finger. Which I never do."

Chase groans. "Dude, you can't be that obvious!"

I go on ignoring him and the others when chuckles of agreement flitter around the table. "Well, she clearly saw it and said she thought I was married. When I told her we'd been separated for a while, she admitted that she would have asked me out if she knew."

"Holy shit. Ballsy, that one," Tyler comments with a smile.

"Ok, then what?" Harley says.

"We talked, and she asked me to dinner. But it was fucked. She ordered a shared appetizer the second we sat down, and I couldn't get out of my head from that point on." I fidget with the label on my beer bottle. Pulling the edges off as they soften with the dripping condensation.

Tyler rolls his eyes at what is obviously a huge tell about my lack of dating experience.

"I mean, she's great. She took every piece of my weird, awkward fumbling in stride. And once we got to talking, it was fine. Outside of the dog thing."

"What dog thing?" Damian says, confused, his brows furrowing.

"She has a fucking Malti-poo she named Beyonce. Wears clothes and everything." I grimace, remembering the photos, as I take a drink from the bottle I've been attacking.

"That's too far, man," Kit says without hesitation.

"It's beside the point though, everything she did I compared to Maddie." I run my hands through my hair, and when I look up and see Harley's all-knowing gaze as he tries to hide his smile, I attempt to distract attention away from it by reaching for a chip.

"Lame as hell date, but at least you took someone out. Didn't get back into the game, but the first one's the hardest, right?" Chase says, chiming in again.

"I mean... I walked her back to the car," I pause before I tell them the rest. It's not the worst thing I've ever done, and they're still here, so I dive in. "We kinda made out before she left." Tyler's mouth falls open at my admission, and I keep going. "And goddamn, I've been so stuck in my rut with Sherry, I forgot that that shit isn't supposed to be mechanical."

"Well, shit," Chase says. "She's fully off the list for me then. Some lines I just can't cross."

"How was it?" Harley asks, not even trying to be subtle with his intentions of proving to me that he was right.

"Fucking great. Until I pulled her against me and realized I'd been picturing Maddie the whole time." Guilt eats at me until I remind myself that she knew it and still went there.

"She didn't even smell right," I admit before adding, "Who the hell thinks like that?" I ask almost rhetorically.

Both Damian and Harley smile back at me while the others look as confused as I feel. Damian answers, putting the rest of us out of our misery, "Someone who is feeling more with his heart than his dick." He raises his bottle to me in a silent cheers. To my happiness or chagrin, I have no idea.

Quiet fills the room as we all sit back. The tension fully gone, but the room silent with what that means for me.

"You were joking about the Beyonce thing, right?" Tyler asks finally, breaking the silence as we all just sit, quietly processing the conversation. "Like she didn't really put clothes on the poor thing, right?"

I cringe, thinking back to the picture with the poor thing in a raincoat and mini boots. "Man, I wish."

"Poor Beyonce."

# Chapter Fourteen

## COSMOPOLITANS

### Maddie

"Come on, Hails! I need to go out. I finally found a sitter Mikey loves. I'm not stressed out about the shop, I haven't heard from Zach in days, and you clearly have nothing better going on. Come with me." I'm pleading with her to go out with me.

There's been some sort of shift in me since the therapeutic experience of listening to all of Zach's messages. Lucas and I had that moment on the field, and I feel like, for the first time in a long time, the future is starting to not scare me so much. Which is, in itself, terrifying, but I'm pretending that that is not the case, and I plan very much on enjoying myself tonight. I got dressed. I did my face. I am ready.

Hails looks up at me through the crack in her arm that's draped across her face. She's tipped upside-down on my couch with her feet hanging over the back and her head off the edge of the cushions.

I plant myself in front of her upside-down body and put a balled-up fist on my upturned hip as I move my foot in an obnoxious tap-tap-tap that I know is riling her up.

"Ugggh. Why me? Go get another sister," she sighs so heavily I can see her chest rise and fall with the effort.

I don't answer. There is no need. This is our dance, and I'm quite happy to swing her around in a messed-up sibling do-si-do.

I crouch down and grin almost as obnoxiously as the foot tapping, while I wait impatiently for her to open her eyes.

Five, four, three, two...

They open right on cue, and she groans, "You're the worst. You know that, right?"

"Absolutely," the smile on my face is brimming with amusement. "Now, go... get... dressed," I say, shoving her off the couch with each word.

Twenty minutes later, and we're in the car on the way to River Rats. It has become our go-to ever since that first night. Not that Hails has forgiven, or forgotten, Mr. Tattoo. But who cares. Watching her squirm under his nonchalance will only make my night better!

The front of the bar is almost welcoming now, and I practically skip my way in with Hails trailing behind me. My mouth watering at the idea of Apple Pie and whisky, and the thought of a visual showdown between my sister and Harley. I haven't told Hailey I know his name yet. This might be a tad mean, but the stand-off the two of them have every time we've come has been better than any sporting event. Honestly, I only refer to him as Mr. Tattoo anyway, so it's not like I'm keeping anything from her. Heck, I call him that to his face.

Smiling to myself, I find us two seats at the far end of the counter. I like it better when we're down at the end of the bar because the people-watching is better. I don't like hearing the conversations, but I love watching.

"Hey, Maddie!" Carly calls from the front. "Be with you guys in a second."

"I'm going to the bathroom. Spare me the inevitable torture and order for me?" Hails says as she puts her bag on the counter to my right and turns to leave. I call to her retreating frame,

"And miss out on the show? Never!" her responding groan is followed only by her flipping me off over her shoulder as she continues on, not even bothering to turn back.

While I wait to order, I watch the people around me, wondering what makes them come here. Is it the drinks? The food? The company? Will my bakery be full of people all the time? Will the locals like me, or will they consider me another tourist attraction?

I'd never admit it, but these thoughts keep me up at night, the worry that I'll fail and that all this will come to an end because I really am not capable of doing things on my own. There's this little monster in my mind that taunts me, telling me that no matter how hard I try, I won't succeed, much like my marriage.

I can even see it. The terrifying outcome of failure. Me needing to fall back on my family to bail me out, failing Mikey, all of it. I frown down at the menu that is starting to blur with tears that I won't let fall over a premature failure.

"Maddie?" a familiar voice grabs my attention, pulling me from the depths of my internal despair. I look up to see Harley's eyes on me. The look on his face and the cliché scene of me almost crying at the counter of a small-town bar have me wondering about the stories he must hear working here night after night. I'm sure my drama, as internal as it is, is barely the tip of the iceberg.

"Oh hey, Mr. Tattoo," I say through a fake-as-all-hell smile.

"I can't believe you're still calling me that." His chuckle warms the space around me, and I smile a genuine smile again.

"I couldn't possibly ruin Hailey's day by telling her your name," I say, letting my fake shock bring out his full smile.

"Is that right?" His deep timbre rolls over me, and I take comfort in the sound of it.

*Maddie: One*

*World: Probably one, but at least it's a tie*

Harley has become a sort of friend over our occasional nights here. He even gives me a new drink every time I'm here, matching my apparent mood to alcohol... though, I usually ask for an Apple Pie by the second one. He's only gotten it wrong once. Apparently, I am not a fan of tequila.

"So, what's on for today?" His curiosity is the best part about him. He doesn't ask anything that he genuinely doesn't want to know. It's dangerous because it makes me want to tell him way too much. Which, now that I think about it, is probably why he's so good at his job.

"Well, I'll have you know I was in a fabulous mood when we left the house," I say, wiping the last of the unshed tears from my eyes, not bothering with the effort of pretending that they weren't there. He saw them.

"And what happened in the twelve minutes between your place and when I walked up?" His hands are busy on the other side of the counter, grabbing unseen items and doing whatever it is that he does.

"Well, I was sitting here, minding my own business," He gives me a look, all raised eyebrows and unvoiced doubts that lets me know there is no way in hell he believes that, but he lets me continue without comment anyway. I smile gratefully and carry on. "Then I was looking around wondering what it will be like when I open the bakery, and this crystal-clear future of me failing spectacularly played out in my mind like it's already set in stone." I sigh as I put my head on the counter with a thump.

I hear a glass slide toward me, and I raise my eyes up to him without lifting my head off the cool counter.

"Maddie, failure is always an option." His tone is soft, but I frown at the words. Sitting up and sliding my hands around the drink.

"That doesn't really make me feel any better," I mumble as I take a sip of the pink liquid floating around in the cocktail glass.

I frown down at the drink, confused. This is a Cosmopolitan.

"Why did you make me a college girl drink?" It's delicious, but I'm not going to tell him that. I'm kinda mad at him for not trying on a night when I really wanted him to.

He looks at me with kind eyes and a kinder smile, hiding a chuckle at my description since it's obvious that that wouldn't fit the mood.

"You can't succeed if you never fail at anything. Otherwise, what does the 'success' even mean?"

"What do you mean?"

"When you first start something, it's new. Even if you expect to fail or do fail, there should still be pride because you learned from it. Maybe you need to give yourself a little leeway. If that," he says, indicating to the pink drink at my lips as I take a quiet sip. "Is a 'college girl drink,' maybe you need to take a little college girl risk. Let some of those expectations go for a night."

I smile at that. It kind of makes sense in a weird way. I could use a little 'college girl risk' mindset. It sounds easy and carefree. Those are things I haven't been in a while.

Harley pats my hand, sets a beer down to the left of me, and moves to walk away.

I raise my brows at the beer, but he just smirks as his body moves farther down the length of the bar.

That's a new smile. A mischievous smile. Weird.

I sip my pink drink and go back to people-watching, only briefly wondering where Hailey went off to. Probably hiding in the bathroom. Chicken.

"What a nice surprise," a deep voice whispers inches from my ear.

I spin faster than the stool is prepared for and am only kept upright by the solid hand at my back holding me onto the seemingly unreliable chair.

"Lucas! What are you doing here?" My heart is in my throat, and my lips part in surprise. An unexpected happy feeling taking over my mood.

"It's my best friend's bar. I'm here at least three nights a week."

Grabbing the beer, he raises it to Harley at the other side of the bar with a devilish smile. His lips close around the edge, and he takes a sip, sitting on the stool while spinning it toward me with an easy smile.

I twist my stool and my eyes find Harley's at the end of the bar, a wide grin on his face. Mother-setter-upper! I might... I might love him, actually. He nods knowingly and goes back to the man in front of him without another look.

College girl risk, right?

I spin my chair, slower this time, so that it's facing Lucas.

"How's life, Mr. James?" I let a sultry tone out when I say it, and instantly worry that it's too much.

He toys with the label on his bottle one-handed as he holds me in a stare that gives me the feeling I get from hot caramel and wicked me-time thoughts.

"Oh, it's much better now." His smile tells me things I want to hear, and I wait a minute, hoping he says them with words.

Lucas openly appraises my body with bedroom eyes, and I feel my usual blush come to my cheeks at the very public assessment. *Someone* has gotten brazen since I last saw them, and I'm not so sure that I mind at all.

His eyes land on my drink, and he chuckles. "What the hell is that?"

"This, I'll have you know, is my new philosophical outlook on life!" I'm teasing him, but it's worth it when his brows furrow.

He leans forward and smells the pink swirling contents of my glass. "A Cosmopolitan is your new outlook on life?" His tone is incredulous and somehow still curious.

"You should be so lucky it is."

He grins at my retort. "Okay, I'll bite." His hand reaches for my glass.

I can't hold in my laugh, and I pull it back against my chest protectively. "You sure you want to ride this wave with me?" I raise my eyebrows seriously. "It could get messy."

"Even better. Give it here, Cupcake." His fingers open and close in a 'give it' motion, and I pass him the Barbie-colored beverage, hoping it distracts him from the blush that creeps up and down my face and chest at his endearment.

He shakes his head and grimaces when he takes an enormous sip and painfully swallows. My eyes inadvertently follow the motion down his neck, and I blame the vodka for my own public appraisal of his body.

"Umm. That's definitely an interesting outlook on life," he says, taking another tentative sip and nodding when the second one goes down easier. The whole scene has me tracing the motion down his throat for another, embarrassing time.

Suddenly I'm becoming a very fast fan of this new outlook.

"So, tell me," he continues without pause. "What is the Cosmopolitan philosophy you mentioned? I'll need you to sell it if I'm going to subject myself to that." His voice is now smooth from the vodka, and he nods toward the mostly empty glass.

The smile on my face must be contagious because he mirrors it. The edges of his lips rising up to meet his tanned cheeks.

"Well, I am a new member of this *very* exclusive club," I reply thoughtfully. "But from what I gather, it's a take-risk mindset, a guilt-free, life-living, no apologies attitude. All with a give-yourself-a-break outlook." Hell, I've just sold myself for a second time. That does sound like fun.

His head tips back as he laughs, the deep chuckle waking up the little butterflies that live in my stomach when he's around. When his hand lands on my thigh, he sends them on an exploratory flight while heat builds in me at his touch.

I lean forward and gesture for him to come closer with a crooked finger. He obliges eagerly. “I’ll tell you a secret, though,” I whisper before I pause and look at him, the effects of the vodka starting to show.

“Go on. I’m all ears,” he whispers back with his eyes on my mouth.

Before the alcohol-fueled bravery leaves, I press on, “I have no idea how to do that.”

“Oh, well, I can help you with that. We’ll do the one thing you can *only* do with that attitude.” He’s deadly serious as he raises a hand and gestures for two more.

“And what is that.” I laugh.

“Truth or Dare.”

Forty minutes, five rounds later, and we’ve *terrorized* Harley’s bar. There are a dozen bowls of bar snacks in front of us that we bribed off of other tables—no money allowed. A collection of phone numbers sit in a pile like a deck of cards from people we have no interest in calling. And far too many secrets have been shared between whispers that are definitely too loud to be kept secret. Hailey finally came back at some point and made a fake excuse about going home. After a knowing look, I could tell she wanted me to be doing exactly what I was doing. A glaring death match between her and Harley took place, much to Lucas’s and my entertainment, but still, she left happy as an unsatisfied clam. Which I decide is firmly Hailey’s fault.

Harley, though, despite that, has been a wonderful sport, and on more than one occasion, I’ve caught him slipping glances at his friend with a smile on his face.

“Okay! One more!” Lucas spins my chair toward him and puts his large hands on my knees. The rough feel of his fingers leaves invisible marks on my skin that I fully plan on tracing later.

“At least two! I’m not going to be the last one in this. No way.” I shake my head in emphasis, making my blond hair fall around my face at the drunken enthusiasm I put into the usually subtle motion. He just smiles at my argument.

Leaning forward in an effort to tell only me, since our voices are beyond controllable, he whispers, "You just want more of my secrets, don't you?"

Lucas's voice is dirty, and the chills it leaves across my skin me has me wanting to know all of him. Especially the parts that make him talk like that. "Fine, I'll admit it, I want them all, but I will settle for one more secret each." I hold out my pinky to swear on it.

Lucas doesn't even look down as he puts his finger in mine. His eyes hold my gaze like letting go will let go of me.

"You first," I whisper.

He still hasn't looked away. He's barely blinking. I can tell he's trying to decide how deep to take this. I'm hoping he picks correctly. I don't want this feeling to end, one wrong move, and we both know it will.

"Have you dreamed about me?" The words are sultry and even dirtier than before. No question about what he's actually asking.

I turn my head away shyly, leaving my drink on the counter. More alcohol won't help me get out of this, so I confess my biggest secret to him. "Yes." It comes out breathless.

His hand is back on my thigh, higher this time, braver. He's leaning toward me, giving me no chance to escape. "When?"

"The rules call for one question, Mr. James."

"Come on, Maddie," he says, my name like a promise. "What's one more?"

"Which time are you asking about?" It leaves me before I think about it.

"Fuck," Lucas runs his hand through his hair and smiles down at me with the look of a teenage boy who just discovered the local make-out spot.

"My turn," I say confidently, straightening my shoulders.

"Same question. Do you dream about me?" I have no capacity for seductive. My curiosity gets the better of me.

"Only when I'm awake."

Holy cookie dough.

Electricity crackles between us, the air growing thick with a tension that neither of us wants to cut. It's a heady feeling, and my fingers itch to touch him.

"I have to pee," I say seconds before I act on the impulse to pull his body toward me. "Pee break." My words slur together as I slide out of my seat and sway slightly when I stand.

"Oh no, you don't, Cupcake," Lucas says as he rises with me and holds me by the shoulders. "There's no way you're making it there on your own."

"Ha! You just want to follow me to the dark hallway. Admit it," I reply, smiling up at him playfully.

His gaze darkens, and he licks his lips, his eyes on mine.

"And if I do?"

There are moments when your brain shuts off, and the decisions you make are made by instinct alone. With my eyes on his face and my hands on his chest...not sure when they got there, I reply before my brain turns back on.

"I think we both want to see where that would go."

With more confidence than I feel, I turn toward the back corner of the bar. His hands land on my hips somewhere along the way, and I'm holding my breath in an attempt to hide how breathless his touch is making me.

I turn the darkened corner to the hallway that leads to the bathrooms. The walls and alcove at the end are decorated from one end to the other with artistic photos and mirrors, each framed in antique gold. Every time I've come back here, I've ended up spending more time than I care to admit looking over the sensual photos and art that were so carefully curated. Though, this time they are the last thing on my mind.

Stopping halfway, I turn toward the radiating force at my back, his hands haven't left my hips this whole time, even with the lack of movement along the way.

Lucas grips me slightly with confident fingers and pulls me to him, our chests coming close enough that the space between is too small to measure. I don't have enough oxygen for words, especially when his hand comes up and tucks a wayward strand of hair behind my ear and lands on my neck.

He tilts my face to his and bends his head down to brush those pillowy lips across mine. Soft and full, they slide back and forth. There's nothing I can do, nothing I *want* to do except fall into this.

Reading my mind, he leans into it, into me. Pressing his lips tightly to mine while holding me to him with a firm grasp on my neck. When his tongue brushes the seam of my mouth, I can't hold in my responding moan of his name as it slips between our shared breaths.

The sound snaps something in him, and the tempo of the kiss changes. Without warning, my back is against the wall, the impact rattling the photos and frames. My hands are in his as he holds them above us with one hand. Kissing my mouth, my neck, my chest, all while his other hand roams down my body.

He is everywhere, in my head, in my mouth, in my thoughts, on my body. It's intoxicating, and I don't want to do anything other than welcome it.

His tongue dances across mine, a combination of soft and hard, alternating when the mood suits him. The electrifying mix of him everywhere builds a fire that pools inside me, only fueled further when his thigh slides between my legs, putting pressure on the ache that's building at a feverish pace. My hands burn with want and need to touch him, to pull him closer. A need I can't define and a need I can't explain. I just need him. I need more. I *need*.

Our pace is building, and neither of us is capable of holding back anymore. The sexual tension that's been building over weeks of small touches and conversations has just added gasoline to the fire that lit that first time we met.

I'm shaking with want and desire when I feel the evidence of his own grind against my center. There's a part of me that isn't above taking this into the bathroom and being a bar cliché. He wouldn't even have to ask. Honestly, it would be quite on par for my college girl mindset and Cosmo outlook.

He lets go of my hands as he slides his to the back of my thighs, kissing me with a passion I've only read about while he lifts me up effortlessly and holds me pressed against the wall. My legs wrap around his waist mindlessly as a frame tips off the adorned wall, hitting another before it falls, causing a wave of them to crash to the floor next to us.

The sound breaks the trance we're trapped in, and he pulls back, chuckling, just enough to rest his forehead on mine. He makes no move to show that he plans on putting me down, and when he squeezes my thighs in his strong grip, I get the feeling he plans just the opposite.

Harley comes flying around the corner with the look of a parent about to break up a set of horny teenagers, and I laugh quietly at how spot on my assessment is.

His face fills with surprise, his eyebrows rising comically when he takes in the broken frames, glass, and photos scattered around us, and me...wrapped around Lucas like a Christmas bow.

Pointing to the mess on the floor with an unhindered smile, Harley says, "You're covering that, James." Shaking his head in what must be disbelief or relief, he leaves without another word.

Lucas meets my eyes, his full of silent promises we made on football fields and things I've dreamed of seeing. "Worth it," he says.

"Without a doubt." I laugh before I plant a final kiss on his lips, deciding Cosmos might be my new favorite drink after tonight.

# Chapter Fifteen

## ACADEMIC AMBIENCE

### Lucas

I don't see Maddie the rest of the week after that night at the bar. That kiss in the hallway has played on repeat inside my head hourly ever since. Kiss is too tame of a word. The whole scene is burned on my brain, taking over every thought I have. It fills me with unease how much I think about it, how much I think about her, as the days go by without seeing her face.

Embarrassingly, I walked by the bakery *twice* this week with the hopes of accidentally running into her. Not that I would ever admit that to anyone but myself. Sadly, it was just her sister in there both times.

Our texting game has gone on all week, though, and I've learned some interesting things.

Her family is very close. She talks to her mom daily, works with her sister, and every day has a story to tell about their antics, and texts her dad constantly. Hearing stories of her life with them makes me admire her more as a mom. It is very clear that Mikey is her entire world, just like how I feel about Jasper.

An excited trepidation fills me when I realize that I'll see her tonight. The parent-teacher night at the school is mandatory, and since Mikey and Jasper are in the same class, there's no doubt that she'll be there.

It doesn't make the day go by any faster, though, and by three o'clock, I'm contemplating texting her and asking if she wants to go together. But that would be weird, and people would talk. Sherry is also going to be there. The realization washes over me like an iceberg on the Titanic.

Speaking of, I shoot off a text.

**Me: See you tonight?**

**Sherry: Why?**

**Me: Parent-Teacher Night?**

**Me: Mandatory School Event?**

**Sherry: Oh, sweetie, I'm at a conference in Tucson.**

**Me: Of course, you are**

**Sherry: What is that supposed to mean???**

**Me: I think you know**

**Sherry: You always do this**

**Me: Can we not? I'll be there. I always am**

**Sherry: You're an asshole, Lucas.**

**Sherry: We can't all have everything together like you do.**

There's no winning this fight. I know from experience that the only way it will end is if I admit that she's not wrong and move on. It doesn't matter, and has never mattered, whether or not I was right or not. Just that she *wasn't* wrong.

I put my phone back in my pocket, not ready to admit defeat yet but not wanting to keep it going. This is the part that ruins me. How long am I going to have to keep this fucked-up relationship with her just because she is Jasper's mom? There's no one else in the world I would keep in my life if they constantly put me down on repeat. I'm instantly disappointed in myself for all the times I willingly, or unwillingly, took her back over the years. Even if it was just for the sex.

I throw myself into work after that, not wanting to have a spare second that I will inevitably fill with emotional weakness and end up apologizing to Sherry.

Diving back into the Anderson project was the best thing I could have done to pass the time. I blink, and Amy comes in to remind me to head out.

I was pleasantly surprised with her the week following our date. She was completely unfazed by my disinterest, and surprisingly, we've hung out and had lunch a few times since then. As friends. I still hate seeing pictures of her poor dog in clothes, but everyone has their thing.

I'm definitely liking this new phase I'm sliding into in life. The lines I am drawing with Sherry are improving—sort of—my games with the guys, Jasper, and Maddie. For the first time since Sherry and I split, I can finally think about where my life will be in the coming years, and not hate myself.

I slide my car into the parking lot of the school and thank God that I found a spot here and didn't have to walk the trek from the secondary lot.

These back-to-school nights are the school's attempt to give us access to the teachers and understand the level of work expected over the year, like we hadn't actually attended school ourselves. It is also an obnoxious time when the single moms on the PTA scout for fresh meat. Us single dads have a spot specified in advance to avoid the cougar-ish hunt. Unfortunately for me, that usually meant getting the pleasure of watching Sherry flaunt herself at other unsuspecting men, all while trying to come home with me. But not tonight.

I'm silently thanking Sherry for blessing me with her absence... now that I think about it.

Walking up the sidewalk to the school's front door, the chatter of other parents mingling by the front doors fills my ears. This is normally where I would be up until the last second, chatting with the others who were putting off going in for whatever reasons they had. Some smoke around the bushes—getting their last fix in before sitting under the authoritative gaze of the teachers and school staff who frown upon the habit. Some just not wanting to participate in the requirements at all. Some hoping to just delay seeing their exes…or maybe that's just me.

Not needing to shield myself this time, I find that I have something to look forward to and walk right in. The telltale smell of academic ambience greets me with open arms as I walk through the hallways.

"Hey, Lucas," Damian calls to me from a group of parents standing in front of a closed door. He's off to the side with Stacey, one of Jasper's friends, Spencer's mom, and Tyler. I glance ahead and see the door they're standing in front of.

117

MR. BRADLEY CLEMENTS

FIFTH GRADE

That's the one.

Jasper didn't have anything particularly special to say about his new teacher. He just mentioned that he was strict and really didn't like it when kids talked too much. Doesn't sound like a trait I'd think a teacher should have, especially a fifth grade one, but as long as he is good at his job, who am I to complain?

Other parents are gathering around the door, all waiting to be let in. I scan the hallways and notice most classrooms are already open, welcomingly, as groups of people walk in. I nod to a few faces I recognize ass we wait for the teacher to open the door. I'm growing increasingly unimpressed as time goes by, but we make idle small talk. Still waiting.

The knob turns and the door opens without preamble. Well, here we go.

A man in a plaid shirt and khakis stands inside the doorway smiling casually as he welcomes us to come in a take a seat. Mr. Clements, I presume. He nods at me as I walk in.

"Please, take a seat in one of the chairs. Tonight is an opportunity to walk an hour in your child's shoes." Something about how he says it has me meeting Damian's equally annoyed gaze. Tyler hides a smile at our displeasure, and the three of us take up seats in the second row.

"Your children are moving out of the phase of nurture and being groomed into what will manifest as their nature." The classroom is silent and full of parents whom I can only assume are as put off by this man as I am.

He continues on, oblivious to the rising distaste, "My job is to guide that process along in an educational sense."

There are a few seats open around us, and I catch him looking at his watch indignantly.

"While we wait for *everyone* to arrive, I'd like you to take a look at the schedules I put on each of your desks." There's an exasperated undertone as he glances back to the door, and I wonder who he's so annoyed to be waiting for.

Having Damian at one side of me and Tyler at the other is oddly reminiscent of our childhood years. We were just missing Kit and Harley. Kit's daughter is a year younger than our kids, so they never shared a teacher, and Harley is an honorary dad, taking his uncle status more seriously than many of the people I know take fatherhood. I don't know how his sister would have survived without him helping take care of his niece.

The school desk is a tight fit for my adult body, and I am briefly taken down memory lane by the size difference. I don't remember the seats being this uncomfortable. Damian has it worse than I do since he's the largest guy I know. His pressed suit adds to the hilarity of him stuffed into the too-small desk. His fingers drum on the desktop, annoyed, and I can't help but take my phone out and snap a picture of him. He looks even more pissed after he catches me doing so, and I know I'll pay for that later, but it is absolutely worth it.

I look at Tyler on the other side of me, and the look on his face screams, "Who the hell is this guy?" My exact thought. We all silently sit looking through the papers he placed on the desks, unsure of what we're waiting for. No parent wants to be the one to ask, obviously, so we all sit here suffering in silence, until a commotion sounds from the hallway beyond the door, and all heads turn in that direction.

"Oh fuck! Get it together, Maddie."

I chuckle at the sound of Maddie's swearing and flustered tone coming from the hallway. Standing to go help her with whatever has put her in such a state, I'm halfway through unfolding myself from the torture device that we're all seated in, when I'm stopped by Mr. Clements's halting hand as he calmly says, "If you'll all please excuse me for a second."

Slowly lowering myself back into the plastic, I can't help but glare at him when I hear a muffled conversation taking place on the other side of the wall.

Every set of eyes in the room is watching the open doorway, waiting to see who, only Tyler and I know, is on the other side.

"I didn't *intend* to arrive late, Mr. Clements." Maddie's voice raises slightly, loud enough for everyone to hear, and a look passes between Tyler and me. It doesn't escape my notice that she seems to already know who he is, and the thought of that bothers me more than it should, considering he's her son's teacher, so it's not like they'd be complete strangers.

The only thing that stops me from getting out of my chair to go break up whatever is going on out there, is Maddie coming around the corner. Though the sight of her slumped shoulders and tempered mood makes me want to get up for an entirely different reason. She takes the first open seat in the front row, smiling softly, and mouthing sorry at me as she slides into the seat. Fitting into it much better than any of the guys with her petite size.

After very obviously waiting for her to sit down, Mr. Clements finally starts walking us through the class schedule and expectations for the semester. He goes over parent communication, and his eyes find Maddie's in open judgment when he mentions how a parent's actions are the best example for a child. The fact that he is calling her out in a public setting like this is disgusting to me, and my blood starts boiling.

This happens two more times before Damian calls him on it, saving me from the risk of spending the night in a cell after pummeling his face in. I can't see her face from my position behind her, but I can only imagine how embarrassed she must feel.

"Mr. Clements, is there a reason you are continuously bringing Ms. Thompson into this?" His voice is laced with authority that could only come from the professional success he's achieved over the years.

"Mr. Jackson is it?" he responds, clearly already knowing the answer. "My stance as a teacher is to aim for the best. I'm only asking that the rest of you do the same."

"We're here to understand the expectations of us as parents. Your belittling of the parents in this room does not instill confidence in your role as an academic advisor to our children." The standoff between the two of them becomes a tangible energy that radiates around the rest of the room. "I'm happy to take my concerns up with the School Board, if I must."

There are nods of agreement around the room.

"I'm happy to listen to your concerns, and I will gladly take them into account, Mr. Jackson." His smile is placating, and not nearly enough of any apology, but the room seems to settle.

The question-and-answer period starts next, and the remaining tension diminishes as we progress through it. When Maddie raises her hand and asks about the field trip schedule for the school year, I hold my breath, praying that the response he chooses to give her shows some semblance of respect.

"Great question, Ms. Thompson," He smiles at her, holding her gaze as we wait for him to answer. "There is a typed-up schedule in the parent packet you were presented with at the beginning of the night."

"Thank you." Her reply is quiet but quick.

"That will conclude our evening, class. Thank you all for coming, and I look forward to getting to know you and your children more over the coming year. Please fill out the contact preference form and other questionnaires and put them on my desk before making your way to the auditorium where you will have a chance to discuss extracurricular activities with some of our other staff."

He takes a seat at his desk, shuffling papers and making notes like the pompous asshole he's portrayed himself to be.

Maddie gets up and makes her way to his desk. I can't concentrate on these papers at all, knowing she's up there talking with the piece of shit. It's not lost on me how messed up it is that I feel this way about my kid's teacher.

Her soft voice fleets in and out of the other conversations going on around me, but I can't make out what they're talking about. She gives him a smile that eases some of the fire in my blood, and I relax a little.

The papers are completely mundane and redundant, but I start to fill them out regardless, only stopping them when the smell of vanilla stops in front of me.

I look up at her warm hazel eyes and smile more genuinely than I have all day.

"Mr. James." Her response is playful and flirty, and I know that her mind is exactly where mine is. The bathroom hallway at River Rats.

"Cupcake," I whisper back mischievously. Her cheeks flush, just like I expected. Just like I had hoped.

"What an interesting night," I comment casually. A not-so-subtle statement of "Can you believe this tool?"

"I agree. My whole week has been just as eventful. I'll tell you all about it later," she says, the words sounding slightly deflated, but with a smile as she looks over her shoulder at Mr. Clements. A clear look of displeasure on his face at our conversation.

The fact that she mentions seeing me later makes me giddier than a teen, but it's tempered by the clear stress in her words. "Anything I can help with? Do we need more Cosmos this evening?"

Her eyes light up at our new inside joke. "As fun as that was, and highly repeatable, I might add, I think I just need to head home tonight. Will you thank your friend for me?" Her hand covers my fingers, and she squeezes before she nods at Damian who is off talking with another group of parents. Waving bye to Tyler, she turns and walks out, looking over her shoulder once to give me one last wave and smile before she rounds the corner.

"Well, that was a fucked-up show of authority if I've ever seen one," Damian says a minute later after he makes his way back to us. I look around, noticing that there are only a few of us left in the room still flipping through papers and wrapping up social conversations. I curse inwardly, noticing a little too late that Mr. Clements is gone too.

"What the fuck was up with his hard-on for Maddie?" Tyler asks far too loudly. "I get the idea they've met before."

"Yeah, me too, and I don't fucking like it." We make our way out into the hall and start walking toward the atrium. "Do you think it's worth filing a complaint?" I direct my words at Damian, keeping them quiet as we pass other parents and faculty.

"Honestly," he says, eyeing me. "Being an asshole to parents isn't something anyone will act on. I say we just keep an eye on it." I nod in agreement, and we keep walking.

We meet up with the rest of the crowd heading toward the front exit, and my gaze catches Mr. Clements as he slips out one of the side doors breaking off from the rest of the crowd.

Weird fucker. I'm pretty sure that leads to the parking lot. I'm not sure what bothers me about it, but I can't shake the need to follow him. "Hey, I'm going to head out. Will you guys let me know if there's anything I miss?" They both nod, and I turn down the hallway without a second thought.

# Chapter Sixteen

## UNDERBAKED CROISSANTS

### Maddie

"Madelyn!" Turning to the sound of my name, I see Mikey's teacher running toward me at a slow jog from the side of the building. I have no idea why I decided to park in the side lot, but the lack of cars and people seemed appealing at the time, even though the walk was so much farther than it could have been. Clearly Mr. Clements knew a shortcut.

I sigh under my breath and wonder why he's here. Hasn't he tortured me enough for one night?

"I was hoping to catch you before you left." He's still a few feet away, but close enough that I finally put my finger on what was bothering me earlier—besides his general shitty attitude. His shirt contrasts horribly with his skin tone. Kind of making his whole skin coloring pasty and washed out.

Hmmm, like an underbaked croissant. Yellow and soft. He really should have picked *any* other color. That pale green is hard to pull off.

His features are an odd combination of too strong a jawline and not enough cheekbone. I will say, they are much more pleasant in the muted light of dusk than they were in his fluorescent-lit classroom. Unfortunate for him really.

"O-kayyyyy," I say once he reaches me. "What's up? I know I skipped the forms but I filled them out when we first met so I didn't think you needed them again." I lean against my car while he pauses and catches his breath. There's a thin line of sweat coating his hairline and accenting his curls.

"No, it's not that." His smile is soft, not meeting his eyes. There's an odd look there. Maybe nerves? Either way, it's starting to make me uncomfortable, and I need to get out of here. Plus, the idea of my bathtub and a glass of wine is calling me, encouraging me even more to hurry this along.

"Okay, well ..."

He cuts me off, "It's just that you're new in town, and I thought you might be interested in going out sometime."

What? He just humiliated me for an hour straight in front of countless others. There's no way I'd even remotely consider doing anything with this jerk, even if he wasn't my son's teacher.

Lost in my disbelief, I barely notice him move until he's closer. So close that I can see his heart pumping in his neck and his chest slowly heaving. The smell of his musky sweat fills my nose, and I hold in a grimace.

Get me out of here. Please. I pray to whatever entity can save me since I don't have the energy for this. Bracing myself for the emotional work this type of conversation takes, I pull up my big girl panties and press on.

"That's really sweet. I'm not really looking to see anyone right now. I just went through a divorce and I'm trying to get settled with my son." I've practiced this exact rejection. Be firm enough that there's no reason to raincheck, but nice enough that no one takes it personally.

There's not a single indication he heard me at all. In fact, he just steps closer. Crossing that line between what's considered joint space and personal space, and that strange smile fills his face again. Being this close to him makes his size overwhelmingly intimidating, and a feeling of claustrophobia that I don't usually suffer from starts to rear its head. It was easier to separate his space and size from mine when he was farther away.

"Oh, come on," he says softly. "You just look like you would be a really good time." His hand moves up to tuck a piece of hair behind my ear before I step back, I turn my head away, rejecting his advance.

"I really do appreciate the tho-"

He cuts me off before I can finish, "Look, being new in a small town is hard, and it would be a shame if you started off with a bad reputation. After tonight we both know that's likely to happen." The look in his eyes is now something I'm all too familiar with and is far scarier than I had thought. It's the look of someone who isn't going to take no for an answer.

"Mr. Clements," my voice is teetering on pleading, this is the sort of trauma you read about other people going through, not what you ever expect to experience yourself. "Why don't we go back inside and maybe talk." Just get him around other people. I try to push past my fear and make an attempt to sidestep him, but his arm shoots out and presses against my car. Caging me in.

He leans forward, his lips against my ear. "Just one date. It will be great, I promise." That empty unemotional smile reaches his eyes, and an excited gleam lights up his face.

His fingers brush my cheek, and I turn my face away for a second time, knowing that it's pointless, but it's my only option of rejecting his touch.

"P-please, stop." Screw pleading. I'll beg. The words barely make sound as they leave my mouth. The train of desperation I'm riding on is moving fast and I have a first-class seat. Yay me.

I'm made aware of the tears staining my cheeks when his fingers brush through them. It's then that I realize, without a doubt that there are worse people in the world than Zach. I never thought I had it as bad as it could be, but this is putting my fucked-up history into a harsh perspective.

"Get the fuck off her! Now!" The familiar voice registers a second before Mr. Clements's body is gone and I can breathe again. The space around me opens up like someone ripped a plastic bag off my face—one that was slowly suffocating me.

Things around me start moving quickly, yet more like a slow-motion scene playing out like it's someone else's life. I'm frozen as I watch it unfold.

Lucas picks him up by his front collar.

Lucas pulls his fist back.

Lucas connects his fist with the asshole's face.

A loud crack like someone snapped a piece of Styrofoam in half.

The sound snaps me back into my body right as my son's teacher cries out in pain. I'm thrust back into my life right then, and the tears begin to fall.

For all the times when I should have stood up for myself but didn't. When I should have cried, but held it in.

Lucas just stares at Mr. Clements as he gets up from a heap on the ground in the parking lot, his back is to me, and I can't see his face. When Mr. Clements starts to back away, holding his mutilated nose, blood drips down his hand and onto his shirt, and I can see Lucas' shoulders stiffen. "Don't you ever fucking come near her again. Your days of teaching our kids are over." His words are resolute, and Brad stiffens when Lucas says them.

My whole body is shaking, and my hands won't even move to wipe my tears. Stupid tears still streaming down my stupid face. I close my eyes against the onslaught, hoping and praying that this is just a nightmare that I'll wake up from. I don't want to watch my new life here become the worst version of itself.

Warm hands move up my arms, and I jolt. My mind zoning out in a pathetic attempt to flee, but reality forces it—and me—back to reality. "Shhhh. I've got you. He's gone." Lucas's voice is a soothing balm on my racing heart, and he turns and wraps me in his safe arms. The heat from his body and the cool metal of my car against my back keeps me firmly in the present while I watch my son's teacher walk away. Once he's gone, I lean my forehead on Lucas's chest. Losing myself in the security he's giving me, focusing on nothing but my breathing. In. Out. Chest up. Chest down.

We stay like that as my tears slow and eventually stop. He makes no effort to stop me before I am ready, or to hurry my grief along so he can move on from this.

He just stands there holding me. I can feel his breath ruffle my hair. The warmth from his hands grounding me.

Lucas is watching me. I can feel it. He can somehow see *me* even through my carefully taped-together mask.

"Why does this happen?" I'm not asking him directly. I just need to say something, so I know my voice works again, and that the meek woman I turned into didn't move in and decide to stay. Again.

"This isn't fucking on you." His voice is harsh. He is furious. Hell, they could probably feel it inside.

"How do you know that?" I yell back, surprising us both. God, now I was pissed. Not at him, just at the world. "You *just* met me. You know nothing about me. When bad things happen enough times to you, it's naïve to think there's anyone else to blame." As soon as the words are out of my mouth, I know I shouldn't have said them. I hang my head in defeat.

"What do you mean?" His words simmer with barely contained rage. "This isn't the first time some asshole has touched you without permission?" There is actual poison in his words. I know it's not directed at me, but it's there. Part of me used to dream of someone who would come rescue me, who would pull his shining sword out and slay my dragons, keep me safe. But there is something more you gain from fighting your own fights, something you *earn* when you win those fights.

"Lucas, everyone has a past. Everyone. Single moms don't just move to small towns where they know no one because it sounds 'nice'." God, I'm tired. Emotionally and physically tired. "Look, I'm going to go home now, and when I wake up tomorrow the world will go back to being a beautiful place and men won't be scary, and I will go about my business." His gaze is unwavering and hard, the stability of it giving me small pieces of comfort.

"Maddie, I'm not just going to walk away after that. I'll drive you home."

"Yeah, okay." There isn't anything in me left to fight or argue.

"Where is Mikey?" The fact that he asks and knows to think about that does something to my battered and bruised heart, even after all this.

"He's at my sister's place. They're having a sleepover." I can make a pretty accurate guess at what they were doing. Junk food, video games, and movies that are one hundred percent way too mature for him. I silently thank her for moving with us.

Getting from the side lot of the school and into Lucas's truck in the main lot is a blur. Some moments clearer than others. Him clicking my seatbelt. Him asking Harley to pick up my car later. Him backing out of the traumatizing parking lot. Me giving him directions.

Lucas doesn't force conversation once inside his truck, and I only know that he keeps glancing at my reflection in the window—the one that I haven't stopped staring out since we started driving.

My purse buzzes more than once from the floor of his truck as we drive down the road, and I have as much interest in looking at who is calling me as I have in prying my eyeballs out with a mixing spoon. I can tell he wants to ask who it is, but I'm relieved when he doesn't.

"Which house?"

"Little blue one on the left." One side of my mouth quirks up when I realize I almost said cozy.

He pulls into the driveway, somehow gliding over the monstrosity of a pothole with a skill that I still haven't mastered even after weeks of running over it daily.

There's weight in his stare. I feel it resting on me as I continue to look out the window like the view is going to solve all of my problems. Once we're parked, he shuts the car off and lets the silence fill the empty space.

"You know," I start, looking at the illuminated windows in the front of my house. "I didn't lead him on." I don't know why it matters that I tell him this truth, but it does. "I barely had a full conversation with him tonight or the one other time we met." The heavy weight of suppressed tears fills my chest again, while my throat works to push them back down.

I startle when Lucas's hand presses on my thigh, and I struggle to turn my burning eyes to his.

"Maddie, even if you had led him around like a dog on a leash, there's no fucking excuse." His voice has no judgment or disgust, which leaves me oddly relieved that he doesn't think less of me.

He continues, "Look, I know it's probably too soon, but you should report him. It's a miracle I let him walk away, but that doesn't mean he should get away with it."

I nod, knowing he's right. He's my kid's teacher, for Pete's sake, and he needs to be dealt with accordingly. But how many damn ripples in the water do I have to cause?

"Damian, the guy you asked me to thank, he's a lawyer and he can help." Lucas pauses. "I may have told him all about you, so really, he'd be happy to help"

I nod again. Knowing the process and the work involved. I'd done it once before and researched it more times than I care to admit.

Lucas unclips my seatbelt again and comes around to open the door for me, his calloused hand helping me down from the height of his truck.

His eyes don't leave me as we make it up the small brick stairs and to the brightly colored front door. I'm starting to wonder if his eyes ever leave me when we're together. I pause with my key in the lock, questioning my choice before I even ask. Deciding being polite is worth more than what any of my neighbors might think, I ask, "Do you want to come in?" He nods and grabs my free hand, placing a kiss on the back of it before I unlock the door and swing it open to let him in.

It feels monumental for some reason. I'm not surprised when his stare meets mine because this is a step that takes us forward, and he knows it. He's not pushing for it, and it makes me like him even more. I gesture to the couch in the middle of the living room. "Want to sit? I'm just going to take a shower, if that's okay?"

His eyes hold mine patiently and I go on, "My room is just through that door," I say pointing down the short hallway off the side of the living room. "I won't be too long. You can watch TV or something." I'm tempted to keep talking so the air does not fill with an uncomfortable silence, but he saves me from having to as he takes my purse from me, setting it on the table in front of the sofa. Before I can say anything else, his hands come up to my shoulders, and he slides my jacket off my arms. Laying it across the back of the couch before spinning me around and walking me toward the room I just indicated.

Crossing the threshold into my safe space takes us another step further. One more important than him just coming inside the house. I feel the lines we spent drawing those first weeks are being erased by the second, and even in my catatonic state, I love every second of it.

Once inside my room I feel him look around before spotting my bathroom in the far corner. His firm hands steer me to the bathroom, stopping in front of the shower. Leaving me facing him, he leans behind the etched glass door and turns the water on, moving the knob around until steam starts to fill the room. There's no space for words at this moment, and we both welcome it.

Pulling out of the shower, he moves to stand in front of me again, his eyes on mine and his body close. Without breaking eye contact, his hands slowly reach down, and he snags the hem of my dress. Holding it between careful fingers, he pauses, giving me time to stop this if I wanted to.

There are a million questions in his stare, the most important one being my agreement. Now, more than ever, it's important to him. No pressure for me to agree. He just waits, with his fingers holding the edge of my sweater dress like he's holding the edges of my heart at this moment.

There aren't many moves left before he'll have my whole heart in his hand. I'm self-aware enough, even after this shit show of a night, to know I'm not ready to give him that yet.

I give him a small nod, and his lips tentatively brush mine, soft and brief, before he slides my dress up my body. Taking his time. Moving it up agonizingly, inch by torturous inch. Lucas's breath comes out soft and labored when he slides it up past my generous hips, revealing my plain underwear.

His fingers graze my soft stomach when he slides the garment past my navel, and I swear he stops breathing when he finally pulls the dress up over my breasts and over my head.

Unable to help himself, his eyes drink in the sight of me in my plain bra and panties. I can't help but wonder what he thinks when he looks at me. Soft from motherhood. Curvy from my profession, and my general lack of exercise. Boring clothes and used goods.

My eyes are glued to his, searching in the depths of his chocolate gaze for any trace of disappointment.

"You're stunning, Maddie." His voice is gravelly and tells me more about his state of mind than the look in his eyes does.

He steps behind me, leaving me in front of the shower as he pauses with his hands on the clasp of my bra. Again, he gives me every chance to stop this before he places a kiss on my shoulder and unclasps my bra, sliding the straps down my arms and onto the floor.

"I won't survive doing the rest." He chuckles, embarrassed. He turns, facing the mirror, to let me undress myself the rest of the way. When I do, I stand back up, looking over my shoulder and meet his eyes in the reflection. His gaze is hooded, heated. I know that neither of us planned this, but I know I wouldn't change it for the world. And right before I get in, I take an emotional leap I'm nowhere ready for.

"Truth or dare?"

He doesn't fidget, doesn't blink, his look glued to mine over my shoulder in the slowly fogging mirror. The reply comes out in a whisper, "Truth."

"I couldn't have done tonight without you." My voice is soft and vulnerable, and I look away before I can see his reaction to them.

"Cupcake..." His hand reaches out to me, and he squeezes my bare hip before he continues. "I'd never have let you." The words imprint themselves on the very essence of my soul, and that last little piece of my heart I'd been holding onto slips into his unsuspecting hands. Not knowing how to feel about that realization, I slide out of his touch and get in.

The shower almost covers his words, and he was probably counting on it, but I hear them anyway when he says, "You won't have to do anything without me ever again."

# Chapter Seventeen

## FUZZY LITTLE PIGS

### Lucas

I close the door behind me as I leave the greatest temptation I've ever faced in my grown adult life. The steam that surrounded Maddie's body was as thick as the words I wished I felt brave enough to say.

Leaving her to shower on her own was the only right choice after tonight, and as much as I want to own her body, I don't want what we have to be tainted by that piece of trash and the events of this evening.

I flinch when I realize that I never texted Damian and Tyler about what happened in the parking lot. The fucker should be dead right now. It's a goddamn miracle that I let him walk away.

**Me: I fucking found BRAD assaulting Maddie in the parking lot**

**Damian: Are you fucking kidding me!**

**Tyler: Where is he?**

**Me: He cornered her against her car and was touching her. I punched his lights out. Follow the trail of blood from the parking lot to whatever hole the weasel crawled back into.**

**Damian: Where is she? We should file a report before he has the audacity to consider reporting you.**

**Tyler: I'll only repeat myself once. Where. Is. He?**

**Me: I don't fucking know. I got her the hell out of there. We're back at her place now. Damien, I'll probably ask you to swing by later to talk her through this. She was pretty rocked. UNDERSTANDABLY.**

**Damian: I'll keep my phone on. You should call Kit.**

**Me: I will, I just want it to be her choice.**

**Tyler: I knew that guy was messed up. Does she need anything?**

**Me: I've got it for now. I'll keep you both posted.**

I set my phone down harder than is necessary and breathe in through my nose, trying to calm the anger that's creeping back up on me. Running my hands through my hair is the one move more telling of my internal torment than any other single thing I do. I pace back and forth in the space between her bed and the closed bathroom door, absentmindedly staring at her room and the pieces of her scattered around it. I inadvertently replay what I walked up on in my head. The whole thing is like some Lifetime movie that you can't get out of your head.

Everything felt off when I saw Mr. Clements sneak away. As soon as I made it outside, I knew. It took more time than I care to admit to track her down. White cars are, unfortunately, the mom standard, and the parking lot was full of them. I have half a mind to go buy her a lime green Beetle just so I know I can always find her.

When I finally saw him, caging her in when every look on her face screamed that she didn't want him anywhere near her, I saw red, and I ran. After that things were a bit hazy in my anger-fueled rage, but I know I punched his face with all the strength I had. I am pretty sure I broke his nose, and he still got off way too easy. But my heart breaks remembering her in shock. She barely responded to me when I wiped the tears off her face. The fact that there's any doubt in her mind that led her to believe that she could have caused this makes me want to punch something again. Or someone, rather.

But fuck, what happened after that. I rub my hands down my face, wiping away every poker face I've ever built up. Her creamy skin and soft curves. My body starts to come back alive, picturing her in those tiny white underwear, surrounded by the thick steam of the shower. Visions of me taking her up against the glass assault my mind, and the impulse to act on them eats away at me.

I have to distract myself, so I look around her quaint bedroom to get my mind off of her quaint body. The room has pieces I would absolutely expect to be here. Photos and trinkets that shed light on small parts of her that you would only learn from living with someone. Her bedroom is a collection of old wood furniture, all of which I could see at local thrift stores, since none of it matches in wood or tone, but somehow it all feels homey and styled just the same.

Her dresser has framed photos of her and Mikey, an older couple who must be her parents, and a photo of her and a brunette who looks just like her. There's also a small glass vase with a single dried wildflower in it, and it makes me wonder why she keeps it. A silver tray neatly displays an array of perfumes, the smell of them finally filling in the aroma that is hidden underneath the aromatic scents of the bakery.

I perch myself on her white bedspread while I wait for her to get out of the shower. Not that I need to remind myself of that anymore, my resolve is already hanging by a thread.

*Jesus, Lucas. Get it together.*

I hear the water shut off and stare at the door before it opens with her standing in the doorway, wrapped in a fluffy white towel. The warm light from the bathroom surrounds her in a halo that makes the soft pale tones of her hair glow like the angel she is. Her cheeks are flushed, and her small hands grasp the terrycloth barrier that rests between us.

Her body closes the distance between us, and there are no words. The smell of her, wet and warm, washes over me, and I place my hands on her hips from my seat on the bed. Whether it's to pull her to me or hold her back, I have no idea. Her face is almost level with mine in this position, and she looks down at me, hazel eyes framed by thick lashes.

"Thank you." She doesn't need to say it, and I open my mouth to tell her so before she stops me. Her lips seal against mine in the most glorious moment.

I pull back, knowing I need to ask, "Look, Maddie..." I hesitate, not knowing how to approach this, but knowing that it will eat me alive if I don't. There is no other option.

Something in my face must give it away because she turns her head away and clutches her towel closer to her chest. Her knuckles going white with the effort. "You said something, and I have to know," I pause in that way I know is becoming predictable to her. "This has happened before." I don't ask the last part. I know. She nods anyway. Her confirmation of the dirty truth I didn't want to hear, but still knew, killing part of my trust in the world in a way that's irreparable.

"Give me a minute, and we'll talk." She places a chaste kiss on my forehead and slides out of my grip for the second time in the last hour. It feels like an omen I try not to read anything into. She pulls some clothes out of the dresser and takes them into the bathroom with her to change. Coming out in an oversized shirt and leggings, she grabs my hand before she pulls me out of the room, into the living room, and settles us both on the couch. Her toes are covered with pink fluffy socks. Like fuzzy little pigs. She tucks herself into the corner of the couch before she turns to face me.

I will never look at those things the same again. The fluffy pink socks will now and forever remind me of her softness and vulnerability in this moment. I stare at her for a minute while I build up the strength to listen.

"Zach and I did not have a relationship that I am proud of. He did things that I would justify for him, but as time went on it got harder and harder to justify his actions. It took me a long time, longer than I care to admit, before I realized that they weren't okay." She tucks a wet strand of her hair behind her ear and shifts a little, trying to find a way to make herself more comfortable while she talks about this. Her tells are too obvious to me, and I wonder when her crystal-clear emotions became even easier to read. I pull her pink-covered feet onto my lap and start rubbing small circles on the bottoms of them while I wait for her to keep going.

Her returning smile is small, but she keeps going, "Small things at first, then a little more and a little more. Each time I would find a reason why it was my fault or explain away his behavior. Or just freeze. It never occurred to me that I *should* say something. Or do anything. That sounds naïve, I know. Standing up for yourself shouldn't be something you need to be taught, right?"

I'm shaking my head, face stoic as fury burns inside me.

Like she can't get this part over soon enough, she keeps going. "How could it be bad if I was happy?"

My hands on her feet are keeping me grounded and I feel my fingers mindlessly make circles on her ankles.

"Anyway, when Zach and I started dating, he was *so* charming." Her eyes roll like she can see through the act looking back at it. "He would wine and dine me. I thought his controlling tendencies were sweet. How romantic was it that he always picked where we ate and made vacation plans for us? Who cares that he never asked me what I wanted?" She shifts again, her nerves on full display before discussing the next part.

"We got pregnant with Mikey on accident. I was on birth control. He seemed so happy and proposed the week we found out in front of both our families. I thought it was like a romance novel at the time."

I'm squeezing her pink fluffy feet, trying to hold everything in so she can finish.

"Even his proposal wasn't a question." She laughs, resigned, like she's realizing it for the first time. "He said I can't wait to call you my wife. Not, 'Will you marry me?' Not, 'Be mine?' After we got married, he stopped hiding his drinking. He started coming home drunk, and eventually coming home drunk and angry. It wasn't until after Mikey was born that he hit me. But it was always 'my fault.'" She sniffles, trying to hide it, and presses on. "I'll save you the horrid details, but about six months before I moved here, I reported him. I went to the police station with my mom. She runs a charity for battered women, and I knew that if anyone would be able to help me, it would be her." I silently thank the woman from afar and smile at Maddie reassuringly.

"He was so mad when the cops came and took him to the station. Once he got out, he begged me to forgive him, and I did, but I told him if it happened one more time, we'd leave. Me and Mikey both."

My smile turns sad when the story clearly has only one outcome, given she's here on a couch in front of me. With me.

"I planned it ahead, filed for the divorce in secret. Since there was a prior report of domestic violence, I was able do it without him. The police report would prevent him from getting custody of Mikey. To be honest, I would have left sooner if I knew all that. While Zach was out of town at a conference, Mikey and I packed up everything we could in a car my mom got for us, left the divorce papers and a filled out, but unfiled domestic abuse report on the counter, and came here."

"Is that who calls you all the time?" Her eyes start to water again. She nods, tucks her knees up, and rests her head on them, hiding her fuzzy socks beneath her. I leave my hand on her leg. Needing the contact. Knowing she does too.

"I know at some point he'll figure out where we are and come find us, but for the first time in so long, Mikey is happy.

I'm happy. Do you think I'm a coward?" Her question comes out sounding insecure.

I don't know how to answer that. I could never forgive Sherry if she took Jasper from me, but there is no universe where I would do the things this guy has done. The answer comes to me with the force of a train, "There's no doubt in my mind that you made the right decision. None." I raise her hand to my mouth and kiss the back of it softly. "That being said, it doesn't sound like it's over if you're worried about him coming back into your life." Her round eyes find mine, and I know the truth I gave her both hurts and scares her. "I'm here now. I'll do whatever I can to help you through all of it."

"Lucas, you're a good one." She smiles genuinely at me, and I feel us push past this barrier, moving to the next level. "I guess I need to report Mr. Clements, don't I?"

I give her a pointed look normally reserved for Jasper, and she laughs at the parental expression, clearly familiar with it.

"Well, let's get it over with."

The next few hours are a blur. Damian calls Kit in and between the two of them they are highly efficient. Kit pulls all the local connections and strings he has to get the whole thing expedited. Tyler has taken Jasper for the night, and I am determined to see this through. The fact that I can act as a witness, and that it happened on school property seals the deal. It always surprises me at how professionally Kit handles his job, and true to that he has the report filed and the next steps lined up in no time at all.

As he finishes tucking away his papers and clipboard, I watch Maddie hesitate with asking him something. Whatever it is seems to be causing more of an issue than the filing of the report.

"Ummm, Kit?" she says softly, causing him to pause and look up in concern. She hesitates and bites on the edge of her nail. "Do reports like this wind up in public record? And if they do, how long does it take until that happens?"

He raises an eyebrow at her familiarity with the process. "Is there a more direct question you want to ask me, Ms. Thompson?"

I watch the exchange in silence, knowing that my input isn't going to help, but seeing exactly what she wants to know without her needing to spell it out. Kit is obviously tracking too.

"My ex-husband and I aren't on the best of terms, and this report being filed could tell him where I am. I'm just trying to weigh how much time I have to prepare for that."

"Are you in danger if he finds you?" Kit looks down at the file in his hand, flipping through the papers clipped to the top, pausing when he reaches a specific one to read its contents. Whatever he sees seems to alter the direction of questioning and his eyes meet mine over her head, laced with concern. "It seems that if that is the case, a restraining order might be worthwhile." His knowing look is an obvious sign that her prior domestic violence report is in whatever file the department pulled together on her before he came here. "I'd be happy to help you get the paperwork filed while I'm here."

I want her to say yes to his offer so badly, but this isn't my call. She has to be the one to take that step.

"I'll think about it."

"You do that. Goodnight, Ms. Thompson. Lucas." He gives me a restrained smile that says we'll be talking about this more, turns and leaves without another word.

"Let's go watch TV." Her hand is in mine again, and she's pulling me back into the house.

Pushing me down into the corner, she slides in after me. Her body nestled up against me as she all but lays in my lap. Whatever this has turned into over the last week, one thing is for sure—this is looking more and more like *something* with each day that passes. Hell, what we went through today has been enough drama to last for several years.

She sighs as she gets comfortable before asking, “Any preference?”

“I’m pretty sure that no matter what you put on, my attention will not be on the TV. Not with you this close to me and in my arms.” I give her a squeeze in emphasis. She laughs, puts on *Jeopardy* reruns, and slides her fuzzy feet between mine. I hear Alex in the background, “Well, thank you, Johnny, Ladies and gentlemen, tonight on *Jeopardy*, we have a real treat for you...”

Maddie rotates her feet between mine and I swear inwardly. Those goddamn fuzzy little pigs are giving me a hard-on from hell.

How lame to think that fuzzy little pigs would be the death of me as a grown man.

# Chapter Eighteen

## INTERNAL WHISKS

### Maddie

This morning's game has left everyone in a fantastic mood. The conversations around our table at Old Sal's are full of laughter, and the boys are out of their minds with the win.

It's been two weeks since the incident with the boys' teacher, and I would be lying if I said I wasn't waiting for the other shoe to drop. When it does, I'm sure it will be a huge steel-toed boot filled with concrete. Brad was arrested after I filed the report, and the school had placed a sweet older lady over the boys' class as a substitute.

For now, I'm riding the train of happiness that left the station after a low that will unfortunately live rent free in my mind… for a very long time. Lucas and I are good. We text constantly. I've even made a new friend in the ever-serious Damian. He was not what I was expecting when Lucas told me one of his lifelong best friends was a lawyer who could help. The guy is intimidating and doesn't seem fazed or even emotionally affected by most things. I mean, I've barely gotten a smirk at any of my one-liners and self-proclaimed punny thoughts. That said, the *one* I did get gave me hope. I'll crack through that crunchy exterior if it kills me.

*Maddie: One thousand*

*World: Who cares? I'm not currently counting.*

Even with Damian's serious front... or at least what I am now out to prove is a front, I can't pretend that the guy isn't *scary*. After Kit, whom I was surprised to find was another one of Lucas's friends, came over, he and Damian took the reins. Apparently, this wasn't the first sexual harassment complaint the school had received about Brad, and no action was ever taken.

Damian offered to come with me when I met with Principal Noll. He just stood in front of his desk, while the rest of us were seated, arms crossed, unbothered by the weighted and incredibly uncomfortable silence, and said nothing. For minutes. He just let his heavy stare weigh down on the poor old man until Principal Noll just started talking, saying things in the hope that Damian would say or do *something*. If it wasn't such a boss move and completely in my favor, I would have been uncomfortable at it being done on my behalf, but truth be told, it really helped get everything rolling at a much more efficient speed.

Damian asked me if I was fine with being at the center of all this before it all went ballistic. Which is a tame word to describe his reaction. The consideration he took in asking me that was not lost on me, and shows his character beyond anything words could possibly say about him. Don't get me wrong, when he first came over that night, it was a lot to process. He sat down in front of me, his ginormous body perched on the edge of my coffee table smack dab in the middle of my living room. His crisp suit was in stark contrast to my eclectic thrifted furniture, and out of place in the very early morning hours. Elbows on his knees and low voice, he made his case, and it was a good one. Between the time that Lucas called him and when he arrived, he came into the house prepped with a file of complaints, profiles, and whatever else he handed over to the office. The idea that this creep was teaching our kids, teaching his *daughter*, was awful.

Once I was on board, Damian took over everything. It wasn't hard to get meetings with whoever he deemed necessary, at least for him. Between Damian and Kit, they clearly had contacts and resources. It surprised me that no matter what time either of them made a call to someone, they picked up. He clearly knew exactly who to tell what and what to do when.

The school board is now under investigation, and the principal and the entire teaching staff are being reviewed.

It was awful watching the security footage of the parking lot. I had to sit through the torture of it with both Kit, and then with the lead detective who was investigating. Both went through minute by minute, asking questions through the whole thing, what he did, what he said, and my responses.

There was something harrowing about seeing how scared I was that opened my eyes. It was a moment I *refuse to* feel or experience again. The woman in that parking lot will never again see the light of day.

Even through all the drama that has filled this week, Lucas and I have continued to move forward. Past something that sits on the surface and down through a few layers of cake… into all the bits of filling. The ones that make up the parts of your life that matter.

Today's game was the perfect move back into the normal routine of life before the bakery's grand opening. The Sweet Shop opens in just under a week, and I'm equally nervous and elated. We're putting the final touches on everything now, so there is barely a spare moment to wallow in everything. Thank God.

Mikey and I are meeting Hails there after this to finish painting the front counter and hang some art. I'm happy Mikey is getting to be part of it and is seeing that all the hard work leads to something we can both be proud of. Despite what my mean evil inner monologue says in the middle of the night when she knows no one else is there.

"All right, Ms. Apple Pie, what can I get you?" Sunny's voice pulls me back to the table with her signature raspy tone. I smile at her and order my usual eggs. All three boys get pancakes.

Lucas and I sit across from the boys, Tyler perched on the end of our booth rounding out our circle.

"So, what are you doing after this, Maddie?" Tyler asks, taking a large sip of his black coffee.

"Mikey and I are going back to the bakery to finish up the punch list before the Grand Opening on Friday. You guys are coming, right?" I turn to look at Lucas and find his eyes already on me, as usual. I've asked them all at least three times this morning alone.

He smiles broadly with a subtle squeeze on my bare thigh under the table. "Wouldn't miss it." A skirt might have been the best—or worst—choice of my morning. Lucas was starting to find ways to touch me even when we were around other people, and I have a feeling that the 'what are we' conversation is right around the corner. Oddly, the thought of it is scaring me less and less.

However, my clothing choices for the day are feeling a little more monumental since the skin on skin gives every small touch and graze of his fingers a whole new meaning. His eyes went wide when I walked out on the field this morning, bakery boxes perched in my hands. It made me feel like a *woman* and not just a mom.

Wardrobe choices aside, I've found myself in such a better headspace lately, so much so that I *almost* answered Zach's call yesterday. There's no avoiding him, and part of me is ready for that. The grown-up part. The other part is planning a quick escape into a hole of Ben & Jerry's. But I have finally faced up to the fact that I either need to file a restraining order and fully remove him from our lives, or confront him and see if things have changed.

"We could come help you if you want?" Tyler offers without a second thought, his golden retriever personality bringing me back with a smile.

"Yes!" Asher and Jasper chime in at the same time.

"I'm always happy to have help!" Leaning forward in a pretend secret, I whisper mischievously to the bouncing row of children, "I'll even pay you both in cookies." Tyler and Lucas both groan loudly at the idea of boys hyped up on sugar, but their excitement is totally worth any shit they will definitely be giving me.

"You're the best, Maddie," Jaspers says easily, and I feel Lucas's hand stiffen on my thigh.

It's fine, Maddie. It doesn't change anything.

*Maddie: Three probably*

*World: Not getting points today since my mood is too good*

Luckily, we're saved from anymore touchy words or comments being said by our food arriving. Sunny glances at Lucas and me knowingly, her eyes slipping to where our bodies disappear innocently under the table as she puts the plates down in front of us. The rest of the table hardly seems to notice when her eyebrows raise in a silent question, and I find myself blushing and shrugging in response. Lucas laughs quietly at my reaction, and his fingers start moving slowly back and forth. I feel my cheeks heat and silently say a prayer to the gods of baked goods and luck that everyone else is distracted by the buttery smells.

By the time we finish our food and pay Sunny at the front counter, my thoughts are so fully on the mental checklist of items I have to get done that I barely register the boys leaving with Tyler and Lucas walking me to my car until he takes my keys from my hand and opens the passenger door for me to get in.

"You do know this is my car, right?" I say teasingly before I move to get in.

"Yes, Maddie, I am fully aware of that," he replies with an impatient hand telling me to hurry up. "Don't we have things to do?"

I smile at him and slide into the seat, my breath catching when he reaches in and snaps the buckle around my waist. His big hand lingers on the clasp, while his body is stretched over mine. His size, his smell… crap, just all of him, takes up all the oxygen in the car, and I can't take my eyes off his face. He rests his forehead on mine and breathes the suffocatingly thick air with me for an eternal minute before he places a quick kiss on my forehead and closes the door.

This level of sexual tension we've been riding since we met is as heavy as pound cake, and there's something decadent about it that makes me think of chocolate and marshmallows.

He handles my car like he's driven it countless times. One hand on the wheel, and his other on my bare thigh. Like he's a magnet and I'm another, pulled together without thought or consideration.

There's a vulnerability I didn't expect to feel once we finally reach the front door of the bakery. The signage went up this week, and the vinyl on the windows got hung yesterday. It looks so close to what I had envisioned in my mind, and I'm filled with equal measures of pride and terror.

The idea that Lucas will see this dream of mine, each thing laid out how I wanted it and planned it to be, leaves me suddenly doubting how well I thought it through. He has his own business. What if it pales in comparison to his expectations?

The boys are brimming with excitement. All of their faces pressed up against the windows while they wait for us to arrive and open the door. I know they won't say it, but they are definitely disappointed with the girly teal. I expected nothing less from three ten-year-old boys. I pause only for a second, with my hand on the brass doorknob before I look over my shoulder at Lucas, searching for any signs of disappointment.

His eyebrows lift at my hesitation, but he just stands there, quiet and patient.

As soon as the door is open, Mikey takes the boys to give them the grand tour, and I preen at how proud he sounds. This really has been a labor of love for both of us.

Tyler and Lucas look around the front of the shop. Tyler turns while he runs his hands over one of the round marble dining tables and takes a seat in the curved wooden chair. Lucas, however, casually walks around looking over the neon pink signage and modern menu stretched out on the wall. His large hands finger one of the plants perched on the counter, and I wish, not for the first time, that I could read his mind like he somehow manages to do with me.

It doesn't take long before the boys come flying through the metal kitchen door and I get everyone right to work, even if it's just so I don't fixate on what Lucas could possibly be thinking.

Tyler gets the lucky job of wrangling the boys, whom I've ever so graciously put in charge of painting the front counter. They are overly thrilled when I open the can of paint and show them the light blue color.

Tyler diligently makes them tape every edge and ledge, clearly having done this before. Leaning over, I whisper a nearly silent thanks to him, not daring to admit how much I love the marble countertop and would hate to see it covered in paint.

Once it's taped up and each kiddo has a cup of paint with a brush tucked in it, I watch Tyler snag a muffin. Happily munching while he 'supervises' the progress.

"Oh no, you don't, good sir!" I exclaim, dragging his butt out of the chair. "You're on hanging duty," I say, gesturing to the collection of hanging plants and framed photos piled in the front corner of the shop.

"Oh, come on," he smiles and grumbles half-heartedly between bites.

I push him over to the pile and leave the drill and hooks on the table in front of him.

"Why does Lucas get to sit back!" Tyler argues, eyeing his earlier chair with longing.

"There will be no sitting for anyone if I have anything to say about it! We have a list to get through." The tsk-tsk of my voice gets him right to work. Not sans grumbles and a longing look back at the pastry counter.

With the boys and Tyler begrudgingly assisting, I walk up to Lucas.

He stands like he always does, tall and not giving anything away. He holds my stare as I stop in front of him, trying not to get *too* close. We aren't hiding anything, but there is still a lot that the two of us have to talk about before I want this anywhere on Mikey's radar. One side of his mouth is upturned as he watches the wheels in my head turn. I'm practically a whisk attachment on a mixer with all the whirl, whirl, whirl, even I can hear coming out of me. My own little internal whisk.

"Yes, Cupcake?"

I try my very best not to appear too affected by those words or the tone that he delivers them in. However, the nickname takes me back to dark hallway and the taste of Cosmos on my lips... and his. "Wanna help me in the kitchen?" I tuck my chin slightly, trying and failing to hide my stupid perpetual blush, but I know by the chuckle that follows that he sees it.

"It would make my day," he replies with an undertone of wicked things to come.

"Don't you two worry about us!" Tyler calls. And I spin toward him to find his face all smiles. "We'll be *finnne.* Take your time with those *appliances*. It's important to make sure they're running right and performing..." What he's saying without actually saying it does not help the blush I'm currently rocking, and I've never been happier to have given children paint and a surface to cover with it.

Lucas shakes his head and laughs at Tyler's not so obvious hit at our impending disappearing act.

"Well, lead the way," he says with a glint in his eyes.

# Chapter Nineteen

## HEALTH INSPECTOR

### Lucas

Maddie turns after she enters, leaning back on one of the two gleaming silver worktables in the middle of her kitchen.

"Well, what do you think?" The softness in her voice is a clear tell that she cares about my answer, and it makes me think before I respond. Her need to please me is something that causes a deep fire to stir inside my heart.

Moving from the swinging door of the kitchen to where she's standing only takes a few steps with my long strides, and I pause once I reach her. Really taking a second to look around. The kitchen is nice. It's clean, new, and organized with borderline obsession. Large silver appliances and ovens line two of the walls, with shelves full of powders and chocolates stacked neatly above gleaming counters on the others.

All of it is centered on the two matching tables, faced back-to-back, one of which Maddie is currently leaning on. Her eyes follow my gaze around the room, looking everywhere I look, and it is becoming incredibly clear that she is trying to see what I see. It would be *very* fun to play cards with her sometime.

I don't have much to compare the kitchen to, and I don't want to give her any semblance of an answer that makes it seem like I'm not impressed. Because I fucking am. Not many people can make something like this from scratch, let alone turn around the dump that this place was before she bought it.

I turn my attention back to her, admiring how her blonde hair glows under the bright lights, the loose waves hanging around the shoulders of her tight white shirt in a way that hugs her curves and leaves very little to my extremely creative imagination. Especially now that I've had my hands on her.

Thank you, Harley. Which reminds me, I still owe him for those broken pictures.

I move my eyes back up to her face, her pretty lips, and her bright eyes, held captive in them for an embarrassingly long minute. In an effort to add some humor to the tension, I whisper, my voice rough and unused, "This is by far the cleanest kitchen I've ever been in." She exhales. Her telltale blush creeping across her cheeks and down her long neck. The sight of the pink on her creamy skin has me wanting to do more to get her little tells to show. I can't imagine that it would take very much to have that blush creeping farther down than her neck. I don't let my eyes leave hers as I close the distance between us and place my hands on either side of her, caging her to the table.

I can smell her this close, and my heart picks up when her gaze inadvertently dips to my lips. She smells like sugar, and I ponder, not for the first time if it's just from what she does or if she just tastes like it.

Swiping my finger across the surface of the spotless table, I pretend to inspect an invisible residue. "Oh, Maddie," I tsk in mock disappointment. "It looks like you missed a spot." Her laugh deepens, causing her chest to briefly graze mine. If I was a lesser man, I would have come on the spot. Especially after watching her in that tight little skirt all day, coupled with the weeks of sexual tension. But I have more restraint than that.

Her eyes are glued to me, not even sparing a second to glance down at my obvious erection, as I move to show her my presented finger. It's spotless, but our game requires she look at it regardless.

Being the playful thing I know she is, she obliges, and her face falls with make-believe shock. Her eyes brighten and she smiles when an idea comes to her. It's not hard to see what she's thinking with those big eyes. My cock jumps with eagerness to see what she does.

"I'm sure there's something I could do to get you to ignore this dirty mess," her voice is seductive as she rolls with playfulness. Her response to my teasing and taunting shouldn't surprise me like it does, but when she continues, I'm barely able to keep standing. "I'd gladly get on my hands and knees to show you just how clean I can get it."

"Fuck, Maddie." I groan. A response that's so telling I hope I'm not losing my game. Clearing my throat from the thick as fuck air between us, I somehow manage to get out, "Seriously though, how in the world do you get it this clean with all the flour?" Our chests are almost touching, and something in the air shifts with our closeness.

I move my fingers to brush hers on the edge of the silver surface, and her breath hitches. Another tell. The feel of her skin on mine where our fingers meet causes electricity to shoot through me, making my heart pound even harder. Not to mention the other overly excited part of my anatomy.

The mix of it all is just enough and too much. The look and feel of her, the smells permeating the air, and the eyes she's giving me in return are all causing things to be increasingly uncomfortable as I shift to try to ease the strain. I suppress another groan.

Jesus, Lucas. You're not in fucking high school. Get it together.

I'm done for. "If you want space, Maddie, you better tell me right now. Because I'm about thirty seconds away from losing what little control I've been holding onto." My hand moves from her fingers with a mind of their own. The pads of them trailing up her bare skin until I cup the back of her neck.

I'm hypnotized by the feel of her when she leans back slightly and rests the weight of her head in my hand. Unable to stop myself, I tilt and run my lips up the column of her exposed throat, my lips searing the skin on the long expanse of soft skin.

"Fifteen seconds," I whisper against her ear with a ragged breath. My lips find the shell, and I suck her lobe into my mouth, biting down slightly in warning when she doesn't respond. She grabs the front of my shirt, pulling me impossibly closer. My body fits against her like it belongs there. The thought has me leaning into our connection. I'm too far gone in her sweetness to do anything else.

A suppressed moan leaves her, and the sound is something that will both haunt me and star in all of my fantasies for the rest of my life. I bite again, this time rewarding her for her involuntary response, and she pulls back, her face flushed with lust and want. "Lucas, the last thing I want from you is space." Her lips land on mine in a quick, hard kiss, her desire bleeding through her skin. Fuck, I'm done for.

She smiles when this time, it's me who doesn't respond, her eyes moving from my face down to my fully erect length, leaving very little to the imagination. "Lucas, I think your thirty-second timer just went off."

This fucking girl. A dam breaks, and I violently crash my lips into hers, my hands move to her full, mouthwatering curves. Her tongue breaches my lips, and the taste of her fills me. Grabbing her hips, I slide her body up mine, giving her a full preview of my 'timer' as I lift her onto the table, not breaking our kiss for even a breath. Her hands tangled in my hair and her center grinding on my now painfully hard cock as her skirt slides up her thighs. She pulls me harder against her, like our bodies touching from head to toe isn't enough to satiate her. It's honestly not.

There's too much and somehow not enough for me to explore, and I give up my purchase on her hips, sliding one greedy hand up the center of her shirt until I find the lace-covered swell of her breast through the thin fabric. "Good God, these are perfect," I try to convey the awe I feel by rolling one of her hardened nipples between my fingers.

That breathy moan is back at the pinch and slight tug, and in an effort to save her shirt from my completely Neanderthal urge to tear it from her body, I lift it up, exposing the sheer white lace and the petal pink where her skin darkens peeking through. The rearranging of her shirt gives both my hands unhindered access to her chest. Leaving her mouth, I move mine down her body, trailing kisses and love bites along the way. Each one eliciting more of a response in her breathy gasps, filling me with a masculine pride when I see the marks I leave behind.

Sucking one of her hardened nipples into my mouth through the lace, I keep up my toying with the other one. Gliding my free hand up the smooth skin of her thigh and under her skirt, I'm eager to see if she is as wet and wanting as her moans tell me she is.

"Lucas." The plea of my name has me abandoning my mouth's new favorite place and swallowing her words with my tongue. My fingers find the smooth silk of her panties, and I groan loudly when I feel her soaking through them.

"You want me, don't you?" I whisper over her moan as I start to stroke her through the silk, her dampness spurring me on. "Look at how wet you are, and I haven't even touched you yet. You're practically begging me."

Shoving the fabric to the side, I use my thumb to circle her clit, gliding my fingers through the outside of her folds, causing that breathy voice to cry out.

"Oh God."

"Tell me what you want, Maddie." I tease her ruthlessly, slowing my movements when I feel her legs start to tremble.

"You! I just want you," she begs in response.

I chuckle as her grasp on my arms tighten. "I'd ask you to prove it, but your wet pussy is all the proof I need." Her panting pleas are getting desperate, and I can feel her legs shaking around me. Knowing she can't hold off much longer, I quicken the pace and drive my fingers into her soaked center over and over until she's shaking and breathless with her need for release.

"Come on, baby girl," I breathe in her ear. "Give me what I want. Come for me."

I pinch her nipple hard at the same time I use the thumb of my other hand to press down on her sensitive bundle of nerves. It throws her over the edge, and her head dips into my neck while she cries out against my skin. Her walls are clamping around my fingers, milking me for all I'm worth, while my fingers ride her through every last shudder of her orgasm.

My cock is harder than I think I ever remember it being, but fuck if that wasn't the hottest time I've ever had in a kitchen.

Pulling my hand from her, I lean back and look into her hooded eyes, soaking in the lust and emotions I see reflected in them.

"Holy cream puffs." She breathes, clearly still wrapping her head around what we just did.

Eyes locked, I open my mouth to tell her—something, maybe even *finally* ask her out—when a voice calls out, and the kitchen door swings inward.

"Maddie Pie? You in here?"

Shit.

Quickly lowering her skirt, I spin around and position myself in front of her, hiding my soaked fingers behind my back as she pulls her top back down over her breasts.

My eyes are met by a brunette photocopy of Maddie. I saw her that night at the bar, but she was on a one-track exit toward the door, and my attention was entirely focused elsewhere. She is identical to my blonde, green-eyed cupcake in almost every way except her hair and height. The infamous Hailey.

"Well, *helloooo* there," she singsongs mischievously when she spots me, her gaze glancing down my body embarrassingly before meeting Maddie's eyes over my shoulder. Her sister's eyebrows raise in question, directed at the head peeking from behind me. Maddie is still seated on the top of the worktable, and that, coupled with my pretty obvious hard-on, conveys way more than it should.

"I was just showing Lucas the kitchen," Maddie squeaks out without prompting, and I turn and look at her with narrowed eyes. Her embarrassment has me wanting to make her scream my name regardless of who walked in.

"Yes, that is very clear," she says with a sisterly grin before adding, "He looks incredibly familiar with his way around the worktable." Hailey's comment is filled with a knowing smirk that promises she'll *never* let this go.

She leaves Maddie with that and turns her attention toward me, "This isn't how I thought our first meeting would go, but I can't say I'd have it any other way." Her teasing is clearly not reserved solely for singling out her sister, and her words have Maddie dropping her head to my shoulder in joint suffering. "You must be Lucas."

Offering my *dry* hand, I give her an uncomfortable left-handed shake that has her eyebrows shooting up again. But mercifully she holds back the obvious questions that are begging to be asked and shakes with me in an awkward move neither of us comments on. Thank God.

"Well, this has been very...enlightening. I think I'll meet you two out front." She gives Maddie an overexaggerated wink before she raises her hands like she's holding a camera and takes an imaginary photo of the two of us without explanation or comment, then promptly turns and leaves. The whole peculiar exchange has Maddie groaning in an entirely different way.

As the door swings shut behind Hailey, I turn, offering to help Maddie down from the table.

"Do I have to ask, or are you going to tell me?" She gives me a confused look before she seems to realize what we both just witnessed and clarifies her sister's quirky behavior.

"Oh, Hailey does that. Whenever she sees something, she wants to remember, she 'snaps' an imaginary photo so she doesn't forget it. I can only imagine the reasons she wants to remember this," she explains while gesturing between the two of us.

I can't help but laugh at the oddness that is these two women. I've never met anyone like them. Maddie, with her quick comebacks and witty retorts, and her sister, with a perpetual look of trouble and an air about her that leaves me wanting to make sure she's never alone with a Sharpie and my face while I'm sleeping.

"That was *mortifying*!" Maddie groans with her face in her hands as she brings me back to the moment.

"I think it was fucking perfect and *highly* repeatable. Although, maybe next time we don't do any family introductions until after your shirt is back down." I wink at her as I finish and pull her into my arms.

"Ha! I'm pretty sure this one incident will be brought up any time I threaten to embarrass Hails. She's locked and loaded on ammunition for the foreseeable future."

The thought of the two of them threatening each other with things like this leaves me chuckling, and I can only use the best my imagination has to offer to come up with what other things they might be holding over one another.

But the look Hailey gave us, and how comfortable she seemed with walking in on what she so clearly walked in on, gives me confidence that whatever they have on each other is substantial.

"I'm willing to put money on us catching her in something that will even the playing field." Maddie's eyes light up at that idea, and suddenly, I have another new goal with this girl.

"Unfortunately, even though there's a ton to do back here, I doubt I'll be able to look at that workbench and picture anything but mind-blowing orgasms in the near future. Time to face the music." She flattens invisible creases on her shirt and straightens her skirt before eyeing the kitchen door.

"You kill me with your compliments," I reply back with more than a hint of cocky confidence as I take her hand in mine and lead us both out the metal swinging door, not so subtly adjusting myself before we face the boys and Tyler.

One thing I am sure of…I will be making this girl mine very soon.

# Chapter Twenty

## JOB HAZARDS

### Maddie

"No one is going to come," I whine.

Hailey doesn't even look up at me from where she is expertly applying her mascara in the staff bathroom. "Just stop it. You know they will. Tell your Debbie Downer and your Negative Nancy to take the day off and leave us be." She grins at her wit before she moves on to putting on lip gloss, smacking her lips with flourish as she finishes and zips up her gold-sequined makeup bag.

I know she's right. There's already been such positive feedback from the local community that I chose to restore so much of the shop while upgrading it to feel new and modern. For weeks I've had daily deliveries up and running to half of the restaurants around town, and it wasn't like I was terrible at this or something. Even with all of my insecurities, I can at least admit to myself that there is a reason I chose to pursue this career path. I tug on my lip with my teeth and try not to wring my hands since that will definitely tell her how in-my-head I am about this.

Hails rolls her eyes at me, knowing without me saying anything. "You've got this. We've got this. Now own it like the bad bitch you are and get out there!" She shoves me out the door of the cramped bathroom and hooks her arm in mine as we make our way out of the kitchen and out to the front of the bakery.

Moving through the room, I adjust the spacing of things I've already adjusted dozens of times. They don't need it and I know that. But I can't help it.

I was... am, so proud of how the whole thing came out, and looking around, I admire the open space. It's a bit of a cross between café vibes and your traditional bakery. There are about a dozen small tables scattered around the main countertop bar. The display case is packed to the brim with everything Josie, the baker I hired, and I could make. Hails had put vases of flowers on every table, and the shelves along the walls had packaged goodies to go, along with jams and other food items from local shops.

There had been an enormous amount of debate over the teal color throughout the shop, but when we tempered it with creamy chic tones and furniture, it felt so happy. I debated hard for the neon pink sign, but it's my favorite part, and honestly, it feels a little rebellious. Looking back at the choice now, I laugh at how monumental that one small decision felt when I made it. But I am the one in control here and it finally feels like all is right with the world.

It's funny how there are points in life where you can see a change in yourself just a few weeks apart, but then there are other times when years go by and nothing changes. In my life outlook of full honesty, I recognize that a lack of change is what held me where I was for so long.

The minutes drag by as people slowly arrive, and not even an hour later I find myself thinking that I had no idea what I was worried about. The shop is packed with people from around town, most of them I know, but some aren't familiar, and I'm shaking hands and smiling like it's the only job I have. Sugar and sweets be damned.

When I see Sunny chatting with one of the other restaurant owners in town, I'm immediately thankful. My Negative Nancy fully had me convinced I would be run out of town by the locals who could smell the city on me a mile away. If I hadn't already been falling in love with this small town and all of its charm, it was becoming very apparent how much I was starting to love the people in it too. Especially since the show of support is so heartfelt. I feel like everyone I've met in the last few months here has shown up. Sunny and Jackie—the brunette waitress from the diner—all the guys from Mikey's football games, Kevin, and even Greg, the grocery store clerk.

What does it say about me that I'm thrilled that even Greg came to my opening? I guess when you start over and have to make a life from scratch, just like a batch of cookies from an untried recipe, it makes sense that you might be worried about the results.

A man with cropped auburn hair makes eye contact with me from the front door. His gray dress pants and pressed button-up shirt make me jittery, and when I see him nod to a camera guy out front, my heart rate spikes, hard.

*Maddie, this is to be expected. You're a business owner. Be happy about free press. Not worried about who will see it.*

The thought that keeps running through my mind is, "What if Zach sees this?" I realize suddenly that the idea doesn't fill me with the same level of fear it once did, and the difference startles me.

What has really changed? The only answer that comes to my mind is, me. I've changed.

I'm stronger. I'm proud of myself. And I will never again let someone walk over me. I smile at my thoughts and take a deep breath.

Well, time to be whisked. Way to go, Maddie.

*Maddie: New store, happy kid, life I can be proud of. Not to mention a new outlook on my deepest fears? A total of like...a LOT.*

*World: Nothing that matters.*

I smile back at the guy and walk over with all my accomplishments perched on my shoulders like a suit of armor.

When I reach him, I give him my most confident smile and hold out my hand.

"Hi! How are you? Thank you for coming." He places his warm palm in mine with a megawatt grin filled with picture-perfect white teeth that unfortunately were much more appealing farther away. Up closer, I'm a little taken aback by how tan he is, and I wonder if he gets it sprayed on or if that's just his usual hue.

"Ms. Thompson. So nice to meet you. I'm Johnny." He waits for me to respond, still shaking my hand, and at my nod and polite smile, he seems a tad disappointed before he continues, "Johnny Lewis. From Channel Eight News."

I turn up my surprise and exclaim with a comical level of enthusiasm, "Oh my! How wonderful of you to make it." I move to grasp his one hands in both of mine with a level of commitment that feels painted on. He seems to need recognition, and I inwardly laugh at how cliché the whole conversation is. When my eagerness appeases his disappointment and replaces it with a genuine smile, he takes over the conversation and I relax right into it.

"We heard about your opening at the station, and I would love to do a short interview with you, announcing you to the locals. Would you be okay with us filming that? I promise it will be easy as pie," he says the last bit with a wink, very proud of his joke. I silently wonder to myself how long it took him to come up with it.

I laugh politely and am happy it comes across the way he wants. He directs me outside, waving and smiling at people as we go. He introduces me to the cameraman and his station coordinator, who fits me with a microphone and talks me through the questions they will be asking. I freeze when they ask what brought me to Camden, but I push through, taking the angle that I wanted a small town to raise my son.

The interview itself is pretty painless after that, and I find myself enjoying the whole process. Especially when he asks me to walk him through the shop. His questions are easy, and I feel like the whole thing goes pretty well.

We stand side by side behind the front counter, both looking head on at the camera. His charming voice booms though the shop as people watch us wrap up. "This is Johnny Lewis coming to you from The Sweet Shop, right off Main Street. I don't know about all of you, but I'm looking forward to mornings filled with muffins made by the charming Madelyn Thompson." He gives me a warm smile and holds up a large blueberry muffin he spent five minutes selecting from the pastry cabinet. As he signs off, I catch Lucas's eyes from over the cameraman's shoulder, and my smile widens when his eyes say in their silent way, "How's it going?" I try to keep my face neutral as I say back "you know, same old same old." He points to the front door, and I see Tyler and the boys outside with Damian and a few others. The kids are playing with balloons and eating cookies. It fills my heart with so much happiness. I pull a Hailey and mentally take a snapshot of this moment.

Johnny tells me that the piece will likely air at some point in the next day or two, and I make a note to keep an eye out for it. There is no way Zach will miss this if my mom or anyone Hailey knows mentions it. There are too many people involved, and I know that shoe I've been worried about is on its way down. I decide not to let the thought scare me out of this moment. I roll my shoulders and spend the rest of the afternoon shaking hands and showing people the results of all my hard work.

All in all, the day flies by, and with a big sigh, I flip the open sign to closed and turn around to look back over the now silent and empty shop. I think over what Hailey said before she kissed me on the cheek, snapped an imaginary photo and left. "You don't need me to say this, but I'm proud of you. You've made a lot of hard choices, and I hope someday I'm as strong as you are."

I grin to myself and lean my head on the back of the closed door. I can't believe I actually did it. This place is everything I dreamed of, and the fact that it's here to stay has me brimming with pride. I hit the lights and walk out the front door, locking it, before I see him.

Lucas is leaning on the light post just in front of the shop, a bundle of wildflowers in one hand, and the other in the pocket of his jeans. His dirty blond hair is tousled perfectly, like always, and the smile on his face is one I want to frame in the back of my mind. His eyes find mine across the dark and empty sidewalk.

"Don't tell me those are for me," I say with a huge smile.

He holds them out for me to take as I cross over to him, taking the bunch of flowers from him and letting the smell fill the corners of this moment, knowing that when I remember it, the smell of those flowers will always be present.

"I'm so proud of you. Today was perfect. You killed it." His words melt my heart, especially since I feel the exact same way, but hubris is not something I'm comfortable with. Better to hear someone else say it.

Lucas's arms snake around me, and he hugs me while he places a soft kiss on the top of my head. "Congratulations, Maddie."

I pull back a little and look up at him through my lashes. "Thank you." I keep going before I overthink and don't say what I'm feeling. "I'm happy you were there today. It meant so much to me. Really."

His smile is the biggest one I've seen on him yet, and I do what Hailey does for the second time tonight, but this time with my hands. It's a little awkward with the flowers, but when I pull back from him and hold my invisible camera up to snap Lucas's 'photo' with a murmured "click, click," that smile only grows. This is something I never want to forget, and now he knows it.

He stays in this moment with me for another minute before he smiles and pulls out his phone. Quickly taking a real picture of the two of us, and then one of me holding the flowers in front of my shop. Then sliding his fingers across the screen as he types out a text.

My phone pings from my back pocket, and I smile at him as I pull it out. I can't hold in my happiness as I read it.

***Lucas: One question. Want to play?***

I type my response, sneaking a glance up at him, loving that he's watching me while I text him back.

**Me: That was a question. Rather anticlimactic of you…**

My eyes are back on him as he reads it and shakes his head with a smile. He eyes me with a look over the top of his phone before types back, only looking up once he's sent it. When my phone pings again, he smiles, waiting for me. I can hear my heart in my ears and his faint breathing in front of me.

**Lucas: How about this one then? Will you go on a date with me?**

I pretend to think about it. Tapping my chin with the finger of my free hand as I pretend to consider his question. His eyes roll back before he taps his foot with make-believe exasperation. My heart pitter patters with nerves that belong to some high schooler, not to a grown woman standing in front of a man who wants her as much as she wants him. I try to calm my shaking hands as I type back.

**Me: Maybe. Ask me in person.**

Lucas reads it and looks up when he's done, walking over to me without pause. He wraps me in his arms. Not knowing what to say, I let my mind wander out loud. "Fancy seeing you here, James," I comment while staring at his handsome face. His laugh tickles my face, and he leans in, to whisper in my ear.

"Maddie, I don't want to fight this anymore. I want you to be mine." His voice sends goosebumps down my spine, and I shiver.

"That's not just a date, Lucas James."

Running his hands down my arms, he looks down at me with a heated gaze that leaves lots of things flittering to the front of my mind.

I take a steadying breath, pushing the thought of those hands sliding to other places to the back of my dirty mind. "But it just so happens that I want that too," I finally say.

"Thank God," he whispers with a thread of relief.

I love that he asked. I love that he asked like this. I love that there isn't anything present or past that scares me from saying yes. The realization that I feel this way hits me with another layer of surprise at just how much I've changed since meeting him.

His fingers settle on my jaw, and he tips my head up toward his. Before he leans in to kiss me, I hear him breathe in the air between us.

"I can never tell if it's you that smells like sugar, or if it just lingers on your skin." His voice is gruff and breathy and it's fueling me.

"Hazards of the job," I say back, my eyes on his mouth, hoping he wants to taste me and find out.

"Never quit," he quips back, putting his nose in my neck and breathing deep.

"Oh, I don't plan on going anywhere."

"I'd follow you if you did, Maddie. I don't do relationships halfway. You're mine now, and I don't plan on letting you or Mikey go anywhere without me."

Not giving me a chance to respond to that monumental proclamation, his lips find mine, soft and full.

I lean into the kiss, knowing that what he is giving me is more than a kiss. It is a promise. Things aren't going to be the same after this.

The quiet realization sits at the back of my mind like a warning. But I ignore it. Happily.

*Maddie: Over the moon*

*World: Fading into the background*

# Chapter Twenty-One

## POMPEII

### Lucas

I don't know why I feel like I'm in fucking high school. But sitting outside her front door building up the freaking courage to just knock has me thrown right back into my teens.

She already said yes. We've been texting nonstop. There's no rejection waiting for me. No dad with threats of a shotgun. I just need to get out of my head.

Running my hands through my hair is an annoying habit I can't seem to shake, even though I know it gives away all semblance of a poker face. This girl just brings it out of me, and I can't seem to get my emotions together when it comes to her. So, before I can psych myself up further, I raise my fist and knock on the brightly colored wooden door.

I hear Maddie exclaim on the other side of it, "Shit!" Her voice sounds pained, and I lean forward trying to figure out what happened before I kick open the door open for no good reason.

She pulls it open before I have a chance and my lips quirk up at the sight of her, bent over grabbing her toes, hopping on one foot. Her hair is tossed over to one side, a wild mane of blonde waves casting a glowing halo around her in the faded light of the kitchen.

"Mikey, honey. I love you more than anything in the world, but I will send you to school shoeless if I trip over these things one more time." He smiles shyly up at me from the couch where he and Hailey are cuddled up with the opening scene of some Marvel movie on in front of them. They both have plates of pizza on their laps and look ready for a movie night in.

"Sorry, Mom." His voice is soft and full of remorse. "Hey, Lucas," Mikey says when he notices me at the door. His wave is easy, and Hailey looks up from the TV with a mischievous smile on her face, giving the impression she knows something I don't.

"Oh hiiii, Lucas," she draws out. "Big plans tonight?" Again, that knowing grin and the seemingly innocent question has me turning toward Maddie, who now has her shoes on and is putting on her earrings at the mirror inside the door. The look Maddie is giving Hailey could set fire to a glacier, and I raise an eyebrow at her questioningly.

"Am I missing something?" I've clearly walked into the middle of an ongoing conversation between the sisters.

"No!" Maddie says too quickly, a flush dusting her cheeks.

Hailey laughs as Mikey shushes her, leaving her apologizing to him and going back to the movie without another glance back at us.

"Ready?" I ask Maddie while looking her over head to toe. She looks stunning in the short flowing black dress. It's tighter on the top and low cut, enough to know that I'll be looking at little else the rest of the night. Her heeled boots give her a little height and really put her tan legs on display. My fingers twitch with the desire to slide them up the smooth skin.

She knows I'm eye fucking the shit out of her, but she leaves me to it as she grabs her bag off the table and smiles at me.

"Be good, babe." She chimes to Mikey, who calls back 'yep' without taking his eyes off the TV.

I openly stare at her and try to tell her silently all the dirty thoughts I'm thinking.

"Let's go, James." She reaches her hand out to me, and I take it without a second thought. I peek at Mikey, wondering what he thinks of all this and find him looking at us with the biggest grin on his face. He gives me a little thumbs up with the most exaggerated wink I've ever seen, and my heart grows two freaking sizes over the fact that he's pepping me up for going on a date with his mom. Shaking my head in sheer shock at the whole thing, I take over and pull her along behind me as she closes the door.

As soon as it clicks shut, a startled cry leaves her lips when I give her hand a small tug and I pull her to my chest, pressing a desperate kiss to her lips. Her breath does that hitch thing I've come to expect whenever I have my hands on her.

"I missed you, Cupcake," I whisper against her lips.

Maddie's face lights up and her smile turns shy before that wit comes flying out. "Looks like I should make you miss me more if this is the hello I get." The breathy tone makes her voice take on a sultry edge, and I quietly promise myself that I'll do everything I can to hear that all night.

Walking her down the steps and to the passenger side of my truck, I open the door and help her up into the raised cab. Another flash of skin and leg leaves me groaning. Which is not helped when I reach across her to secure the buckle, and my body makes contact with her in a variety of innocent ways, all of which leave a trail of dirty thoughts in their wake.

I get myself together before I make it around the other side and up into the truck.

Jesus, Lucas, don't fucking blow it.

"So? Where to, Mr. James?" she says curiously, pulling me out of the trance her body has put me in.

Leaving her hanging, I just wink in response and put the car in reverse, backing out of her driveway. The dip my truck hits on the way out is hardly noticeable, but she braces like it's going to shake the very core of the earth.

Twenty minutes later we walk through the door of River Rats and toward one of the booths at the back that I had asked Harley to leave open for us.

I find myself shaking away nerves again, wiping my sweaty palms on the sides of my jeans. We've spent so much time together already, but there's something about this being official and formal that makes me feel out of my element. I'm in my late thirties and have not truly dated since high school.

I relax a little when I see that Harley came through, and the two Cosmos I asked for are sitting on the table waiting for us. They set her off smiling like this is the best night of her life, and my chest fills with pride that I've done something right already.

"Expecting more hallway catastrophes tonight?" Her tone is teasing, and the memory of her in my arms, pressed against that wall, fills all the space I have inside my mind for sensible thought.

"A man can only hope," I quip back, bringing that telltale hue back to the forefront of her cheeks.

We sit and chat about all the small things in life, and we talk more about the opening and how business has been since that day. Her joy is contagious, lighting up the features on her face like a Christmas tree. Her wide eyes and animated smiles are leaving indents on my heart. I tell her about my architecture firm and how the Anderson project is moving along. The questions she asks are intelligent and thoughtful, and I find myself thinking that Sherry and I never talked like this.

Harley keeps the drinks coming and sends over food, but amazingly the conversation never stops. It's easy. The only people I've been able to talk to like this are Harley and Tyler, and maybe the rest of the guys on occasion. But I know for damn certain that they will never look at me like she does—with fire in her eyes and promises in her stare.

When we finish eating, I grab her hand, pulling her out of

the bar with a wave to Harley. He winks at me but says nothing as we make our way out the door.

River Rats is off to the right of the town center, and a block from the harbor. It's Friday night, so there are people out walking around. A variety of music from restaurants and other bars filters onto the sidewalk as we walk toward the pier. We've hit the last bit of the tourist season in Camden, with fall well underway and young couples everywhere.

Maddie and I start off walking side by side, shoulders bumping innocently, but the second her fingers brush mine haphazardly, I grab onto them and hold her hand in mine. Our conversation quiets and settles into an easy lull that has us watching the people meandering around us.

The harbor has little stands lined up at the entrance and benches all along the boardwalk that ends situated out over the bay. Twinkle lights are strung up between each of the concession booths, and the laughter and conversations around us only add to the atmosphere.

We make our way to the end of the dock. It's a little darker this far out, farther away from the crowd and from the music that softly slips from the stores. It's like a soundtrack playing behind a movie scene, especially when Maddie leans against the railing, elbows resting on the worn wood, with the breeze in her hair. She closes her eyes and breathes in deeply.

"The smell out here always reminds me of what home should smell like." She looks so happy with her eyes closed and face turned up toward the sea breeze.

"This has always been one of my favorite spots," I say, not taking my eyes off her profile. "The view is perfect." There's definitely a double meaning behind my words, and she hears them just fine. Her eyes open and land squarely on mine.

"Tell me something, Lucas, something that makes you *you*." Those green eyes are deep with questions. She's probably not even sure what they are, but she wants to know more, and I know the feeling.

"You want more of my ingredients?" I counter teasingly. "That was a tit-for-tat game, Cupcake." I lean on the railing next to her, bringing our faces closer together, our arms brushing with innocent touches that leave shivers on my skin.

She laughs and turns around, leaning her head back toward the stars and closing her eyes as she breathes in the salty breeze when it gusts her hair. The way the golden strands stand out on the black sea below her is something that belongs in paintings or to be written about in country songs. She takes her time, not in a rush to move on from this quiet moment before she opens her eyes again and smiles warmly at me.

"All right then, James, but you first."

I love it when she calls me that. Playfully scolding me, like I'm teetering on the edge of trouble and only she knows it.

"First concert?" I ask without thinking.

"Oh... hmmm." Her face scrunches as she tries to remember. "John Mayer, I was thirteen and listened to 'Your Body is a Wonderland' on repeat." Her head shakes as she remembers that last little bit. "You?"

"Third Eye Blind." She laughs at that and starts humming the opening 'doo, doo, doo' to "Semi-Charmed Life" as she nods her head to the invisible beat of the drums. I can't hold in my chuckle as I sing it with her, going off with the opening chorus rap without a hitch. Her head tips back again as her chest rises and falls tauntingly with her throaty laugh.

"Okay, my turn. Last meal on earth?" Her eyes turn serious like this question will make or break her opinion of me.

"Good God, woman, probably those brownies you make." I groan as I say it, eyes rolling back in my head.

"Understandable," is all she says back with a nod. She thinks for a second and then follows it with, "Though, I don't think I could leave this world without having tacos before I go.

The good kind, made on a truck or at a stand, by someone who has only done that over and over again for years."

"Kids?" I say, turning things a little more seriously, mostly because I'm dying to know.

She thinks on that for a second and I can tell it's something she's given a lot of thought, especially when she answers without additional hesitancy. "Well, I've got Mikey, obviously, and I've always wanted a family and a ton of grandkids. With the right person I'd have however many we wanted. As long as it was what we wanted." Her answer hits me squarely in the center of my chest, and I give just as much honesty back before I even think about it.

"Sherry and I never discussed kids before Jasper. One day she brought me the test with its little life-altering plus sign, and the direction of our lives changed in an instant. So, I agree with you completely. Jasper is everything I never knew I needed, and if he was all I had I would be a happy man, but I have more love to give, you know?" I look at her, hoping to see she gets it, and am not even a little shocked when everything on her face says she feels the exact same way.

Her fingers start to glide back and forth on my arm that's resting next to hers. It's a mindless motion. I don't think she knows she's doing it. Her eyes are far away, deep in thought as she considers her next question.

She comes back to the moment, continuing our game, "Biggest regret?"

The question has a dozen answers coming to the front of my mind before I can process them. But the more I look at each one, the more I realize I don't really regret any of them.

Jasper? Couldn't regret him if I tried. Quitting football? Not really. Sherry? Not even her, I got Jasper out of that.

The only thing in this moment I regret is not moving forward with Maddie the second I met her. I grab her hand in mine and spin around, pulling her into my arms, my eyes on her green ones. "Not meeting you a minute sooner."

Her breath catches at my admission, and her eyes fall to my lips. I take that as all the invitation I need and lower my mouth to her lush pink one. The kiss starts slowly, a soft press, before my tongue slides against hers in question. She responds instantly, gliding across mine passionately, tangling the two of us. Connecting our hearts a little more now that our bodies are touching after hours of honesty. Her hands grab at my shirt, pulling me toward her as my own hands slide up her arms to weave through the soft strands of her hair. The kiss is all consuming and honest, with the world and the crowds fading away around us.

"Let's get out of here," I breathe against her lips, my hands in her hair and hers on my chest. My heart is pounding, and her finger mindlessly taps on my chest in time to the beat of it. I should be surprised that she's perfectly in sync with the very core of me, but I'm not.

It doesn't hit me until we're on my porch that this is a moment I won't come back from. I'm not sure I would have come back from her regardless, but this will take things further than anything we've done yet.

I unlock the door with one hand and lead her in with the other. As soon as the door shuts, the silence between us grows. Filling with the sexual tension that's been building since the dock.

She sets her purse down on the table inside the door and turns her body toward mine.

Wordlessly I reach out and slide my hands around her waist, looking down at her flushed cheeks and parted lips. I waste no time and kiss her senseless, all while walking her backwards until we reach the couch. The second the backs of her legs hit the edge, I pull her flush against me. I've had my hands on her before, but this time it's different, it's more and I can feel the air growing thick between us.

Her body is so responsive to mine, and when I press into her with my hips, a moan leaves her, filling the space between our mouths and echoing in my head on repeat.

I slide my arms from her waist down to the front of her dress, my fingers toying with the hem of it. A repeat move from that intimate moment in her bathroom. Her tongue dances across mine as the backs of my fingers slide against her thighs, just as I pictured doing when I saw them for the first time. My fingertips slide higher with each brush across the silky expanse of skin. When her dress is almost at her hips, my fingers hit the soft satin of her panties and I groan.

"Take it off, James," she breathes between kisses, and I take the desperate command like gospel and continue the slide of the fabric up over her hips and stomach, eyeing each inch of creamy skin like a starved man. In a way, I am one. Starved for her.

Her shoulders shake, trying to get the dress off in a hurry, when I pull it up over her chest and over her head, exposing her lace bra. Her breath is heavy and hitches almost comically when I toss the dress to the side and fall to my knees in front of her.

"I think it's time to find out if you taste as sweet as you smell, Cupcake," my voice is gruff and heady, and she shivers when my breath puffs against her, ghosting over her exposed skin and the arousal that's soaked through the lace that covers her.

"Lucas," she breathes, my name on her lips like a plea or a prayer, I can't tell which. Maybe a bit of both.

Hooking my fingers on each side of the material at her hips, I pause as I place a reverent kiss to her center. It's a silent question and pause, giving her every opportunity to tell me to stop before there's no chance of me holding back. Her fingers dive into my hair and pull me close while she grips onto the ends like a lifeline.

Fuck it. I slide the fabric down her legs, getting an eye full of her perfect pussy as I worship every bit of exposed skin with my gaze while I move her underwear down her legs and out from under her. Swiping them off the floor, I tuck them into the back pocket of my jeans before I give her the undivided attention she deserves.

"Ass on the couch, Maddie," I say as I pull her hips toward me while I drag her down. A whoosh leaves her when she lands on the edge of the cushion.

"Tell me what you want, I need to hear you say it" The words are dirty and come out rough.

Maddie's eyes flare, adding to the perpetual flushed cheeks, making them look like an even deeper shade of pink. "You. I want you." she says, her voice is edged with lust, and it spurs me on, I want to drag this out. I want her to want me as much as I want her. I need her to *need* me with the burning fire that I need her.

"Sweetness, you're going to have to be more specific than that. Where?" I kiss the inside of one of her thighs, nipping it before I move lower down her leg. She huffs in frustration and her hips arch off the couch, a silent command that I'm having none of. Putting one hand across the expanse of her stomach, I press her into the cushion and kiss my way down one of her legs, worshiping each inch of skin my mouth touches. "Here?" I ask the question in a taunting tone, kissing the edge of her ankle, knowing this is nowhere near where she wants me.

"No," she pouts in a dejected breath. Her pouting is cute, but it'll do nothing to get me where she needs me without asking. I slide my thumb over her stomach and down to her clit as I press, circling slowly, causing her to shift farther toward me.

"Use your big girl words," I whisper against her other leg as I nip at the inside of that knee.

"Goddamn it, Lucas, I want your mouth on my pussy," she practically yells it, and I chuckle against her skin.

"All you have to do is ask, Maddie." Sliding my other hand up her leg, I push her knees apart before I swipe my tongue straight up the center of her. Her gasp fills the silence in the room, and I take mental note of every reaction she has, categorizing her little tells like I'm playing the highest-stakes game of my life.

She's so responsive to my touch, and I feast on her with an enthusiasm I haven't had since college. It doesn't take much before she's grinding my face and calling my name out like it's the only word in her vocabulary. And I love every second of it.

I feel her reaching the edge of the precipice I've been hurtling her toward, and when her legs start shaking, I suck on her clit, sending her over the edge with a cry. The sound of her coming is a song made just for me, and I ride her through every last contraction of her core, slowing my licks and sucks as she comes down from the high. I would spend every second of my life between her legs, happily. Who needs food and water? Not me. Oxygen? No, thank you.

"Fuck." She laughs, throwing an arm over her eyes in embarrassment. "I'm pretty sure your neighbors called the cops on us during that." I rise from the floor and fold my body over hers, spread out along my couch. Prying her arm away from her eyes, I thread my fingers through hers and kiss the back of her hand, and then smile with a shit-eating grin I earned the fuck out of.

"Let them. I'm confident that whoever is sent to check on your status would find you very much alive and in an undeniable post-orgasmic high." She laughs and leans forward to kiss me, not even close to finished with us. Good, babe. Because I'm nowhere near done.

"Take me to bed, Lucas. As *incredible* as that was, I'd like to fuck you now." She kisses me hungrily, grinding her hips in invitation.

"When did you get such a dirty mouth?" My voice is a soft reprimand, and her eyes flare when I finish with, "Keep it up and I'll fill it with something suitable for the filth coming out of it."

She closes her mouth demurely with an innocent smirk that does not belong in this space, and I kiss her for it before murmuring, "Good girl," against her lips and pulling her up with me.

When we walk through the door to my bedroom, her eyes fly across the dresser and bookshelf that line one wall. Without a doubt I would bet that the second she's not distracted, she will be snooping through anything she can find. I love the idea and am half tempted to let her do so... especially naked, so that the image of her among all my things will stay with me whenever I touch anything.

I nudge her to the end of my bed and reach around her to unclasp her bra, sliding the straps down her arms one at a time. The front of it holds on by a thread, the curve of her breasts seated in the cups just enough that it hangs onto her.

The sight is erotic, knowing I could breathe a sigh and my breath alone would cause it to fall. Brushing my thumbs down her shoulders, I slide them toward the front of the swells of her breasts, knocking the undergarment to the floor without flourish or thought.

Her nipples are hard and just the right shade of dusky pink. I nudge the hardened peaks with the edge of my thumbs, loving how she leans toward me and how her chest rises with each swipe. So responsive.

"Look at you, so eager and wanting," I praise, openly admiring her naked body and how crude it looks next to my fully clothed one.

She sees it too and huffs when she says, "I need you naked, Lucas." Her hands tug at my shirt, and I happily put her out of her misery, reaching over my head to grab the back by the neck and pulling it off with one long tug.

Her hands slide down the front of my exposed chest, nails trailing and leaving little white lines behind them. The need she shows in that one move radiates through me. Nails trailing back up in a long, sensual stroke, she stops when she wraps her hands around my arms and squeezes. I can see her appreciation and her hunger in that hooded gaze.

There's no more room left between us for foreplay.

Sliding a jeans-clad leg between her thighs, I press her backward with it until she falls into the center of my bed. Her light hair fanning out across my gray bedding.

Pulling a condom out of my wallet, I rid myself of my jeans and boxers before I'm naked, taking more time than I'd prefer sliding the condom down my length. The time I've let pass in my single life shows how out of practice I've gotten. Not that I expect that to be a problem going forward.

Leaning down, I rest my body above hers, propping my weight on my forearms so she can breathe.

Her knees fall wide to give me space between her, and the fit feels fucking perfect. Letting my eyes fall to hers, I notch myself at her entrance, giving her a second to adjust to my size. Her inhale is the only sound in the room, and without another audible word, just the silent looks that we let pass between us, I slide in slowly. It takes everything in me to go inch by inch and not just seat myself to the hilt. When her breath catches halfway through, I whisper encouraging praises that leave her relaxing into me.

"You can take me, baby, I know you can." The words of praise cause her to clench around the inches I have inside her and I groan.

When I thrust a little farther in, her gasp has me halting. "Touch yourself, sweetness, let me in." Kissing her neck below her ear, I worship the spot that causes her to gasp each time I've done it. When her hand slides between us and she starts rubbing her sensitive nub, I feel her body give in to mine and I slide the rest of the way in.

We groan in unison.

There is something about the emotional connection we've built being solidified by our bodies that closes a circle she's been building around my heart. If I wasn't already hers before this, I am now. She's telling me everything I need to know with her body's reactions, and all the little tells have me really start to move. Her hips rise to meet me each time, and I feel her clench around me, knowing it's not going to take much to get us both there.

I feel the telltale tingle at the base of my spine, and the building of pressure up my legs and down my back. It's been an embarrassingly short minute, but she is right there with me. Her breaths quickening and her core squeezing around me. There is no way I'm finishing this without her.

Propping myself up, I cup her breast with one hand and roll her tightened bud between my fingers, tugging and playing with it as I deepen my thrusts.

"Lucas, I'm almost there. I'm going to come." She's out of breath and panting, her eyes hooded with lust as they hold mine. She closes them when I twist again, and that won't do. I want to see the look on her face as we come apart together.

"Eyes on me, Cupcake," I demand, causing her eyes to fly open and hold mine. She's there. I can feel it. I can see it...and I'm right behind her.

"Come for me, baby." The harsh command and another tug on her nipple sends her cresting, and I feel her contract around me. She calls my name as she comes in a throaty prayer that pushes me over that precipice right with her.

My orgasm hits me like a freight train. The out-of-body experience becoming the highest level of escapism I never want to leave.

I collapse down, sliding to one side so I don't crush her with the full weight of me as we both struggle to catch our breaths.

"Holy cake pops." Her chest is rising and falling in time with mine and I laugh at the comment, expecting such a thing to come from her.

"Pretty sure that was way better than cake." My voice is just at breathless as hers.

"Oh yes, and pie. Way, way, WAY better than pie." She laughs at our little inside joke and tips her head to the side to place a kiss on my exposed neck.

We lie there in peaceful silence before I get us both up and into the shower to clean up. I set the water temperature and pull her in after me, taking time to wash her down and clean us both up before I jump out to get us towels. I wrap mine around my waist and set hers and one of my shirts and sweats on the counter for her, giving her a moment to herself.

Putting on my favorite loose joggers, I head into the living room. Last time it was just the two of us and a couch, we watched reruns of *Jeopardy* and I find myself cueing it up on the TV before I hear a buzzing coming from somewhere in the room.

Jasper is at Tyler's, and I know he would rather die than cockblock me, unless there was blood or broken bones, so I'm pretty confident it's not my phone. The buzzing stops, and I continue flipping through the TV app when it starts again. Getting up, I go over to Maddie's bag, and sure enough it's coming from her phone.

"Maddie?" I call, but I can hear the shower still running, and I assume that she's still in there. The ringing stops and I go to turn back around, not wanting to cross some line.

When the buzzing goes off for the third time, I can't ignore it and know that I should at least see who's calling her over and over again. My mind is instantly on Mikey and Hailey. What if something happened to them, or if there was an accident at the shop?

I reach inside her small black purse to pull it out, loving that there's a Nerf bullet inside the small bag, tangled between her car keys. I absentmindedly wonder how long it's been there, and in my mind, I can see Mikey handing it to her and her just slipping it into her purse mindlessly. It's a wholesome thought, and it's so *her* that it takes the thawing she's done on my frozen heart to another level.

Looking down at her phone I'm shocked to see 'ZACH do NOT answer' flash across the front of her screen with the angry buzz. It goes to voicemail, and the screen lights up with notifications of six missed calls from him and even more text messages.

Before I think twice, I slide my thumb across the phone, unlocking it, and a wave of messages fill the screen.

**Zach: You can't hide from me, Madelyn! Answer your fucking phone.**

**Zach: Do you think I won't come get you? That I don't know where you are?**

**Zach *link to the news story of the bakery opening***

**Zach: I'm giving you a chance to beg me before I come there and bring your spoiled ass home.**

**Zach: Fine. You asked for it. We'll do this my way.**

I scroll back, through countless messages. My anger rising with each one.

I can't hear myself think, the only sound filling my thoughts and my mind is the blood pumping loudly in my ears, each pump louder than the last with my rising anger. There are months of these messages. She barely responds, and when she does, it's with one-word answers, or asking him to stop contacting her.

The further back I go, the more I see red. How has she never mentioned this? How has she let this go on? I have so many questions, and the need to put my fist through his face fills me.

When she rounds the corner from my room, I stand frozen with her phone in my hand. Guilt washing over my anger. The missed calls and the endless slew of angry texts are causing my blood to boil like an impending eruption, and I have nowhere, no one... to take it out on.

“What happened? Is everything okay?” Her voice is worried when she sees me standing there with what I can only imagine is a death glare on my face. She looks like a vision in my shirt and sweats, her wet hair hanging around her face, and the smell of my body wash on her skin filling the room.

I shake my head to clear what the look of her in front of me is doing. She looks so fully *mine*. In my house, in my clothes, with my smell on her skin.

Then I remember that her asshole ex was texting and calling her the whole time I was inside her. The whole time I was with her. My heart is open to all of her, not knowing this has been lurking in the dark corners.

“How fucking long has this been going on, Maddie?” The words are as vicious as I feel on the inside, but they come out directed at her. I’m not mad at her but I can’t separate this out in my head. My thoughts are tangled up in each other. Even more tangled we were in each other just minutes ago.

“What are you talking about? What happened?” Her steps pick up and she hurries around to where I’m standing, coming to a standstill when she sees that it’s her phone in my hands and not my own.

The color drains from her face and her worry is replaced with cold, hard anger.

“Why are you holding my phone?” The words come out robotic and void of their usual tilt and emotions. Not a single sign of the joking and witty Maddie I normally see. I run my hand through my hair pulling on the ends as I grip the device in my other.

"It was ringing incessantly, and I was worried it was Hailey with Mikey. But apparently it is your daily session of abuse." I know I'm exaggerating, and I should probably be asking her about this rather than making assumptions that are just going to break both of our hearts, but I can't stop now.

Her fingers are warm and slightly damp from the shower when she takes her phone out of my hands.

"You think reading these," she says, holding up the offending device, "instead of asking me about them is going to tell you the full story?" She doesn't mention the invasion of privacy. She doesn't mention that I crossed a pretty hard line. No, her only talking point is that I'm not asking her about it.

It hits me immediately that she's too good for me, and that thought has me wanting to prove her right. I'm on a crashing plane, and like countless times from my past, I can't stop it, I'm too angry. I have to go down with it.

Maddie holds her phone in her hand looking down at the messages I so clearly scrolled through. When she sees just how far back I went, she drops the phone to her side and hangs her head, wet strands dangling around her face, a cold silence filling the room.

"Why the fuck do you sit back and let him talk to you like that? You're worth far more than being someone's fucking punching bag!" I'm yelling at her. I can't help it. She should stand up for herself. "How is he *supposed* to treat you if allow him to do that...if you never stand up for yourself?"

The look she gives me could wilt flowers and burn paper.

"Stand up for myself. Okay. Sure." The coldness that fills her face as she moves around the couch and grabs her sweater, leaves a chill over my skin, and is an omen of how badly I am fucking this up. Coming around the other side by the front door, she continues, eyes not leaving mine for even a second. "What do you see happening if I respond to that? Do you think I haven't tried? Do you think I've just sat there and 'taken it' when he gets like this? You want to call me out? Tell me I'm lying there and *welcoming* it, that I should have *stopped* him from yelling at me? From hitting me? From making me feel insignificant around my son? Why the hell do you think I left?" She throws her phone into her bag so angrily it almost bounces right back out.

"I don't need to explain myself to you, Lucas," Her fury is so apparent on her face, eyes burning, and cheeks heated. "It's easy to look at someone else's life and point out their flaws and mistakes, but I've gone through enough of those moments, learned from enough of them to know that I don't have to sit by and listen." She turns without another word and leaves, taking my stupid dumb heart with her.

The door slams in my face and I stand frozen wondering how I could have possibly messed up this royally from where we were not even thirty minutes ago.

There's not a chance in hell I would ever side with her piece of shit ex, but that's basically what I just fucking told her. I violated her privacy and then sided with the worst person in her life.

I know I've fucked up even before her text comes in, but when it does it's like a dagger straight through my heart. I don't think about how much she's already tied herself around that part of me. I don't think about what it means. I don't think about the four-letter word that I just laid waste to at the thought. I just grab my phone off the front table and look down at the message, knowing that no matter what it says, this is absolutely my fault.

**Maddie: One question, since clearly, you're all-knowing… what would you do now?**

Jesus, Lucas. Fucking fix this. Fix this now.

# Chapter Twenty-Two

## TAPED-UP KALEIDOSCOPE

### Maddie

I cry for the whole first block of my walk home. Not a cute cry. An ugly, soul-wrenching sob that is embarrassing even to myself, and even though I'm the only one around, it's mortifying.

I know that when I calm down, I'll probably be able to see where Lucas is coming from. Even for Zach, those texts were bad, and Lucas is nothing if not committed. He scrolled pretty far back, painting an ugly picture of the verbal abuse that I've been allowing at this point.

As I round the corner a block-and-a-half from my house, I hear a car pull up beside me and slow down. It's no surprise when I glance over and see Lucas's truck.

I'm a mess and he'll notice the second he sees me. My eyes are puffy, and my nose is running. His clothes are way too big, and I left my shoes at his house. I look down at my pink toenails and dirty feet. The realization that I probably look like a bum has the tears flowing down my cheeks again. The anger I felt at his place is nowhere in sight. I wipe at the tears viciously, trying to get myself together before he gets to me.

I hear his car door slam with the engine still running before his large frame flies around the front of the cab. Suddenly he's standing in front of me, heartbreak and regret on his face.

"God, Maddie, I'm so fucking sorry. I'm a fucking idiot." His hands are on my arms, and I lift my eyes to him.

The sight of me and what I can only picture my face looks like causes a new wave of anguish to wash over his features.

"Fuck!" He screams it as he lets me go and turns, throwing his hands in his hair and pulling on the ends like they're offending him.

I don't say anything. What should I say? Should I apologize? If I'm being honest with myself, I don't feel like saying sorry. I'm tired of *being* sorry. That realization is my own personal line in the sand, and there's no way in hell I'm going to say those two words.

He's back in front of me, taking my hands in his. His glassy eyes on mine.

"I shouldn't have done that. I shouldn't have yelled at you or done anything but ask you what *you* need." His pause is weighted, and his breath is loud on the quiet street. "I just... I had no idea." Silence surrounds us.

That last line hits me. He really didn't. No one knows that it's like this, really. I guess Hails has an inkling, but even she doesn't *really* know. I've kept this to myself. Choosing to suffer alone. Shielding my son from Zach's vengeance and hatred. I've never seen the point in making anyone else go through this with me. It sucks enough for one person, why would I ever drag someone else into this hell with me?

I offer him a small smile that seems to pain him even further. "Of course, you didn't know." No time to lie to yourself now, Maddie. "I didn't tell you." I go on, wanting to fix this rift between us more than I want my next breath. "I haven't told anyone. Why would I share that?" My hand gestures to the air like the text messages and voicemails are hanging in front of us. I guess in a way, they are. Their ugly words fill the space and surround us like an unwanted caress in the area that grew between us while he read them.

"We need to do something." His voice is desperate and tortured.

"It does seem like it, doesn't it." While my voice is thoughtful, and the oddly rational response in the emotional moment doesn't throw him. I figure he seems to like me enough to not be swayed by such a quick mood change.

Honestly, I haven't really had a second to process the fact that he sent that link to that news story that aired. This is the other shoe. Definitely concrete-filled and steel-toed.

"Please come back with me." Lucas tugs me slightly, urging me into his arms. I go willingly. I don't want Zach to keep ruining things in my life, and if I let him come between me and Lucas, he'll always be there. Waiting to ruin the small moments and the big ones. Lucas's big arms wrap around my body, and I take my fist real breath since the moment I had realized what he was reading. His embrace feels more like home than anything ever has, and I welcome it.

When I came out of the shower, wrapped in pieces of him and the smell I'd been dreaming of for weeks, I realized that was the word that kept evading me when I tried to pinpoint how he makes me feel. *Home.*

With his knowing gazes and he chivalrous actions. His dirty words and thoughtful inclinations. I wasn't worried about who we would see or where we were going when I was with him.

His loving eyes are pleading when his hand tips under my chin and lifts my eyes up to his. His silent words say how sorry he is. Sorry. A word I feel neither of us is ready for just yet, but I see it just the same. I see how much he wants me to hear it through his guilt-ridden eyes and almost forgotten questions.

I nod and let him put me back in his truck for the third time tonight.

On the drive back to his place, I shoot Hailey a screenshot of Zach's texts. Something about Lucas seeing how vicious Zach is, and has been, has my filter fading away. Her response is outrage. Rightfully so. She offers to take Mikey to our mom's for the weekend, and something in my chest relaxes at the suggestion, even though I know I won't take her up on it. I knew waiting for this exact response from him was weighing me down, but I don't think I realized just how much.

Lucas's hand rests on my thigh, and I get the feeling that he's worried I'll fade away if he isn't touching me. I don't mind. The anger seeped out of me with all the crying and with each step I took as I walked away. It left me with the words we didn't say but insinuated. The touch is reassuring against the chaotic thoughts in my mind.

As soon as we're back to his place, he sets us up on his couch, wrapping his arms around me as he presses play on *Jeopardy* reruns. There's a stillness hanging in the air while we both wait for the other to say something, knowing that we can only not talk about it for so long. So, I dive in. "You might as well ask." Turning my head, I look at him over my shoulder. Not surprised, but pleased to find that his eyes are on me and not on Alex Trebek.

"Do you have a suggestion of where I should start?" His words are gentle and soft, betraying the heaviness of the topic matter completely.

"When in doubt, the beginning is a surefire place to begin." I've said a similar thing to him before, and a wave of déjà vu washes over me.

"All right." His simple answer is a peace offering, an olive branch from his earlier misstep, and I take it willingly.

I smile at him and thread my fingers through his, looking at the size difference between them. I ponder where to start. We've touched on some of this, but after tonight there's no chance it's going to be enough without full transparency.

"When?" The one word is a grunt he pushes out like it pains him to ask. It's not a full question, though, and I have to pick through what he already knows to really get what he's trying to figure out.

I don't want to make him suffer through it, but it's better if I know what he needs to hear to move on from this. "When did it start?" He nods once, brushing the back of my head as he does so, resting his chin on my shoulder while he pulls me closer in his lap.

"I guess it was fine for the first few months. Like I told you, we met in college, and after a few weeks of dating I started seeing little signs that things weren't as 'put together' as I thought. Honestly, I don't think he even realized it. It would be an empty bourbon bottle on the counter after I got up in the morning, or calls from a bar at two AM. At the time I just assumed that those were isolated incidents. He had a rough day, or a meeting that went south. Or he was just blowing off steam. But that's the risk, isn't it?" My rhetorical question hangs in the air.

"When I got the positive pregnancy test, he insisted I move in with him. We had to *become* the family we were going to be. This was a hard line for him. I took it as a romantic gesture and leaned into it. What a whirlwind romance, right?"

Lucas responds with a nod and lifts our entwined hands to his mouth, leaving gentle kisses on the tops of each of my fingers.

"After Mikey was born, he would only get mad when he was drunk, but those nights started few and far between. When Mikey turned three, I suggested that I go back to school so I could get back on the path I was on before we got derailed. He *hated* that. It was the first time I felt like the curtain was really pulled back."

I swallow, letting the memory wash over me. The weight of it settles in my chest and I struggle to push past it. "Even before it got physical, he promised me he'd never hurt me, but I don't think he realized that he already had. That it didn't need to be a physical hit to put cracks in our fracturing frame."

Lucas is silent but his fingers are busy, tracing patterns on the backs of my hands, the soothing, repetitive motion lulling me through this fiendish nightmare of a storybook.

"It got more frequent after that. His work started suffering from the alcohol, he showed up to a showing drunk, and the more stressed he was, the more he drank. I fought my way back into school even after all that. I'd have my sister, or my mom watch Mikey at nights. After I graduated, a friend of my mom's gave me a position at her bakery when Mikey started school. Zach didn't want me to work, and he insisted on checking in on me during the day. Tracking my location, showing up randomly. I think he was scared I would leave way before I even thought of it."

"About a year ago he lost a huge deal he had been counting on. I suggested the alcohol wasn't helping things. *Definitely* the wrong thing to say."

Lucas tenses behind me. "What did he do?" The words are low, the volume downplaying the wrath they hold.

"It just go to be too much. I know I shouldn't say 'just' but I've spent so long justifying it and coming up with reasons why he did that I can't help it." I pause, swallowing and turning in his arms so I can see his face. His hair is tousled along his forehead from where he's been pulling at it, and his eyes are anguished. I need to get the rest out and get this over with. I haven't laid this out for anyone so deeply before, and it really doesn't make me feel like I made choices that I am be proud of. Honestly, I sound a bit cowardly playing it back.

"It got worse after that, and at some point I woke up. I called my mom and I caved. Not in so many words as this, but I didn't need them. She didn't need them. She called one of her contacts and he helped me file a report. I told him he had one more chance after that. I gave him that chance, and he blew it. I left a copy of a filled-out report that I *threatened* to file with photos attached and our submitted divorce papers. All in a neat little bow on the counter and then I fled. We stayed with my mom for a few weeks while I prepared to make sure he couldn't find us for a while. He didn't come to get us because I'm sure he thought it was a phase. I had already failed to 'woman-up' so many other times, what would make this one different? I opened new bank accounts, got a new car, deleted my social media, fell off the face of *his* earth. I'm lucky to have a little family money that helped us restart our lives. It didn't deter him though, he somehow tracked down my new phone number two weeks after I left, and he hasn't stopped calling since then. It comes in waves, but I know that if I filed that domestic abuse report, he'd never see Mikey again, and I was too weak to decide that for Mikey. Not permanently."

"What changed?" His question is out the second I finish.

"I guess when I saw that video of Brad and me in the parking lot, I decided enough was enough." I pause, knowing I can't take back my next admission. "And you."

"Oh, Cupcake." His lips press into my hair, and I say the last little bit before I chicken out. My heart reaching the end of this open-heart surgery I was putting it through. "I didn't... don't want to start something with you with one foot in my past. I don't fool around. I'm not made for a relationship I can't see being permanent."

His warm eyes bore straight through me and into my soul, seeing the truth of those words in my stare and on my heart. His hand touches my face, and he tilts my chin toward him, sealing his lips on mine. Pouring all his emotion into the kiss.

I pull back and he lets me, still holding my face. "I know it's messy. I told you that in the beginning, that was why I asked you to give me time."

"Maddie, life is messy. You can't fit the things that shape a person into boxes. And I'll tell you right now that everyone... Every. Single. Person. No matter how it looks on the outside, has their own kaleidoscope of shapes that don't even *resemble* tidy boxes." His fingers brush my cheek soothingly as he presses on, his eyes holding mine with rapt attention, "And what a stunning compilation of colors and shapes you are. I don't want anything less or different than you. Give me all your shapes. All the colors. All the mess. Because you fit with me."

His words break a dam in me. I've been a patchwork of taped-up wounds and cracks that I've covered up over the years, all barely holding together my tattered heart. I guess in some way I've always been fine with my taped-up kaleidoscope heart, as he calls it.

But now it feels special.

Knowing that Lucas wants it. And wants me.

# Chapter Twenty-Three

## OFFENSIVE ACCESSORIES

### Lucas

“Dad?” Jasper’s voice is hesitant as he stands, stirring the slightly cloudy spaghetti water.

I stop cutting the cucumber I am currently slicing and look up at him, being pulled out of the hypnotic lull of memories from this weekend. I haven’t been able to look at my couch without seeing Maddie spread across it, her body begging to be touched and her all-telling flush covering her face and chest. We spent even more time on that couch doing even more things after she told me everything. The couch. The kitchen. The bedroom.

Actually, now that I think about it, I really shouldn’t be thinking about it too hard if I don’t want to be running back to my room to calm myself down. Shaking my head slightly, I clear the alluring sights from behind my eyes and focus on Jasper.

His fingers rub at a spot on the counter, and I stop cutting the vegetables I’ve been murdering to give him more of my attention, knowing he’s debating asking me whatever is hanging around in his mind. My instincts have always told me that undivided attention is the best thing you can give someone when the truth seems hard, and he is almost never introspective unless he’s worried about his impact on others.

His eyes flick to me and back to the pasta before he says anything. I give him time. I know from experience that he'll get there. Courage is learned, not inherited.

I see his shoulders straighten and his eyes gain a bit of steel right before he starts talking, readying himself to ask whatever he's been mulling over.

"Do you think I'm the reason you and mom didn't stay together?" His question is a punch to the gut, not a surprise, but painful, nonetheless. He's asked it before, but he was much younger, and I fully thought we were past it.

Putting the knife down, I walk around the island and pull him by his shoulders so he's facing me, eye to eye. He grew a ton over the summer, so it's easier now, and it doesn't escape me how quickly my time with him is ticking away.

"There is nothing in the world you could have done to make Mom and me what we are." He nods like he knows this. I know he does, but his head hangs...so I keep going. "You are the only thing we *ever* agreed on, and the *one* thing that was always right with us." I smile at him trying my best to convey how true those words are with a look.

"Really?" The self-doubt radiates through him as he glances at me before looking back down, not feeling brave enough to make eye contact. The whole conversation is causing things to stir in my chest.

"Really," I say back, pulling him in for a hug. "Can I ask where this is coming from?"

"I just don't want you to be alone forever, and I was worried you were staying by yourself because of me." His words shred me. The innocent honesty of them cuts straight to my frozen center. Here I was thinking that I was doing what was right for him by not moving on. Not giving him an insecurity he has nothing to do with.

I laugh at myself, causing him to look up at me in shock. "I'm so sorry, bud. I kinda thought you wanted the opposite?"

Now it's his turn to look at me in surprise. "You think I wanted you to be *alone*?"

God, I love this kid.

"Well, when you put it like that, no."

He laughs at me. Laughs.

"Dad. Come on. Who wants to be alone? What are you going to do when I move out?" He's incredulous and I can't help but wonder...when did ten become so grown up?

I laugh at his very astute observation, which makes his smile grow. "You have a very valid point."

He turns back to the pasta water that's quietly bubbling on the stove, leaving me staring at his back when he says subtly and half-heartedly, "You should ask Maddie out."

He's trying to be innocent and coy with his request, and after my shock wears off at his direct suggestion, I smile at the obviousness of it, loving that after that adult conversation there's still some growing up to do. "Oh really. Why's that?"

He gives me one of my looks over his shoulder. The one I use on him when I know he's full of shit. Which is exactly what he's looking at me and saying right this second. It's an entire face full of 'are you kidding me?', 'nice try', and 'really?' All rolled into one.

I laugh again and go back to cutting. "Been talking to Mikey, have you?" I briefly look up and see him glancing over his shoulder, biting his lip. Fully busted.

I toss the cucumbers into the salad and take it over to the table.

The timer goes off on my phone for the pasta water, and I walk back to the kitchen, pulling a strainer out while Jasper grabs the pasta sauce.

"What do you think of her?" I ask casually.

"Who? Maddie?"

I nod and strain the water while he grabs the cheese from

the fridge. It's killing me to remain casual about this conversation since it could change or make everything.

"I like her. She's pretty funny, and Mikey is really cool. Plus, she makes those cookies and all the other sweets." He pauses again, toying with another thought before he says it. I want to nudge him to tell me so bad, but I wait. Letting him get there at his own pace.

"Also, you're different around her." He doesn't put anything into the words. Like he knows they might make me uncomfortable. Just lets them fall out of his mouth like we're having a conversation about the weather.

"How so?" I ask, trying not to let my emotions show.

"Well, you smile a lot," he chuckles at that before going on, "You also stare at her, and when you do, it kinda looks like you can't believe she's standing there. Uncle Harley said that's how you know you really like someone. You can't believe they're real."

I shake my head at that guy's thoughtful tidbits. He's a man of so few words, but when he fucking says them these days, they're prolific. Especially lately.

I think on what he just said while Jasper carries the plates to the table. The words float around in my mind. He's not wrong.

Maddie is a wonder. A wonder of sunshine and sugar rolled in a happy outlook that can't be tainted, even with all the dark things the world has thrown at her. I can't help but be sucked into wanting to wake up with her in my arms. Even asleep this weekend, she had a smile on her face. Her features are softer in the safety of her dreams, but the curve of her mouth speaks of all of the secrets and dreams that keep her going. I watched her as she stirred, her body wrapped around mine like a puzzle piece. As she slowly woke up, that smile grew when she saw me openly staring at her.

My reverie is cut short when the front door opens and Sherry walks in. All the happy thoughts in my head float away, replaced by annoyance that she still fucking does that. Just walks in. Like she owns the place. Like it's her home. Like she thinks she belongs here.

I shove the thoughts down, not wanting to turn the mood sour when there is at least the possibility that we can get through the meal without being at each other's throats.

"Oh, my baby!" Her shrill voice calls when she sees Jasper from the door. She yells the words like there's an audience she's trying to impress, and I roll my eyes as subtly as I can while I bring the rest of the food to the table.

Jasper goes over and gives her a hug and starts to tell her about school and his latest game. The only time I see parts of what attracted me to her are when they talk like this. As much as she and I are oil and water, she loves Jasper as much as she can, and I don't think her intentions are ever selfish... at least when they come to him.

They sit side by side at the table, across from me. Her big brown eyes land on me while he tells her about the touchdown, he made last weekend. I give her a terse smile that usually does nothing but seem to annoy her. I am relieved when she slides past it, just moving on to ask Jasper about his friends and what he's learning about in school.

She pulls a bottle of wine out from her purse on the floor while he talks, and I magically hold in any further eye rolls when she makes a motion for me to get her a glass. I give myself a pat on the back as I get up and get it without comment. Honestly, that's growth.

The meal goes on. As long as Sherry is talking with Jasper and busy with her wine, she's fine. It's what comes after that pushes us to uncomfortable places.

I watch her while they chat. Her long, chocolate hair is down in waves, and she's in her trademark athletic gear. The Pilates studio she runs has always kept her body toned, and the selfish part of me hates her for it. She's doesn't let anyone, or anything come in the way of *her*. Even after she had Jasper, she barely waited the full six weeks of recovery before she was in class three hours a day, 'getting her body back'. I'm not mad that she took care of herself. I'm jealous as fuck that she's somehow always able to put herself first. But actually, I'm not. I wouldn't trade what I have with Jasper for the world.

I know I'm riling myself up and I should absolutely fucking stop. Laying out traps in my mind is not a safe strategy when maneuvering minefields.

Once we finish eating, Sherry sends Jasper off to get ready for bed and stays back to 'help' clean up after dinner. Which means she watches me do it while she drinks and loads her verbal BB gun with whatever ammunition she's been mulling over during our time apart.

I suppress a groan when she starts with, "I heard the most interesting thing in town yesterday." I look over at her, a dare in my eyes as I start collecting the plates. I used to be affected by her very presence. The toned curves and tight clothes bringing back visions of the two of us together. But now the sight of her in a spot Maddie stood not that long ago annoys me.

"How unusual for you." The words are clipped and cold. But I know where she is headed, what she 'heard', and I have less than zero interest in going there with her.

In standard toxic, wine-infused fashion, Sherry continues like she hasn't heard me. "Jessica was at Harley's bar on Friday and told me the *damnedest* thing." Her hand slides through her long waves and she throws them over her shoulder while she holds my stare, leaving the door open for me to defend myself or admit things. Like what I'm doing is wrong.

Joke's on her, I have nothing to fucking admit or own up to.

Her gaze tightens as her stare turns to a glare, twirling her glass in her hands. I can see her irritation mounting. The wine fuels her, making her bolder than she already is. Like a fucking bull with a chip on its shoulder, taunting the matador with dramatic huffs.

I start rinsing the dishes in the sink, ignoring her taunts and leaving her to stew.

"Aren't you going to admit to it!" She pushes me, setting her glass down with a rattle. I lift my eyes to the glass, checking for shards before I go back to the mindless motions of household duties. I know she hates it. Not giving her attention when she feels like she deserves it is the quickest way to a Sherry tantrum. I can practically see her stomping her feet with child-like annoyance. But I'm not doing this anymore.

"There is nothing you could have heard that's any of your business." I finally say, remembering Jasper is awake. I'm impressed at the evenness with which I get the words out.

Unfortunately, that doesn't help what's fueling her.

"I can't believe you're seeing someone, and you haven't told me." Her voice pitches at the end of her whining complaint, belying the amount of alcohol she's had—not that it's much of a mystery when only *one* person is drinking from a dwindling bottle.

"Again, I'm still confused how any of that would be your business." The direction of this conversation is starting to press beyond annoyance. There is nothing for me to feel guilty about. No matter how much she pretends otherwise.

Jasper saves me, temporarily, from any further hounding when he walks out, showered and ready for bed. I doubt he cleaned anything with a shower that fast, but I silently thank him in my head for delaying the rest of this conversation.

While Sherry takes him back to his room to read to him and do whatever it is she does, I finish cleaning up the kitchen, trying my best not to work myself up even more.

When she comes down the hall a while later, her moves are loose, and I know that the dead and gone bottle has put more than a little bit of elastic in her steps. Steeling myself for the inevitable, I take a prematurely defeated seat on the couch. My new favorite place in my house.

"So, who is she?" Her words are venomous.

"Way to ease into the questions, Sher."

"I didn't think you had it in you to get back out there. Did you meet her on an app? I can't imagine anyone we know would want to go out with you." She waves her hand as she talks, like the idea is preposterous. I consider throwing Amy in her face for more than a minute before I decide against it. I really don't owe her anything, even if it's tempting.

"Sher, I really don't want to get into this with you. I already told you I was moving on and I have. When it's relevant for you to meet her, you will. But I'm not going there with you tonight." It's more words than she deserves, but I'm done, and I don't want to have this conversation anymore.

Unfortunately, I have no idea why I thought I could talk to her like a grown adult. She rears back like I've slapped her.

"You say that like it's serious." There are fake tears in her throat.

"*Again*," I over-enunciate the word when I say it, "I'm not sure how that is *any* of your goddamn business!" I don't mean to shout. It doesn't do anything but spur her on. But like Maddie said, why would I sit here and let someone else point out my flaws or mistakes. I, of all people, am already aware of them.

I watch Sherry from the couch as she sips her wine and changes her tactics. It's like putting on a movie you've seen a hundred times. I hate it so much. I wish I could set fire to the proverbial tape and never watch it play again.

"You can't actually expect it to work out?" The words are incredulous and wound me in that special way only she has mastered. I inwardly pray to any god that may or may not be listening in hopes that that's all she has to say, but my half-hearted attempt goes unanswered as she continues.

"How could you have a relationship with someone you barely know when you couldn't even make it work with me? And we've known each other almost our whole lives." She slides down to sit on the seat next to me and leans toward me, her hand gliding down my arm before I can flinch away from her. "Though it is incredibly sexy watching you come out of your shell again."

I look over at her disgusted. "Sherry," I say the one word to get her attention. She looks up from where she is eyeing my body. Once her eyes slowly make their way up my frame and I have her attention, I say the only two words worth saying. "Get out."

Her cheeks turn red in anger, and she sets her empty glass on my coffee table before she stands and grabs her bag from the counter, making zero effort to hide her rage.

As I watch her collect her things, I wonder how many more 'family dinners' are going to end like this before I reach my limit and stop having them altogether. I suddenly realize I accomplish nothing from these Tuesday nights other than letting her flay me open and pick me apart, like a bird with a fish. I feel hollow and useless after every single one. Why? To appease her sense of 'family'? It sort of hits me like a gut punch that what I've been doing with Sherry isn't that much different from what has been going on with Maddie and Zach.

She moves to the door in a huff, and I call her name before she opens it. "Sherry?" She turns, eyes burning with my rejection and dismissal. "Until you're willing to grant me the respect I deserve as a human being, not to mention the father of your child, we won't be having these dinners again."

Suddenly, like taking off a tie that's been tied too tight, I can breathe again. I don't bother watching her leave, though she slams the door with enough emphasis that I'm sure my nosey neighbors heard three houses down. My chest lifts and I close my eyes, laying my head on the back of the couch.

A chuckle breaks free, and before I know it, I'm laughing alone on my couch, the weight and fear of having to face music that I never wanted to hear finally coming off my shoulders. I run my hands through my hair and look around my house. It hits me hard that this is *my* home. My safe space. And I can finally have it be that again. Running my hands around my neck, trying to touch a physical change that I can so clearly feel, I take in a deep breath. I decide that I'm never putting on a fucking tie again, the clothing item is now and indefinitely an offensive accessory.

An hour later when the sitter arrives, I feel better than I have in years, and I walk into our weekly poker night with a smile on my face.

"What the fuck is on your face, James?" Damian calls to me with a hint of amused disgust while he waves in my general direction. I shake my head at him and leave the grin plastered for all to see. I feel like I've earned it and it's not going anywhere if I can help it.

The game is at Tyler's this week, and I swipe a beer from the counter before I settle in at one of the mismatched chairs around his kitchen table. The wood is worn from it being used, the way furniture in a home should be. Harley and Tyler sit next to Damian, while we wait for Kit and Chase to show up.

"I've got an update for you," Damian's contemplative tone says, fully moving on from my smile. All eyes move to him in question. Once he sees the undivided attention, he goes on without preamble. "Mr. Clements's replacement has been hired. Principal Noll is on probation, and I've been elected by the school board to hold quarterly reviews of all teachers for the next twelve months, plus overseeing all new hires." A collective sigh goes around the room at his words.

"Since Maddie didn't want to press charges, he's walking, but there seems to be no intent from him to stay around." Another worry weighing down my life lifts at this. One asshole down. One to go. The look on my face must give something away and Harley pinpoints on it. "What?"

I meet the eyes of each of my closest friends. Knowing that there's nothing I could say to them that they would take anywhere else. It's the type of trust that takes a lifetime to build.

"I finally asked her out and we went out on Friday." Looks of surprise fill the faces looking back at me, not Harley's because he obviously knew that already. "It was amazing. She's funny and smart and sexy." Harley lowers his eyes with a chuckle at that last part.

"Break any décor at other local establishments on this date?" His teasing tone causing chuckles at my expense. Oh yeah. Clearly, they all heard about that.

Kit and Chase walk through the doorway, arms laden with drinks and snacks. They sit down and Kit grabs the cards, starting to shuffle the deck without question.

We say casual hellos and Tyler updates them on the topic matter, but I don't answer Harley's *hilarious* question. Instead, I pick up right where I left off, "At the end of the night we took things to the *next level,* and it was fucking perfect."

Chase wags his eyebrows, "Man! You're finally getting out there!" Tyler and him high five at that and I ignore them, getting to the point. "I came out while she was in the shower and her phone was blowing up." Harley and Damian's eyes are glued to mine. I know they get a sense of where this is going, and neither of them like it. It's moments like this where you can really gauge where the maturity lies in the group.

"Of course, I was worried it was something about Mikey or her shop, so I pulled her phone out of her bag." Everyone groans. Heads shaking.

"You fucking didn't!" Chase yells in disbelief at the same time Tyler and Kit call out "No!"

A new wave of guilt eats at me for that invasion of privacy, but I press on. "Don't worry. It gets worse."

"Her fucking ex was blowing up her phone. He had been calling her over and over, and the goddamn texts he was sending her, and his voicemails still make my blood boil."

Damian's dark eyes look like he wants to say something, but he's debating hard, and I turn my full attention on him telling him with a look to spit it out.

"I did some digging after the school incident. She mentioned a few things in passing, but I can tell you right now that her ex-husband is a nasty piece of work." He even says the words like they taste bad, spitting them out and taking a large sip of his drink once they've left his mouth.

"What did you do, Lucas?" Harley asks quietly, but he already knows. He knows me better than anyone, and there's not a chance in hell that I would have ever handled that smoothly.

"I lost it," I hang my head, running my hands through my hair. We've given up on cards at this point, and I nod to Kit telling him to deal. His hands start moving across the table, and Tyler passes out the chips.

"What the fuck does that mean?" I don't take the defensive tone Tyler spits at me personally. We've all fallen under her spell, and I wouldn't want them to react any other way to something like that.

"He was threatening her, even sent her a news clip from the opening, told her he knew where she was, and that he was coming after her. I was so fucking mad."

Damian's face goes all business at that comment. He's grown protective of her during the time they spent together reviewing the ins and outs of the situation with the other slimy fucker whose name I can't even think without wanting to commit murder.

This next part pains me to admit, but I can't give these guys a half truth, "I told her she needed to stand up for herself. That he was only going to treat how she demanded she be treated. It was like every step forward I've taken to get my anger in check over the years went out the fucking window. She left. Rightfully so. I chased after her and apologized on my knees."

I shake my head as I look down at the cards in front of me. A seven and a two. Full crap hand. Pretty much what I deserve in this moment.

"But once we started talking, she told me everything... this guy makes that asshole *Brad* look like a harmless cakewalk." I don't say more than that. It's her story to tell, if and when she wants to. "He's going to come here. He's not done with her. He has made that very clear. And I hate it because there is absolutely nothing I can do to stop it. I just have to sit by and wait. She's the one in control of this situation and it fucking sucks."

There are murmurs of disgust all around the table before Chase and Kit throw some chips down and the play starts to move.

"Did you tell her about Sherry?" I look up at Harley when he asks, but he's looking at his cards and doesn't meet my eyes. It's not a question entirely out of left field, but it snags my attention regardless.

"Not in depth, but I will say that I reached my limit with Sherry tonight." This causes his eyes to raise from what I'm guessing is as shitty of a hand as my own. He folds and waits for me to continue.

I slide my useless cards to the center before I go on, "She came out swinging tonight, telling me she heard about me seeing someone. You should have heard her. She kept saying it like I was cheating on her. When she stormed out, I told her that when I was ready for her to meet Maddie, I would tell her. She was livid. Mostly that I was finally serious about someone else. It was the final straw. I told her not to come back until she starts respecting me as the father of her son and as a fucking human being." Pride fills me as I recall that freeing exchange.

Whoops and laughs fill the air.

Harley smiles at me across the table. Knowing more so than the rest of them how much growth this is for me—and knowing the reason lies solely with my sugar-covered woman.

"Those Thompson women are something else," he says finally, moving to reorganize his chips. My eyebrows hit my hairline at that, and *all* heads swing toward him.

"Excuse me?" Tyler starts. "Did you just reference a woman?"

"You *clearly* haven't met Hailey," Harley says defensively as Damian and Kit face off, flipping their cards silently, one at a time before Damian slides the chips in the center toward his stacks.

I can't contain my laugh. Sounds like they've had a few run-ins and I mentally figure out when I can get to the bar next to hear about them.

Chase eyes me as the deal moves to him and he starts to pass the cards around. "You serious about her then?"

I take a swig of my beer, letting the bubbles wash away the taste of talking about one of the worst moments in my life. "I wouldn't have started it with her if I wasn't." He shakes his head in disbelief at that. I've never understood how our views on women could be so far apart considering we were raised by the same loving parents.

Harley raises his bottle with one hand, holding his cards in the other. "To moving on."

I smile at this as I tip my beer toward him and take another sip. "Damn straight." He smiles back before I say, "Now it's your turn next to settle down."

The look he gives me is abhorrent, but the chuckles around the table at his expense has him shaking his head. "It'll be a cold day in hell before I let a woman back in my head."

I look up, confused at him. "It's not your head you should be worried about." The table falls silent, and he sets his bottle down. "It's when they hit your heart that you should be concerned."

# Chapter Twenty-Four

## WORD SEARCH

### Maddie

**Me: What are you doing?**

**Lucas: Waiting in line to order lunch at Old Sal's. The lady in front of me is still debating.**

The smile on my face could probably be seen from some spy satellite in the sky, but I love how much my cheeks hurt at the end of the night. Like a kid with a huge piece of birthday cake.

I know that a fallout is imminent, but I am happily riding my current euphoric high.

**Me: What did she order?**

**Lucas: Wait… why? Lol**

**Me: I feel like someone who puts thought into what they order would only eat food that made them exceptionally happy**

**Lucas: Hold please…**

**Me: Holding**

I see the dots appear and then disappear.

**Lucas: *image***

**Lucas: How did you know?**

As soon as the image loads, a slice of the cheesecake I dropped off at Sal's earlier this week fills the screen of my phone. Classic cheesecake with glazed strawberries on the top. I pride myself on that recipe, getting the top not to crack was a struggle, but it was one of the first real hurdles I overcame that made me feel like I could do this.

**Me: I know people… and desserts. Those glazed strawberries are almost the exact color of her shirt!**

**Lucas: What dessert would I order?**

**Me: Brownies for sure. Gooey chocolate brownies.**

**Lucas: Absolutely**

I don't know when this whole thing stopped being scary, but with Lucas it's been easy.

**Me: Stop bothering me now ;) I'm a very important business owner and must get back to work**

**Lucas: How dare I disturb you, your majesty**

Laughing at his playful response, I go back to Josie and detail what we have left to do for the day. Hiring her was one of the best decisions I made, and she is a true professional at this.

She's in her mid-twenties but is as stern as they come. I occasionally wonder if she was just born missing her sense of humor, or if they beat it out of her in culinary school. She trained in France, and the only time I see her face show any hint of emotion, is when she talks about that. Her stoic features aren't helped by her tight bun and straight back. Somehow, she looks more put together after a nine-hour shift then I do at the start of any day of the week. Even with all that, I worship the ground she walks on with the level of skill and talent she brings. I was even able to expand the menu with her repertoire.

That being said, I know that she finds my personality a tad exhausting. But luckily for me, she finds Hailey even more so, leaving me with harmless eye rolls and all her verbal frustration taken out on Hails.

Once we go over the shop's to-do list and inventory, she updates me on the restaurant orders we have left to fill for the day and leaves me to go over marketing with Hailey. I try my best to get out of her way and let her work, but when I see the trash overflowing, I wrap it up and leave her to her tasks. Tying the bag closed, I laugh with a huge smile at the *glamorous* life being a business owner grants me. The thing I never realized when I dreamed of owning my own business was the straight fact that when it's yours there is no job that is beneath you and no job you won't do.

Flinging the giant bag over my shoulder, I walk down the narrow hallway to the back door. Kicking it open with my foot, promising myself for what must be the eighth time this week, that next time I will take the trash out *before* it's too heavy to lift.

The smell of alleyways has always been a mystery to me. Even in Boston—when you walk by one downtown, the smell always creeps its way right to the edge of where the darkened hole meets the sidewalk. Like the stench knows to stay in the darkened shadows between the buildings.

I'm sure there's some deep analogy that I could relate to all things 'trash' in life and how they hide in dark places. But as I ponder what it could be, my thoughts leave me worrying it's an omen of things to come, so I try to think of more positive things.

Owning a business is the American dream I remind myself as I'm hit with another wave of rotting death as I open the lid. You lead a glamorous life, Maddie... You are a successful, ba-dass bitch.

The smile on my face is a closed-mouth one because... well, ewww. But it fills my face all the same, and I go to put the bag in just as something moves out of the corner of my vision and I turn and look as a shadow comes into view.

Zach's full frame fills my line of sight.

"Fitting finding you out here with the trash," he says as his eyes roam down my body, pausing on my flour-covered apron and filling with open disgust at the mess on the front of it. I drop the bag to the ground with a clatter.

"What are you doing here?" I'm shocked yet proud that the words actually come out of my mouth, even though they could be a little more forceful.

"I was very, *very* clear in my messages to you." He's smiling now, a look of vengeful promises amid the mirth. I'm torn out of the moment wondering how that same look, that same motion, is what I found so appealing about him in the beginning. I realize that intention and conveyance is everything. Two words can sound and seem entirely different with just a look and a vocal shift.

Zach has changed in the months since I saw him last. His hair is longer, and his beard is more rugged than he normally kept it. It makes me uneasy. He was always so proud of being put together. Messy made him uncomfortable. I hold in a crazed laugh at that realization, wondering what is coming over me.

How did he ever want to be with me? Me with my messy hair and messy thoughts. I never made my bed or put my dirty laundry in the hamper. My life and emotions are chaotic. And I love that part of me.

I'm startled when I see him move as he begins to make his way closer to me. I wasted time looking him over, my mini-mental breakdown and assessment giving him the already sky-high upper hand.

"I was tolerant of your tantrum in the beginning. You packaged your threats so nicely when you left. You must have thought you were pretty clever going behind my back with the divorce papers." The tone he's using has the hairs on my arms raising. It's not his usual, drunken, threatening tone. It's more subtle. More sure of himself.

His volatile nature was always what scared me toward the end. Those instances felt like a roller coaster I never asked to be on, but now he seems like he is on cruise control, riding the anger like he has it honed to a sharpened blade.

I take a step back when his features become discernable. His approach is slow—me, the wounded animal and he the predator that was going in for the kill. It is suddenly obvious how calculated he is.

"Madelyn, it was childish to ignore my calls." He pauses, the silence and uncertainty causing my anxiety to rise. "You probably felt like such a big girl when you hung up on me or ignored my texts." He says the words, 'big girl' with a taunt, mocking me with little effort.

I don't say anything back. There's nothing I can say that will make this better, and it's no use reasoning with him. So, I keep my mouth shut. No good will come of enraging him in person.

"I'm not even mad you took, Michael." He laughs at what I'm sure is a confused look on my face, the way he would laugh at a child. His eyes are alight now. Filled with a joke I'm clearly not in on. I can't look away, he's moving closer, and each step raises my heart rate, leaving it pounding on my chest like a drum.

"You think it was the news story that led me to you, don't you?" The pounding stops. My heart plummets. He's at me now, his sinister smile filling his face, his almost black eyes holding me in their grasp as he pulls me in with his words. "The second you enrolled him in school, I found out where you were. I've made a few visits to keep an eye on you. Even watched you whore it up at his football games. Flirting with everyone in sight. I watched you waste your money and *my* time—time you should have still been with me—on this dump," he says the last words while he motions to the back of the shop. All my accomplishments suddenly looking dingy under his scrutiny.

My eyes widen at his admission, and I wonder how I could have been so stupid. My blood is rushing in my ears, and I can't calm my erratic breathing. I've never had a panic attack, but I briefly wonder if that's what I'm feeling. Or is this what a heart attack feels like? A stroke, maybe? I've dealt with drunk Zach, angry Zach, even asshole Zach, but sinister Zach is a new one and I'm internally freaking out.

He continues while I flounder in front of him, a fish out of water. "It was like you tried to do and pick *everything* I wouldn't. Thinking that made me less real in your life? That house, so different from ours. Football of all things? You know I hate that game." He reaches out for my face, his fingers trailing the loose strand of hair that was always hanging along my jaw.

Him touching me is something I can't stomach, and I try to stop him with my words. "Zach..." I don't know why I try that of all things, why his name is the only word that I can utter, but it turns his glare a little manic and he lunges forward, closing the small space between our faces. My ass hits the concrete wall behind me as I rear back, pushed like a magnetic force away from him. The impact against the cold hard surface is like a livewire to my system.

"Don't you dare, Maddie," he yells into my face at the top of his lungs, his cruise control finally glitching. He slams the wall behind me with his fist, no sign of pain registering on his face, and when his hand lowers, his knuckles are bloody.

The threadbare restraint he had is broken, and his chest starts heaving. There are breaking points that are invisible and ones that are so apparent any stranger passing would see them. Zach just hit the latter.

"I let you have the freedom you craved, but I'm *done*. I let you 'play house' by yourself. Taste what your solitary life would feel like. You can run from *us* but I'm here to bring you back. And one way or another, you are coming home with me."

Venom. That's the only description I can use to explain how he says those words. Spewed with venom. Their position and potency shooting into me and pulling me from the fog I've been in since he stepped out of the shadows.

But I am not that scared girl that left him.

I am not weak or alone.

And I will not let him define or dictate my life anymore.

"You have given me nothing," I spit. My voice and intentions matching the strength that I feel inside me now.

"I *took* my life back. My freedom, my house... our home, does not, and will not, ever include you again," I say the words with shaky confidence, but I believe them and that's what matters. I have to believe them. It doesn't matter if he does. If Lucas does, if Mikey or my mom or Hailey does. I have to believe them for them to mean something. And I do.

He laughs. Eyes holding mine, without a trace of humor on his face. "See, such a 'big girl." Pressing his body into mine, he grabs my shoulders. "I think this will be a fun new side of you for us."

Pulling my hand back, I put force behind it before I pull back and slap him. His head jerking from the impact. He clutches his hand to his reddening face and levels me with a glare that should leave me quaking in the concrete-filled boots that I knew would one day make their appearance. But it doesn't.

Maybe it was that word again. The word 'us' that put the proverbial nail in the coffin. But it is time I stop letting him run my life with that word and all the other hateful ones he uses.

No matter how many times he says it, there is no *us* in 'me', or in 'mine', or even in 'we'. And while there are plenty other words inside those, I am done playing word search with this man.

Word search is for Sunday mornings, with coffee, and donuts with your loved ones.

Not describing fucked-up, abusive relationships.

# Chapter Twenty-Five

## CUPCAKES?

### Lucas

Lunch time at the office is usually a group affair, but since we finished the Anderson project this week, I am taking a minute to myself. Sal's is the go-to regardless of a group lunch or a solo one, but that is when we eat out and not in. I sent Amy and the rest of the office home early today since we've been pulling constant late nights this week leading up to the presentation.

Saying I feel relieved that it went well is beyond an understatement. Part of my generally pessimistic state of mind had me worried that I would be spending the next two weeks doing a full redo of the entire set of plans. The fact that it only came back with minor edits makes me want to go a little easier on myself, but that is always easier said than done.

Turning the corner, I let my mind wander to other areas where I am most definitely being harder on myself than necessary. My role as a father is an easy punching bag and a go-to favorite but even on that front I've been feeling more stable. It definitely helps that I don't have Sherry in my face this week pointing out my flaws... whether real or imagined.

The crisp air blows through my hair and I take in deep breaths on my way to Old Sal's.

Walking through the wooden door brings back a wave of nostalgia whenever I enter. It's like taking a trip down memory lane multiple times a week. But I guess that's what happens when you move back to the town you grew up in. I am one of those people who craves the small-town life. Sometimes I like to think that it craves me back.

Jackie takes my order less than a minute after I plop myself on a stool at the bar counter. Sliding an iced tea in front of me, she puts my request in and returns to the lunch chaos.

The sounds from patrons' conversations fill my ears, mostly from the older ladies behind me. The grocery store apparently had no good lettuce this week, and Tyler was seen in the parking lot giving yet another 'young lady' his number. I give the old set of birds noisily clucking about him a glare over my shoulder. I realizing in the moment that it used to not bother me, but ever since I decided to move on and start looking at my options again, the idea of someone else having an opinion on the dating scene that has nothing to do with them grates on me more and more.

Only one of them notices, but the eyebrow she gives me back says she is *completely* willing to tackle me on the subject and has more than once given her opinion about *my* actions in life. Shaking my head, I ignore her and go back to my tea.

I'm halfway through a million thoughts when Sunny comes out from the kitchen and stops in front of me, sliding over my plate of food. Her hands on her round hips isn't a new sight, and even though I haven't seen it in a while, it leaves me chuckling.

"Okay, you old hen... what have I done now?" Her brow quirks at my title for her, but I leave her stewing in it, not wanting to explain how the old ladies gossiping behind me sounded more like a group of birds than respectable ladies. Call it maturity, or life experience, but I know for a fact that she'll call me out for 'having something to hide' if I complain about their gossip.

Familiar with my antics, she groans and gets to the point, while I grab a fry and start munching, annoying her further with my silence.

"Is there something you want to tell me?" Her raspy voice has no volume control, and the old bitties go quiet, no longer being subtle with their eavesdropping.

"Oh, that's right! I was asking around about someone new in town," I lead, my poker face falling into place like a second skin. "They haven't been here too long and, while I know them, I wanted to get things a little more formal before I commit to anything."

Her eyes light up and she starts grinning, probably thinking that I walked right into her plan with all her teasing. I smile back and swipe another fry, dragging it through the ketchup on my plate.

"That new plumber down the street said he'd give me a great deal to replace the faucet in my kitchen." I barely flinch when the rag thrown over her shoulder smacks me in the arm. She's had one in that same spot nearly every time I've seen her, and I've only ever seen her whack unsuspecting fools with it.

"Lucas, don't you give me that. I've known you your whole life. You can't leave me in the dark about someone new." Her voice doesn't shy away from scolding me for daring to have boundaries around my personal life, and damn, if I don't kinda love her more for it. Eyeing the ladies over my shoulder who are now openly staring, I look back at her, deciding it doesn't really matter. They'll find out soon enough anyway. Hell, they probably already know.

"Sunny, it's new, but yes to your implied question. She's wonderful. I won't lie, or beat around the bush. I'm happy for the first time in a long time." The truth comes easy, and I smile.

She doesn't miss that. This woman misses only the things she chooses to miss.

"I'm happy for you," she says as she pats my arm with one

hand while she starts wiping down the already-spotless counter, and *not* with the rag on her shoulder.

Not interested in giving the town gossips any more ammunition, I wipe my mouth and stand to leave, pausing when she obviously stops wiping and fidgets while she thinks something over in her head.

"If you have to think that much before you ask, I'm probably not going to like it, so just say it and put us both out of our misery," I tell her as I place my money on the counter where my plate was seconds before.

She rolls her eyes at me and clears her throat, continuing, "There was a strange man here asking around about Maddie and her shop yesterday. I didn't want to say anything to her when she dropped off this morning because, well honestly, I wasn't sure what to think and I didn't want to scare her because he seemed sort of off. But I figured you should know." Her hesitancy only adds a thickness to her already-lowered voice. This is not something that needs to spread around town, and her discretion is appreciated.

Her words leave me on edge. I know who it is. It has to be her ex, and the fallout that's coming with him kicks my heart up a notch. Running my hands through my hair, I don't even try to temper my obvious tell. This isn't a poker game. This is my life. And Maddie's.

Pulling my keys out of my pocket, I turn to leave, giving her a second of my scattered attention to say, "Thanks for the heads up, Sunny. I appreciate it." I put my hand on hers for reassurance. If only she knew that it was for me and not for her.

I turn and leave the diner without another word. There's no doubt that I have somewhere more pressing to be with this information.

I walk through the door of Maddie's bakery less than fifteen minutes later, startling the hell out of Hailey when I barge into the back office without a knock or introduction.

"Where is Maddie? I need to find her...NOW!" My voice is harsh, and she jumps out of her skin clutching her chest.

"Good God, Lucas! What the hell? I haven't seen her for a bit. She was working with Josie." Her shock at my initial surprise fades when she sees the look on my face. Standing, she leaves her laptop open to the bakery's social media pages and follows me out the door.

I fly through the kitchen, Hailey hot on my tail, shouting at Josie, asking where Maddie went. Her stoic face looks up in shock at the intensity we're both wielding. She tells us she went out back and we race through the back hallway.

The sight that hits me when we find Maddie, and a man who must be Zach, breaks my heart and makes it soar all at the same time.

Zach stands a few feet away from her, clutching his face, which is as red as Maddie's, but for a very different reason. The smack from her slapping him is still echoing in the alleyway, and I feel more pride than I care to admit.

"You piece of useless shit!" Hailey screams at him, causing both Maddie and Zach to turn their eyes toward us. "How dare you?! How dare you come here after everything!" She's charging up to him without hesitancy, her hands shaking, and her voice quaking. She is clearly *not* afraid of him in the slightest.

To add comic relief to a situation where it has no place, both Maddie and Zach roll their eyes at her dramatics. He steps away, reminding me that he was standing close to her in the first place.

"I see *you* haven't changed, Hailey," he starts, looking from Hailey to me before he goes on, feet moving away from her as he talks. Looking back to Maddie, he says, "And you, spewing private things to *anyone* who will listen." I don't miss the emphasis he puts on anyone, like I'm the one in this situation who doesn't belong.

Maddie glares at him as she slides out from the wall and makes her way over to Hailey and me. "The only one doing anything wrong in this situation is you." Her words are angry, but her composure remains, and I make a note to tell her how proud I am as soon as this is over.

He glares right back and shows no sign of being fazed at her words. I'm not even surprised that he is exactly what I pictured. She never described him to me, but the horrible attitude and persona fills up so much of his image that he could look like a Greek God, and it wouldn't matter. His dark jeans and fitted tee look pressed. I instantly feel sorry for his dry cleaner. What kind of pompous asshole presses a t-shirt or jeans?

I pull her closer as Hailey stands by Maddie with a caring hand resting on her arm. Our support for her provides a shield from the violent wave that surrounds us.

"Get out of here, Zach. I won't change my mind, and I'm this close to filing those papers." The words are spoken quietly but she doesn't back down when she says them, holding his face with her eyes.

The gruff sound of frustration that he throws back is background noise as I look down at her, the only truly important thing in this alleyway. I know he leaves when Hailey visibly relaxes. I cup Maddie's face with my hand, wiping away the tears with my thumb. "I am so sorry I wasn't here sooner. That *this* happened at all."

She shakes her head and smiles at me, and then Hailey, who is still standing next to us. A tripod to our embrace.

"What in the world is so funny, you lunatic?" Hailey says incredulously at Maddie's grin.

"You came at him, Hails! Even I was scared for him." She's joking, but it lightens the mood, and the air around us thins out, some tension leaving at the ease with which she's handling it all.

"Are you really okay?" I know I shouldn't be worried, but I can't help asking.

"Surprisingly, I am." She sounds like she barely believes it herself. "I had built him up so high in my head, but I think over the last few months I've had the time to focus on building up myself instead."

She doesn't need me to fight this battle for her and she just proved that. Not that she had anything to prove to anyone but herself.

"What happened?" The words leave me before I think them through, and Hailey's nodding tells me she was about to ask the same thing.

"I came out with the trash, and he was just standing there." Maddie looks at Hailey before she drops the bomb that we all knew was coming. "He's known we were here the whole time, Hails. He was just doing what he always does. Letting me *think* I was making progress, while he just stood by waiting to take it all away from me." There's no sadness in her tone. Just acceptance of the shitty hand she's been dealt.

"He told me that one way or another, Mikey and I were coming back with him, said that he let me 'play house' alone. He actually used those words too. *Let me*. He's never *let me* do anything!" I can see latent anger start to bubble up out of her. She turns her face away from Hailey and toward me, realizing that I'm standing there in the middle of the afternoon. "Wait... How did you know to come?"

I shake my head, knowing that I will be putting Sunny on a fucking pedestal whenever I see her next. Fuck, all of these women belong on pedestals. Well, not the old gossipy women, but still. "I was having lunch at Sal's and Sunny told me someone had been asking around about you and Mikey. I came straight here. I pictured the worst in my head but I should have known you had it under control." She glows at my praise, and I smile a truly carefree smile back.

"I think I'd like to go eat the remainder of the pastry cabinet and then spend the night with some wine." She looks at both of us in invitation.

"There's nothing I'd rather do, Cupcake." Hailey's eyebrow quirks up at my nickname for Maddie, but she says nothing.

We all turn and make our way back to the bakery before Maddie turns and slides out from under my arm. Heading back, she bends over to pick up the black trash bag on the ground next to the dumpster. Heaving it over the side with a grunt, she wipes her hands on her apron and walks back over.

With a tight smile, she leans in front of us and reaches to open the door, pausing to say over her shoulder, "Just making sure the trash actually makes it to the garbage for a change." Her smile hits me in the chest before she chirps, "Cupcakes, anyone?" Like nothing ever happened.

# Chapter Twenty-Six

## OPERATION MOTHER

### Maddie

I almost don't recognize the person I've become over the last several months, and on more than one occasion I've found myself wondering if it is a good thing or a bad thing. Am I going to curdle like old milk, or is this like when you accidentally pour a tablespoon of vanilla instead of a teaspoon and everything suddenly turns out better? The fact that I made it through that moment with Zach in the alleyway and came out unscathed, honestly better than unscathed, freaking added to my armor. I've found a whole new person in my reflection, and it is not lost on me that I wear a little pride when I see myself in that overly honest and judgmental glass.

I mean, I know that part of moving on is truly getting over your past, but after our run in, the only emotion I feel toward Zach is indifference. The poor guy is like someone giving me the option between spinach and a brownie. And sorry, not sorry, Popeye, but there is no way I'm remotely interested in bitter greens.

Full indifference.

There was a layer of guilt I immediately looked for when I finally realized I neither cared, nor didn't. I finally let myself admit that not caring for Zach was way better than worrying about him.

I had been so focused, for so long, on whether or not I was going to hurt myself or hurt Mikey *because* I was hurting Zach. I never even considered that it shouldn't matter to me what his feelings were. He no longer deserves my emotions or my worry. That realization alone gave me so much power.

Lucas and Hails, on the other hand, care. They care *very, very* much. Care like it is sprinkles in a funfetti cake, both unable to see anything but that. Lucas has insisted on me texting him when I get home, when I leave the shop, if and when I hear from Zach... which I haven't, and he has come over to my place every night this week. I'm really a fan of his attention regardless of the situation, so I'm making lemon bars out of lemons with this one. The fact that Zach has known where we were this whole time creeped Hailey out to no end. To the point where the nosey pain in my butt tattled to our mom. This inevitably ended up in very long phone calls and increasingly frequent texts, like the one I am actively staring at, trying to figure out how to answer.

**Mom: Has he contacted you again?**

**Mom: Do I need to come out there?**

**Mom: Should I call your father?**

Yowza. Big fat no, thank you.

I plop my forehead down on the metal table in the center of the kitchen with an overly dramatic 'thump' and sigh. It's two o'clock, and Josie is on her lunch break.

I was perfectly content to take five minutes and sit here staring at the walls, pondering my life instead of doing the never-ending list of tasks that *never* seemed to shrink. But now the real world is calling me back, and playing phone tag with my mom is unfortunately no longer an option. Clearly.

*Maddie: Sitting on nothin, batting nil, picking sixes, and bowling zeros? So essentially nothing. Maybe less than nothing? But I'm an optimist, so maybe just missing points?*

*World: I dunno... seven?*

I'm about to lift from the cool metal and answer her when my phone rings and I groan.

Why me world? Why me?

*Come on, Maddie. Pull up those big girl pants and get it together.*

I answer without looking, knowing that one way or another that the call will either make me happy or add to my somewhat defeated mood. And between the two, there's only so much I can do about it all anyway.

"Hello? Ms. Thompson?" the formal voice on the phone asks questioningly.

"Yep, this is she," I try to use my usual chipper phone-voice and not my 'I'm-laying-on-the-table-in-my-kitchen' voice. Fingers crossed that I succeeded.

"This is the reception office at Knox Elementary School. We were hoping you could come in for a meeting today? Principal Noll requested I call you directly and that we schedule it for as soon as possible." I bang my head twice on the table in response, giving up entirely on my earlier attempts at sounding put together.

"Umm, sure, is everything okay? What time were you thinking?" Goodbye phone voice. Hello table banging tone.

*World: Definitely eight*

*Maddie: Why do I care again?*

Once the receptionist reassures me that it will be a quick meeting but better in person, we settle on a time that works for both of us, I know I can't put off my endless list anymore, so my mom, lucky me, will have to wait. By the time I make it out of the shop, just before four, I am already running late, not sure what they expect for a last-minute meeting.

When I pull into the parking lot, I don't even *pretend* that I'm actively looking for a spot on the other side of the lot from where the Brad incident occurred. I decide it's actually okay to recognize and admit that I do not have any interest in being near that moment again, let alone right in the same spot. Driving even farther across the lot, I park as far as I can from the other end.

As soon as I make it to the office, I try to brush off the perpetual dusting of flour that seems to seep through my apron and onto my clothes no matter how neat I try to be in the kitchen.

"Good afternoon, can I help you?"

Looking up, I find myself face to face with the put-together voice that called me not even two hours ago. Ms. Laurel—the receptionist, is definitely as composed as her tone, with her wispy white hair pulled up into a bun. She peers up at me through spectacles and I chuckle to myself thinking that there is no way she wears glasses. Her looks and persona firmly categorize them as spectacles.

I smile back before saying, "I have an appointment with Principal Noll."

"Oh, you must be Ms. Thompson. Principal Noll is waiting for you in his office, I'll take you back." She turns and walks away without preamble, and I follow obligingly.

Her sharp double knock on the wooden door is followed by a flustered clatter, and a rushed, "One second!" The door flies open a moment later, and a disheveled Principal Noll stands in front of me. Looking over at the space beyond his brown wrinkled suit, I'm not shocked to find the chaos inside his office a perfect match to his rumpled appearance and behavior. He stands with a pile of folders stacked in his hands, and nods at me to enter. He sets them down on the floor next to even more piles of paper, all while he proceeds to remove the remaining stacks from his desk and from the chairs in front of it.

"Please take a seat, Ms. Thompson," Principal Noll begins, gesturing to the worn leather seat in front of him. The image of Brad in the chair next to the one he just cleared assaults my mind and I shake my head once. Turning my attention to the other side of his desk, I pretend I didn't just get a full body shiver at the memory.

"I'm sorry to make you come all the way down here, but we were concerned and thought an in-person meeting would be best."

I stare back at him blankly, willing him to just get on with it before my mind fills in his ever-growing blanks with the worst. I chose not to comment on the fact that he does not specify who the hell 'we' includes.

Looking a little off put and uncomfortable with my silence, he goes on. "We found Mikey on the edge of the playground, by himself with his head in his hands. He was not responsive to the staff and seemed quite upset. We are required to bring this to your attention." My good mood plummets as his words sink in, but he goes on, completely unaware of the chill filling my bones and my biggest fears creeping out of the shadows of my mind. "With everything that has happened in the last few months, I wanted to meet with you personally and not leave it to the school counselor." I feel myself nodding along as he speaks, a bobble head perched on the dashboard of a car, stuck in motion from the world around it. Nod. Nod. Nod.

Again, this unfortunate old man waits for me as I let the silence fill with my repeated motions and churning thoughts. Clearing his throat, once again he goes on. It snags my attention that silence clearly bothers him, but I can't seem to care about that little tidbit of information. Especially since it does nothing for me at this moment. "The counselor talked to him after the incident, and while he wasn't eager to share, he did say that he was speaking to his father through the fence at the edge of the school."

My chest seizes at his words. There is no doubt in my mind that this is officially the final straw. I am done with this man. He can fuck with me all he wants but he brought Mikey into this. So. I'm. Finished.

The ice in my veins starts to heat, and anger fills all the nooks and crannies that make up the space inside me. What is it Ana said in the *Frozen* movie? Only true love thaws? My one true fucking love is my son, and this man was threatening that. I'm not thawing. I head straight to boiling.

Officially snapped out of my mental freeze, I blink and say, "You waited *hours* to bring this to my attention! I would have come in straight away if it hadn't been so downplayed! With everything that's happened this year I would expect a little more care." Principal Noll looks remorseful as his face reddens with embarrassment.

Waving off his too-little-too-late apology, I go on, "I am already working on a resolution for this... issue, but I'm confident Mikey will be back to normal soon." It's not until after the words are out that I realize how true they are and how *done* I am with people messing with my kid.

"Sounds good. I also... since you're here, I would like to update you on what we've done since... well, you know." Looking once again like he would rather be any other place than in this room with me, he picks up a stack of papers on his desk and shuffles them, putting them back in the corner of his desk. "Umm. Well, let me just get Mr. Jackson."

He distractedly picks up his desk phone and calls his assistant, asking her if she wouldn't mind sending Damian in. I rein in any look of surprise that he is just hanging around in the principal's office, but my disbelief is quickly replaced when I remember that fact that I don't know anyone else who would have tackled the issue like he did. Part of me hopes that I am never on the receiving end of his focus. Though, I'm sure there is some woman in his future who will turn that into something worth coveting, and whoever it ends up being will be one lucky lady.

Damian opens the door without a knock or introduction, like he owns the space, and undoes his suit jacket with one hand before taking a seat in the chair next to me. Principal Noll's entire demeanor, along with the feeling in the room, shifts from a chaotic state of perpetually uncomfortable to one of cold, hard focus. The thought of where he would have sat if I had a significant other sitting there flits through my mind before I inwardly shake the hopeful image away. Because the man I wish was sitting there in my head hasn't asked for the job yet, and parenting is never something that someone should be forced into. Willing and eager applicants only, please.

Damian reaches over and squeezes my arm in a reassuring gesture that is at odds with his overall persona, and Principal Noll stiffens at the contact. Reacting like he smacked me, instead of the friendly calming touch.

"Hi, Maddie," he says, ignoring the practically quaking man in front of us.

"Hello to yourself, Damian," I say back with a smile. "Fancy seeing you here."

He smiles at my teasing quip and volleys back, "I'd say we have to stop meeting like this, but I do enjoy your company."

I hear the sharp intake of breath from our innocent banter as Noll inhales and exhales at every comment. Containing my laughter is not as easy as it is for Damian, but I like the look of glee in his eyes, even though the rest of his face looks as stoic as usual.

"Mr. Jackson, I was hoping you wouldn't mind letting Ms. Thompson know the steps we have taken to resolve the issue she was unfortunately involved in, as well as the good news we have on that same front."

I can't help but admire the old man as he speaks, somehow

his words are practiced enough that he sounds impartial and thorough, all while remaining politically correct.

Damian only raises a single eyebrow in response and then turns to me. "Well, as you can see, *Ms. Thompson*," he says, putting emphasis on the name Principal Noll called me by as he gestures to the stacks of files and papers scattered around the office. "In coordination with the School Board, my office has pulled and reviewed all of the employment files and records for every single teacher and staff member here at the school." Damian straightens his shirt before going on while Principal Noll swallows loudly in the nearly soundless room. "Mr. Clements was terminated immediately, as you know. Since then, I have personally reviewed and interviewed every candidate that the school has proposed to fill his position with, and this week we finally settled on a suitable replacement. While her final interview with my office isn't until next week, I am unequivocally certain that she at least *qualifies* for the job. After reviewing her references and her resume, I am happy with what I have seen so far."

"The substitute seems okay, was she not an option?"

"Unfortunately, not, but rest assured, I am doing everything I can to make sure that our children will have the best candidate possible, especially considering what they've endured with their previous teacher."

It's pretty easy to read between the lines, and I can hear the words 'piece of shit' through all pretenses used to describe Brad. It is funny to watch Damian go into full legal mode, not that I've ever truly seen him out of it. But the degree of professionalism he exudes imbues a confidence that I wish I could mirror someday.

"Thank you for coming all this way, Ms. Thompson. Please let me know if you need anything else on that other matter, and we will inform you immediately if anything else comes up." Principal Noll is basically dismissing us with this comment.

Damian turns toward me at the mention of the other topic of discussion, the one he was not privy to. I nod to him slightly, telling him without words I will catch him up, and we both stand. Neither of us comments when Principal Noll sighs in relief and rises to his feet.

As soon as we are both out the door, I turn to face Damian with a grin on my face. I'm about to ask him for help, again, and as unfortunate as the topic is, I had a surprisingly good time watching that entire interaction. But life being what it is and him being who he is, my enthusiasm is not met.

"I feel like I'm going to be very displeased at whatever you are about to tell me."

He doesn't ask if I *want* to tell him, which is probably why my mouth opens to spit it out the second the words leave his lips. Not that he needs to. I all but wrote it on my forehead with the earlier look we shared.

"Let's get out of here first. I can't shake the feeling that the receptionist is itching to assign me detention."

"Why do I get the idea you could somehow make detention enjoyable?"

"Because you have been lucky enough to experience my charming personality."

He doesn't respond but leads me out past the front desk and down the hall to the parking lot. We make small talk on the way to my car. When he sees where I parked, he nods in agreement, like my decision is something he approves of. Or at least understands. It honestly makes it seem even more okay getting his approval.

Leaning back against my driver's door, I run him through the incident at the shop, what Principal Noll told me, and then briefly what I left Zach with when I left him. I tell him about the one domestic report I had filed, and when I finish the look on his face brings a little bit of perspective to my situation. When I mention the entire reason, I came here in the first place, and the line that it so obviously crosses, the anger that radiates off him is palpable.

"What the fuck did Lucas say about all this?" his voice has dropped, taking on a gravelly edge that I'm sure instills fear, like the one that was bearing down on Principal Noll that entire meeting.

"Well, as I'm sure you can imagine, he was not in love with the whole situation. I was frankly surprised that he didn't tackle Zach when he found him cornering me in the alley. But I had just slapped him, so that probably helped..." I stop my rambling and look up at him.

"Do you think I can make this go away for good? I know I have the grounds to do it, but I've always been worried that if I go through with everything, it still won't be enough. That he'll just keep coming back. And what if it does work and then he changes and comes around?"

His face says he didn't miss the fact that I avoided saying the words 'restraining order' or being too specific. When he goes on without commenting on it, my shoulders relax.

"Maddie, I think that you have not only had grounds for a very long time, you also should have followed through with it in the beginning. The only question we need to discuss is, are you ready to do it now?"

It's the right question. It's also the hard question. I'm about to take away his position in Mikey's life. His position as a father. That is not something I take lightly. Which is why... well, one of the reasons, I have put off even considering it for so long. Who am I to make that decision? I think through all of what we've gone through and that icy fire that was in my veins from earlier flares to life.

Who am I to make that decision? I am his mother. I am the one who will keep him safe and happy. I am someone who deserves to be happy and have a happy life worth living. I say those words over and over.

I am his mother. I am *his* mother. I *am* his mother. I am his *mother.*

My new motto rings in my head, like those four words are molding all my thoughts and all my actions, because I've done all of these things for exactly that reason without acknowledging it until this moment. My job is to keep him safe. Even without the emotional weight I've been willing to carry, Mikey has been and always will be my top priority.

Damian's eyes have tracked the whole thought progression on my face, and when mine finally focus and meet his, he smiles.

My responding nod is all it takes to set things in motion.

Operation Mother is a go.

# Chapter Twenty-Seven

## TALK OF THE TOWN

### Lucas

"Listen up! We're down by six. You all need to keep your head in the game and push through their defensive line. I can tell you all the plays I want, but if the execution isn't there, we won't win." The faces looking up at me though the grates in their helmets look a little defeated, but I'm not going to mince words and then tell them they played their best when I know they have more to give.

"Coach," Asher starts. "Those guys are pummeling us. We haven't scored since the first half." A chorus of mumbles sounds around him as half the team in the huddle nods in agreement.

I've never gone easy on them, and I'm not going to start now.

"Here's the deal, we're going to run a variation of the double reverse," I explain, showing them the play I have printed out on my clipboard. "I know it sounds tricky, but if we execute it right, we'll have a clear shot at the end zone, and we can take this game back."

I see a lot of blank stares in front of me, and I know they need more. This is one play we haven't gotten to practice as much as I had hoped, but I know they can do it. And even if I have to use our last timeout to make sure they're tracking, I will.

"First, we're going to send our quarterback, Jasper, in motion, pretending to go for a handoff." Sliding my finger across the image of the play, I show them the direction. "Jasper, you fake the ball to the Archer, and instead hand it to the first receiver. Spencer, that's you." He nods in response and stretches his neck, getting himself ready. That's a tell we'll have to work on next year, but the fact that he's in the zone has me pressing on with more drive.

"So, Spencer, you'll run the opposite way with the ball. Wait for a second, and then pitch the ball to Cash, ..." I pause, making sure they're keeping up. "Then, Cash, once you have the ball, you throw to Mikey who will have moved over to the opposite side of the field," I continue, nodding to Mikey. "You should have a straight shot at the end zone. Blockers, you all have to create space for him." Laughter lights up around the huddle at that last part, because Mikey is small. Fast as hell, but small. There's confidence building in their faces and posture, and I know this is as good as I can hope for. "I know it may seem a bit complicated, but we've practiced this before, and we can pull it off. So, let's dig deep and execute it. Time to show everyone what we're made of and bring home this win!"

The team cheers when I finish, excitement now replacing their nerves and fear of defeat. I throw my hand in the center, signaling the end of the huddle. Small palms fly on top of mine and the boys all cry out "Titans," before they break off and move into position in the center of the field.

From the first snap of the ball, I can tell that huddle is exactly what they needed. They are pushing harder, running, dodging, and tackling their way toward this win. Pacing along the sideline, I let my chest fill with a bit of pride at their obvious determination. Not that I'd ever show it. I do my damnedest to keep my shit together. Can't let anything slip now.

The boys run the play perfectly. The ball is hiked to Jasper who fakes a handoff, while Spencer runs back behind him and snags it before the other team has a second to register what is happening. He takes off in the opposite direction. The rest of the play runs like clockwork and, with just seconds to spare, they do it. The blockers take down everyone in their path, and Mikey sails through a hole in the line that most kids wouldn't fit through. His legs beating as he races down the field and through the end zone. The crowd bursts into a frenzy of cheers, and Mikey throws his fist into the air. The guys around him slap his back at the advantage he just gave us.

But they aren't done yet, and I yell at them to line up, not caring about the emotion in my voice. I want this victory as much as they do. And they still have to score the extra point to put it over the top.

I yell to the ref for a quick substitution, and I tell Jasper we're going back to Mikey one more time to seal this one up. Nothing fancy, no trickery. Just a straight shot up the gut to bring it home. There are only a few seconds left in the game, and we only get one shot at this.

The boys line up. I can feel my heart pounding in my chest, but the rest of the world seems to be moving in slow motion. Jasper takes the hike and quickly hands the ball to Mikey in the backfield. From where I'm standing it looks like the hole, he's supposed to run through has suddenly turned into a brick wall of defenders. My heart sinks. We didn't come this far to get a tie.

Mikey bounces off the first defender, unfazed, and quickly spins out to his right. He speeds around the line and hits the open field, only one man to beat on his way to the end zone. With a final burst of speed, Mikey stretches past the arms of his would-be tackler and races across the line for the score.

The whistle blows and everyone loses it. The ref throws his arms straight up and the team, almost in sync, throws their helmets down. The kids all run into the end zone, tackling each other, cheering over the win.

The last few seconds on the clock fall away and the game is called. We're officially in the playoffs, and I'm beyond proud at these kids.

Watching the boys smack each other on the back, pass around high fives and supportive comments at both our team and the opposing one, I can't help but wonder if this will become one of those moments that will stay with them for years to come. An instance that reminds them what they are capable of, even when the odds seem stacked against them or their confidence is low.

Turning my head, I see Maddie and Hailey grasping each other in a ridiculous hug as they bounce up and down in glee. Maddie's bright hair is glowing in the fall sun. But even that can't compare with the glow on her face as she stares at Mikey, the last-minute hero of the game.

The sight of her on this field, with everything that has happened since, then leaves my heart aching. Not in a way that is unpleasant or even painful. It just feels... full. Satisfied, if a heart can be that way.

So much of my life leading up to meeting her felt exactly like that—a lead up. Like my steps were taking me toward her. Invisible strings pulling us together. I ponder it sometimes, after Jasper is in bed and I am alone with my thoughts. What made her land on this town out of all the options she could have had? How did Mikey wind up on my team? The coaches are selected at random after all. Even the boys being in the same class. It *kills* me to think what would have happened with Brad had I not been at that parent- teacher night. What if I hadn't watched him talk down to her all night and then decided to follow him out the door?

My thoughts pull me like a magnet to her, and my feet are moving me across the grass before I even make the decision to do so. Pete and his opinions on next year can wait a minute or two.

Her eyes meet mine over Hailey's shoulder, and I give the tiny brunette a playful shove to kick her out of Maddie's arms so I can pull Maddie into mine.

Not caring who sees us, I close my arms around her back and look down into those big eyes. "What's this for?" she asks as she wraps her arms around me and squeezes back, like it is just the two of us and not a sea of parents who are undoubtedly staring at my unusual PDA.

"I was just watching you and thinking about the day we met."

She laughs and smiles up at me through her lashes. "I swore you moved in slow motion that day." She shakes her head, that comment feeling like a steroid injection to my ego. "I couldn't keep my eyes off you the entire practice. You make hot chocolate look cold, James."

"Cupcake, my thoughts were much less gentlemanly and definitely not on how fast or slow you were moving."

She laughs and hits my shoulder as the boys come up and starts taking cupcakes and treats out of the bakery boxes stacked next to where we had left Hailey standing. Maddie had become the unofficial treat mom. Mostly because she brought treats regardless of who was assigned to do so, and after three games of telling all the boys they had to eat the regular snacks first, so they didn't hurt anyone's feelings, I gave up and stopped asking anyone else to bring anything.

For the thousandth time, I mentally praise my earlier self for not giving up on recruiting Tyler to be the assistant coach, because that savior of a man has fielded all the parent conversations by the time we're finished. So, when I see Pete leaving the field without talking to me, I send up a prayer.

Before I know it, it's just Tyler, Hailey, and us, almost like that very first practice, the rest of the parents having left while we cleaned up.

With Maddie's hand in mine, Hailey and Tyler chatting on their own, and the boys trailing behind us, we make our way off the field and to the deserted parking lot. The whole thing seeming like a picturesque family moment I don't want to move past. Leave me forever in this space with these people and I would die a happy man.

I squeeze Maddie's hand and she looks over from watching the boys walk side by side. There are words in my smile I am too nervous to say. They feel right, but saying them changes things, and it's too perfect to mess up, so I just smile down at her and place a kiss on her head, deciding to enjoy the moment as it is.

I feel her stiffen before I see it, and Hailey calls out, "You've got to be fucking kidding me!"

"Auntie Hails, you can't swear in front of other people!" Mikey calls back to her, but all my attention is stuck on Maddie as I follow her glare to the direction of our cars.

I'm not surprised to see Zach leaning on the side of her car with his arms crossed over his chest. His dark hair and stupid pressed pants making him look like the put-together asshole I already think he is. My head whips back to the boys and Tyler. They stopped a few paces behind us, and Tyler has Hailey by the shoulders, the tension in his flexed fingers telling me how much he is holding her back.

He's moved the boys behind him, and I catch Mikey's head peeking out from behind Tyler's back uncertainly.

Looking at me, his words slice across the silence in the parking lot like a hot knife through butter. "Just filling all my shoes, aren't you?"

"I don't know what you're hoping to accomplish here. But this is not the time or the place for this discussion."

"You think I give a fuck what you think is appropriate? That's my fucking wife your arm is around. My son you're cheering on like he's yours." He spits the words, making anger fill my veins at his audacity. Who the fuck would talk like this in front of kids? Or strangers, for that matter?

He laughs venomously at Hailey's useless attempts to go at him, her shoulders fully restrained by Tyler now.

"Zach, I am not your wife." Something inside me relaxes at Maddie's words. I knew she was over him and that she filed the divorce papers, but hearing her say these words has a fire burning in my chest. She doesn't hold back her disdain when she talks, and I'm proud of her, even if I hate the fact that any of us are in this current conversation.

His face morphs at those words. "You think you have grounds to take my fucking son from me?"

My head flies to her in question. What is he talking about? Zach continues and I catch up quickly.

"Pretty clever you figured out where I was staying. Sending them in to be served with my take-out was even more clever. You clearly hired a professional this time."

Keeping my eyes on Zach, I take a step in front of Maddie, causing his gaze to flare. "We aren't doing this here. Set up a time and a place and she *might* grant you a meeting, but you're done cornering her in shitty situations." His actions are so similar to Sherry's that I can see right through them, and I'm man enough to call him out on them.

I expect it when he takes a step toward me with his fist clenched, and I take a matching one, putting more space between him and Maddie. I've dealt with a few drunks in my day, and even though it is clear he can handle the majority of his liquor, his anger is his biggest tell. Add in the sweat covering his brow, and the way he continuously shifts his feet to keep himself steady, and I have everything I need to read him like a children's book.

I hear Maddie step back and I don't turn to look to see if she's walked over to the boys and Tyler. Taking my eyes off of Zach would not be my smartest move.

My step forward flipped a switch inside him. Or it might have been the fact that I am protecting Maddie. Either way, there is only one way out of this now, and I try to prepare myself when his hands ball up even tighter. He moves away from the car, taking two giant steps toward me.

The anger in his eyes is apparent. I had never exactly thought through whether or not I'd end up on the receiving end of it, but here we were, and if I am certain of anything, it is that I regret none of my decisions that put me here.

He doesn't slow his strides and his fist rears back. The strength in his arm is wound up, and my entire body tenses in anticipation. My mind is ready to dodge the blow, but before I can react, Zach's fist connects with my jaw.

The force of it has me stumbling back, feeling the sting of pain radiating through my cheek and my chin. I have been punched before, but this is different. This is personal. This fucking matters to me. Zach barely registers the hit even though I know his knuckles must be hurting. Not as much as my jaw, but punching someone doesn't just hurt the one on the receiving end. Zach is still seething with anger, ready to throw another hit. I can see it. His chest angles slightly toward me. His body is shaking. There is nowhere for his rage to go except out. And I am the only person here he'll be getting his hands on.

I don't want to do this in front of the kids. If I rail on him just because he is a drunk asshole, I'm setting a precedent for them. As much as it fucking hurts, I have to be the better man in this situation. I have to be the *only* man in this situation.

The second hit is worse than the first, and I'm knocked back another step, keeling over to try to catch my breath as I stare right at him. My face still stings from the impact of the first punch, and that second hit landed below my eye. The swelling is already starting, and I can feel the pressure building up around the sensitive flesh. My fingers reach up and I gently probe the area, biting my cheek and looking at Zach with unrestrained hatred when my fingers come away bloody. Normally an attacker holds something in the tank. Either out of fear of hurting the person in front of them too much, or from the fear of hurting themselves. Zach is holding nothing back. He is either too drunk to know he should, or the more likely option... he's out for blood.

When Zach takes another step toward me, thinking he can catch me either unaware or unprepared, I snap upright and lunge forward, swinging my arm around in a powerful arc. The sound comes first when my fist connects with his cheek. The dull thump rings out around the empty lot as the impact reverberates through both our bodies.

When I pull back, hoping the one hit was enough to put an end to this, Zach has staggered back, stunned, and there's a fresh cut on his bottom lip, where my fist landed. I chuckle at the sight. Those really are the worst... next to a hit in the eye, that is.

"Fine..." He spits, blood leaving his mouth and landing on the pavement in front of me. "You can have the trash." He rubs his lip with his thumb before adding with a vicious grin. "Just a piece of advice though, she likes it rough."

The second his words register, I'm back on him. My fist ramming again and again into his smug, piece-of-shit face. He gets the upper hand momentarily and throws me to the ground, the gravel pinching into my back barely registers when his fist connects with my side and then my cheek.

I don't hear Maddie calling out to me or hear Tyler trying to pry him off me. Though I know both of those things happen. I barely register the sirens when they arrive, and only hear the cops when they finally separate us.

Eyes swollen, I lift my head slightly and look up through the puffy lids to see Kit standing over me, hands on his hips, blond hair falling around his eyes.

"You look like *absolute* shit, James."

"Makes sense," I reply, laying my head back down on the concrete. "I'd say you should see the other guy, but the fucker probably looks better than me."

Kit laughs at that and runs his fingers through his long hair that always seems to be in his face.

"He definitely seemed to be winning that fight." Holding a hand out to me, he helps me up before landing another verbal blow. "Whoever taught you to fight clearly forgot to mention that you're supposed to hit them back."

I look around for the kids, but I don't see them or Hailey, and I pray that she took them home before the fists started flying.

I look around the parking lot and I can't find Maddie, either. A sense of panic fills me. Kit puts me out of my misery and nods behind me. I turn quickly and see her and Tyler sitting on the curb a few feet behind us. Steve, the deputy sheriff, is squatting in front of them with a pad of paper and a pen flying across it as he writes down whatever she is saying. Tyler sees me watching them, and nods at me with a small smile.

"You know how fucked this is, right?" Kit says.

I poke at my swollen face with my fingers and prod my cheek with my tongue from the other side, wincing as it causes pain to radiate across my face. "Unfortunately, yes."

"Procedure says that even though it was obviously self-defense, I've got to detain you and take you down to the station to take your official statement. None of it is permanent, but you're in for a very long night of godawful paperwork."

I groan and he nods. "Yep. You, my friend, are going to be the talk of the town for at least a month."

I shake my head and slap my hand on his shoulder, giving it a squeeze before I make my way over to Maddie and Tyler.

Steve is wrapping up when we get there. His grandfatherly voice brings back memories of general teenage trouble. "Thank you for all this, Maddie, this whole thing seems rather cut and dry, but it would be very helpful if you could come down to the station and give a formal statement. You, too, Tyler."

Hearing me come up behind them, he looks over his shoulder and stands, giving me a disappointed stare. "Lucas James, this was not how I wanted to spend my evening. I do have a real job, you know." His scolding tone makes me chuckle. Not a cool move, Lucas. But what can I say? He said that like I'm out getting into fights every night of the week... and like this isn't his *actual* job.

I picture him at his desk down at the station. Feet propped up on the worn metal surface, a donut in his hand while he reads the paper he's already read twice that day.

"No problem, boss," I say, giving Steve a wink as I hold my hand out to Maddie. She eyes it cautiously before taking it and letting me help her up.

"Don't make this night any harder for yourself, son," Steve scolds me before he adds, "I'll give you two a minute."

Kit laughs as Tyler stands and moves over to him, nudging him toward the cars. Thankfully, he takes the older man's cue and gives us some space.

Maddie punches me in the shoulder as she shouts, "What were you thinking!" I act like she hurt me when I wince at her light hit, and her eyes go wide at the sound of pain.

"Oh no! I'm so sorry," she cries out, reaching for my shoulder and running her fingers over it, checking for more injuries.

Once she's satisfied I'm going to live, she shoves me and looks up at my undoubtedly ugly and battered mug. So much passes over her face before she grabs my shirt and pulls me toward her, kissing my lips with enough force that I actually struggle to hold in my wince.

"What in the world made you do that?" She mumbles against my lips before she pulls back with tears falling from her puffy eyes. The sight of them causes me more pain than my current physical state. I'm so sick of this man making her cry, and tonight I only helped him.

Wiping away her tears with my thumbs, I slide my palms down her neck and rub them up and down her arms. I don't answer her right away, and she shakes her head at me before laying it on my chest, causing my breath to hitch and another fucking look of worry to fill her face.

"I can't touch you anywhere without you being in pain, can I?"

I raise my eyebrow at that. "Well, Maddie I've got at least one place that you can absolutely touch, pain free."

"You are the absolute worst." Her words don't sound like she means it. They actually sound like the opposite.

"Sadly, though, Kit has just informed me that my night is now spoken for."

"Steve did say that he wants me to go down and file a report too."

That brings back to what Zach said, before everything went to shit. "Care to tell me what the hell he was talking about?"

I desperately want to know, especially since it seems like that's what pushed the fucker over the edge tonight. Not that he could have any viable excuse for his behavior.

Her face fills with guilt. "I was going to tell you tonight." She pauses and I give her time to get her words together. "He showed up at Mikey's school last week and was talking to him on the playground, through the fence."

I spin around looking for him again. Ready to go another round. Her hand on my arm brings me back, and she quickly presses on.

"Mikey is fine. He was just upset. But as soon as I heard about it from the school, I met with Damian and he helped me compile and file *everything*. My old report with the pictures. The recent incidents...everything. We filed a restraining order and had it delivered to him. The court date is three weeks from now, and if he doesn't show, it's done." She pauses to think, to breathe, having rushed through all the words. "Well, it's done regardless after today."

Her smile melts me, and I pull her back into me. Wrapping her around my arms. Having her there, cradled against me, feels like home, and with all the turbulence of the night, the feeling is a great comfort.

"Maddie, I am so proud of you." I whisper the words against her hair, breathing in her scent.

Kit clears his throat from behind me. "As cute as the two of you are—despite your wreck of a face, I'd like to get this show on the road so I can get home before the sun comes up."

I spin with Maddie in my arms, loving how she chuckles at Kit's poorly timed joke.

"Aw, you think I'm cute. Thanks, Kit."

"Don't make me put the cuffs on you," he threatens halfheartedly.

"Oh, I'd actually pay to see that!" Maddie chirps, clearly coming out of the emotional moment we were just in.

I glare at her, and Kit laughs.

"I'll get you your own pair as a souvenir from tonight."

She beams at him from inside my arms. "Don't you toy with me, Kit." There is far too much excitement in her voice.

"Excuse me, miss," I interrupt her. "If you think you'll be using those on me, you are sorely mistaken."

She sighs dramatically, patting my good cheek with one of her hands. "What a shame. So pretty, but afraid of a little challenge."

My eyes darken and I level them on her, causing her breathing to pause. "Is that a dare, Cupcake?"

She clears her throat. "Maybe it is, James." Visions of us dance in my head. Handcuffs playing a part in a few of them.

"Kit!" I shout over my shoulder while keeping my eyes on her. "Get me the hell out of here."

# Chapter Twenty-Eight

## COFFEE CAKE

### MADDIE

Finalizing the report at the station was easy. Hell, I was a freaking seasoned vet at it now. Kit and Steve were not mincing words when they said it would take all night. It really did.

By the time we got back to the house, both boys were passed out in Mikey's bed, and Hailey was on the couch, with Tyler long gone.

Splitting up, Lucas goes to make sure the boys are situated as I carefully lay a throw over Hails, trying desperately not to wake her up. She stirs when the blanket touches her anyway and one eye cracks open as she repositions herself on the cushion, pulling the blanket up to her chin when she does.

"You okay, Maddie Pie?" Her voice is soft from sleep, but the concern comes through and my heart cinches at the fact that my baby sister is worried about me.

"You know me, Hails, I'll always make the best of a bad thing. No ruined cupcakes in my house. Those bad boys get made into cake pops." My whispered words are deflecting as all hell, but she knows to expect that and nods anyway, reaching out and squeezing my arm before she mumbles she loves me and rolls over.

I creep my way down the hallway, hoping the old wood floors don't creak and wake anyone up. Coming up on Mikey's door, I peek in and see Lucas sitting on the end of the bed watching both boys sleep. I wish there had been an opportunity to talk to them before they fell asleep. But as I watch Lucas deep in thought, looking at them, I give myself a minute to just observe. His hair is a mess, and his eye seems to have stopped swelling. Thank the chocolate gods he can still see out of it. Despite that, though, seeing him in Mikey's room with the boys is causing all sorts of feels to creep up from those butterfly dens living in my stomach.

Whether he senses me standing there or can hear me breathing, I'll never know, but when he turns, his eyes land right on mine, knowing exactly where I am. Tonight did things to us. To our relationship. There are things in life you move on or change from, never sliding back into who you were before they happened, but becoming someone new. This is one of those. No matter where we wind up, he was there for me tonight, fought for me, protected me. Stood up for Mikey. How many times have I wished for that in the past decade? Prayed to be loved and supported? More times than I had prayed to the afore-mentioned chocolate gods, and in my industry, that is at least twice a day.

Not veering, and without hesitation, he stands and walks over to where I'm standing, hand sliding across my jaw and into my hair without pause. He pulls me to his mouth before my next blink, and his lips move onto mine. He doesn't rush it, taking his time. Doorway be damned. Sleeping boys forgotten.

The feel of him taking his time, his full lips pressed against mine while his tongue toys with my own, makes me feel worshiped. Honestly, it makes me feel loved.

Knowing tonight isn't the place for declarations, I pour the words into my kiss, pressing my body against his. He flinches when my teeth snag his bottom lip, and I pull back, apologizing before I even see his face. "I am so, so, so sorry." My whisper is breathless, and I'm surprised he can hear the words when they whoosh out of my mouth.

"You never have to apologize for kissing me, Maddie, No matter what state I'm in."

"I mean, have you seen your face? Probably not the best idea to put too much pressure on it." I blush as soon as the words are out. Maybe a tad too much left to be implied in that, Maddie.

Hanging my head in a silent prayer, he doesn't comment and only chuckles.

"Are you suggesting you put something heavier on my face than your lips?" The words are dirty, and his tone is dirtier. Lucky me.

Being the true gentleman that he is, though, he doesn't leave me to wallow in my mortification. "I think it's time for bed." The words make sense, and when I feel the disappointment they bring, I remind myself, it's the middle of the night.

He holds out his hand, and I take it without a second thought as he pulls me out of the room.

"Why do you look so sad, Cupcake?" His words are a whisper in my ear from behind me.

Of course, he saw that. "I'm just not sure I'm quite ready to go to sleep." I don't turn around to look at him as I say the words. I'm braver when I can't see all the things that he doesn't say out loud.

Leaning into me, his lips press on the spot below my ear, sliding his arm around my waist, resting over my navel, he breathes quietly, "I never said sleep, I said *bed.*"

My heart flips and a warm feeling builds in my center when his fingers start to brush under the hem of my shirt, the tips of them sliding under the edge of my jeans. Taking my silence as only someone who cares about a person would, he backpedals, his motions stilling. "We don't have to. Tonight was a lot. I'm happy as long as I'm with you."

Men. I just *specifically* said I wasn't interested in sleep.

Taking his hand from around my waist, I use it to drag him forward, down the hall, and to my room. Creaks in the floor be damned.

Once we cross the threshold, the entire mood shifts and me leading him anywhere becomes a pretense. His large body blocks the doorway before he turns and softly closes the door behind him. Even though this isn't exactly new, I am starting to feel like I will always have butterflies when he is around. Especially when he looks at me the way he is now.

Unreasonably nervous, my feet shuffle when he walks toward me, the look in his eyes turning to a mischievous twinkle.

When Lucas stops in front of me, his fingers reach out and gently brush my hair out of my face. His fingers barely graze my cheek, but his touch still sends a wave of warmth throughout my body. He doesn't hold back, leaning in and pressing his lips against mine, adding gasoline to the small flame his touch is already building in my core. Pulling me down onto the bed, his leg tangles between mine and he uses the leverage to roll us from our sides and pins me beneath him. He settles his thigh more firmly between mine, and raises his chest off my body, propping it up with his forearms so they rest on either side of my face.

The look he gives me.

It's hot and bubbly and tells me all the things he wants and plans to do. "You're mine, Maddie. Body and soul, I'm not sure I could give you up for anything at this point." Placing his lips at the spot he always finds beneath my ear, he breathes in deep before he kisses it reverently.

After tonight there is no way I can sit back and let him worship me the way he does. Even if he does it better than I can ever possibly bake. No, I want to worship him back.

Lucas did something for me today that I have been too cowardly to do for myself. All while making me proud to be with him. He thought of my well-being and my kid's well-being, and put both over his own. To the temporary detriment of his beautiful face.

Sliding my hand down his chest, I slip my fingers down the front of his jeans and cup him. His face raises from the crook of my neck, and I meet his battered and bruised face. "I want to take care of you, Lucas."

Shoving him lightly to the side, I nudge him onto his back before I straddle him. Trying to move softly so I don't harm him any more than he already is, I gently grasp his face and kiss him, pouring every ounce of gratitude and passion possible into it before I pull back.

With deft fingers, I tug at the hem of his shirt, encouraging him to sit up and let me take it off. His tan skin is soft and warm, and I graze my nails lightly down his chest as he falls back on the bed.

"I have to say, Cupcake. I really, really like you on top of me."

I laugh at the sincerity of his words and bend down to pepper kisses down his chest. When I reach below his navel and start to undo the button on his pants, he swears, and I find myself lingering a little longer to see if I can make him do it again. The power of this position might get to my head if I'm not careful.

True to his nature, he doesn't disappoint, and just as I feel him move his hands to tug me up and take control. I free his hard length from his boxers. He really *does* like me on top.

Lucas groans audibly when I take the tip of him in my mouth. The taste coating my tongue as I give him a few exploratory passes, listening to his ragged breathing pick up when I find the tempo and pressure he likes.

I am no expert at this. Not by a long shot. And it has definitely been a while since I was even remotely interested in putting this kind of work into someone. But I have read enough romance novels that motions are almost intuitive. Lucky for me, despite being a sealed vault with his emotions, he is currently an open book, and I am reading every obvious breath, groan, and gasp.

His hand slides through the curtain of hair that falls around my face, and when he pushes it back to watch me, I meet his gaze dead on.

"Fuck, Maddie." His voice is throaty with lust and his fingers grip my roots, spurring me on to take him deeper.

When he tugs slightly, I moan at the friction and his hips jerk in response.

"Cupcake I'm getting close."

His words give me confidence and I narrow my eyes at the determined look on his face as I suck harder. His groan fills the quiet room before he grits out, "Fuck. I'm not going to last much longer." He tries to pull away, letting go of my head in the process, and giving me the option to stop. But that's not what I started this for. I dig my fingers into his hips and pull him closer, running my tongue along his slit. I swirl it before taking him all the way and putting everything I have into finishing him off.

I need him to let go. To let me take care of him. I need him to feel how much I want him.

Neither of us blink or look away from one another. The heat in his gaze is turning me on, and I know he can tell. So many emotions and feelings pass in our silent conversation. I hear his breathing stop a second before his release hits my tongue and his eyes finally close. The salty heat of it coating my mouth before I swallow it down and lick my lips.

Lucas pulls me up and kisses me passionately before either of us has a second to catch our breath. "Clothes. Off. Now." His commanding tone is laced with urgency. One I am happy to oblige.

Lucas is already basically naked, and kicks off his boxers that had landed somewhere around his ankles while I was on my knees. Taking over my attempts at ridding myself of my shirt, he yanks it over my head and pulls me down on top of him as he falls backward onto the bed.

I have no idea how he's ready again, but I'm not letting that stop us.

His chest rises and falls against mine as we both struggle to catch our breath.

The heat in his gaze tells me how much of a warm-up that was, but the tempo starts to change, and the look that passes over his face is anything but rushed and frantic.

Without taking his eyes off mine, he angles my leg and slides into me before he whispers, "You really are mine, Maddie. I meant every word. Body. Soul. Mind. Everything."

I can't find words that seem right enough to follow that. I give him back the only fitting response: I kiss him with everything I have as my hips begin to rock against his.

Our kisses and hands are laced with emotions and feelings that are too big for the moment, expressed in breathy pants that go in time with his hips as they thrust in steady beats. Hitting that spot that sends me climbing towards my release.

His hands find my chest as he expertly plays with my sensitive nipples. He squeezes harder until he pushes me over the edge. His breathing hitches again before he follows right behind me and I collapse against him, letting him hold me as we both come down from the physical and emotional high.

While his warm body holds mine, it surprises me that I don't feel the need to roll over or send him 'back to his side' of the bed, like I've always done with other men in the past. My fingertips just trail across his chest while his play in my hair. The content silence surrounds us like a warm blanket.

Before long, his breathing grows heavy and levels out as he drifts off, and I wonder what he dreams of as he sleeps. I read somewhere once that people will dream about what you tell them when they're sleeping, and the selfish part of me wants him to only think of me whether he's awake or asleep.

Without moving too much, I tip my face toward his ear and take a deep breath, knowing that even if I don't say it, I'm thinking it.

I inhale slowly before I finally do it. My lips stop a hair's breadth from his ear, I exhale slowly, "I'm pretty sure I love you, Lucas James." I look at him, checking to make sure he's still sleeping, hoping whatever he was dreaming of is replaced by me and what I just told him.

Laying my head down, I settle in and hope my own dreams are just as happy as I feel right now.

---

No one comments on the fact that Lucas is in his boxers when the boys come into the kitchen the next morning. And Hailey, outside of a silent snapped imaginary photo, leaves with a flippant wave over her shoulder and grumbles about the coffee not being good enough.

There was no discussion on spending the weekend together, we just did it. Lucas and Jasper fit in like they were always meant to be there.

I'm not sure how he managed it, but at some point, while I was getting ready to make pancakes, Lucas showered and got dressed, the scent of my bodywash wafting around him and fresh clothes on his body.

The batter sits in the bowl forgotten when the memory of his caramel-colored skin assaults my perfectly unsuspecting brain. I'm only brought back to the task when Lucas dips his finger into the messy bowl and pulls it out, licking a sweet dollop off the end. My cheeks heat further, and I set the whisk down so I can catch my breath.

I never realized how erotic my entire career is. Lucas could eat an eclair and my mouth would water. I let the image of him doing so fill my mind. How he'd lick the cream off his lips. Or maybe his thumb would wipe some glaze off and he'd offer it to me. Fuck, I should give him a donut.

I groan.

Me time thoughts do *not* belong in the kitchen making pancakes.... Unless they do and I've been doing it wrong all along?

Lucas's chuckle snaps me back and I look up from the pale batter to see him shaking his head with a devilish grin on his face.

"Care to share?" Just like in my sticky fantasy, his thumb slides along his firm bottom lip and he sucks it into his mouth with a raised eyebrow.

I groan even louder and start to take my now heightened sexual frustration out on the pancakes, knowing they are beyond overmixed and will be flat as all hell. But at least something will be deflated this morning.

The boys don't notice how flat the pancakes are. I, on the other hand, will never look at them the same way again. I decide I'm fine with that as I watch all three of the people at my table shovel them into their delighted, greedy mouths. The house is full and happy with Lucas and Jasper here, and I am floating on a cloud of whipped cream, hoping I can keep it like this forever.

After we clean up, the boys call for games and I'm happy to oblige. You don't truly know someone until you play Monopoly with them... but like the feelings in my heart that I can't quite verbalize, I know we've got to work up to those Monopoly moments.

The four of us settle on Uno, sitting in a circle on the living room floor, the old worn coffee table in the middle of us. Scattered cards cover most of its imperfections, and the soft glow of a Marvel movie plays on the television in the background. Every time it was one of the boys' turns, I'd look up and see Lucas making eyes at me, the deep pools leaving me caught up and embarrassed when I have to be reminded it is my turn for the fifth time. Luckily, both the boys are too caught up in the game to notice, or perhaps just too polite to comment.

It is funny to watch these two friends settle into whatever their relationship is becoming so easily. Neither of them asks us any uncomfortable questions, and given how much I am already reading into everything. I am beyond happy about it.

Jasper and Mikey were all for Lucas' suggestion that he teach us all to play poker, but being who I am, I was not about to admit that I don't want to lose to my ten-year-old the first time I play, so I said it is probably better if we play an 'age-appropriate' game, much to all three of their overly dramatic disappointment. Turns out Uno is plenty. They are all fiercely competitive, shouting out card combinations and cheering when they win a hand. Lucas included.

When the game becomes gang up on Maddie, I threaten to never bake another brownie and suddenly, would you look at that, I'm in the lead.

The afternoon turned into a blur of movies about superheroes, board games, and food. I learned things that you can only learn from living life with someone. Lucas hates mushrooms, Jasper likes ranch on his pizza, and Mikey has always wanted a sibling.

I don't know how I never thought about this before. When they boys start talking at dinner, pizza slices stacked on the paper plates in front of them, Jasper asks Mikey if he's ever had a bunk bed.

A bunk bed. Simple.

Easy life question.

Mikey, my sweet boy, replies, "No," which of course I knew, but he follows it up with, "I always wanted one." He pauses. Chewing his pizza, deep in thought. "Seems like the only way to share a room with a brother." My mouth hits the table.

Jasper, the sweet brown-haired angel he is, didn't bat an eyelash at this. Instead, he just responded like they talk about this sort of stuff daily, "Did you ever want a brother?" The conversation flows between the two of them like water, easy and at the whims of the directions they push it. "Oh yeah, always. Who wouldn't?"

I swear my mouth is so far open, I look like one of those clown attractions at the carnival. The ones where the clown's tongue is the entrance, and you have to walk into its mouth.

Lucas puts his hand on my leg, the touch causing my head to snap in his direction. Leaning forward, he whispers, "You're going to catch something if you leave your mouth open for too long."

The thought pings back and forth in my head the rest of the night. Along with a heavy feeling of regret. I can't shake the idea that I made this perfect kid miss out on something because I wasn't brave enough to move on.

Lucas was patient with me the rest of the night, clearly seeing that I had moved into my head after dinner, so when I spit out the thought that had been at the end of the tracks on every train tonight, he doesn't seem even a little surprised.

"Do you want more kids?" I blurt out. I don't mean to say it like I do. It just falls out of my mouth, not even sounding like a question, even though I mean it that way. It honestly sounds more like a demand.

He looks over at me as he pauses to think about it, his arms crossed over his chest, leaving me with a view I should probably be appreciating more, rather than inwardly spinning on things.

"I feel like we've talked about this already?" His words aren't harsh or mean. More confused.

"I know, we did. You're right. I just..."

I try not to think about how he'll react when I ask. Just spit it out, Maddie.

"Do you want them with me? Or would you...?" I feel like I've stepped in something unpleasant, and I can't take a step forward from the mess I just spit up.

Pushing his body off the wall, he towers over me and smiles with more emotion than I know what to do with.

"I would have a dozen kids with you if that's what you wanted."

He laughs before he adds on, "I'd hate sharing you with fourteen people, but if that's what you wanted, I'd happily do it."

I can't hold back the smile that fills my face. It stretches and stretches, and my cheeks start to hurt.

Leaning forward, he kisses me quickly before pulling back a little to look at my face. "Was that the right answer?"

"Oh, one hundred percent."

The boys come flying down the hallway with Jasper's bag in tow. Mikey and I watch Jasper and Lucas climb into his truck, and I can't help but feel like this was the best weekend of my life.

---

Kit wasn't joking when he said that Lucas would be the talk of the town. What he failed to mention was that I would be too. The bakery is busier than ever with rumors of all the drama, and despite the embarrassing reasons for it, I am welcoming the business and how busy it is keeping me.

As I clear off the tables in the front of the shop, my mind wanders back to the weekend, the one that came after what I am now referring to as 'Zach meets Lucas 2'. Well, at least in my head... I'd *never* call it that out loud to anyone else.

I'm so engrossed in my happy cloud of whipped cream that I barely notice the woman standing next to the table I'm cleaning until I almost run into her.

"So sorry," I mumble as I move to slide past her.

"You *really* don't know who I am?" I look her over and realize she that does look familiar, but I have no name to go with the face in front of me.

"I'm sorry, have we met?" Despite her snarky comment, my genuine confusion prevents me from being offended.

Her hand is propped on her hip, and I can't help the way I check out her toned body. She's covered head to toe in designer athletic wear, and her spotless white sneakers are practically glowing under the lights of the shop. My first conversation with Lucas comes to my mind as I stare at her shoes, I know whole-heartedly that she would never stoop low enough to play in the grass. Stains would ruin the carefully put together appearance. My eyes don't leave her feet when I see she's one of those women whose ankles look good at the bottom of leggings. Like the rest of her isn't enough? She has to have attractive ankles too? Brutal.

I give her the friendliest smile I can muster through my jealousy before she finally responds.

"I'm guess I'm not surprised. Lucas was never one to overshare with people who don't matter." Her words slap me across the face before I really register what she said.

Looking back over her, it finally hits me. Hits me, like a drink in the face. The dark hair. Big brown eyes. Just like Jasper.

Sherry.

I'm only slightly pissed that Lucas just *happened* to leave out the fact that she is stunning. Rude.

She must see the recognition in my face because her smile shifts and turns into effortless confidence. But I don't need a mean girl to ruin my good mood. Be above it, Maddie.

*Maddie: Fifteen. Why? Because it sounds like a lot.*

*World: Two. Mostly because of her ankles.*

"Did you need something?" I respond casually, ignoring her earlier jab before turning to wipe down the next table, and giving her my back. She walks around it, her annoyance flashing as she crosses her arms in a way that pushes her chest up and out of her sports bra.

*Maddie: I still say fifteen, but a fifteen with a B cup.*

*World: Three. Because she does not have a B cup.*

She fires her shots at me before I can walk away, or ask her to leave, or even build up a defense to not care.

"Lucas is not made for drama, and from what I hear, from what *everyone* hears, you have got a ton of it. What kind of man, with a kid, would want to bring that into their home?" Her judgy face looks me up and down, pausing on my dirty apron and messy ponytail. When she gets to my old Converse she just raises an eyebrow like my tried-and-true Chucks offend her somehow.

"I am still one hundred percent in Jasper's life, and I can tell you right now, no washed-up-leftover from a failed marriage is going to take my place in his life." She leans in and I flinch. "I know you're probably falling for him. Hard. Anyone would." Her eyes land on mine, and I know she still loves him by the rage that lives in that stare.

"Has he told you he loves you yet?" I try not to let her get to me. I try so unbelievably hard. When I don't respond, she nods. "Didn't think so."

Picking up her bag that I never even saw her put down, she flips her ponytail over her shoulder and finishes with, "He and I aren't done. He won't tell you what you want to hear, what you're dying to hear because the three of us are still a family. We always will be, and you have no place in it."

Without another glance back, she turns to leave, and I just watch her go, my dirty rag clutched to my disheveled, chubby-ankled chest.

A throat clears next to me, and I don't realize my eyes are full of unshed tears until I have to blink them away to see who it is.

Harley stands with his hands in his pockets, with his eyes on me. I don't know how much of that he heard, but judging by the look on his face, he heard enough of it to embarrass the hell out of me.

"Come sit with me." He turns and waves to Josie, who nods and starts making him a drink. Wow, I wonder how often he's in here?

He takes me around the corner from the front counter and pulls out a chair from a table in the far back. I wait for him to sit down before I realize he pulled it out for me. It faces the back wall of the shop rather than the front, and the thoughtfulness of that one thing makes me reach around and wrap him in a giant hug. He stiffens when my arms go around him, caging him a little but not caring even a bit. His trapped hand awkwardly pats my back before I let him go with a sniffle and sit down.

Leaving me, he grabs his coffee and a slice of coffee cake from the counter and comes back, setting them down while looking at me as I wipe my eyes on the bottom of my apron. It's odd. I'm usually very good at telling what desserts people will order, and I *never* would have pegged him for the coffee cake type. More like a standard croissant guy.

These small-town men seem to have all the patience in the world. He just sits there with me, not rushing me to talk about it, just letting me get to wherever I need to be before I start.

I stare at him. His tattoo-covered arms are unusually on display, and his hair is casually styled on the top of his head. Worn jeans and boots made up the rest of his casual, day-off look, and I admire how he can look put together in something that would make me look like a hobo.

He sips his coffee in silence, and I find myself wanting to tell him what is eating at me. Maybe because he doesn't insist that I *have* to? Who knows. Maybe it's just because of who he is.

"Why does she have to be so pretty?" The words are kind of

whinny, and it's embarrassing. He laughs at me, not even pretending to hold it in. He just does it.

I start to laugh too, because what else is there to do?

The mean girls in my high school were nicer than her and they at least had acne and bad hair days. I was somehow positive Sherry never did.

"She's not very nice, is she?" I make a face when I ask, and he shakes his head.

"No, she's not. Never has been, actually." He breaks off a piece of his coffee cake and tosses it into his mouth. Something about the coffee cake still bothers me, but I can't put my finger on it.

"You know," he says, between chewing, his jaw becoming more prominent as he does.

"Sherry was always the pretty girl in high school, but she was calculated. She picked Lucas because he was your standard jock. Captain of the football team, everyone liked him, good grades, letterman-jacket-wearing guy. I don't think he ever thought they would end up as anything more than a short term, high-school couple."

This all tracks with what Lucas has told me, but somehow doesn't make it better, because she is still very obviously in his life.

"For all her flaws, she's never pretended to be anything she isn't. What you undoubtedly faced today is exactly who she is; although, I imagine she turned it up a few notches because you intimidate her."

"What?!" I practically yell the words at him. How could I possibly wave a candle at all...well, all that. Let alone intimidate her into anything.

He just looks at me, his face blank as he munches away between sips of his coffee.

"The fact that you have no idea what I'm talking about is

part of what she could never be. The most important person to Sherry is, and will always be, Sherry. And deep down, she knows you can give Lucas things she never could."

I'm not entirely sure how to process this. I would never pretend that I didn't or couldn't use improvement. I mean who doesn't have flaws? But I also know what's important to me, and when to put other people's ahead of my own.

Harley looks toward the kitchen doors over my shoulder and I decide I'll ponder what he's thinking about later.

"You can let her get to you, or you can take what you and Lucas have and focus on that. Lucas is a good man, flawed like the rest of us, but Jasper is proof of his ability to love. I was kinda hoping that you would be proof that he is capable of getting that level of love and care back."

His words hit that dark corner inside me that wants to adopt all the kitties at the shelter or send money to those commercials about the dogs that need saving. They also hit that glowing part that had me whispering secrets in Lucas's ear in the middle of the night.

Not wanting to share my secrets with the world before I share them with the people who matter, I deflect.

"And what about you, Mr. Tattoo?" He doesn't comment on the obvious statement... or question? He really was asking something without directly asking. I shrug one shoulder and smile down into the rag I had abandoned on my lap.

Chuckling, he pushes his now-empty plate in front of him and drains the rest of his coffee.

"I guess we're all waiting for that kind of love, aren't we?" Standing up, he looks down at me with a knowing quirk of his face, telling me that I had already spilled the secrets I was trying to keep. My face said it all, even if the words never came out.

"Come by the bar soon. I've got a new drink for you to try."

I stare at his empty plate before the curiosity gets the better of me and I ask, "Why the coffee cake?" He pauses his steps and turns back with a shrug that mirrored my own just minutes ago, obvious and telling.

"Why not?"

I smile, wondering if I'm onto something, and I feel like he confirms when his eyes subtly glance at the kitchen door again.

"You know..." I say, pondering. "Not many people know that the coffee cake is the only thing in the shop that isn't made by me or Josie."

His face gives nothing away now. A mask slides into place. He lifts his wrist and fiddles with his watch. As Lucas would say, he's trying to hide his tells.

"I'll see you soon, Maddie. Maybe then we can talk about coffee cake, and feelings, and we can both get our questions answered."

My head tips down and I laugh, shaking my head at him.

I turn in my chair and watch him leave, my eyebrows raising in surprise when he grabs a to-go box from Josie at the front counter. He leaves without another glance back, and I have a feeling that if I wasn't there, he'd be looking back at that kitchen door again.

Grabbing my rag and his plate, I carry both behind the counter and wait for Josie to finish with the customer she is currently helping. When she finishes, my stoic baker turns to me impatiently, waiting for me to ask whatever it was I was rather impatiently waiting to discuss.

"What did he take to go?"

She seems surprised at my question, but goes back to moving things around in the display case, taking out empty trays and replacing them with full ones.

"The same thing he takes every day."

I wait for her to go on, knowing that if I ask again, she'll just get testy with me, even though it was she who didn't answer my question.

"He buys whatever coffee cake we have left whenever he comes in." She shrugs like this oddity is completely normal, and then looks confused when a huge, stupid smile breaks across my face.

I'll bet he does...

"Have you mentioned this to Hailey?" I say casually, trying to keep my cool even though I know for a fact my smile gives away far too much.

"No, but she's becoming increasingly irritated. She was so adamant that no one else make her recipe, and now she's having to make double batches every day. And before you say anything, I *have* continued to offer my help."

I pat her shoulder consolingly, causing her to stiffen. "I have no doubt."

Ohhhh, this is going to be so much fun.

# Chapter Twenty-Nine

## PUZZLE PIECES

### Lucas

I've dodged about a dozen of Sherry's calls and texts. She has been begging to come stop by the house, to come over for dinner, or meet for lunch. Honestly, she would have come grocery shopping with me if I'd let her.

Well, for her it was begging, for anyone else it would be insulting, but I am choosing to call it what it is.

I don't want to hear what she thinks she is entitled to say about my life. The reality is that there is nothing for her to give input on. She is entitled to say *nothing* about my life.

I know that she's heard about my visit to the station and has probably dug her manicured claws into whoever she could find to get any piece of real or imagined dirt on what happened. The fact that she is trying so hard means she thinks she has something she can use to control me, and that is a hard pass.

Too much thinking about Sherry leaves me missing Maddie. I pull out my phone, bringing up our most recent texts.

**Me: Coke or Pepsi?**

**Maddie: Iced tea…**

**Me: It doesn't count if you don't actually answer the question.**

**Me: I get to go again…**

**Maddie: lol that seems like a made-up rule**

**Maddie: But I'll allow it…**

**Me: City or small town?**

**Maddie: Which one are you in?**

She is good at this. Her playfulness constantly brings out my own, and I find myself itching to bring it out of her whenever she is around.

This morning is the last game of the season, and no matter what the outcome is, I am already proud as hell of these boys. They have grown so much over the last few months. But if today wasn't so pivotal for the kids, I would absolutely be spending my Saturday morning wrapped around Maddie's body.

Instead, I decide I'll just count down the hours until I can see her at the game.

---

My heart is heavy as I stand on the sidelines watching the team as they huddle together, the disappointment etched across their young faces breaks my heart. Especially after everything they put into the season. There is no way we are coming back from this game. We are down three touchdowns and have just under three minutes left to play.

The fact that we made it to the playoffs at all is something they should be proud of, but as the clock continues to run down, their posture and movements become more and more strained. The pang of defeat lingers in the air as the clock moved under one minute and the other team takes a knee. The final whistle blows, marking the end of a hard-fought game... and a hard-fought season. For everyone.

I rally myself as they trudge off the field, their hearts sinking. Fuck. I feel it too. I have poured hours of my time and energy into coaching these kids, nurturing their skills, and instilling them with a sense of confidence and teamwork. Losing is never easy, but witnessing these players' sadness is harder than losing myself.

So many of their friends and family line the edges of field, and even though it didn't surprise me, I still had to look twice when I saw Sherry on the sidelines.

Our team holds it together through the end-of-game line up, shaking hands with the other group of kids. The whole time I can't help but notice Pete off to the side, red-faced and full of rage, pacing his way through the grass, his hands holding onto the loops of his belt with a white- knuckled grip. But this is how it is every year. Whether we win or lose, Pete loses his shit. I almost wouldn't let Cash be on my team this year because of it, but what kind of asshole punishes a kid for his fathers' behavior? Pete seems to think, at the end of every game we lose, that the loss is solely my fault, blaming my play-calling, my coaching, my drills, whatever he can think of for the team's shortcomings.

With a heavy sigh, I decide it's better to cut him off at the pass before the kids get wind of it. Their already-struggling egos don't need to take another hit right now. His words spew at me when he sees me coming, but I am numb to the sting of his accusatory tone. "Hey, Pete, let's talk," I say calmly, cutting him off like he wasn't just swearing at me at a ten-year-old football game. Grabbing his shoulder, resting my thumb right below his collar bone, I squeeze, causing him to stop as I drag him off to the side away from the other parents. Tyler is managing the huddle, kneeling in front of the kids with his wide smile and calm, reassuring words. He has them, and it is on me to have this conversation with Pete.

Trying to remain calm, I give Pete one last squeeze before I lean in. Leveling him with weighted words, carried on an undertone of 'don't fuck with me.'

"I understand you're frustrated, but it's important to remember that these kids are ten. They played their hearts out, and second place is leaps and bounds from where we were last year."

Pete rears back, taking a deep breath like whatever he has to say will take up all the available air between us. I cut him off with another squeeze and go on, adding another level of venom to my tone. "The *main* focus here is not on winning, but on teaching these kids important values. Values like teamwork and sportsmanship. And from the looks of it, Pete, it seems like you could benefit from these values as well."

He pauses his rampage to look at me like I've lost my mind, completely taken aback by my composed response.

"They need to learn how to win, too!" he yells in my face, spit flying, his voice echoing across the now-silent field.

I look over at the parents and players, some of whom are openly staring at us. Maddie and Sherry included.

I nod, knowing my image in how this is handled is more important than ever. After last week, the last thing I can afford is to fucking fly off the handle at this man who so rightfully deserves it. I reposition us so he is facing the parents, and my back is to the silent crowd and prying eyes. "Cash is a good kid. Hell, he's talented and could actually play down the road on travel or high school teams if he's coached well..." I pause, knowing my praise of his son is the only thing keeping him quiet.

"But know this, I will ban you from *every* single game, practice, and team in the goddamn county if you keep carrying on like a petulant child." With that, I turn and leave him to the consequences of his actions and walk back toward the team, where they are huddled eating cookies.

"Listen up," I say as I reach them and kneel down on the grass, grabbing an offered cookie from between Mikey's fingers. "This game was rough. We had some bad fumbles and it got away from us. But one game does not define an entire season.

For me, as your coach, I want you to embrace the lessons you learn from defeat." These are big words, but they matter, and I want to make sure they are listening to the whole reason I do this. I make sure all of their eyes are on me, letting them chew through their emotions while they do so. "Setbacks are steppingstones toward growth. You're not always going to win in life, but if you can get through things like this, and be comfortable getting back up after you lose, I know you will always be successful in whatever game you have the opportunity to play." I put my hand in the center, making contact with every set of eyes around me.

Cash puts his hand on last, his eyes glossy but his mouth drawn in a firm line. Meeting my eyes, he says quietly, "To playing the game." The entire team yells it back and emotion chokes me.

Hanging my head while I put myself back together, I don't rise up until everyone is gone, running back to their parents with far more life than when they left the field moments ago.

I make my way over to where the parents are gathered, and I see Sherry off to one side and Maddie on the other.

As soon as I'm in front of Maddie, her face makes my steps falter. She looks upset and I internally want to strangle myself for even talking to Pete. I should have let Tyler handle it. I should have just sent him home. I should have done a million things. I can only imagine how much that would trigger her after last week. I reach out to grab her, wanting to make it right, but she pulls back and my heart plummets.

"I can't right now, Lucas." Her gaze falls to the ground, and she shakes her head while she tucks that perpetual flyaway strand behind her ear.

Her eyes widen and turn glassy, and I know deep down that everything suddenly got worse, but I don't fully know why.

She moves to leave, and I grasp her arm, pressing my body to her side. I can smell her this close, and it fills the spaces left from the chaotic emotions of today. "Please...don't. You can't keep running. Please tell me what's wrong."

Her head just shakes at me, and she walks away, but not before I see tears falling down her cheeks.

I hear Sherry call my name before I can run after Maddie, calling my attention over to where she and a group of other parents are waving me over.

Jesus, Lucas. Get your shit together.

Knowing I can't get out of here before I talk to these people, I hurry over and try to get it over with quickly.

Halfway through the seemingly endless conversations that just go on and on, Sherry pipes in and offers to take Jasper home. I nod and let them leave since I'm clearly stuck here saying the same three things over and over. 'Yeah, what a season' and 'Next year is our year', followed by 'the kids played so well.'

It's another twenty minutes before I get out of the parent conversations, and another ten to pack everything up and get to my truck. The second I'm buckled in, I call Maddie, swearing when she doesn't answer, half tempted to drive to her place, or the shop since I know Saturday afternoons are busy for her. The thought that Sherry is at my house without me has me heading that way instead.

I shoot Maddie a text as I begin my mindless route home.

**Me: Please, call me. I couldn't let Pete get away with that in front of the kids.**

When I walk through the front door, I'm not surprised to see Sherry on my couch, her feet curled under her and her loose sweater hanging off one shoulder. This is exactly what I was worried I'd walk in on. Her acting like my house is *home* to her. She takes the phrase 'make yourself at home' far too literally, and considering I've never said those words to her, the sight in front of me is even more outrageous.

She looks up at me through her thick lashes and painted

face. "I'm so happy you're home," she says sweetly, standing and making her way over to me.

I take a step backwards when she does. "Thanks for bringing Jasper back." I turn and open the door in an obvious dismissal.

Her responding laugh is airy and completely in denial of my demand that she leaves. It pisses me off.

"I was actually hoping we could talk." She leans on the back of the couch instead of getting her things, and I shut the door, not wanting nosey neighbors to hear this when I don't even want to participate.

"I don't have anything to talk to you about, Sher." Cold. The words are cold. The tone says, 'not fucking interested'. And the look on my face says don't fucking go there.

She ignores it all.

"Lucas, I'm just going to say it, because we've beat around things so many times in our relationship..."

I cut her off fast. "We do not have a relationship."

She sighs like I'm tiring her while she stares at me for a long minute. Maybe the longest stare of my life. Or the most torturous one, at least.

"We could, you know."

I respond with an eye roll that is so complete it leaves my head hurting.

"Lucas, we have both grown up so much since everything happened. We were so good together, we just needed to live some life separately... and we have."

"Sherry, I told you last time you were here, but I'll gladly tell you again. I'm with someone else now. I've moved on."

She shakes her head like I'm a juvenile child and not a grown man who can make his own decisions.

"That's fine, spend your time with her. Get it out of your system. I had to do the same thing." She waves her hand through the air, passing my comment off as a big fat nothing.

"This is not a fling or something to get out of my system. I'm in love with her. Jasper loves her. She's not going anywhere."

Her face falls as soon as the 'L' word leaves my mouth and she eyes the door, her hands fidgeting in her lap. The difference between that and the confident stance she had moments ago causes my heart to thump.

I immediately think of Maddie, and I realize her response after the game probably had nothing to do with me confronting Pete.

"Sherry, what did you do?"

"Nothing." She spits her answer out before I finish asking. I've dealt with the guilty version of this woman more times than any man should, so I know exactly what this is. "Sherry." My growl makes her jump, and her defenses rise.

"I thought she was a fling, Lucas!" Her fight is back. This woman is a roller coaster, and I am finally getting off the ride.

"What did you do?" I ask one more time, knowing that I can't ask the question any differently in the state I'm in—one-track minded with frustration burning through me.

When she still remains silent, I press on. "You look guilty as all hell, and we both know what you're capable of." My words sting, and they were meant to. She obviously came ready for a fight.

Her words fly out. "I heard all about the shit from last week. Everyone in town is talking about it, Lucas. It was mortifying, hearing them talk about you with another girl. Standing up for her like you never did for me. So... I went to find her. To introduce myself."

I have no thoughts in my head as she spills it all, the puzzle pieces quickly falling into place.

"I told her that at the end of the day, your focus has always been your family and we..." she gestures between us. "We're family. We always will be."

"You talked to her at the game..." It's the only thing that makes sense. I tried so hard to handle Pete quietly, the way I should. Now that she's laid all this bare, there is no way my conversation with him was what upset Maddie.

Sherry looks appropriately embarrassed, and I take it as a sign that there's still a semblance of a soul left in her selfish body.

"Sherry, if there is any hope for me not hating you for the rest of our lives, it hangs in this one moment. What. Did. You. Do?"

I can see the shift in when she finally registers that our relationship is over. She nods before she drops the bomb that I realize already exploded in my face.

"I may have gone to the bakery the other day and mentioned that you and I were going to be together in the long run." Guilt bleeds through her words as she adds on "When I saw her at the game, I told her you invited me. That you loved Jasper... and *our* family." She picks up her bag and starts to walk toward the door. "Lucas, I'm not sorry I tried. I might have fucked us up, but I still want a happily ever after. It's a shame that it won't be with you." When she reaches me, she places a small kiss on my cheek, one that finally feels like goodbye.

I let her open the door beside me, numbed by the events of the day, frustrated that I keep messing things up, and only slightly hopeful that I still have time to fix it.

Surprising me—and the rest of the universe—Sherry gives me a piece of that hope back. While she's halfway out the door, she says quietly, "It's easy to fall for you, Lucas, trust me. I owe you at least one truth after all we've been through. It hurts me to say it, but she loves you, Lucas. She loves you, the way you love other people. Completely." She looks away and doesn't meet my eyes when she closes the door without another word.

I suddenly realize that there is somewhere else I need to be, but I have one stop to make on my way there.

# Chapter Thirty

## EXPLOSIVES

### Maddie

There are plenty of things I *should* be doing. Actually...there are a *million* things I should be doing. But I'm not doing a single one of them. No, I am sitting in the back office. Face down, on a desk. My face is covered in sticky tears, causing the stack of receipts I am lying on to glue themselves to my cheeks. I could not care less. I am a mess, what does it matter if I look like one too?

I can't hate her. Not really. She is a mother. A protector... and as judgy as I want to be about her methods, I can respect her for it. I don't have to respect her bounce-back, pre-baby body or her dumb ankles. Those I will let myself be petty about for the remainder of my days. But not the rest. I can see where she was coming from when it comes to her kid. And her family.

When Sherry came up to me at the game, I was hoping it was to at least pretend to like me or to support me and Lucas. You know, maybe you *think*, 'I hate your face.' But, you say and *act* like, 'You, fellow sister, have my respect for being a woman.'

That, however, is not what happened.

No. She walked up all tight and put together while casually dropping that Lucas 'really *wanted* me here' and that they were 'celebrating as a family after.' Basically... 'hi, lesser human...' stab, stab, stab.

I swear I missed the second half of the game because I was too busy watching her. How she held herself, how she talked to other people, the whole time comparing her to how I do those same things. Suddenly I realized exactly how bad my posture is, and that no matter what set of leggings I wear, I will never look like she did in them. And that my shoes aren't as crisp.

*Maddie: Minus seven... one for each day of the week*

*World: Nine. One for each day of the week, plus two for her damn ankles.*

I hate how I feel about myself right now. My dramatics are high, my self-esteem is low, and I currently felt like two-day-old brownie batter stuck to the bottom of a forgotten bowl. Solid, useless, and looking a little like crap.

It's not that everything about today was awful. Honestly, outside of the Sherry thing, I know exactly what pushed this pity party over the edge. It hurt when he told me I couldn't keep running. Like that's what I do... run from my problems. It hurts worse than it should because we both know that's exactly what I have done.

Until lately, it was the only thing I knew how to do. So that's what I did.

It is an icy cold realization that the bravest thing I have ever done is run from Zach. Or it was, up until I stood up to him in that back alleyway... the same alley I have avoided like the plague since it happened. I'm not even sure who has been taking out the trash lately, but it sure as hell isn't me.

I'm terrified that I'm a placeholder for Lucas when all I want is to be the real deal. I can see his face when I close my eyes. The warm depths of his smile, the constantly out-of-place hair that flops like it's intentional. His tanned skin that I can't look at without thinking of caramel.

This is the exact problem. My life has been on this one-way track of living it the best I can, and now here I am. Faced with this man, who walked into my world with so little effort, and now he has me comparing something I've been making for a decade to him, and not the other way around. I'll never be able to make caramel again if... if Sherry is right. All I'd see if I do is him.

Imagine that...like, sorry, people, this bakery steers clear of caramel. And all men with warm eyes and a sense of humor.

Is this the switch you look for when you try to decide what someone means to you? Your life reminds you of them and not the other way around? Not that I am trying to delude myself. I'm totally over the moon about him.

I am entirely and wholeheartedly in love with Lucas James.

I groan to myself and internally wish I had grabbed something from the display cabinet before I came back here. I could use some emotionally soothing treats, but there is no going back out there now.

Mikey is out there chilling with Hailey. Josie is running the shop, like a well-buttered cake pan. Lucas is, hopefully not... but probably riding toward happily ever after with Sherry, like I want to be. So, I am just going to sit here and wallow, like it is my new full-time job.

My phone rings, and I raise my face off my desk to answer it, peeling damp yellow papers off my cheeks as I do so.

"Hey, honey." My mom's sweet songbird voice calls from the other side.

"Oh, hi, Mom."

"It's nice to hear that you are... in fact, alive and well, Maddie Pie." The tsking tone she used to chide me with as a child makes me smile now, wrapping me in nostalgic comfort.

"I'm sorry. I know I'm terrible about calling."

"That's fine, sweetie. That's why we have your sister." She's joking, but also not at the same time. No one could spill secrets like Hailey, and she is always the first person to out you for your shit... if you have shit that needs to be outed. Which I apparently do.

I laugh and say, "What do you want to know?" Trying my best to get the point, so my self–abasement can continue in peace.

"Well, honey... there are just *so* many options." It's just like her to leave it at that and not press or do anything specific but imply that there is something *I* am not telling her. Her silence always makes me want to fill it with words so that she doesn't fill it with presumptions that are often far worse than what actually happened. This time that might not be the case, though.

I shake my head and start at the beginning, the real beginning. The one that started years ago. The one that she had seen, but that I'd never admitted to. By the time I get to what happened after the game today and my current position-—both figurative and literal—we're both sniffling.

She's quiet on the other end, and I pull the phone back to make sure the call didn't get disconnected.

"I am so proud of you, honey." She clears her throat, and that usual bell-like voice sounds raw and unused. "I've seen a lot of women go through things like this, and I will tell you what I have told every single one of them." Her pause fills the room, even though she can only be heard through the small speaker on my phone. "You are not defined by or made of the things that *happen* to you." Her words are like a shot into my heart.

"You are made into who you are each time you get back up when the forces in the world try to push you down, each time you pick *you* over the pain. No matter where you go in life or what *happens* to you, the only person who can change who you are, is you."

There are slow tears inching down my cheeks. I knew that her work over the years has shown her some of the darkest parts of the world. Her words are so powerful and so true they leave an imprint on my soul. Tattooed on my brain and stamped on my heart. I know I'll never forget them.

She goes on, letting me have my thoughts and my silence. "You deserve to be happy, Maddie. Happy and loved. Both you and Mikey. Never settle for less than that, sweetie. Never."

"Mom. I love you. So, so much."

"I love you too, sweetie. Let's plan a visit soon. It sounds like you'll be staying there for a while, and it's probably time for me to come see it, you, and my grandson in person." The 'it' in that sentence being a man and not the charming town. My mind immediately goes to all the places I should take her. There's so much about this town I have come to love, and I wanted her to see all the best parts of it. And the man who is undoubtably keeping me here.

"That sounds great, Mom."

I hang up, put my phone on the desk and stare at the wall, lost in my thoughts and the weight of the words my mom has left me with.

The door behind me opens, and Hailey pops her head around it, followed by Mikey right behind her. They look like a scene out of a comic book or a movie with the door barely open and just their heads floating inside it.

When the tears in my eyes register on both of their faces, the two people closest to me come flying in, wrapping me in loving arms and a wild tangle of hair.

"Mom, why are you crying?"

"Well," I mumble against his hair, pressing a kiss to the top of it. "Technically I just *finished* crying."

Hailey pulls back and rolls her eyes at me while she leans against one side of the desk.

"Pointing out semantics isn't sexy," she quips, tucking her long brown hair behind her ears and giving me her signature look of full sass.

"Gross, Auntie Hails... also, what are semantics?" Mikey

says from below both of us.

"Excellent question, Mikey. Two points for asking." Her praise causes him to pull out of my arms and lean on the desk next to me, almost mirroring his crazy aunt's positioning. He shifts uncomfortably since his height doesn't give him the same resting point, but he stays there nonetheless.

"Semantics are *useless* specifics, used by people who are trying not to explain themselves..." she levels me with a pointed stare, and I can't help but laugh at her. Leaving the chuckle as my only answer, I rub some of the tears from my face and fire back, making sure I have her full sisterly attention before I do.

"We should really be talking about your terrible habit of tattling... to Mom."

Her face fills with a pained look full of guilt. I let her wallow in it especially when Mikey chimes in with a 'burrrrrn.' He is used to our banter, and I am happy that we grew up so close. I couldn't have done the last few years without her, and I wouldn't have wanted to.

Mikey lifts his body onto the table so he's sitting on top of it and looks down at me, now taller in his new position.

"Are you sad because you love Lucas, but Jasper's mom came to the game?"

Hailey's mouth falls open with a surprised gasp, and I just stare at this horribly observant child of mine, whom I want to hug and kiss until he begs me to stop.

"What would you think if I said yes?"

He smiles back at me before saying with a grin, "That I knew it! Lucas is really cool, and Jasper says he really likes you. Do you think he loves you too?"

"Okay, now, Mikey..." Hails says saving me from the torture of my ten-year-old's honesty and curiosity.

'No, wait!" he says, sliding away from her when she goes to reach for his shoulders to guide him out of the room. "Listen! This is important, I promise." She lets up and raises her hands in surrender. "Don't be mad at me for saying this, but I've always known Dad was a bad guy...but Lucas isn't." He's staring at me with so much intensity, and I don't want to look away.

"Oh, honey."

"It's okay, Mom. Really. I'm good. I'm happy." He bites the edge of his bottom lip, thinking his thoughts through for the first time since he walked in.

"Ugh, just spit it out, kid," Hails says, putting us both out of our misery.

"Don't you want to be with him?" he blurts. "Like if you love him, don't you want to be with him?"

"Of course, I do." I try to put how I feel into words that won't make him grow up too fast, or worse, grow up jaded.

"It's just...it's not just me I have to worry about." I put my hand on his leg and squeeze it.

He shakes his head at me, the motion somewhere between chiding and slightly disappointed in my answer. I catch Hailey's eyes and shrug at the same time she does, both of us wondering where he got his maturity from. "Mom, if you love him and he makes you happy, that's all I could ever want."

Hailey cracks before I do and pulls us both into another group hug.

Looking at Mikey, she says, "Little man, if I ever find love, promise me you'll point it out to me too if I don't notice?"

He smiles at her. "Auntie Hails, I have a feeling he'd have to drop a bomb for you to notice, but don't worry, I'll help."

I laugh to myself at his joke, not wanting to give him any ideas. Hailey, on the other hand, laughs out loud, encouraging the naughty behavior.

"For the love of all things, could both of you please stay away from explosives."

"Sure, Mom, anything you say." He gives me a wink.

I see them high five out of the corner of my eye and decide I'll worry about that another day.

# Chapter Thirty-One

## GIFT BAGS

### Lucas

I stand outside the shop just like I did the night of the opening.

One hand in my pocket, and one gripping a bunch of flowers. Flowers that I tortured the florist with while she was making them. Again, just like the night of the opening. I wanted them exactly right. At least this time she knew what to expect and charged me extra for the 'work'. But it doesn't bother me. They are perfect.

I've watched people trickle out of the shop and stared like a creep while Josie started the process of closing up. The sun is just starting to set when she *finally* turns the open sign to 'closed', grabs her bag and leaves. I wave to her as she walks to her car, but she seems more interested in leaving than she is in why I am standing outside instead of going in.

I see Maddie move about through the front windows as she leaves the kitchen, the metal door swinging closed behind her. That kitchen has been a repeated location for my fantasies since the afternoon we spent in it, and I am eagerly hoping for a repeat in the near future.

Hitting the lights as she goes, I can't help but admire Maddie in the lone glow of the neon sign behind the counter. The way the light bounces off her hair turns it a light shade of pink, and I find myself loving that she always leaves that one on.

She finally makes her way to the door, and I meet her eyes through the glass. Her smile is shy and questioning, but I don't move. I want to do this out here, where I first asked her out.

I had a ton of time today to figure out how I wanted this to go and what I wanted to say. With how out of control I feel about my emotions, knowing that I can control these small things makes me feel a little better.

She opens the door and steps out, walking toward me. She's beautiful. With her light hair and freckled nose. I love how simply she accepts her beauty, not changing the way she looks with makeup or overdoing her hair, just accentuating it. It's one of the million-and-one things that hooked me.

"Fancy seeing you here, James." She chooses the same words from the night I asked her out, and the fact that she knows what I'm doing is another reason I feel the way I do about her.

I run my empty hand through my hair to calm my nerves. Who would have thought that I'd have such obvious tells?

I'm so certain of what I have to say—nerves aside, that there is no turning back. "Maddie," I begin, my voice steady, but filled with an unmistakable level of vulnerability. She doesn't let me go on, cutting me off.

"Lucas, I am so sorry." Her lip goes between her teeth in thought before she adds, "I just got so wrapped up in my head and what I thought you wanted, and what I thought of myself, that I let appearances seem more truthful than actions. I should have talked to you. I should have told your ex to take her drama elsewhere...I should have told you what I was feeling. But first, why the heck did you leave out the fact that she has a completely photoshopped body? Very rude of you, James." Her love-filled gaze turns to a glare at the last part, and I shake my head with a quiet smile.

"Wrapping paper will never make a present better than it is." I sound like a fortune cookie, but I don't care.

"Spoken like someone who uses gift bags." Her eyes go comically wide before she says, "You're a gift bag present wrapper, aren't you? Are all our Christmas presents are going to be under the tree in gift bags and tissue paper? That might be a hard line for me, James." She's obviously joking, but I make a note to watch as many tutorials as I can on the subject of wrapping gifts as soon as she's distracted.

Part of what she just said sticks with me though. "Are we going to be spending a lot of Christmases together?" I try to make the words sound confident and not vulnerable, but when her expression turns curious and emotion flickers in her eyes, I know I've failed.

"Lucas, I plan on spending as many holidays as I can with you. Get ready for National Donut Day."

"I'm pretty sure you'd celebrate that one without me anyway," I remark, my eyes going pointedly to the shop and its pink glow behind her.

"Okay, fine, National Goat Day will also be an annual tradition that we add to the calendar."

I love her banter with me. The fact that she's turned this whole argument and fight into something light and easy is part of what makes her so unique.

I take a step closer, my fingers tightening around the stems of the flowers and drawing in a deep breath. "Cupcake, I was so confused earlier and I didn't know where things went off..." She opens her mouth to speak, and I hold up my hand not wanting to wait a second longer to say what I'm trying to get to.

"Sherry told me," I explain, and her eyes narrow at the mention of my ex, leaving me openly laughing. I had a feeling that was going to be a sore subject for a bit.

"Don't worry, she left right after." My words are placating and appease the glare...for now.

I take another step closer. "I realized at some point over the last few days...maybe weeks? I don't actually remember when it was suddenly different, but at some point, it hit me that there isn't anything or anyone I wouldn't fight, or take on, or do for you." I'm rambling and I'm a little frustrated that I'm messing this up.

*Come on, James.*

"Whenever it happened, I realized that my problems in relationships haven't come from my inability to love or be loved. It came from my never having found the person I was meant to love the way I love you."

Her eyes go wide, and she smiles at me, one that will forever be branded on my mind.

"I love you, Maddie. I love you today, and tomorrow, and on Christmas, and on National Donut Day, and National Goat Day too."

She has happy tears, and I cross the last few steps between us to wipe one away as it falls. Holding her face in my hand, I tilt her head up toward mine.

She swallows and whispers, "I love you too, Lucas."

Leaning down, I kiss her to show her all the ways I truly love her in this one moment. She pulls back and looks up at me, her eyes catching on my lips before they land on my eyes.

"I'm scared." Her words, so full of honesty, cause her whisper to catch, and I can't take it. I kiss her again, hoping to take the fear away with it.

The corners of her lips turn up against mine, knowing what I'm doing without even seeing the look in my eyes. "I've got you, Cupcake, and together we can get through anything."

"How do you know we're going to make it?" she whispers between kisses. "That we aren't going to just keep repeating the mistakes from before?"

I pull back so she can see all of my face and not just my mouth when I tell her the most important thing, I think I might ever say. "Maddie, relationships aren't built on what you do when everything is perfect or easy, they are built on how you handle things when they aren't."

She doesn't blink or move at my words.

"We, luckily or unluckily, have gone through some rough moments already, and through each and every one of them, there's not a thing I would change about you. Not a single thing about you or your life that I don't love." I drop the flowers to the ground and grasp both sides of her face in my hands. "If you were perfect in our worst moments, I can't wait to see you at our best." I pull my face to hers and kiss her. I kiss her like she's the oxygen I need to breathe. I kiss her like she's what keeps my heart beating. I kiss her like the world depends on it. When her body melts into mine, I realize that she is every one of those things and more.

Our relationship might not have been wrapped in a pretty bow until now, but no matter how we package it, it is everything I never knew I wanted and then some.

No gift bags required.

# Epilogue

## Maddie

"Run!" I scream at the top of my lungs, surprising both Pete and I at how loud I am. The boys take off down the field at a sprint, one of them clutching the ball under his arm, surrounded by the other members of the team as they break away from the defensive line and race toward the end zone. My heart is in my throat, and I hear the other parents around me hollering and cheering them on.

The other team is hot on their tails, and I watch the not-so-little legs of these ever-growing kids push harder as they near the end of the field. This game has been a close one, and seeing how excited everyone has been to get the season started, it is the perfect beginning. Not to mention the fact that the boys have been pushing to practice with Lucas for months. They started getting ready for this season earlier since they now have each other to play with all the time.

The second the ball crosses over the white line at the end of the field, the sidelines go wild with cheers.

I turn and high five Pete, his face still beet red from screaming. His wife is behind us shaking her head at our 'antics' as she calls them, but as usual we ignore her and scream anyway. The folding chairs Hailey and I are perched on creak as we bounce up and down clapping. She was almost as excited as I was to come to this game, even though I know that sports are definitely not her thing.

Looking over at her, my heart fills with gratitude and emotion when I see that her smile is as big as mine. I was a little shocked, but equally happy, at how many of our friends came out for the boys' opening game of the season. Harley, Kit, and Damian are all here. Surprisingly, Chase showed up on time. Heck, Sunny even took time off from the diner to come. I know Lucas says it isn't the most important thing, but the fact that the boys are winning really makes the whole experience that much more special.

I glance across the field and find Lucas standing with the team. His head raises and his eyes find mine like he can feel them on his skin. Knowing him, he probably can.

That man still sees everything, even after a year with him it still surprises me. He smiles at me from the end zone, our stare holding a little longer than is probably appropriate, but it's never bothered me before, and it doesn't bother me now. Through his gaze I can see him say, "I love you, Cupcake." I smile back with a wink, saying, 'I love you too."

Turning back to the boys, he crouches down in the middle of all of them, and I can't hold in my happiness that this is my life. That I have these boys and that man. That I'm surrounded by my closest friends with no worries in sight. It's crazy what can change in a year.

This time last year, Mikey and I were coming for his first practice, scared and alone in a new town with nothing but each other.

The boys break away with a yell and line up for the final play. Their helmets shine in the early fall sun. The weather hasn't turned yet, and we've been soaking up the last of the sunny days while we spend our weekends at the beach and with the boys, playing catch or having picnics.

Lucas and I are so good. Jasper and Mikey are getting along great with our little blended family. We've even made it through a few Sherry dinners without any drama. It sounds like she's been seeing someone, and it's created a much healthier dynamic between her and Lucas. I haven't heard from Zach outside of one email months ago where he told me he was getting help, and though I'd never admit it to anyone but myself, not having that constant stress in my life has made a huge difference. I don't even cringe when my phone rings anymore.

The whistle blows, and our team sends the ball off one last time. I'm pretty sure all they have to do is make sure the other team can't run the ball back and score. We all watch as our defense tackles the other team's runner before he can even get going. When the final whistle blows, our entire sideline breaks out in cheers. Hailey and I cheer the loudest. Obviously.

I turn to Hailey, and she gives me a smile that makes me do a double-take. It is without a doubt her 'I've got a secret' smile. Which I, of all people, would know anywhere. Her hands raise up to her face, holding her invisible camera. Lately, whenever she does this, I find myself doing the same right back because anything she wants to remember is worth remembering. She takes her *picture* with a soft 'click, click' and I smile back at her with a questioning eyebrow. Shaking her head, she nods to the other side of me, and I turn to around to a sea of people I had no idea were all looking at me.

Mikey and Jasper are both standing on the sideline of the field, hands behind their backs. Helmets off and sweaty hair plastered all over their foreheads. All of our friends and family are standing behind them, and every single face in the crowd in front of me is smiling. I'm more than a little surprised to see that everyone moved to one spot, much less that they are all staring at me like I'm about to give a speech. But I don't get a second to ask the boys what I am missing because they pull their hands out from behind their backs, and they both reach to hand me something.

Mikey hands me the game ball, and Jasper passes me a bunch of picture-perfect wildflowers. The ones Lucas has taken to giving me since our first date. I take them with a smile and hear a throat clear behind me.

Turning around, to where Hailey was just standing, I see Lucas on one knee, a ring in his hand and a look on his face that I will never forget for as long as I live.

"Maddie," he starts, pausing to clear his throat one last time. "I never thought that I would find someone I could love the way I love you. You are everything bright and wonderful in my world. My life started over when I met you." His eyes mist with tears that we both know he'd never let fall and I choke back a sob when he takes my left hand in his.

"I stumbled across you a year ago today, on this very field, and since that moment you've changed everything for me. You showed me I could love again... and oh, how I love you. I want to show you and Mikey just how much every day for the rest of our lives." I feel the tears falling down my face and can hear the chuckles and sniffles from our friends and family behind me.

"Will you marry me?" There is so much emotion in those four words, and I'm nodding yes even before he finishes. When he does, a laugh leaves him as he takes out the ring and slides it onto my finger.

He stands up and pulls me to him as cheers go off behind us. I can hear Mikey and Jasper above them all, whooping and hollering, and it makes the moment even more perfect.

"I'm still going to need a verbal answer," Lucas says into my hair with a chuckle.

"Yes! A million times, yes," I call out through the tears and emotions filling my chest, making the laughter behind us start up again.

He pulls me back and looks down into my eyes.

"I love you, Cupcake." His voice is gruff and full of emotion as he presses a kiss into my mouth. Jasper and Mikey join in on our hug, and I kiss both of them on the tops of their sweaty heads.

Looking down at the ring on my finger, I grin at how perfect it is. The emerald solitaire sparkles brightly on a dainty halo band. Of course, Lucas would pick something so perfect. "How did you two keep this from me?" I say to the boys nestled in our arms.

"Oh, they almost gave it away more times than I can count. The day we all went to pick the ring, I swore I was going to have to change tactics and propose that night!" Lucas replies for them with a laugh.

The grin on Mikey's face is comical. "Why do you think we asked for SpaghettiOs so often?" he says.

"Or kept trying to get Ring Pops at the grocery store?" Jasper adds.

"I think the worst was when the two of you suggested we watch *The Ring* and *The Proposal* back-to-back," Lucas supplies, looking pained at the memory.

I laugh at that one because I was beyond confused that night and I remember it vividly. I made Lucas look at what they were watching on their iPads just in case.

I squeeze them tight before they run off to talk to the rest of the people waiting for us.

"There's no going back now, Cupcake." Lucas says, inspecting my hand. "You're officially mine forever."

"I'm pretty sure it's not legal until after the wedding," I say back with a grin. It's clear he does not like that, and he raises his eyebrow at me in that way he does when I know I'm asking for it.

I turn and look up at him through my lashes. "I'm yours, with or without a ring, James." "Forever..." he says back with a smile. "And always," I reply, before kissing him, just like I plan to do for the rest of our lives.

The End

# Acknowledgements

There is no real way to correctly or adequately give thanks to all the people who helped me through this process. And while an attempt is a thoughtful gesture, the people who have encouraged and inspired me know who they are and just how much I love them.

That being said. Their love and support deserve at least an effort.

First and foremost, my husband is and always has been my biggest supporter. The number of things I have heard him tell someone I am 'incredible' at are comical and straight-up lies. But the fact that he believes it each and every time makes me brave enough to try. As if his perpetual praise wasn't enough, the poor guy has spent the last decade being incessantly teased over a 'romantic' email I *accidentally* sent to another 'Matt' at the office, and he has never once been anything but proud of my *poetic* composition. While my initial attempts at writing said 'romantic' email were half-hearted and juvenile, it truly does paint the perfect picture of how dedicated and supportive he has been of anything I do.

When it came down to my terrible usage of tenses, my jokes that fell flat, and my lowest lows he was there to talk me through them and help me pick myself back up. Just like he does whenever I need it. Matt. You are the love of my life and my best friend. There will always be a bit of you in the love stories I tell because you've given me the kind of love worth writing about.

To my kids. My beautiful, smart, little hurricanes. You all are the reasons I do everything I do. Thank you for filling in all the corners of my heart and soul. I hope you find the kind of love you can read about in books or even better, the kind your dad and I have.

My family has listened to lots of 'ideas' and artistic ventures that I have had over the years and they have all been supportive of every single one. This was no exception. Thank you all for asking for updates, telling people about it, and even reading it (as embarrassing as that is and will be.)

Lyns, you really are my best friend and that will always be true. Thank you for giving me a brood of redheaded nephews to love and my 6-ft 2" chicken-loving whim twin. Speaking of... Cru, you might have been the first person to have read any of this. You were far more encouraging and enthusiastic than you should have been, and I love you for it. This wouldn't be here without that little boost of encouragement.

Through my love of romance and reading I found my very own family of friends. These girls are something special and unless you know them and get to see them the way I do you are missing out.

Kaymie. What in the world would I do without you? I would have deleted 90% of this book and never finished it, and that's the best-case scenario. Thank you for late late-night text talk downs. For early morning brainstorming and for showing me that we can laugh through the tears that these characters of ours put us through. Please don't get eaten by a giant spider before I convince you to move back home.

Syd, Steph, and Sav... I don't know what your mama put into making you three but there is something special about all of you. You guys are somehow the life of the party, the devils on my shoulder in Mexico, my responsible friends, epic mama figures, and the angels guiding me through tough conversations. Being in the orbit of all that you guys do makes me a better person.

Britt, you're a real-life Snow White, the nicest person in the world, and the most supportive sounding board. I can't wait to read your stories and give you back all the love and support you've given me.

Tracy, thanks for the tips... you know EXACTLY which ones I mean.

Thank you to both my editor, Elaine, and designer Kari. Elaine, you somehow mastered the skill of pointing out my (very obvious) mistakes without making me feel like a failure before I ever got going. Kari, I don't know how you did it with such ease, but you made making my perfect cover look effortless.

Lastly, thank you to my characters. We had a lot of ups and downs over the last year. Lucas and Maddie, you both had stories to tell, and I did my best to listen. To the rest of you...don't worry, I'm coming for you.

Love,
Britt

# About the Author

An ever-evolving artist and a true hopeless romantic, Britt is thrilled to share her first novel with the world.

Since she started making New Year's Resolutions in High School, completing and publishing a novel has been on every single list.

Ironically, between working full-time and being a mom of four, Britt finally achieved this goal when she found herself busier in life than ever. As it goes, inspiration struck and she couldn't wait any longer to put the stories in her head to pen and paper (or rather a keyboard and screen).

Britt's hope is to continue to share stories that will make you laugh, cry, and smile, all while giving you a chance to share in her characters' intimate moments, obsess over their quirks and imperfections, and embrace the challenges they overcome to find love and happiness.

Britt is a coffee lover, an 80s action-movies and rom-com fanatic, married to her best friend, and still always finds time to read as many books as she can get her hands on.

Made in the USA
Las Vegas, NV
03 April 2024

88166737R00204